SWISH

Tom Carter

PRAISE FOR TOM CARTER:

"I really loved this one!"
-Author Leigh Kenny on *The Doctor Will See You Now*

"Kept me guessing until the very last page."
-Author Sarah Jules on *The Doctor Will See You Now*

"I did not see that twist coming!"
-Author Brianna Raine on *The Doctor Will See You Now*

"This book is a masterpiece and a must read!"
-Rae In Wonderland Blog on *SWISH*

"A must read if you enjoy books about fallen angels, supernatural forces, and the balance between good and evil."
-My Fantasy Bookshelf Blog on *SWISH*

"I'm just going to say it was brilliant."
-Well Worth A Read Blog

PROLOGUE

Tom Lewis was driving to his death.

Or, at least, that's what it felt like.

He speeds down the deserted country lane, driving dangerously fast considering the weather conditions. The road ahead is pitch black and the truck's headlights are rendered useless by the ferocity of the storm. Tom leans forward and squints through the blurred windscreen, his wipers on full speed in a futile attempt to clear his view. As fast as the water is swept away, a new torrent arrives to ruin his millisecond of unobscured vision. Every minute or so the thudding sound of the golf ball-sized raindrops fades into the background as apocalyptic thunderclaps echo around him. He knows they're coming, he can feel the rumble, but still, each one causes him an involuntary jump. The dark horizon ahead is illuminated, not by the warm glow of his headlights, but by forks of lightning that seem to strike the very road he travels down. Shiftily, he scans his surroundings; the trees creating shadow monsters. Their bare, spiny branches reaching out in an effort to grab his truck and drag it into the dark hell it looks as if they're crawling from.

This is how Noah must have felt for forty days and forty nights.

I could do with one of those James Bond cars, the ones that turn into submarines when they hit the water, Tom thinks. Any other day he would have chuckled to himself, but not today.

Tom was in his forties, and it was easy to see just by looking at his face that he has worked his whole life. He looks at least ten years older than his actual age. His hair graying, and his face lined and weathered from the constant outdoor work he has done since he was a teenager. It would be hard to see that right now though, as he sits in the shadowed driver's seat of his battered old Ford truck.

Even though he has a nagging feeling deep in the pit of his stomach–a feeling urging him to turn around, head back to the quiet solitude, not to mentioned safety, of his home–he continues his treacherous journey. The feeling of apprehension hangs in the pit of his stomach like a bolder. Constantly checking his mirrors and his watch, his eyes darting from side to side as if looking for someone. He grips the wheel so tight his skin stretches as his knuckles strain to penetrate his skin.

Moments later a large brick building looms into view, the only thing that can be seen through the rain. It's huge. From this distance, it looks like a prison. A massive structure of nothing but gray breezeblocks and barred windows. A fork of lightning strikes the land beside the building, bringing it to life for a matter of seconds before it returns to a silhouette in the night.

Is it a prison? he thinks.

He begins to slow the truck as he approaches its pothole-ridden driveway. His dull headlights illuminate a big brass sign embedded into the brickwork out front.

'Bethel Bible Village Children's Home.'

Tom stops to read it. Then looks over his shoulder to make sure he isn't being followed. He then winds down his window and scans the sky looking intently for something up in the darkness. His eyebrows are furrowed and his eyes unblinking despite getting splattered from the rain. Seeing nothing, he winds the window back up and continues up the long winding driveway. Enormous double doors sit at the top of a flight of concrete steps. On each side hangs an external lamp, but only one of them seems to be working properly. The other, flickering on and off, seemingly upset by the weather. Tom can just about see windows scattered around the front of the building, but it's hard to make out any other detail as every one of them resides in darkness. Once again, the sky lights up as if it's the Fourth of July, creating a beastly face of the building's front; windows for eyes, and an entryway creating an open mouth with the wooden double doors as sharp, cannibalistic teeth. Stopping his truck at the foot of the steps, he kills the engine. The deafening sound of his roaring beast stops immediately. All that can be heard is the barrage of rain beating against the concrete ground and the roof of his rusty truck.

Close up, the huge prison-like structure is intimidating, and he pauses to control his breathing. He drags the palms of his hands down the length of his dirty jeans to rid them of panicked sweat. He was a man on a mission. Driving as if he had just escaped from the gates of hell to make it here. But now he hears an unexpected, questioning voice arise from deep within himself. A voice telling him to turn and go. To pack a bag and lose himself. He shakes his head to dislodge the voice that is gradually becoming dominant.

Driven, literally, by adrenaline and a deep-rooted fear on his way here, like he was part of a high-speed chase, now he just sits and scans the front door. A knocker, in the shape of some growling demonic figure, catches his eye. His heart races in his chest and doubt fills his mind as he wonders whether he should get out of the truck. His doubt turns to anger and frustration as he punches the steering wheel. Closing his weary eyes, he takes a deep breath–steadying his shaking hands.

"Why me?" Tom asks himself aloud.

Out of nowhere, a light illuminates his face. Holding his hand up to shield his eyes, he can see someone has opened the front door and is standing ominously in the entryway.

Brilliant. Too late now.

Tom yanks the keys from the ignition and pulls his thick outdoor coat over his head as he jumps from the truck's cab and runs up the stairs leading to the front door.

Under the shelter of the porch, Tom gets his first look at who has come to greet him. The home's warden. Dressed like some kind of security guard–dark gray trousers and a dark gray shirt, a utility belt carrying a baton, torch and other useless items. *Who does he think he is, Batman?* Tom takes him in, tips of his toes to the top of his head, which doesn't take long considering how vertically challenged the man is. He can't be much older than a teenager. Out of school a few months at most. Pimples scatter his pale white face in an effort to create some kind of human connect-the-dots. The seven ginger hairs on his top lip are each an inch apart, 'grown' no doubt to make himself look older to colleagues and guests. The warden runs his hand over his already messed up hair, undoubtedly cut by his mother considering the different lengths. A chunk on the crown stands on end, he tries to flatten it several times to no effect, and it pings directly back up doing nothing to quash the schoolboy look.

"Helluva night, Mr. Lewis," the warden says. "It's like God himself has opened the floodgates."

Tom doesn't answer. He gives the warden a hard look as if he had said something stupid. The warden seems uncomfortable under Tom's penetrating stare. Tom pushes past him, brushing shoulders in his haste, a little more aggressive than he intended, but he isn't here to make small talk. He takes off down the hall, not knowing, but hoping he's going in the right direction.

"Let's move this along," Tom calls to the warden. "I've got a long drive ahead of me."

"Er yes...of course," the warden calls after him as he slams the door and jogs to catch up. "This way, Mr. Lewis," the warden adds as if taking back control. He gets in front of Tom and keeps his half-jog, half-walk going.

"Tom."

"Excuse me?"

"Call me Tom," Tom says flatly. "I ain't never been called Mr. Lewis in my life, don't see why it should start now."

The warden nods uncomfortably. The air is thick with unease and Tom finds it hard to catch his breath.

They both walk down a long oppressive corridor, the warden leading the way with Tom only half a step behind him. As they walk, Tom takes the opportunity to scan the bare walls, not that there's much to look at. Nothing hangs on them, except the gray paint that is peeling away. *Is everything gray here?* Tom wonders to himself.

The lights are uncovered. Bare bulbs emitting a harsh, flickering glare.

At the end of the world's longest corridor, Tom can see a window. When they reach it, they stop and look through into what can only be described as a type of day room. The window is like those you see in hospitals, where happy parents and family members can view the new addition to their families. Where rows of new-born babies can be found. The big difference here is that the people looking through the window are anything but happy. These are unwanted children.

Tom looks tense. The warden, nervous.

In the day room another bare bulb harshly lights up another gray room. Inside are not sweet chubby cheeked babies, but kids of all ages, from three or four up to what looks to be teenagers of around sixteen years of age. Kids that have been abandoned by their parents for one reason or another and failed by the system. Kids that have to spend what is supposed to be the happiest time of their lives, alone. They should be out enjoying themselves, looking forward to what the world has in store for them, but instead, they have been left here, forgotten by society. Left to rot in a prison masquerading as a children's home.

The warden and Tom stand looking through the internal window. Tom studies the kids. They all sit in little groups scattered around the small room. Some are gathered around a small old-fashioned television that blares out cartoons in a corner. Others around a broken table tennis table, taking turns to knock a ball across a non-existent net. None of them look to be having a good time–they all seem institutionalized, joyless...staring instead of looking.

A P.A. system crackles static outside the room before a muffled, unintelligible voice echoes down the corridor. Tom can't make head nor tail of what is said, but one of the teenage children in the room obviously does. He looks up at the speaker, then turns to look at the children he's sitting with. His face betrays no telling expression as he heavily lifts himself from the hard-plastic seat and exits through a side door. Tom turns and gives the warden a quizzical look. The warden's face remains passive as he continues to stare through the window at the children, as if he's looking at animals in a zoo.

Eventually, the warden points out a little girl. The only person in the room not sitting with anyone. Her hands are neatly clasped together, her back is ramrod straight as she stares down at her lap, seemingly oblivious to the other children in the room with her. She sits, oddly composed.

"She's a strange one," the warden begins. "As you know, her mother was killed in an accident. Nobody knows who her father is. She hasn't spoken a word since she's been here and doesn't mix with the other kids. County Sheriff put her here until they could track down kin. I gotta be honest, I thought she'd be here with us for a good few years. Took 'em a while to track you down."

"Her mother and I hadn't spoken since we were kids," answers Tom, not even looking at the warden. Never taking his eyes away from the motionless little girl.

"So, you've never met your niece?" Queries the warden.

"No. You say she's a strange one. I don't want no trouble."

"There won't be any, I'm sure of it," the warden answers quickly. Too quickly. "You'll be doin' us a favor, dang, you'll be doin' the county a favor. She needs a home and you're her uncle...she just don't fit in here."

"I don't know the first thing about raising a kid," Tom whispers, mostly to himself.

"Nothin' to it. You ever had a pet?" the warden raised his eyebrows. He seems to genuinely think that owning a pet is a good start on the road to parenthood.

Tom doesn't answer.

The warden turns his eyes away from Tom. Both men just stare through the glass at Tom's niece, a little girl he has never met in his life and who he now has to raise. In normal circumstances he would have said no, but these aren't normal circumstances. He would have had zero problem with leaving her here. She may be blood, but she's nothing to him. He's never even laid eyes on her, and he isn't exactly the paternal type. In fact, he really doesn't like kids, kin or not. But after that visit from...from that...thing. He doesn't have a choice.

The whole time they've been at the window looking, she hasn't once averted her gaze from her lap. Staring constantly at her clasped hands resting on her legs, or the sheet of paper that rests under them. Tom stands with his hands folded against his chest, as if guarding himself from something.

"What's that on her lap?"

"Oh, yeah, she likes to draw." The warden starts to fumble in his back pocket. "She may not have said anything, but she's doodled loadsa these."

He hands Tom some crumpled sheets of paper and his heart sinks to the pits of his stomach. They're drawings of monsters. Demons with wings.

Looks like I'm not the only person whose had these dreams. Or visits.

"Her name?" asks Tom, shoving the drawings into the warden's chest.

"Beg pardon?"

"Her name, what is it?"

"Oh, yes, of course," the warden says in surprise, forgetting they've never met. "It's Abigail. Abigail Lewis."

Tom allows himself a small nod. As he does so, Abigail's head snaps up from her lap and looks directly through the glass. She looks up with such speed and purpose it's as if she heard her name mentioned, which is impossible, Tom thought... right?

She continues to stare, unblinking. A penetrating gaze that makes him feel as if she's staring into his very soul, a stare which makes him start to feel increasingly uncomfortable. A cold shiver runs up the length of his spine causing him to shudder. He can't turn his eyes away from her, as if she's hypnotizing him. He tries to look elsewhere, but it's impossible. He tries with all his might–he grits his teeth, sweat starts to prickle his brow, his face starts to grow red–but still he can't look away.

"Mr. Lewis, is everything okay?" asks the warden.

Tom can't answer. He wants to, but his mouth won't form the words.

"Mr. Lewis? *Tom?*"

Suddenly, Abigail looks away and finally Tom can blink. He lets out a huge breath that had been lodged in his chest. He leans on the window for support while he composes himself.

Looking up at his niece, who now looks off into the corner of the room, her fingers gently rubbing a gold necklace that hangs loosely around her thin neck. The warden puts a hand on his back which Tom immediately shakes off. He turns and heads back along the ominous and imposing gray corridor. The front door looks so far away, as if the corridor gets smaller and smaller. Like they're in a circus fun house. But there's nothing fun about this place.

Not one thing.

"Get her stuff and bring her to my truck. I'll be waiting," Tom says over his shoulder.

1

11 years later.

"Shit!"

I step away from the broken China plate and stare in disbelief at the shattered pieces. *Brilliant, exactly what I need first thing in the morning.* I pull a miniscule shard of plate from my finger and wrap some paper towel around the smallest of wounds. I watch as the watery pink blood starts to seep its way through the white paper. Soaking it up until it eventually becomes a thick red gloop. I wrap another piece around my finger. Double the thickness to contain the life juice that is exiting.

I bend my finger to hold the paper towel in place and search under the sink for the dustpan. I offer a quick glance over my shoulder to make sure my uncle isn't there. That's the last thing I need before school, him accusing me of doing this on purpose and gifting me a new bruise to accompany my bleeding finger. Depending on what mood he's in and what kind of night he had, it's a strong possibility. I sweep the remains of the plate up and empty them into the trash. As I do so, I notice the half dozen empty beer cans piled on top of each other, like bodies abandoned on a battleground. All that remains from Uncle Tom's one-man party. They were guzzled last night, but this inevitably means his hangover will have him in one of his 'cheerier' moods.

The new bruise is looking more likely by the second.

I pack the dustpan away and scan the kitchen, checking to see how much more cleaning I've got to do before heading off to school. A mass of wood greets my eyes, exactly what you'd expect from an old farmhouse. Dark wooden floorboards, wooden beams above my head, low enough to bang your head on if you weren't only five feet four inches. Wooden walls, bare of any kind of homely materials. No family photos or reminders of my mum–Tom's sister. It's not like I can't remember what she looks like, her face is burned into my brain. But still, it would be nice to walk down the stairs that lead into the kitchen and see her, welcoming me in the mornings. To have some recognition in this world that she had lived, that she was here. Something other than me of course.

It's not like I'm going to make any lasting impact, though.

I start to clear away the rest of the plates and cups from the (also wooden) breakfast table, emptying the leftover food into the bin. Mostly mine as I barely eat what I cook for breakfast. Yet I cook it all the same. Habit, I suppose. I put the plates and cutlery into the kitchen sink ready for me to wash up when I get home from school. As I do, I hear a shuffle behind me and immediately my body tenses up. I can feel my uncle's stare scorching the back of my head. Most days he just leaves me alone, but on days like this, when his red-hot gaze is searing into my skull–I know he's angry about something and it's me that'll get the brunt of it. I carry on as if I don't know he's there, my heart thumping a drum beat in my chest. I'll wait for him to make the first move. I'm in no hurry to be shouted at for something I haven't even done.

Grabbing myself a banana and a bottle of water, I shove them into my book bag; this'll be my real breakfast for the morning.

The atmosphere becomes heavier, like a weight pushing my shoulders down. The fact I'm ignoring his presence eventually becomes too much for him to handle and he finally ends the silence. His gravelly voice causing me to flinch slightly.

"You better not be complaining at that school that you're hungry." He barks at me from the kitchen doorway. I nervously look at him, leaning on the frame that leads from the kitchen to the living area. There's no door there, it's all open plan, making the whole downstairs almost one huge room. I look beyond him not wanting to make eye contact and focus on the tattered furniture in the living room. A red armchair–*his* red armchair–with fabric sticking out from all angles. Frayed and ripped. It makes me itch just looking at it, but I suppose when you're numbed by alcohol, you don't take much notice.

"When do I ever moan? About anything?"

He doesn't answer me. He knows I'm right. Instead, he takes a different avenue, hoping this one will reach a point where he can, in his mind, legitimately shout at me.

"This place is a mess, make sure you clean it up before you head off to that damn school."

I take my eyes away from the living room and focus them on him. The effects of last night's drinking session are still on his face. It must be so much fun partying on your own. Then again, who am I to talk? It's not like I'm hemorrhaging buddies myself. His hair, greasy and matted looks wet as it sticks to his forehead. Three or four-day old stubble prickles his skin. It sounds like sandpaper when he runs his calloused hands over it.

"I'll do it," I answer him calmly. "You know I will. It'll have to be afterschool though. I can't be late again."

"That place is a waste of time; I need you here. I can't do everythin'," he shouts, as if I'm here to solely be his maid.

"School is important to me, you know I want to go to college."

"I had the decency to take you in, about time you started repaying that favor. I coulda left ya in that home to rot. I don't spend all day bustin' my ass on this here farm, so you'd have a place to sleep and food in the cupboards, to then have to come in and clean this place as well. You know the rules, girl, everythin' inside these four walls is your responsibility!" he hollers, his finger pointing at me from the other side of the table.

"Yeah, real decent of you to take me in so I can be your slave...not all heroes wear capes, right?" As soon as the words leave my lips, I know I've made a mistake. I've given him exactly what he wanted. An excuse.

His eyes turn from gray to red in an instant. Becoming a monster fueled by rage, he runs from the kitchen doorway to where I'm standing at the sink. He knocks over two chairs in his haste to get to me, but he doesn't care, he's a bull charging a red rag. I back up as far as I can. I'm almost sitting in the sink, and I can't retreat any further. Within seconds his face is millimeters from mine, his nicotine breath on my skin causes me to heave. Nostrils flaring like a rabid animal, his anger causes saliva to dribble from his lips onto his chin. He's aged a lot in the past eleven years, the lines on his face becoming the human equivalent of the Grand Canyon—his graying hair now yellowed, discolored from years of smoking. The seconds he's in front of my face feel like hours. I squeeze my eyes tight shut, waiting for the blow to come. The anticipation almost as bad as the actual contact.

Then...nothing. I hear him shuffle away and I open my eyes to find him standing at the kitchen door to my left that leads outside to the farm.

"Just get it done." He opens the back door and disappears, slamming it shut behind him.

I release a long-drawn-out breath, and my hand immediately goes to my necklace. Stroking the broken angel wings that hang on the thin gold chain I wear every day. My mother's last gift to me. I compose myself, tying to slow my heart rate.

Once I've finished making the kitchen look reasonably clean, I check my watch–definitely can't be late again this week. No watch. I race upstairs to get it and as I enter my room, I pass the full-length mirror and stop to have a quick look. I don't know why I bother, what I see looking back only depresses me. Not because I feel I'm ugly or anything like that, I guess I'm kind of pretty. Years of working on a farm have kept me fit. I'm not cheerleading material though, which can be a problem when you live in a town as obsessed with football as this one. Harton, Texas can be like that. It's Football, God, Family. In that order. If you're a guy you're on the football team, if you're a girl then you cheer for the team. If you do neither, well, basically you don't exist.

At first glance it becomes obvious to anyone with even re-motely decent eyesight that I haven't had any kind of new cloth-ing in years. Uncle Tom wouldn't spend a dime on me. I don't think he'd feed me either if he could get away with it. My t-shirts are faded and too small, some are even ripped. Jeans almost too short. I'm lucky that when he bought them originally, he got a pair a couple sizes too big from a thrift store. All of this wouldn't be so bad if he'd let me get a job. I don't want handouts; I have no problem with paying my way. He just won't let me. You would think that if he wasn't going to buy me some clothes, nothing major, just a few t-shirts, then he'd let me buy them myself, but no. Apparently, I'm needed here on the farm so I can't get a job; thus, no money, which equals no new clothes. For anyone still at school or who can remember your school years, well, let's just say teenagers are nasty and most of them don't need any ammo to start picking on you. When you actually give them a reason, all that does is make their job that much easier. I may as well wear a sign saying–*Easy target. Come pick on me.*

I take one more quick look at my make-up-less, albeit tan face, and thick brown hair that's pulled tightly back into a pony and wonder to myself, *why even bother?*

Once I'm done being disappointed with what the mirror has to offer, I grab my watch and cell phone from my bedside cabinet. A quick look at the time–07:48am. The bus will be at the main road in two minutes. Considering it can take almost double that time to reach the end of the long and winding dirt track that goes from the farm to the main road, I think it's safe to say, despite my best efforts, I'm screwed.

I race down the stairs at a speed that most people would describe as unsafe. If I had a concerned parent, they'd probably be yelling at me to slow down. Instead, I have an ass-hat of an uncle who'd probably like nothing more than if I fell and broke my neck. His main concern would be who would do his cleaning for him. Luckily for me I've always been more agile than most so the fear of falling never really enters my head. Jumping the last few stairs, I head directly into the kitchen, grab my bag off the table and sling it over my shoulder. Then I scoop up a handful of textbooks I never had time to pack and slam the backdoor as I struggle out of it.

Another quick glance at my watch–7:49 a.m. "Dang it."

I half run, half walk down the long dusty farm track. On either side of me as I jog, separating the track from the towering cornfields is an old wooden fence—a fence that has definitely seen better days. It's almost falling down and wearing away after years of being battered by bad storms and scorched by the harsh Texas sun. The towering cornfields behind the fence seem to stretch out for miles. I'm not sure how far back they go in terms of acreage–I've never been interested enough to ask. They sway in the slight breeze that sweeps across the open farmland, looming high and ominously over my head.

It's so dense I'm sure you could hide in it and never be found.

The faster I try to walk the harder it becomes. My book bag starts to cut into my shoulder with the weight. It feels as if the strap is trying to sever my arm at the shoulder, while the load of textbooks starts to slowly slip from my fingers with every step I take. The burning heat causing my hands to become slick with sweat. I round the corner and can finally see the main road. Relief washes over me as I notice a couple of kids waiting there for the school bus. I go to check my watch once again. As I lift my hand to scan my wrist, it happens. I drop everything. All the books I was struggling to carry slip out of my hands, and I see it all as if in slow motion. They collide with the floor kicking up a cloud of dust like someone has set off a smoke bomb. I let my bag slip off my shoulder and crouch down, trying to gather it all back up as fast as possible. As I do so I hear the distant roar of an engine. I look up to see it's there–the school bus. I collect everything I dropped as quickly as possible, heave my bag back on to my shoulder with what little strength I seem to have left, and take off as fast as I can. I manage to pick up speed in my desperation, but it's no good. I'm not fast enough.

"No...no..." I mutter to myself. My voice gets louder as I now start to shout toward the bus. "Wait! *Wait*!" I know it's no use. They're not going to hear me. I want to wave my hands, try to catch someone's eye and get their attention, but with the ton of books I'm carrying it's impossible. Even if the kids on the bus noticed me, they weren't likely to tell the driver, it's not like any of them are my friends.

With that, in what seems like a few seconds, I'm at the main road and in the distance, I can see the bus rounding the corner toward the town. I take a second and consider going back to the farm and asking my uncle for a ride to school. This prompts my first real smile of the morning.

I've got more chance of sprouting wings and flying there myself.

I look down at the books in my hand for the first time since picking them up. They're filthy. Covered in a thick layer of dust and dirt. To make matters worse, I've clutched them so tight to myself that my white t-shirt is also covered in dirt.

"Brilliant," I say out loud. "That's all I need on top of everything else." I look up to the heavens and think about asking, *why me?*

It's not like I'll get an answer though.

Sighing, I bend down and try to dust the books off as best I can before squeezing them into the bookbag that's already too heavy. That's all I need now, for the strap to snap completely. No idea how I'd get to school if I had to try and carry the books in my arms.

There's a dark thought at the back of my mind, one that's always there, like a towering shadow, like the monster in the closet. With the terrible luck I have, I know that missing the bus isn't the only thing that is going to go wrong today. The day has barely begun, and I have already been shouted out, missed my bus, dropped my books and dirtied my clothes. To add insult to injury my book bag is about to snap and fall to the floor in a heap.

This is all I need after a terrible night's sleep on account of the nightmares.

No! I think to myself—I won't let those thoughts come back to me while I'm awake, while I'm in charge of where my thoughts go. When I'm asleep is one thing. I'm not in control then, but I'll be damned if I'm going to let my day be bombarded with the horrors that plague me in my sleep.

I push the thoughts deep down into the recesses of my mind, back down with the shadowy thought that my life couldn't get any worse. I try not to let those self-pitying woes make their way above ground. I know my life could be worse—but it could be better, too. So, I push them as far down in my mind as I can and just keep moving forwards.

That's all anyone can ever do.

I stand at the end of the track, just looking. I look at the dust kicked up by the bus that still hasn't had time to settle. I just watch it, out of breath and close to tears. I drop my bookbag onto the floor and it hits with a thud that would make any passer-by think the bag was full of rocks instead of books. I lean forward and place my hands on my knees and try to catch my breath.

I use all my strength, which for someone of my size is quite considerable (more benefits of working on a farm) and lift my bag onto my shoulder. Wiping the tears from my eyes with my dusty hands, I refuse to let them fall to my cheeks, and I slowly begin my trek to school. There's no point in rushing now. I'm already going to miss first period, at the very least.

2

I make it to school in one, disheveled piece. My shirt sticking to me as if someone has just thrown a cup of water over me. Not a good look I can assure you. Just standing outside in the Texas heat is bad enough. Having to trek a couple miles in it is almost torture. The silver lining though is my bag didn't break.

Thank God for small favors.

I stand at the bottom of the stairs leading to the school's entrance. First period is already over and second has begun.

Twelve concrete steps lead up to the main school access point. Oddly, the main reception desk doesn't sit inside the main entrance doors, but at a different doorway just off to the right-hand side. Luckily, I don't have to go through there. If I did, I would have to explain to Mrs. Huckstepp why I'm late, again. A sign hanging above the main entrance reads, '*Main Entrance. Students and School Staff Only.*' To the right of that is another door, a smaller glass door that has the words, '*Main Reception*' printed on it. Above the door is sign jutting out from the brick wall which reads, '*Main Reception and Visitors Entrance.*'

I've always found it a little confusing, why the main entrance and the main reception are two different places, but what do I know? At the bottom of the concrete steps is a brick wall that travels around the front of the school building. It starts at the edge of the school and travels all the way along the front of the building and stops at the steps. The wide steps are separated by a metal hand railing. Students are supposed to walk up one side and down the other. The same rule is meant to apply to each and every staircase in the school building. The idea being it will make things run smoother. People will get where they need to go quicker and there will be less accidents. Kind of like driving on the road. In reality, though, teenagers are idiots who like to think they are making a stand against the *man* by defying every rule set by people in authority; even the rules that make sense. So, they don't walk up one side and down the other, they run up and down whatever side they choose causing not only queues, tailbacks and accidents, but the occasional fist fight or war of words.

On the wall at the bottom of the stairs, drilled into the face of the brickwork is another sign—they do love their signs at this school. Huge chrome plated letters glittering in the morning sun, blinding students and visitors alike when the rays catch it just right. Almost every morning you can see a swarm of students, all with their hands in front of their faces shielding their eyes from the blinding reflection burning its way into their retinas. The sign reads, '*Harton High School.*' Then in smaller chrome letters underneath, '*Home of Excellence.*'

I heave my bag back up off the floor and the pain sears through my shoulder again. I imagine a warm knife slicing through butter, except in this case the butter is my flesh. I climb the stairs, red faced from the heat, shirt sticking to me as if it's been sprayed on, and head to the main entrance (not the main reception). The climb up the stairs feels like I'm reaching the peak of Mount Everest after that marathon journey to school. I don't know exactly how long it is, but it must be at least two miles. I reach the door and laboriously pull it open. The cool breeze from the air conditioning unit hits me in the face.

I stand and let it wash over me. I feel like a drug addict finally getting a fix after what seems like a lifetime of denying his body the chemicals it most desperately craved. I step inside and raise my arms out like a cross, stretched out like someone has freeze framed me in the middle of doing a jumping jack. My sweaty armpits need the air conditioning almost as much as my blood red, tomato looking face. I've heard that saying before, 'Women don't sweat, they glow.' Well, I'm here to tell you, that's bullshit. A big old pack of lies. We sweat, especially in a hundred-degree heat when you've had to walk a few miles carrying a bag of what might as well be breezeblocks. I'll let you into another secret as well; we stink. That's right, B.O. isn't just reserved for the Y chromosome. Oh, no. Us ladies can kick up a stench when we want to, yessir.

I stand for what seems like ages, letting the coolness wash over me like waves from the ocean. Hoping against all hope that somehow, someway, the air conditioning unit will blow some of the smell away. It's bad enough people already assume you smell of cow dung because you live on a farm. I don't really want to add body odor to the list of slurs they like to throw my way. It's a futile attempt. I'll have to wait until gym class when I can have a shower.

I make my way down the corridor passing a bank of lockers on my left. Most of the lockers have some kind of decoration on them. Artwork produced by the owner. Pictures of themselves with their significant other (this choice of decoration seems to change from week to week as people bounce from one boyfriend or girlfriend to another). Pictures of famous popstars and films stars, or if you're some kind of athlete then you'll usually find their jersey number painted onto their locker door.

If you want to look into the psyche of any teenager, then all you have to do is look at their locker décor. Mine, on the other hand, is bare. Now, I know what I just said about delving deep into the psyche of teenager's blah blah blah, and I promise you my bare locker door doesn't correlate with me having nothing going on upstairs. No–I have plenty of activity in the brain department. I guess I'm just not an expressive person, especially when it comes to pointless decorations. I don't really want people knowing my deepest thoughts. I'd rather remain a closed book.

I reach my locker which is near the end of the corridor by the water fountain and all those thoughts I had about decorating my locker go out of the window. It turns out my locker *is* decorated.

Just not by me.

The bright red spray paint catches my eye first. It shines against the metallic locker door. It's glistening as if still wet; this wasn't done that long ago. Droplets roll down my locker door and drip on to the floor. I look at the small pool of it by my feet. It looks like blood. I raise my eyes back to the locker door, reading the kind message someone has taken the time to write.

Trash.

That's it? I mean as insults go that's tame, hardly worth it really. They say worse than that to my face. I raise my eyebrows a bit, not sure whether to be insulted by the artwork because they're calling me trash, insulted because they couldn't come up with something better, or slightly flattered someone has taken the time out of their day to purchase the tin of spray paint, and strategically plan this work of art. Instead, I just stand and stare at it until a voice behind jerks me from my thousand-yard stare.

"Not your handiwork I trust, Abby."

Shit.

I know the voice immediately. Mr. Heaver–The Principal.

Without even turning to look at him, I answer. "Not really my style, Mr. Heaver. It's too plain, I'd have used more colors, more Fauvist if you like." I throw out as if I'm really thinking about the style, as if I'm an art critic judging someone's pride and joy at an expensive Manhattan art gallery. Finger tapping my chin, head tilted slightly to the side, eyes squinting. Trying as hard as possible to pretend that I'm not in the least bothered.

"I admire your stoicism young lady," he replies with what seems to be a little sadness in his voice. Great, he feels sorrow for me. That's all I need. Pity.

I finally turn to look at him. Mr. Heaver is in his mid-forties, or he looks to be at least, I don't know exactly. He's a kindly looking man if not a little scruffy. You wouldn't think looking at him he'd have the authority to handle the students at a busy, overcrowded high school, but when push comes to shove, he has a penetrating stare and an uncomfortable stillness that demands respect. He's always unshaven with a speckle of gray dotted throughout the black of his beard. It's not a nice, groomed beard either–it just looks as if he hasn't shaved in a few days, and it's gotten out of hand. In addition to this he seems to be a collector of ugly ties. Every day he wears a different tie that doesn't remotely go with the shirt he's wearing. They're never a respectable plain color either. They always have some out-landish pattern covering them, or worse–animals. Today seems to be a collection of cats jumping in the air holding lightsabers with the words '*Star Paws*' splashed across the bottom. That one actually isn't too bad. I mean, who doesn't love cats–or *Star Wars* for that matter? It probably wouldn't look so bad if it wasn't for the fact he's wearing the same shirt he has had on for the last three days. Complete with the same spaghetti stain that was there yesterday. I mean the guy changes his ties daily, but not his shirts. Strange.

Anyway, as principals go, he seems to be decent enough.

"Have you any idea who did this, Abby?" he asks, using that penetrating stare I told you about. "Any idea at all?"

It could be anyone really, it's not as if I have a huge group of friends. But in truth, I know who it is. There's one group in particular who seem to take great pleasure in trying to make my time at school a living hell. "No idea, Mr. Heaver," I lie, not wanting to make matters worse by dobbing them in. He nods with a slight smile on his face, understanding, and knowing full well that I have an idea who the culprit is.

"Well, be that as it may, you're late again. Let's go to my office, you've missed first period anyway." He holds his arm out to the side of him indicating that I should lead the way to his office. It's not the first time I've been in there.

Mr. Heavers office is pretty much what you'd expect of any principal's office. A large desk sits at the back in front of a window. I've always found this strange, why would you have your office laid out in a way where your back was to the window? Isn't the whole purpose of a window to look out of it? Oh, well, not my office. Behind the desk sits a large leather chair that looks extremely comfortable. On the other side, the side where I'll be sitting, are two smaller, much less comfortable chairs. I wonder to myself if this is something that is done on purpose. Sitting down speaking to an authority figure can be intimidating for students, even parents at times, especially if they're called in because their child is in trouble. Maybe sticking them in chairs that make it feel like you're taking part in some kind of torture technique gives even more of the upper hand to the person on the other side of the desk, the person in the lazy boy.

Behind where Mr. Heaver sits, hung on the small section of wall in between the two large windows is a selection of certificates listing his qualifications. Either because he's extremely vain and likes to look at how intelligent he is, or because he wants whoever is on the opposite side of his desk to know that he's actually qualified for the position he holds and not some imposter. Which, on first glance, wouldn't be that far-fetched.

I sit down (uncomfortably) and look toward Mr. Heaver who slowly and deliberately eases himself into his chair letting out a huge sigh of satisfaction. *Show off.* He leans forward, hands clasped together, and looks me directly in the eye. I look around the room, at the huge book cabinet along the right-hand side of his office, filled with books that no human can possibly have had the time to read.

I carry on looking around, avoiding his gaze. I turn my head to the left this time, this wall is covered with framed photographs, some old black and white ones of which I assume must be family members, and a few of Mr. Heaver himself shaking hands with various people who I assume are meant to be important.

"Abby." My name exits his lips firmly. I turn and look at him, not saying a word, but knowing I can't avoid talking to him forever. He gives me a sympathetic smile. He just looks at me for a while, then lets out another sigh. "This can't go on, Abby. You've been late, what, a dozen times this semester? I've got to make a report of it...you know I do...it's going to affect your grades."

I look at him for a second or two, then turn my head to stare moodily out of the window. What can I say? Plead with him to not record my tardiness? As if it would make any difference, he's obviously made up his mind.

His office overlooks the school parking lot, not the best view I must say, maybe that's why he has his desk facing the other way. A silver car drives around aimlessly looking for a space. I'm not sure what make the car is, but it looks brand-new so probably not a student. From up here I can see a space right at the end of the lot, next to what looks like an old hippie campervan. That's probably the reason the driver of the silver car can't see it, hidden behind the hippie mobile.

I hear Mr. Heaver let out a heavy sigh once more, more to get my attention I think than actual exasperation. I turn again to look at him. I know what's coming next–this is old ground which we have both walked over at least half a dozen times.

"Is there anything you'd like to tell me? Anything at all?" Mr. Heaver asks nicely.

I look directly into his eyes and pull my best *really, we're going to go there,* face. I see his eyes move from my face down to my body. Not in a creepy way, more of a concerned way. The expression on his face is that of an old lady looking at a three-legged puppy. I realize immediately I'm being scrutinized and self-consciously fold my arms and stare defiantly back at him; or what I assume is defiant, it probably just looks like resting bitch face.

"What happened to your arms, Abby?" he enquires quietly. Softly, like a doctor talking to a patient.

I look at the bruises up and down my upper arms. Unsuccessfully, I try to pull the sleeves of my t-shirt down to cover at least some of them. A futile attempt considering he has already seen them.

"Nothing," I answer moodily. "I live on a farm...you get bruises."

Mr. Heaver leans forward and rubs his forehead, rises from his nice comfy chair (if I had a chair like that, I'd never leave it. It looks more comfortable than my bed) and walks over to his office window. He stands there for a minute or two, saying nothing.

"Doesn't that silver car see the space down the end there? Next to Mr. Watkins, Camper," he says all of a sudden. The van belongs to Watkins. I should have known, really. He's always wearing really brightly colored shirts and always smells of weed, like, so much. You'd get buzzed just standing next to him.

"When did you move into the old Gibson place? Eight months ago?" he says without turning to face me.

"Six."

"Hmm...In all that time, I've never met your uncle..." He finally turns, hands clasped behind his back looking at me. "Maybe I should."

"Why?" I almost shout at him. "He doesn't even want me going to school in the first place. As if he's going to care I've been late a few times."

Mr. Heaver walks around his desk and casually sits on the edge–well half sits and half stands. He looks uncomfortable.

"You're an exceptionally bright student, Abigail. Someone has got to start looking after your interests...if you can't make it to school on time and you continually miss first and sometime second period, well, you're going to flunk. I think...I think it's either time I sit down and have a little chat with your uncle...or...or you go and see..."

"I'm not going to a shrink!" I answer, before he can get the words out. I knew it was coming, he has mentioned this to me a few times before, but he has never used a meeting with Tom to blackmail me into it.

"An educational psychologist," he emphasizes. "And, Abby, it's either one or the other."

3

A hurricane of sound hits me as I walk through the double doors into the school cafeteria. I'm walking on autopilot in a daze. I had absolutely no intention of seeing an Educational Psychologist, but now I've been backed into a corner. This wasn't the first-time Mr. Heaver–evil genius that he seems to be–had brought up seeing a shrink, and let's not sugar coat things here, he can paint it up in whichever way he likes, but at the end of the day, it's a shrink. I'm usually prepared to just shoot him down when this suggestion comes up, but it looks as if he has found another gear and is fighting dirty. He has never, not once, mentioned meeting my uncle and he has never given me an ultimatum. Or let's call it what it is, blackmail. He blackmailed me. *I should go to the Sheriff's office.* Now I have no choice. As much as I don't want to see a shrink, I'd rather that then a letter sent home requesting Uncle Tom come to the school. There's only two ways that will end. He either opens the letter and gives me a beating before coming to the school and causing a scene. Or he opens the letter and gives me a beating before throwing it in the trash and forgetting about it. Either way, I get the back of his hand.

The noise finally reaches a roar loud enough to pull me from my troubled thoughts. I feel like a gladiator walking into the Coliseum, about to do battle for my life. That's how high school can feel for a teenager who is terminally bullied. I look around the cafeteria which to be honest is quite big considering I now live in a small hick town. It's basically a gym hall which about half an hour before lunch sees the kitchen staff wheel in big round tables and plastic chairs, along with a table filled with hot plates to keep the rubbery food warm.

All the tables are occupied and from a distance it's quite amazing to see the different cliques of students. A table full of goths sit grouped in the corner, all in animated conversation. For some reason, I've always assumed goths were like, moody people. These guys look pretty happy to me, who knew? Another table is full of what can only be described as red necks, complete with the plaid shirts, dirty vests and trucker hats. Next to that table sits the jocks and the cheerleaders. The only two groups of people that seem to overlap. I know this all sounds like a cliché, but at the end of the day this is high school–it's the home of the cliché. Seeing as I don't belong to any of these groups of people, I stand looking for the only place I can really sit–next to the only real friend I have–Sam.

I suppose it makes perfect sense that Sam and I would be suited to each other as friends. Neither of us has any other friends. I'm new to the school so obviously didn't know anyone and although Sam has always gone to this school, her quiet bookish nature made it hard for her to mix. Even sitting here now at lunchtime her head is buried in a book. In addition to this, her overprotective mother made it hard for her to make any lasting friendships. She's stopped from doing any kind of activity that could cause her harm, or what her mother *believes* could cause her harm. This includes normal everyday tasks for teenagers such as sports. She doesn't even have to bring a note anymore because it's an unwritten rule. Her mother–Janet Neeves–caused such a fuss one parent teacher night about how taking part in sports could cause serious damage to her daughter's health, not just in the event that she fell over or took a knock or something, but because her asthma is so bad that walking up a flight of stairs makes her feel faint.

Her mother was only looking out for her, but it seems to have done more harm than good.

I make my way over to the table in the farthest corner of the cafeteria, it's not one of the big round ones which accommodates a huge group of friends. It literally has space for two, maybe three people if you squeeze in. I don't even think it's there for people to eat their lunch on, it's just an old table chucked in the corner out of the way Sam and I have just claimed it as our own. I say claimed, actually it's just that nobody else wants to sit on it, their social circles are far too big.

Today she's reading *Salem's Lot* by Stephen King. Again.

She loves Stephen King and is constantly recommending books of his for me to read and then getting extremely annoyed when I tell her I haven't got the time to read them. It isn't like I don't want to read them; I just don't have that kind of time. His books are like, super long. Between school and my chores, I have to keep my reading material to a lot less than a thousand pages. It always makes me laugh that she's so obsessed with him. For a person as quiet and meek as Sam is in real life, she does love a good scare when it comes to movies or books.

"Hey." I drop my book bag on to the table with a *thud*. It's not as heavy as this morning seeing as I've managed to leave some of my books in my locker, but it still feels like a ton weight.

"Hey," Sam replies without even lifting her head out of her book. Her eyes rapidly moving from left to right, scanning the pages at lightning speed, desperate to find out what's going on in the small town of Jerusalem's Lot. She's probably read the novel two or three times already. I managed to watch the movie late one night.

I sit and look at her a while, she's completely captivated by the words in front of her. Her eyes widen behind her thick framed glasses. Slowly she pulls her inhaler from her pocket and without even looking, subconsciously, as if the act has now become second nature to her, places the pump between her lips, pushes the top and inhales deeply. She clamps her mouth shut, swallows and again without ever taking her eyes from the page, places it back in her pocket.

"Scary bit?" Lines crease my forehead in a slight frown.

She nods.

"It's just a book. They're just words." I try and fail to get her attention.

Her answer is to hold a finger up and aim it toward me in a sign that tells me *wait* –she wants to finish her chapter. I sit back in my seat and get a banana from my lunch bag. I look at Sam and then back down at myself. We're both wearing very similar clothes in terms of style, but we look completely different. Sam is much smaller than I am and while we're both wearing jeans and a t-shirt with sneakers, hers are much newer and much cleaner than mine. Her shirt fits and isn't faded, her jeans are the right length, and her sneakers are actually white. Unlike mine, which *were* white and have now faded to a dull gray and are covered with dust and dirt from the farm.

Sam's parents are relatively well off and think nothing of spending money on their daughter. Her father, Stanley Neeves was the local dentist, the only one in town so he earns a pretty penny. Sam's shirt today–Wonder Woman. She finds herself in that unfortunate category of being ridiculed for the same thing over the last few years of her life, but for completely different reasons. She used to be called a geek or a nerd because she wore pop culture tops and read comic books. Now she's ridiculed because going to the movies to watch a superhero film and going to the comic bookstore with your buddies is considered cool, or geek cool if that's a thing. Apparently, Sam isn't geek enough or cool enough to wear these kinds of tops or go to the comic bookstore now that it's for the masses.

It's a fickle world we live in.

Finally, as I take the last bite of my over ripe banana, she closes her book and places it on the table in front of her and responds to my remarks from moments ago as if we have been in full flow conversation and not sat in silence for the last three minutes.

"For any other writer, it may just be words on a page, but for the *master*..." she taps her finger on the cover of her book right on top of King's name, "...it isn't. It's visceral, it's graphic, it's terrifying, it's...alive. It's like a movie playing before your eyes...but...in your head."

"Isn't that the same as any book though?" I ask.

"No," she replies, kind of disgusted at me. "Nobody can conjure up an image as graphic as Stephen King. He's a genius."

"Fine, he's a genius, Whatevs."

"Maybe if you took the time to read one of his novels..."

Here we go again. "I've told you. I. Don't. Have. The. Time. Maybe when I'm away at college." I flash her a huge smile. She bites into her sandwich and chews slowly, placing the sandwich down nicely next to her book. Waiting for the next bite. A loud roar is heard from a nearby table. I look over to see the jocks and cheerleaders, all laughing and looking toward us. Never a good sign. I hear a hiss of air and turn to see Sam has had another puff on her inhaler. She's made uneasy by the eyes of the beautiful and popular angled our way. I turn my back, trying to ignore them. Sam tries to do the same by looking at me, but I can see her eyes every so often flitter toward that table.

"So, I...er...didn't see you in home room this morning. Were you late again?" Sam tries to make normal conversation, but there's a tremble in her voice. Not bad, but enough for me to notice.

"Yeah, damn bus drove straight past me again."

"Did Mr. Heaver find out?" she asks, concern in her voice.

"Yeah. He caught me at my locker, which someone was kind enough to decorate for me."

"Yeah, saw that. Sorry."

I shake my head to her in an unspoken reply of *don't worry about it, it's not your fault.* I know she's been there.

"He asked me who I thought did it."

"And...?" she enquires, leaning forward a bit, eyebrows raised.

I shake my head slightly. "I said I had no clue, although..." I look over toward the table of jocks and cheerleaders. The table we refer to as the Missing Link table, and my eyes focus in on Mia. Mia is–of course–the head cheerleader, very pretty–in a doll like way. Her hair is golden blonde and always perfectly styled, and her make up is never out of place. "It wouldn't take Sherlock Holmes to figure out who was behind it." I turn back to Sam. "It's just not worth the aggravation that would come with dropping her as a suspect."

"Yeah, I suppo..." Sam begins to mumble, looking down at the floor.

Before she can finish her sentence, someone from across the cafeteria shouts out, drowning out the end of what she was saying.

"Hey, farm girl! Milk this!" A loud male voice echoes around the room.

I don't immediately recognize who it belongs to until I turn around. Over at the missing link table, all eyes are aimed to myself and Sam, but mainly me, seeing as he used the flattering moniker of 'farm girl'. Brad is standing up, his letterman jacket on, of course. He's the school's quarterback so wearing his letterman jacket at all times is kind of the law. Probably sleeps in it. In his hand he's holding a carton of milk, his arm is pulled back as if he's launching a grenade or his prized possession–a football. As you can imagine, he has a pretty good right arm considering he's QB one. He may not be able to write or spell, but damn he can throw.

What happens next seems to happen in slow motion. It's like time has slowed down and I was in *The Matrix.* I'm 'The One,' except in this instance, the one has no discernible skill to get her out of this situation. All of Brad's friends look on wide eyed, all with goofy grins or outright euphoric smiles on their faces. I look to Sam who is sporting a look of pure terror as if one of Mr. King's monsters had leapt straight from the page and was about to attack her right here in the school cafeteria. I turn back to see Brad's arm fly forward and the milk carton leave the palm of his hand, then exit the tips of his fingers and float through the air. Slowly, or what seemed to be slowly, everyone at his table rises from their seats, eager to see the entertainment that's about to happen. You'd think seeing that everything seemed to have slowed down to a snail's pace, I would have been able to prevent what was going to happen next. Get out of the way. Dodge it.

Wrong.

Splat!

You know when you're reading a comic or watching one of those cheesy old Batman shows from the sixties, and you see words like 'Biff' or 'Pow?' You'd think, *that isn't what a fight would sound like.* Well, trust me, in this instance, the exact sound of that carton of milk hitting the table and bursting open to cover myself and Sam in stinking, wet milk was exactly that. *Splat!*

The jocks and cheerleaders laugh uproariously. Mia jumps up and flings her arms around Brad's neck. Squeezing the life from him in a celebratory hug as if he has just won them an all-important high school football game.

Taking a deep breath, I calmly start to wipe myself down with some napkins that are on the table. I look over at Sam who is wiping milk from her glasses. She slowly puts them back on and notices something on the table–her book, covered in milk. Pools of it sit on the hardcover. The pages soaked through. Sam picks it up and holds it out in front of her with her thumb and forefinger, draining the milk away from it. It's not good, the pages are ruined and even when they dry, they're going to smell, and we all know what dried milk smells like–vomit. Behind her glasses I can see tears begin to form. Immediately, I grab her by the arm and lift her to her feet. She picks up her bag with her free hand, still holding her prized book in her other. We leave our lunch bags on the table. No time to tidy up today. I lead her through the crowds of people, most of whom are now pointing and laughing at us. There are a few sympathetic faces, but not many. I race to the exit as fast as possible, before Sam's tears can spill over and become real. Before anyone, especially Brad, Mia and their gang of cavemen and women can see what effect they have over us.

"Don't let them see you're upset," I say to Sam as we exit the cafeteria. "Whatever you do, don't ever let them see that."

4

You'd be forgiven for thinking that after the way my day has gone so far that it couldn't get any worse. Well, you would be wrong. Last class of the day. Gym. As you can imagine this isn't my favorite class. Not because I'm not good at it, I'm actually pretty sporty. As I mentioned before, growing up on farms does have its benefits. I'm stronger and faster than most girls my age, hell, I'm stronger than most boys too. It's just that this class seems to give the girls that already dislike me ample opportunity to turn their verbal assaults into physical ones. I mean, most sports are contact sports, right? Mia and her gang of cheerleading zombies use that as an excuse to knock me on my ass at every turn while trying to disguise it as some kind of lame sporting move. "Sorry, Miss Pelly. I was going for the ball," was Mia's favorite line. Didn't matter the ball was at the other end of the court. Or we were playing a sport that didn't even have a ball.

Sam sits by me in the locker room as I change. Basketball today. She sits close by while I pull on my vest. Closer than usual. As if for protection. She sits clutching her inhaler tight, strangling the neck of the pump. She looks miserable. She had a good cry in the girl's toilets while we dried our clothes out. We managed to get them mostly dry, but that hasn't erased the fact that our clothes now have stains all over them and we stink.

Worse still for Sam is that her book looks to be ruined. Some of the pages were stuck together and when she tried to pry them apart, they ripped. This made me angrier than getting the milk thrown over me. Sam wouldn't hurt a fly, literally. She's against fly squatters; she thinks its animal cruelty. To top it all off, she's worried her parents will find out. I suspect she will just tell them she spilled milk down herself at lunch. No one wants to admit to their parents that they're being bullied, even if it's the right thing to do. Luckily for me this is one of the only times having a guardian that doesn't care what goes on in your life is a benefit.

"Go and sit outside, Sam." She looks at me like a deer caught in the headlights of a fast-approaching truck. "You'll be okay," I reassure her. "They'll be in the gym."

"What about you, though?" She whispers with real concern in her voice.

"Oh, I'll be okay. I can handle it, nothing I ain't used to," I reply with fake bravado.

Sam gives me a sympathetic nod, has a puff on her inhaler and slowly gets up and leaves. I watch her go and for the first time I wish I had asthma or some other chronic issue that stopped me from taking part in gym class. It would be so much easier.

As I'm having this thought something, or someone to be more accurate, violently pushes me into the locker. Luckily my good reflexes signal me to raise my hands, so I don't break my nose. I spin around fast to see who the attacker is and am not shocked in the slightest to see Mia standing there with two of her goons, Stacey and Lydia, flanking her like two bodyguards. Stacey and Lydia are, of course, cheerleaders, but much taller than Mia—and less pretty if I am honest. Mia only comes up to their shoulders which is why she uses them as enforcers. Their very presence scares most people. These two girls are definitely at the bottom of the pyramid, not just when it comes to intelligence, but when it comes to cheerleading as well. No way the others could balance them if they were near the top. As with most bully's, Mia never acts alone, or at all in some cases. Yeah, she's always the most vocal of the group, but when it comes to getting physical, she mostly leaves those tasks to Stacey and Lydia who are both dumber than a bag of rocks. This way Mia never has to get her hands dirty and has plausible deniability. If something ever comes back on them or on the rare occasion a teacher catches them in the act, she can always flutter her eyelashes and in her doll-like voice proclaim, *'It wasn't me.'*

Unless, of course, it's during gym class. That way she can knock into whoever she likes and innocently claim she was just being clumsy.

Yeah, I know, criminal mastermind.

"Watch where you're walking, farm girl," she screeches at me in mock offence as if I've just walked into her. "I don't want to get any of your hillbilly, cow dung smell on me."

I take a step forward, fists clenched, but as I do, *Bevis and Butthead* move forward and stand just slightly in front of Mia, blocking my access.

"Go for it," she taunts, a little smile playing on her lips, knowing she will never have to fight her own battles.

Just once I'd like to catch her on her own and plant my fist squarely on her nose. I know, I know. It's not the most sensible and grown-up thing to do, but for at least five seconds I'll feel satisfied.

Mia takes a step through the middle of her henchwomen and starts to stare me down, eyes locked on mine. "It was a big mistake, you coming to this school."

I say nothing, I just hold her gaze with a hard look of my own. No way I'm giving her the satisfaction of being the first to look away. What seems like hours pass, but in reality, it's about ten seconds. Finally, Mia flinches and looks off to the side. While I know I will lose the war, I can claim a little victory in this small locker room battle. I turn back to face my locker and then another fierce push in the back sends me careering into it again. Mia must be really pissed off this time because it was her that pushed me, getting her hands dirty on one of the rare occasions that rage takes over. She must have felt the same as I did, this was a battle she had lost, and I didn't even have to get physical to win it.

When you spend your days losing, you must hold on to these small victories.

"Who the hell do you think you're turning your back on, bitch?" she roars.

This time I don't care one single bit that Stacey and Lydia are standing there. I see red and with a lightning speed I didn't know I possessed I lunge toward her grabbing her by her shoulders, ready to throw her into her locker just the same as she did with me. Stacey and Lydia grab one of my arms in each of theirs and pull me away from Mia. I may be strong, but one of me against two giantesses is not good odds. They pin me to my locker and hold me in place as Mia walks slowly toward me, fists clenched. She looks angrier than I've ever seen her before. She isn't used to people fighting back. Just as she gets within about a foot of me, a voice stops her.

"Come on, girls, break it up," the voice of Miss Pelly, the gym teacher shouts. "Save it for the court, that's where we let our frustrations out." She stands there with her hands on her hips just watching. Stacey and Lydia let go of my arms and the four of us just stare at each other. "Let's go!" roars Miss Pelly again.

"Of course, Miss Pelly. We were just horsing around, building up a bit of competition for the game today," Mia says cheerily with a huge smile plastered across her face.

Miss Pelly doesn't answer, she just continues to stand there like an army drill sergeant.

"See you on the court," Mia then whispers to me.

"Yeah, see you on the court," Lydia copies substantially louder, not intelligent enough to know that she should use hushed tones.

"Move it!" Miss Pelly shouts.

"Idiot," Mia hisses at Lydia as they exit the changing rooms.

I turn around and close my locker door. I hear Miss Pelly take a few steps closer to me.

"Those girls always giving you a hard time, Lewis?" she says to me in her deep voice using only my last name like she does with most of the students.

I turn to look at her. She's a big woman. Not just tall, but well built. Her shoulders are wider than most men's. She always wears her hair tight in a bun, and I have never seen her wearing anything other than sports clothing. She always stands very powerful, legs shoulder width apart and fists clenched on her hips, a stern look on her face. Without knowing it I would bet all I own that she has served in the army or some other branch of the military. She just has that air of authority about her, unlike other teachers. She very rarely has to raise her voice, but when she does, you listen. It isn't a request, it's a command. The only way I can describe her is Mrs. Trunchball like, from the Roald Dahl novel Matilda. Not in personality, but the way she looks. She seems much nicer than Trunchball.

"Nothing I can't handle," I say confidently.

"I see. I like that attitude, but asking for help doesn't make you weak."

"I know," I reply.

"If you wanted, we could go and see Mr. Heaver together and talk."

"No!" I almost shout, cutting her off mid-sentence. "No, it's fine," I say more softly this time. "It's nothing, just normal school stuff. Nothing to worry about. Thanks, anyway." I turn and walk away, not wanting to get into it any further. The last thing I need is Heaver having more excuses to bring in Uncle Tom.

I stand on the periphery of the basketball game, resigned to the fact that nobody is going to pass me the ball. Not because I'm not good, but because these games are based more on popularity than skill. Friends pass to friends and seeing as my only friend was sitting outside, it's unlikely that I'm going to see the ball. I look out of the window as I stand there. There's one spectator sitting on the banked seating, periodically sucking on her inhaler as she watches over an empty field.

Sam looks deep in thought and deeply troubled. I worry about her sometimes, the bullying she has to endure seems to really get to her. I can shrug it off to a certain degree, even though it's not nice, but it seems to really take its toll on Sam. I do wonder if it would be better if we weren't friends. She would still have to deal with the likes of Mia, Brad, and their gang of Neanderthals, but maybe, if I wasn't her friend, it wouldn't be as bad as it has been lately. It's a horrible thought. She's my only friend in the world, and not having her to talk to when I get to school would be an absolute nightmare, but I would avoid her like the plague if it made things better for her.

I'm yanked from this horrible thought by the loud ring of Miss Pelly huffing and puffing on the whistle, which is dangling around her neck. The sound echoes throughout the hall, vibrating off the walls and ringing in my ears long after she has taken the whistle from her lips.

"Time Out!" she bellows as I wiggle my little finger in my ear in a futile attempt to dislodge the ringing that seems to have set up camp in my eardrum.

The opposing team, which consists of Mia and her gang, have called a time out. The group in a huddle, arms over each other's shoulders as they whisper tactics. Every now and then I catch Mia glance over her shoulders in my direction, that same smirk I've seen a dozen times playing on her pink glossed lips. This isn't going to end well, I can feel it. An air of dread hangs over me like a storm cloud. The huddle breaks and the team take their positions on the court. Mia steps off the court with the basketball in her hands, ready to get the game going again. She throws the ball to Lydia who starts to dribble slowly down court. I barely move as the rest of my team take up stances in an attempt to retrieve the ball. Lydia stops and whips the ball cross court to Mia who is now standing about halfway down. Mia uncharacteristically fumbles the ball in her attempt to catch it mid-air and scrambles it in my direction. The ball dribbles its way across the floor until it stops directly at my feet. I'm so surprised at first that I'm rooted to the spot. The same feeling seems to overcome the rest of my team, and the opposition for that matter. Everyone just stares at me for what feels like an eternity. I bend down slowly and pick the ball up and hold it in my hands until a loud booming voice echoes around the gym causing me to jump slightly.

"What you waiting for, Lewis? An invitation?! Get a move on," Miss Pelly shouts.

I start to bounce the ball on the spot, my right arm the only thing that's moving. Slowly at first and then I start to pick up a little speed. I feel like Michael J. Fox in that ancient movie, Teen Wolf. I start to advance on the opposing team, all of which seem to still be standing there in shock–is it shock?– that I actually have the ball.

We are in unprecedented territory.

"Face up!" Lydia screams to her teammates, and they listen immediately.

A couple of the girls start to advance on me, but I pivot and dance around them with relative ease. First one, then another. I pick up the pace so that I'm running to the basket with the ball, I start to get a smile on my face knowing I'm going to make a basket. I start to hear chants of encouragement from my team and it causes me to look around at them, this is the first time this has happened and I don't want to miss out on it. I want to get a mental picture. The split-second I use to turn around is all the chance Mia needs to strike. She sticks her leg out in front of me, I see it, but it's no good, it's too late and I can't dodge it. My foot collides with hers and as if in slow motion I start to fall toward the floor. The ball comes spilling from my hands, which I am now starting to feel was Mia's plan all along. As I hit the floor, I look up to see the ball slowly roll off the court and out of play. A few groans from my team can be heard from behind me, but that's as far as the protests and shouts of anger go. If it had been anyone else who had fouled me, they'd have gathered around Miss Pelly like a pack of wolves baying for blood. They won't do that against Mia, they know better. It would be social suicide.

Miss Pelly's whistle rings out around the gym once more, this time I am too preoccupied with the pain in my hands and knees to be concerned about my momentary deafness again.

"Foul!" Miss Pelly bellows as she marches over and pushes her way through the crowd of girls who now stand around me laughing frantically. For the most part the laughing dies down to a little snicker as Miss Pelly stands, hands on her hips looking down at me, she then turns to Mia.

"Playing a bit fast and loose with the tackles weren't we, Watts?" she asks with her eyebrows raised in an accusatory stare.

"Sorry, Miss," Mia answers sweetly, a slight smile still playing on the corners of her mouth. "Looks like I'm having a clumsy day, my timing is all off."

"Is that right? And that's all it is, of course?" enquires Miss Pelly suspiciously.

Mia's hand shoots up to her chest in a theatrical attempt at looking hurt.

"Miss Pelly, I'm offended. That you think I would do something so cruel on purpose...I would never..." Mia stops mid-sentence and rushes over to me with her hand outstretched in a showy, over the top performance. She must be going for an Oscar. I stare at her hand and then look up at her face, one of my eyebrows raised. Mia's face holds nothing but a look of concern for my wellbeing. I look around and everyone else, including Miss Pelly, look on as if they're eagerly waiting to see what unfolds. "Abigail, I'm so sorry. I hope you're not hurt. I'm such a klutz sometimes." She stands with her puppy dog eyes, looking down at me, taking her act to the next level. An act I'm not buying for a second.

"Really? I don't recall ever seeing you be even remotely clumsy. I'm sure they wouldn't let you be the top of the cheerleading pyramid if you were."

"We all have our moments, I suppose. Come on, let me help you up." She advances closer almost jabbing her hand into my face, her eyes focused intently on mine.

I look around again and everyone stands almost motionless, a few whispers bouncing their way around the group of onlookers, all eager to see what I'm going to do. A quick thought flashes through my mind. Slap her hand away and tell her the last thing I would ever want is her help and that I know full well that there was nothing accidental or clumsy about that challenge, but I know I'm not going to. That's exactly what she wants. For me to come off looking the bad guy while she looks like the innocent victim who's only trying to help. Trying to atone for her misdemeanors. The thing is, everyone else also knows this and Mia knows that they know. No one will say anything to her though. So, on the surface she comes across as the winner, if there is such a thing as a winner in a situation such as this. I go for the more diplomatic approach. I reach my right hand up and clasp it in her waiting, helping hand. She looks shocked. The shock then gives way to another look, a look of pure anger. It's only brief. Too fast for anyone else to have noticed and then it's gone. Her fake innocent smile returns, and she pulls me to my feet squeezing my hand much harder than she really needs to. Well, two can play at that game. I give her hand an almighty squeeze, my farm work coming in useful for a change. She lets out a little yelp and snatches her hand from mine, nursing it to her chest.

"Sorry," I say without a hint of remorse. "Sometimes I don't know my own strength."

"It's fine," she replies through gritted teeth as her bodyguards flank her on either side.

The silence in the gym is by then deafening until Miss Pelly cuts through it with her knife-like vocals.

"Lewis, how's that knee? You need to visit the nurse?"

"No, I'll be fine."

"Excellent. Watts, how's that hand? Do you need medical attention? Bandage? Mommy?"

"Of course, not! She isn't *that* strong."

"Good. Now…" Miss Pelly starts, but is cut off by the sound of the bell indicating that gym class is over and thankfully, with it, the school day. Once the bell dies down Miss Pelly carries on. "Okay, that looks like we're done for the day. Who wants to hang back and help me put the equipment away?"

Mia, Lydia and Stacey turn heel and head directly for the changing rooms making it completely obvious that they have no intention of helping. Everyone else in the class is a little more subtle with their attempts at getting out of clean up duty. They just avert their eyes and look anywhere but directly at Miss Pelly. Some of the girls start studying the walls, some start to study their nails, obviously interested in what damage playing basketball may have done to their extensions and manicures. Something that is not really a problem for me considering my nails are always bitten down to the quick. Others have become increasingly interested in bits of dust that are floating in the sunlight that streams in through the high windows of the gym.

"I'll help," I offer. I'm in absolutely no rush to get out of here, especially as Mr. Heaver sent a note to me in my third period Biology class to let me know he has arranged an appointment for me after school with some shrink. Or *Educational Psychologist* as he likes to put it. On top of that, I have no real desire to be in the locker rooms with Mia.

"Thank you, Abby. I was starting to worry we would have a stampede of helpers." Miss Pelly eyes up the rest of the class. "Go on, get yourselves changed."

They almost sprint from the room, not waiting to be told twice.

I take my time rounding up the scattering of basketballs we had out from free-throw practice and the brightly-colored bibs from when we were running drills. We pack everything away in the equipment room and lock the doors. Miss Pelly thanks me for my help and I slowly make my way to the locker room. I look up at the clock to see it's been fifteen minutes since class ended, which should be more than enough time for Mia to have changed and left the locker room.

The locker room is almost empty when I walk in. A few girls are milling around talking and packing their sports gear away. They look at me when I enter, but shiftily avert their gaze to avoid eye contact. I make my way around to my gym locker. Sam can usually be found sitting on the wooden bench by my locker waiting for me, but today the bench is empty. Earlier I told her about the appointment Heaver had so *thoughtfully* arranged for me so she should just make her way straight home after last period. I hope she made it away before Mia had finished changing.

I look up to my locker door and stop dead in my tracks, my heart plummeting to the bottom of my stomach. The door looms ominously open and the lock has been broken. No wonder everyone was staring at me when I walked in. They probably watched Mia doing it, but once again, no one was brave enough to stand up to her. Tentatively, I make my way over to my locker door, not particularly in any rush to see what they've planted in there. Once I reach the door, I take a deep breath, bracing myself for what I'll find. A spider? A dead animal? Food? I close my eyes briefly, steadying myself, and then pull the door all the way open, peer in and find...nothing. I don't know whether to be pleased or not. Not only have they *not* put anything in my locker—no dead animals, no spiders, no food poured over my clothes. There's nothing in there. Nothing at all.

Not even my belongings.

Once the momentary relief has worn off, the reality and dread sets in. Where are my clothes? And my bag?

I look around again at the last few girls lingering in the changing room, each one seems to be very interested in the rotting décor that adorns the room. Looking up at the flickering fluorescent bulbs or studying the peeling paint. Anything but look my way. I think about asking aloud to no one in particular, if they have any idea where my belongings have gone or if they have any idea who may have taken them. Even though it wouldn't take Batman to figure it out.

In the end I don't bother. I know full well that even if they wanted to help me, they wouldn't have the courage to. Admitting they knew where my clothes and bag were would also be admitting they knew who took them and there's no way they're going to willingly offer up Mia's name. They know it will get back to her which means that their school lives, and even their home lives because of social media, would be made a misery. To be honest, even if I thought they'd tell me, I'm not sure I want to put them in that position. So, I do what I always do. I let my frustrations out in an audible sigh, slam the rough wooden locker door, take a deep breath and start my search of the locker room.

I walk up and down the aisles searching the empty lockers as I go past. Apart from the occasional candy bar wrapper or soda bottle, all I see is dust and cobwebs. It crosses my mind that the cleaners don't seem to spend a great deal of time tending to the girl's locker room, but that's the least of my concerns right now. I get to the last aisle of lockers and shut the last door after investigating its emptiness. My worst fear seeming more likely as each second slowly ticks by. I move past the last door and look beyond the bank of lockers, through the tiled archway and into the girl's shower and rest rooms.

My chest tightens. I rub my eyes. It's been a long day.

As much as I want to find my belongings, I silently pray to myself that I won't find them through that archway. I take a few steps closer and stop just outside, looking up at the broken, dirty tiles that seem to be a visual representation of how I am feeling in that exact moment.

I step through the arch and look immediately to my left, through another archway to the shower room. Six showers stretch out before me. Each with a small door and a small partition separating each one and providing you with a tiny amount of privacy. Almost prison like, or so I'd assume. The small doors to each shower are all wide open and all empty. Puddles of water sit on the floor as droplets slowly trickle down the walls and wooden doors. I turn to my right and start to make my way down the tiled floor to another archway located on my right.

The toilets.

As I walk down the corridor, I poke my head over the top of the bins to check whether my belongings had been thrown in there. That's the type of hilarious joke your stereotypical school bully would play.

Again, nothing.

My brain starts racing, and it's becoming increasingly likely that there are really only two options left. My stuff is either not in the locker room at all and has been taken elsewhere, or they're in one of these toilet cubicles. I pray for the former, but I know it's going to be the latter. I don't need to have the power of second sight to see where this is going.

I turn into the arch on the right-hand side and look at the four cubicles that stretch out before me. The door to each one is closed, but the third cubicle from the left catches my eyes immediately. A pool of water spills out from the cubicle, under the door and out onto the tiled floor. I stand for what seems to be forever, but in reality, is probably less than three seconds. Then, apprehensively I trudge toward the door of the cubicle with the small swimming pool spilling from it. Slowly, I push the door open. I feel as if I'm a character in a horror movie waiting for someone to jump out at them from behind the door. But ultimately what I find is much worse than Ghost Face or Freddy Kruger. The toilet is overflowing with water, spilling over the sides and cascading like a small, less beautiful waterfall. My school bag sits on the floor next to the toilet basin, like the Titanic sinking in a sea of dirty water. In the bowl itself I can see my clothes, just floating. Someone (Mia. Or more than likely one of her goons) has stuffed them into the toilet and pulled the flush. My jeans and T-shirt have blocked the toilet and caused the mini flood.

I walk over to the toilet and stand looking in. I close my eyes, grit my teeth and reach in. What I wouldn't give right now for a pair of rubber gloves. The big ones that go all the way up to your shoulder, the ones that vets use to...you know.

Pulling my soaking ball of clothing out, I lean my back against the cubicle partition. I want to slide down into the pool of water and sob. I can feel it swelling in my tight chest like a wave in the ocean. But I don't. If I allow myself to wallow in the self-pity, I fear I'll never stop. Instead, I turn and splash my way out of the restroom, my bag and clothes leaving a trail of water behind me–like a character in a fairy tale leaving breadcrumbs to find their way back.

This day literally couldn't get any worse.

5

Dr. Ainsley–Child Psychologist

I stand looking at the gold plaque which is screwed to the wall next to a huge brown wooden door. It's sparkling clean, as if it has only just been polished. The scorching sun causes a blinding glare to be reflected off the plaque. It doesn't stop me seeing my reflection looking back at me though, even if the reflection does come back distorted, wavy, as if I'm looking at myself in a mirror in Willy Wonka's chocolate factory. I look back at myself, unsmiling, bored. All the way here, the long walk from school, I was convincing myself I would smile my way through the appointment in the hopes that the doctor will see I'm a happy 'normal' child who has absolutely no need to be seeing a child psychologist. Upon looking at my reflection though, I know my face will betray me. There's no way I can convince anyone, even myself, that I'm okay with being here.

I clench my fist tight, wrapping my fingers around the plastic bag which holds my wet clothes. Another reason why I decided to walk to Dr. Ainsley's office instead of getting the school bus. Having to travel on a bus full of school children while still wearing my gym kit–which consists of a vest, shorts and sneakers–while carrying a bag full of wet toilet flushed clothes. No thanks, I'd rather walk and take the back streets.

Dragging my feet, as if any such delay will result in me not having to attend the appointment, I walk to the door and ring the bell. After a couple of seconds there's a loud buzzing as the door is electronically unlocked from inside. I push it open and slowly walk in. I stand looking at the corridor which stretches before me, I feel as if I need to squint at the white walls. The brightness is blinding. Like I'm looking directly into freshly fallen snow. Not that I've personally experienced that, you don't get much snow here, just the blistering heat. Several pictures hang on the wall. All happy, feel-good photographs and paintings depicting smiling faces or people having a good time. Other than that, it's flowers. Pictures of flowers hang on each wall, sit in small frames on tiny corner tables, and vases filled with all different colored flowers. Dr. Ainsley must be a florist in her spare time. I suppose these are here to put you at ease. I'm here to tell you, they don't work.

As I round the corner, I reach what can only be described as a waiting room. A very small waiting room. Two plastic chairs sit next to each other with their backrests touching the white-washed walls. Next to the chairs is a small table with a selection of magazines stacked on top of them. The magazines are stacked immaculately. It looks as if Dr. Ainsley used a ruler to make sure they were straight. That's some serious OCD right there. Oddly, considering how perfect the magazines were stacked, each and every one of them is about three years old and faded. You'd have thought that someone who took that much time and effort to make sure their magazines, picture and flowers were that carefully arranged and selected, would have also taken the time to make sure the waiting room reading material was at least published this year.

I take one of the plastic chairs and wait for my turn. I'm not in the chair more than a minute when the oak door leading to what I assume is Dr. Ainsley's office opens. I expect to see a troubled young soul walk out, a young girl of about my age with a tissue pressed to her face to soak up the tears caused by the dragging up of memories from days gone by. Instead, out walks a woman who, if I had to hazard a guess, is in her early thirties. Her blonde hair rests on the shoulders of her black Levi's shirt. Along with the shirt, she's wearing white Levi's jeans and black boots. She's too old to be exiting an appointment with a child psychologist, so this casually dressed woman must be Dr. Ainsley. I have no idea why, but I was expecting a sixty-year-old woman in a pants suit. I'll admit, her appearance has thrown me a little.

"Miss Lewis, I presume. Come in, take a seat," Dr. Ainsley says with a smile on her face displaying a set of perfect white teeth.

Without saying a word, I get up, plastic bag full of wet clothes still firmly in my grip. Out of the corner of my eye I can see her look me up and down, but she doesn't let whatever it is she's thinking appear on her face. Her expression stays the same–a happy, welcoming smile.

I walk into her office, and I hear the door click closed behind me.

"Please," she gestures with her hand for me to sit.

I have a quick glance around the room expecting to see an office much like Mr. Heaver's, but I'm surprised that isn't the case at all. Yes, there are small similarities. Dr. Ainsley has some framed certificates on the wall letting all her patients know she didn't go to clown college. Yes, she has a bookcase with tombstone sized reading material, but that's where the similarities end. She has a small desk. Nothing like the size of Mr. Heaver's. *I wonder what he's trying to overcompensate for*, I think to myself with a wry smile. The floor is covered with a beige carpet which along with the oak-colored painted walls gives the room a real warmth, which considering the heat outside you'd think would be too much, but it's oddly comforting. There's a sofa and an armchair which makes it look more like a cosy room in somebody's house rather than a doctor's office.

Out of the corner of my eye, I notice her watching me, surveying me, so I turn and head toward the bookcase and pretend I'm studying her reading material when, in all honesty, I'm not paying the slightest bit of attention to any of them. I just need to get away from her penetrating gaze.

"Do you read much, Abby? Is it okay for me to call you Abby or would you prefer Abigail?" Dr. Ainsley asks politely.

"Abby's fine."

"So, do you...read much, I mean?" she asks again. Probably trying to find out if my reading material of choice is any indication to whether I'm crazy.

"A bit, I suppose. Not as much as my friend, Sam. She always has her head buried in a book. I don't really have the time." I start to take in what books are actually on the shelves. They seem to all be medical books, which I suppose is to be expected.

"I certainly wouldn't want to read any of these books," I say dismissively.

"They're an acquired taste," she replies with a laugh in her voice. "I can't say with all honesty I read them out of pleasure. It's good to keep up with current trends, though."

"Trends?" I ask quizzically, turning around for the first time. I notice she's now sitting down in the leather armchair at the other end of the room. A small circular table is on her righthand side with a lamp, a jug of water and two small glasses on it. A leather binder sits unzipped on her lap with sheets of paper inside covered in scratchy writing which is too far away–and far too untidy–for me to read. "There are trends in the world of Psychology?"

"Of course. There's always some stuffy old professor somewhere coming up with a new way of doing things or who spends a few years doing some research and then believes that that's the *only* way of doing things," she replies.

"You sound kind of dismissive of your own profession," I observe with my eyebrows raised. "Makes me think that my initial thoughts on coming here being pointless were right. Especially if my therapist thinks this is all a bit of a fad."

"I didn't say that, now did I? When you've done this job for a few years and met many different children and teenagers all suffering in their unique way, you realize you can't really use one formula to help all of them. People are different, their problems are different. So, I like to do things my way. That being said, I can't very well criticize the methods of other doctors if I don't read their theories, now, can I?" she answers, still smiling.

"S'pose not."

"Why don't you come and sit," she says to me once again, motioning with her hand to the leather sofa opposite.

Slowly, I trudge across the soft carpet and fall onto the sofa, dropping my plastic bag of wet clothes on the floor next to my feet. I can see Dr. Ainsley examining the bag, but I pretend not to notice. I just look at my hands clasped on my lap, waiting for her to begin. The sooner she starts, the sooner this'll be over. But the silence drags on. After what seems like an eternity, I look up from my hands to see her staring at me with what I can only describe as a pitiful smile on her face. We sit, staring at each other until I can't take the silence any longer.

"Are you not going to say anything?" I blurt out.

"Are you?" she replies, calmly.

"I'm the crazy one, remember. Isn't it you that's supposed to ask me questions?"

"Is that what you think, you're here because you're crazy?" she asks quizzically, her brow furrowed, and head tilted slightly as if she's really concerned and not just doing this for a paycheck.

"Isn't that why people come here, or in my case, sent here? Because they're crazy?" I ask.

"Not even remotely. Some people just want someone to talk to, to help them resolve some issue they may be holding on to, some stuff that may have been weighing them down, for years even."

"Seems like a lot of effort, and a lot of money I'd assume, just to have a chat with someone." It comes out more harshly than I intended. I look up thinking I may have hurt Dr. Ainsley's feelings, but the expression on her face is soft, kindly even. She smiles as if to say she has heard this all before.

"Well, luckily," she says as she shifts in her seat and takes a sip of water, "you don't have to pay a penny–one of the benefits of being advised to come by your principal instead of making the appointment privately–so you may as well make the most of it, don't you agree?"

I answer with a shrug that must come across as extremely childish, like a toddler who doesn't get what she wants on Christmas morning. She briefly looks down at her notes, her head doesn't move, but her eyes angle downward in a way that makes me think she doesn't really want me to notice.

"Mr. Heaver has mentioned you're having a few problems at school. Someone spray-painted your locker today, is that right?"

I answer with a small nod and a sigh, an audible, theatrical one. My way of letting her know I don't really want to talk about this. In my head, that's less rude than actually saying I don't want to talk about it. But deep down, I know it's probably worse.

"Is this a regular occurrence for you?" she presses on, undeterred.

"What? Having problems at school? Happens to everyone. I don't see why, in my case, it seems to be a big deal."

"Everyone can have some issues at school, I agree. You can't be friends with everyone, but having your locker vandalized seems to be a bit extreme."

I don't answer. What can I say? Yes, it's hard. People calling me names and throwing stuff at me, putting my clothes into the toilet and pulling the flush. Laughing at me and pushing past me in the school hallway. But even with all that, being at school seems like heaven compared to being at home where I'm reminded day in and day out that my uncle doesn't want me there. That I have a lifetime of being shouted at and doing chores and on occasion, being hit. If I open that door, if I break down the wall that's keeping all of those feelings at bay, then I'll crumble, and I refuse to do that. I refuse to let them win. Even though, by building it up inside, by letting the storm clouds gather, they've probably won anyway.

After a couple minutes of silence, Dr. Ainsley tries a different subject seeing as she's getting no joy from this line of questioning.

"Okay, Mr. Heaver said you're constantly turning up to school late. Is everything okay at home?"

"At least I'm turning up."

"Well, that's one way of looking at it," Dr. Ainsley replies. "But from what I hear, it could affect your grades, and for a bright young girl like yourself, you don't want anything to cause you any problems when applying for colleges. Are you planning on going to college?"

Again, my response is to give no response at all. I know I'm being rude, and I don't want to, but I also don't want to talk about any of this. I just want to get out of here. I want this over.

She waits again and then presses on. "What about those bruises on your arms, how did you get those?"

I automatically cross my arms in a pointless attempt to hide the bruises, much the same way I did in Heaver's office. It's becoming all too much of a habit. I angle my body away from Dr. Ainsley and look out of her office window. The blistering sun that's been there all day, which was scorching down on me before I came into her office, seems to be disappearing. There's a light glow outside, but a strange wind is starting to pick up. I can see the leaves on the trees beginning to sway and clouds start to form, covering the once bright sunlight. My attention is pulled from the outside world and the ever-encroaching gray skies by Dr. Ainsley. This time it's her that lets out what I can only determine as a fed-up sigh.

I try not to turn my head to look, but from the corner of my eye I can see she has placed her leather binder on the small table next to her and is taking another sip of water. She uncrosses her legs and then re-crosses them the opposite way. After composing, herself she carries on.

"Abby," she says, quietly.

I don't answer or turn around. I look toward the clock on her office wall. I've been here twenty minutes of a one-hour appointment.

"Look, Abby," she says, louder this time. She sounds as if she's losing her patience slightly, but hides it well. "I know this must be difficult for you, but you've got to be a little more co-operative. As I understand things, it's either this or a suspension from school. Am I right?"

"But what is *this?*" I turn to face her again. "I'm not going through the cliché of telling you about my life, about my feelings. What possible insight could you have into that, what help could you ever be? You're a stranger, you don't know me. How could you be of any help whatsoever?!"

"I completely understand that, Abby. Lots of people feel like that. Which is why we have to open a dialogue with each other, let me get to know you. This isn't something we can achieve in one appointment with each other. It takes time. But if I am going to help, I need you to be more responsive." She waits for a few seconds and then carries on. "How about telling me why you're carrying around a bag of wet clothes? Or why you're dressed like that. I know it's warm out, but that isn't exactly normal school attire, is it?"

"Who said I'm normal?" I shoot back. *You wanted responsive, there, that's a response.*

"Come on, Abby," she replies sitting back in her chair. "You can do better than that. From what I can tell, you seem to have a problem with relationships, creating them or sustaining them. Relationships with your peers...with family maybe?"

"I don't have a family."

"Really? I thought you lived with your mom's brother. Your uncle."

"It takes more than blood to make you family," I say, not making eye contact.

Dr. Ainsley looks down at her notes and rubs her forehead slightly. As she looks back up, she places her fake smile back on her face. I turn to look away hoping she didn't see me looking, back to my surly teenager expression.

"Okay, let's try something different. What do you like to do in your spare time? Any hobbies?" she says in a lighter tone than before, hoping to come across as if this was just coffee shop chit chat. I don't answer, partly because I'm still trying to make it clear I don't want to partake in this pointless exercise, but also because, well, I don't do anything in my spare time. I don't have spare time. I have chores.

"How about dreams, then. Do you ever remember any of those?" she presses on, catching me slightly off guard. I try and regain my composure before she notices the shock on my face. I fail.

"Dreams? Is this going to be some Freudian trip now? You got no ideas of your own, gotta steal someone else's?" I reply with a little venom in my voice.

Dr. Ainsley doesn't seem fazed. I suppose being a child psychologist she's used to bratty teenagers. She continues to stare at me. She places her glass down on the small table next to her chair. There's a ring of water on the table where the glass sat moments before. I wonder to myself why she doesn't have a coaster. I would have thought someone who keeps their office this organized and clean would have been quite strict when it came to things like this.

"Well, do you? Remember any?" her voice is almost a whisper, but it's loud enough to pull me away from her wet tabletop and back to looking at her. She has her elbow resting on the arm of her leather chair and her chin resting on the palm of her hand. If I were sitting like that at school I'd be told to straighten up and pay attention, but Dr. Ainsley doesn't look bored, she looks interested. Staring at me intently as if she hasn't wanted anything in life more that she wanted my answer to this question.

"Yeah, I dream...and sometimes I remember them, or to be more specific, I remember *it*. It's always the same dream," I answer, earnestly for the first time, my guard coming down ever so slightly. Right before I revert to my default moody teenage persona. "Why? You wanna hear so you can tell me I'm 'harboring resentment' for..."

"For what?" Dr. Ainsley cuts in before I get a chance to finish my sentence. "For your mother dying in that car accident? For you escaping without so much as a scratch? For being left in that home, alone?" I look at her as if she had just sprouted wings in front of me, completely in shock that she knows all this information. "Yes, it's all here, Abby. Everything," she continues as I look down at the floor, the wind completely taken out of me as if I have just been sucker-punched. "Tell me about your dream. You say it's the same dream every night?"

I nod. The only reply I can manage.

"Talk to me, Abigail. What have you got to lose?"

I try to run the option over in my head. Whether telling her could be of any help whatsoever, but my brain is a muddle. I can't form a coherent thought. Silence drags on and, before I know it, words come spewing from my lips. There's no thought behind them, they just come fast and frantic. The dream that keeps me up at night, the dream—no, the nightmare-that plagues me when I'm awake.

"It's like I'm in another world. Maybe I'm subconsciously trying to escape this one, but it's a world that feels..." I pause, not sure whether I should bother carrying on.

"Feels what?" Dr. Ainsley urges me to continue.

"Feels...too familiar. Like I've been there. It's this world, but it's not. It's like a hell on earth." I close my eyes as I visualize the nightmare. I don't have to think too hard. It's not like I have to drag it up from the recesses of my memory bank. It's at the front, ever present, ever threatening to crash its way through my thoughts. "There're bodies on the floor. Surrounding me. Kids I go to school with. I'm in a room. I don't know where, but the roof has caved in. The sky, it isn't normal, it's red. Not the red you get when there's a beautiful sunset. Its blood red. Creatures are flying about in the sky, like bugs, but much, much bigger. They look like people with wings, but I can't make out their faces."

"What happens next?"

"I keep looking over my shoulder, around the empty room. Someone–or something–is following me. I try to run, but I trip and land face first on the floor. I look next to me and see what I tripped on. My best friend, Sam. She's dead. I try to scramble away, but as I roll over this...this huge shadow looms over me. It seems to cover the whole sky. It's...a person. A man. He stands over me, huge wings stretch from his back and cover the sky..." I stop, my heart racing, mouth dry.

"And then...?" Dr. Ainsley says. The sound of her pencil scratching against her notebook as she furiously tries to keep up, sounds like nails on a chalkboard. It's annoying.

I open my eyes and take a deep breath in an attempt to bring my heart rate down to semi-normal. I look over at her, perched on the edge of her seat, eyes wide as she studies me. Her pencil is armed and at the ready, hovering just above her cream-colored paper. I notice how thick the paper looks, and think to myself that it must be expensive. Then I realize how much business she probably gets. There must be loads of children and teenagers out there that have been damaged by their parents. Or bullies at school.

I stand up and grab my bag, all the while her eyes follow me, her mouth slightly open as if she's about to say something, but I get there first.

"I'm sorry, I can't do this," I say as I head towards the exit.

"Abby, please..."

"Look, I'm sorry, but I don't know you, so I'm not going to start opening up. Besides, it's a dream. It has no bearing on my real life. How could it?"

I reach the wooden door and yank it open.

"You can come back anytime, Abby. I really think I can help you."

What she says stops me in my tracks. For a minute, I consider going back, sitting down, and really talking to her. Dr. Ainsley sounds like she really wants to help, not just faking it because it's her job, but genuine concern rattles in her voice. The thought of finishing that story, though...

The details of my nightmare flash before me and my decision is made.

"Thanks for the talk." I slam the door shut behind me.

6

I decide to walk home for the same reason I walked to my appointment. I'm going to be in major trouble for being late, but the thought of running into some of my fellow students on the bus while dressed in my gym clothes and carrying a bag of my sopping wet jeans is enough to send me into a panic attack. Sure, Mia has probably already told everyone what happened, but why give them a visual to go with the story? It's a long walk, and I've done it once today already, but I don't mind. Plus, I need some time to think. It's bad enough that every time I close my eyes to sleep, my nightmare rears its ugly head, having to drag it up so Dr. Ainsley could hear it was another experience altogether.

I'm sure Dr. Ainsley wants to help, she's a doctor, why wouldn't she? It's literally her job to help people. I just don't see what spilling my guts to an absolute stranger is going to do. Except maybe make her think I *am* crazy. Sometimes, I think that myself. Maybe I'm losing my mind.

I wish my mum were here. I've been thinking about her a lot lately, which is odd. I don't really remember her, so I find it strange that I've been thinking that things would be better if she were here. Maybe they wouldn't. Maybe they would be worse, but I doubt it. She's my mum. Surely, she would know what to do.

The only thing I have to remember her by is my necklace. I automatically raise my hand to it. My fingers run over the gold angel wings, one of which is broken. I like to think that this was her way of giving me a guardian angel for protection.

Well, whoever this angel is, they've failed.

I slowly walk down the quiet back street, ignoring the tall corn that sways on the opposite side of the road. If you've never seen it before, it would amaze you. The corn towers over the average person and stretches as far as the eye can see. It dances lightly to Mother Nature's tune of the whistling wind. It's a sight to behold. Unless, like me, you see it every day of your life, in which case, it's just corn. It's a stark contrast to the side of the road where I'm walking, which is just dense woodland. Even in the middle of the day it looks like night in there.

I'm pushed as far over from the road as possible. There's no sidewalk here, so I'm basically walking on the outskirts of the woods to avoid any oncoming traffic. Twigs and leaves crunch under my feet as I do my best to avoid stepping on animal turds, or worse, roadkill. I look up ahead and can see the trees starting to clear as an opening presents itself. A building appears through the gaps in the trees, but I barely take any notice. I've walked this backroad so many times in the six months I lived here. I've seen everything. I don't stop, but I briefly glance up and have a quick look at the run down, battered old church. The cross hanging from the top, the broken windows, the scattering of beer cans. The white wooden slats, chipped, the paint peeling away in flakes. The cracks in religion obvious for the world to see. The top, blackened with only remnants of a roof left.

Some budding arsonist has been here practicing his craft.

Apparently, years ago, this was the only church in town, which is shocking to me considering how religious this community is. It's never been something that has appealed to me–religion. I wish it did. It must be nice to have that kind of faith. That comfort. If there is a God, though, he has a right sadistic sense of humor. One quick look in a newspaper or on social media is evidence enough of that.

From what I can gather from books I've read in the school library of town history, on a Sunday there would be so many people here that they couldn't all fit in for the weekly service. Some people would have to stand outside. This was considered a hazard, so they built a new, bigger church further in town and this one was just kind of...forgotten. That's what happens to things once people have no use for them anymore. They get forgotten. I can kind of relate.

As I pass the church something odd catches my eye. Something new. Frowning, I turn and take a couple of steps into the woodland. When you know a place like that back of your hand, catching the smallest glimpse of something new gets your attention. I see something on the floor partially obscured by a fallen tree. Another couple of steps though and I stop dead in my tracks. Lying prostrate on the floor, unmoving, eyes wide but lifeless, tongue hanging from the side of its mouth, is a deer. It's definitely dead, but it looks so alive. There's no blood, it hasn't been hit by a truck or a car. There are no injuries on it at all. It looks frozen.

I look around hoping to see someone, but the road is empty, not one car has driven past in the time I've been walking down it. It's one of the reasons I love to come this way. I'm alone. Now though, alone doesn't feel comforting. Now it feels panic-inducing.

I frown as I look at the beautiful animal lying motionless before me. I raise my head, thinking that when I get home, I should call the local vet or something. He may not be able to save her, but he might know what to do with the body instead of just leaving it here for other, less beautiful animals to snack on. As I look up, though, something else piques my interest. Something...more.

I take a few steps further, past the deer and the old church. I can't make out what I'm looking at, so continue to walk. My heart is beating so fast, I'm sure someone will hear it even though there isn't anyone around for miles. What I see next is even more confusing than the deer. A huge patch of grass at the side of the church is burnt. It's as black as coal and in the shape of a circle. A perfect circle.

"How is that possible?" I whisper quietly. It's like those people that go around making crop circles. How do they get the shape so perfect?

Scattered around the burnt circle is dozens, no, hundreds of dead birds. The place looks like an animal graveyard.

I look around at this horror movie scene that is spread before my eyes, and a shiver runs up my spine. Starting at my tailbone and travelling all the way to my crown. Despite the warmth of the weather, even with the overcast that appeared, the shiver causes goosebumps to appear on my forearms. I can feel my blood pumping in my ears. It's deafening. I want to turn and run from the woods, but my feet won't move. I'm frozen to the spot.

My mind goes blank.

A veil of darkness slowly drops over my eyes.

The sound of a truck echoes as it skids across the empty road. It seems to break me free of whatever trance I was in, and I run from the woods back out into the open. I look up and down, but find only emptiness. I turn to look back into the woods and the church. From this angle, I can't see much, just the deer's legs poking out from behind a tree, the burnt grass and dead birds are all but invisible from here. I take a deep breath and try to compose myself, and then I notice how dark it is. I look up and the sun is setting, a dull glow hangs in the air as dusk settles in.

"How? I was only in there seconds."

Wasn't I?

Momentarily forgetting what I've just seen, I take off at a run down the road toward the farm.

Tom's going to be so angry.

7

I finally make it home. It's pitch dark out by now and I've no idea where the time has gone. I stand in front of the farmhouse, hesitant to go in. I know I'm going to be in trouble for being late and not getting my chores done. My only hope of escaping being shouted at–or worse–is that he's already drunk and passed out in his tattered old chair.

I look up into the sky. Pretty much a clear night. A small misting of cloud travels its way across the full moon. Not enough to obscure the light it provides, but just enough to be noticeable. Seeing as there's no streetlights down our country road, on nights like this, the only light we get is from the moon. When it can't be seen due to heavy clouds, you'd need a torch just to find the front door.

The moon eerily shines across the farm, and while scary, it's also beautiful. I know I never really take the time to appreciate just how beautiful it is, but tonight I can't seem to help it. Maybe it's the horrors of what I witnessed back at the church. Maybe I'm just putting off walking through the door. I take a deep breath and, much like when I was back at Dr. Ainsley's office, decide that putting it off is only going to make things worse. I head for the side door that leads into the kitchen. Maybe that way I can avoid him if he's watching television or passed out. I try to be as quiet as possible, taking catlike steps to the door, but it's no good. No matter how light I step, the gravel beneath my sneaker's crunch and echo into the night, giving me away.

From here, I can faintly hear the sound of the horses snorting in the barn. I want to run in there and spend the night with them. I seem to talk with them more than I do anyone other than Sam.

As silently as possible, I turn the door handle and open it a crack. Peering through, I look at the empty kitchen. The main light is off, but the lamp in the hallway illuminates the kitchen creating a warm glow. It looks very homely–quite the opposite of what it actually is. I open the door a little wider, and through the large archway that opens the kitchen up to the entrance hall and stairs, I scan the surroundings, looking for my uncle.

I can't see him.

I turn my body sideways and slip through. Turning my back on the kitchen so I can put all my concentration into silently closing the door, I turn the handle and fit the door into the gap without the latch clicking.

"Where the hell have you been? You any idea of the time?" my uncle's voice booms through the silent farmhouse. The walls seem to shake. It's like when a truck thunders its way down a deserted, quiet country lane. The roar of the engine brings the world around it to life.

Fear roots me to the spot. I don't want to turn around, but I know I have no choice. If I don't turn willingly, he'll come over and turn me himself. I slowly swivel on the spot, my eyes initially never leaving the floor. Once I have one-eightied my position, I lift my head from the floor and look at my uncle. As my eyes travel up his hunched body, I notice he's still wearing the clothes he had on this morning. His work clothes. His white socks are now a dull gray and have more than one hole in them. Dirty jeans he doesn't bother to wash because 'they'll just get dirty again,' and his red flannel shirt completely open revealing a nicotine and beer-stained vest. His unshaven face is complete with red blotches that compliment his bloodshot eyes. I steal a look past him and notice the pile of empty beer cans stacked next to his moth-eaten armchair.

Great.

We stand staring at each other. Two cowboys in the wild west, except this cowboy can't help but tremble.

"Y'all deaf now? Where ya been, girl?" his booming voice causes me to jump, again. I expect him to be slurring his words, but I suppose the half dozen or so empty cans aren't enough to penetrate the tolerance he has built up. I try to kid myself that his reaction to what time I have come home is due to concern for my wellbeing. But I know that couldn't be further from the truth. His main issue is probably that I haven't managed to get my chores done. "This place is a mess. You were supposed to get it tidied up after school, I can't do everyfin' on this farm. I told ya that."

There you go.

"I'm sorry, I got held up at school," I manage to reply.

For the first time through his rage, he seems to notice what I'm wearing and if it's possible, it makes him angrier. "You walked home like that?"

I look down at myself. It feels as if heat is penetrating from his eyes and burning its way through me. Like Superman using his heat vision.

"I didn't have a choice. There was...there was an accident at school and my clothes they...they got wet," I answer, holding up the plastic bag full of now dry clothes, too scared to tell him the truth. "Luckily, we had gym last period so I could just wear my gym clothes home."

"Your clothes gettin' wet has caused you to be hours late?"

"The school bus broke down," I answer as quick as I can.

"I don't believe ya," he says through gritted teeth.

"I don't care," I answer as I quickly push my way past him and half walk half run up the stairs, immediately regretting the outburst.

I don't look back, but I can hear him behind me as his feet stomp on the wooden floor, following me up the stairs. I slam my bedroom door as he's halfway through shouting at me. His raised voice becoming a muffled echo as the door partially dampens his shouting.

"Don't you dare walk away from me. You get your ass out here and finish your damn chores."

I grab a chair and wedge it under the door handle. It's a huge oak chair from the dining room downstairs. When my uncle questioned why I brought it up here, I'd told him it was so I had somewhere to sit when I'm doing my homework, which is partially true. The main reason was for situations exactly like this.

I take a step back from the door and watch in fear as the handle goes up and down, up and down. The chair digs into the floor as the handle hits the back rest, stopping it from opening fully.

"You're already in enough trouble, girl. Don't you go makin' it worse."

Judging by his mood, I'm not sure it can get any worse. I slide my window up and scramble out onto the flat roof. I turn around and lower myself off and nimbly swing from it as I drop onto the ground outside. For anyone watching, it would become immediately obvious that this isn't the first time I've done this. I can still hear his shouts for me to open the door, but they slowly fade away as I take off at a run and disappear through tall swaying crops, hoping that by the time I come back home, he'll be asleep.

8

I'm deep in the woods that are at the back of our land.

I sit staring at the river that runs in front of me. The sound of the water trickling over the rocks is pure peace. More than once, I've fallen asleep here listening to it. Now, I sit with a blanket covering my knees and hug both to my chest. It isn't cold really, but now the sun has set, there does seem to be a slight chill in the air. I look over at the small black patch of grass on the floor, bits of bark and twigs are scattered around it. The remnants of an old fire. I consider lighting another, but know I won't be here long enough to warrant it. I'll make do with the blanket and the lean to shelter I've created from the roof of an old tent.

This is my favorite place. My safe place. I love coming here and listening to the river, lighting a small fire and cooking some sausages. I'm quite the Grizzly Adam's when I want to be. My favorite times are when it's raining. The sound of the drops splashing in the river or hammering against my makeshift roof is so satisfyingly relaxing. Really, at the end of the day, anywhere is better than home when he's in one of his moods.

Suddenly, as if by some kind of sixth sense, I become aware I'm not alone. I don't know how, there was no noise, but I get that *feeling* you get. That creepy feeling that someone is watching you. A shiver runs up my spine as I start to think he's found me. That Uncle Tom has somehow managed to track me down and now he knows about my sanctuary. The thought of not being able to escape here in the future upsets me more than knowing how much trouble I'm going to be in. So much trouble that he has decided to come out and get me instead of waiting at home.

He's never done this before.

My eyes dart around the trees, scanning the area for him. At first, I see nothing, but I know someone is there. My eyes continue moving left and right, looking out across the river into the dense woodland opposite. And then I see him, standing there. It isn't my uncle. In fact, I have no idea who it is. He isn't looking at me. He just stares into the river, watching the water flow much in the same way I do.

He looks to be about my age, a year older maybe. His scruffy blond hair sits on his broad shoulders. He looks tall. Taller than a lot of the guys at my school. His skin is a ghostly white that seems to shine in the darkness. He looks as if he's made from porcelain. His blond hair making him look like some kind of pale surfer, completely at odds with the buzz cuts most kids seem to wear around these parts. I sit and stare at him, not able to tear my eyes away. He may be the most beautiful person I have ever seen. He looks completely out of place in this rural backwater of a town. Like he should be gracing the catwalk of some fashion show in Los Angeles. Even though he's only wearing a white V-neck and black jeans, it sits on him much better than it would anyone else. He looks like a model. Anyone else would look like they've just walked off a construction site.

Suddenly, he looks directly at me.

"Oh, hey, I'm sorry, I didn't expect anyone else to be out here. I hope I didn't scare you."

I don't answer him right away. I try to collect my thoughts. It can be scary enough being a girl and coming across a stranger in a public place, let alone isolated in the woods–where no one can hear you scream. I continue to look at him nervously, eyes unblinking. Like a rabbit caught in headlights. My mind fighting against the happiness I feel that there is a small body of water separating us, the other part upset he's too far away to touch.

"Are you okay?" he asks.

I can't place his accent. It's American, but not redneck enough to be from this town. He's definitely not from the South.

I hear his feet shuffle in the grass and twigs as he moves to walk around the lake. I flinch at the thought of him coming across to my camp and slowly crawl back under my shelter even further. He stops.

"Relax. I come in peace." His hands raised, palms facing me in a 'I surrender' pose.

"I'm fine," I manage after another long pause. "I just didn't expect anyone to be out here. No one ever is."

"It looks like you'd know. Got yourself a nice little apartment there," he waves his hands at my cabin in the woods.

"Sometimes it's nice to be alone."

"I'm sorry, I didn't mean to disturb you. We all need alone time. I'll get going."

"No, wait!" I blurt out, shocking even myself. Suddenly, I'm standing up without realizing it, no idea what I should do next. At first, I didn't want him here, now two minutes later, I don't want him to leave. "You don't have to go."

He looks across the lake at me and a small smile plays on his lips. One side of his mouth arches up revealing the whitest teeth I have ever seen in my life. My insides feel as if they're on fire.

"I just thought I would do a little exploring, get to know the place. We've just moved into the old Anderson place upon the hill. You know it?"

I take a deep breath before I answer. The way he looks seems to have gotten me a little flustered. Not just the way he looks, but the way he looks at *me.*

"Yes...I mean...no. Well, kinda. I've only been in the neighborhood a few months myself, and it's been empty ever since I've been here. Only ever passed it once."

"So, we're both new, huh?" he says to me, that smile still flirting on his lips.

I find myself managing to smile back at him, the butterflies having a full-on shindig in my belly. "I guess so."

We stand staring at each other from across the lake, both smiling. Although, I'm sure the look on my face makes me look much goofier than the male model smirk he has on his. For the first time, it dawns on me how I must look compared to him, my faded vest that's a size too small, my gym shorts that have definitely seen better days. I'm not sure whether the clothes I wore to school would have been any better, but for the first time in my life I wish I had them on. My smile falters as I self-consciously (and futilely) try to cover myself. My right leg crossing over my left and my arms automatically fold in front of me. Something I have learnt to do over the years to cover the hand marks where my uncle has drunkenly grabbed me. Working on a farm also helps. Easy to pass them off as everyday injuries. If the person doesn't look that close of course and see each individual finger mark perfectly formed into dark blue, and eventually, yellowy brown dots.

"Well...I suppose I better be getting back," he eventually says. "That chicken coop isn't going to clean itself."

"I feel your pain."

He turns and starts to walk away, waving a hand over his shoulder. I look down at the floor, glad he's gone, not wanting him to linger too long in my current state, but also not wanting him to go.

"Hopefully I'll see you around. Stay safe...Abigail."

And then he's gone, disappearing amongst the trees as quick as he seemed to have appeared. I turn and head back into my safe haven, and then stop dead in my tracks. I don't even know his name. Being startled by him and in all the confusion I forgot to even ask. I was too busy looking at his face to even concern myself with it, yet somehow, he knew mine. I didn't give it to him. At least, I'm pretty sure I didn't. So how did he know it? And what did he mean by 'stay safe'? Was that just because I am out here, deep in the woods, alone? Or something else?

I turn back toward the dense woodland and just stare. Scanning the tree line, seeing nothing. No indication that anyone was here at all. I look down at the ground where he stood and see the disturbed leaves, a patch scattered where he was standing. A line trails off into the trees where he had walked and then, the further I study, it just stops. The line where he had walked just comes to an end. A huge patch of leaves directly in front of it, undisturbed, as if he just stopped and...disappeared.

9

I urge my legs to move faster, but it's no use, I'm at top speed. Puffing and panting, almost completely out of breath, but I don't dare to stop. I have to just power through and fight the sharp pain that's starting to stab in my lungs. I start to get that metallic taste in the back of my throat that I get when I'm running cross country during gym. That's usually the point where I have to stop, but that isn't an option here. Stopping surely means death. I continue to run through the corridors of my school like a girl possessed—I use my hands as both weapon and shield as I simultaneously try to push the doors open and also stop them from pinging back and hitting me in the face. I fail on both counts. My arms not moving fast enough cause me to fumble the door. I run headfirst into it and the pain through my nose causes my eyes to water.

Any other day I would stop to nurse it. But not today.

The sky, a blood red that causes an eerie scarlet glow to cover everything underneath. Like a blanket of blood. I fight the urge to look over my shoulder, knowing full well that it would slow me down, but it's hard. I'm desperate to know how close my assailant is. The shrieks and cries of the creatures flying overhead seem to rattle my eardrums—it sends a shiver up my spine and for the first time I think no matter how far I run, it'll never be far enough.

Unable to fight it any longer I steal a glance over my shoulder, and there it is. I can't see who, or more accurately, what it is, but it's gaining on me with every stride it takes. It's like a scene from a horror movie. Even though I'm running at full speed, it still gains on me. I push my way through the last set of doors and sprint into the hall. I look around at the scene before me. This hall is usually used for school dances and theatre performances. Tonight though, it's home to something much more sinister. Bodies lay scattered about the room. Blood pools around them. I notice Sam lying unmoving on the floor, her eyes wide but lifeless. I try to run toward her, but my foot catches on the outstretched arm of another body. For a moment, I feel like I am flying as I soar through the air, until the impact of the ground causes every bone in my body to shake and rattle. My teeth clatter together as my chin collides with the hard wood floor. I try to get up and an intense, sharp pain shoots from my ankle all the way up my leg. It's broken. I'm no doctor, but I know this much.

I hear 'the shape' slowly make its way across the floor in my direction. Its shoes clip clopping with every step. In seconds it will be on me.

So, this is it, this is how I'm going to die, during some kind of crazy apocalypse. I feel like I'm living in Sunnydale. Is this my own personal Hellmouth?

Then I hear footsteps behind me. I look over my shoulder in the opposite direction of my pursuer. Someone else is here. I scan behind me, my eyes pleading for help, and find nothing but a shadow. The red glow from the blood sky obscures my vision. The figure bends down and I see what it is for the first time. Or more accurately, who it is. It's him, the blond-haired boy I met at the lake–the stranger whose name I don't even know.

"If you want to live, I suggest you come with me." He looks up behind me. Whatever has been chasing me is almost upon us. "Now."

I wake up.

My heart is beating faster than it ever has before, like a marching band rehearsing inside me. My vest and shorts stick to me, my skin slick with sweat. I lay in bed and try to compose myself. This was the same dream–sorry, nightmare–I always have, but this time, there were differences. This time there was someone there to help me. As usual after one of these nightmares my hand immediately goes to my mother's necklace. I rub the wings between my fingers. I don't know why, but it always seems to soothe me.

I swing my legs out of my bed and sit on the edge. I look at the clock on my dresser–05:30am. I have a little while before my alarm will sound, but I lean over and turn it off, I won't be going back to sleep now. I pull the curtain back slightly and see my uncle in the morning glow dumping feed into the chicken coup. I've got time to have a nice hot shower before starting breakfast, which is good. I don't want to start him off in a bad mood first thing. I got lucky yesterday. By the time I had returned from the lake he had managed to down another few cans of beer and was passed out in his chair, he would have forgotten all about it this morning. That's how things usually go.

I will say this about him, for someone who drinks as much as he does, he never oversleeps. He's always up and out on the farm bright and early. That's either very impressive or he knows unless he does his job, he won't be able to afford anymore beer.

I lower the curtain and grab my wash bag and head to the bathroom. Maybe today I'll have enough time to get ready, do breakfast and be on time for my bus.

10

I was wrong.

I stand rooted to the spot, half in disbelief and half in exasperation. I trade my books from one arm to the other and pull my phone out to double check the time. Brilliant, just my luck–it's come early for once. Okay, just by a minute, but early is early. I suppose it didn't help that my uncle wasn't happy with his eggs, so I had to redo them, but still, I really thought I was going to make it this time.

I take a deep breath, slowly rub my necklace, and fight back tears. The deep breath seems to work, and the tears stay away, for now.

A rustle in the corn causes me to snap my head around. I study the corn unable to shake the feeling that I'm being watched. It sways and hisses in the breeze, looming over me ominously, as if it's alive. It looks like...*is that someone in the field? Lurking behind the corn?* "Uncle Tom...Is that you?" I try to shout, but only a raspy whisper floats from my lips. I swallow hard and consider taking a step farther in to investigate. As I lift my foot to step forward a strong gust of wind comes causing the corn to sway and bend all over the place. The gust is unusually strong considering how calm and sunny the day had been only moments ago. My hair whips my face. The animals start vocalising their discomfort. Pigs grunting, horses snorting and stamping their feet. I hold my arm across my face as dust billows around me, like a mini tornado starting to form. The weathervane atop the barn starts to spin with such ferocity I fear it may come loose and take off, soaring trough the sky and impaling some unsuspecting farmer. I stumble back as the huge trees in the woodland opposite creak as if about to snap.

Then–it stops.

Just ends, as if someone has unplugged a hugely powerful fan. I look again, my eyes piercing through the gaps in the now unmoving cornfield. There's nothing there. *C'mon Abby, get a grip on yourself.*

A shiver runs down my spine and I decide it's time to move on. I'm going to be late enough as it is. I just hope that my being late again doesn't result in Mr. Heaver thinking another appointment with Dr. Ainsley would be the answer to me getting the bus on time.

I start to make my way to school on foot, kicking up dirt and dust as I go not worrying about my already filthy sneakers. I make sure to keep to the side of the road, as far right as possible, there's no point in tempting fate and playing chicken with traffic.

I reach the burnt-out church and can't help, but stop to inspect the animal graveyard once again. Part of me expects to see the place all cleaned up, that someone may have called the town council and complained but I know that'll never happen. Nobody else has probably seen it. Not only is this a quiet road, but the vehicles that do go past probably don't even stop for a second look. The footfall down this quiet street is non-existent. If it wasn't for my run in with Tom, I would have remembered to report it myself.

The deer looks even worse than before, rotted away or eaten by other animals maybe. I can't help but marvel once again at the number of dead birds here. What could have done something like this? To kill this many birds in what must have been an instant, considering how they're all lying in the same area.

Once again, I seem to fall into some kind of trance as I look on the horrific scene before me. This time though I'm pulled out of it relatively quickly, almost immediately in fact as the roar of a truck echoes through the surrounding trees.

I turn and continue my journey realizing that if I don't start to pick up the pace, I won't just be late–I'll be *really* late.

The truck starts to get closer. I can hear it coming up behind me and it's so loud it seems as if the ground beneath me is shaking. I'm not sure whether it's loud because it's old or because it's so quiet. One glance over my shoulder answers the questions for me: it's a little of both.

Still looking over my shoulder I use my hand to shield the sun from my eyes. I can't make out if it's dark green or black. What I can see are all the dents and scratches. It must be from the sixties. I'm sure a car enthusiast would call it a classic, the best I can do is recognize that it is a Chevrolet. Other than that, I'm at a loss. I turn back around and power walk, ignoring the Chevy earthquake that is almost upon me. The closer it gets I can hear it slow down as if it's going to come to a stop near me and I become aware of how alone I actually am. *'In the woods, no one can hear your screams.'* I think to myself again. I wish I was one of those girls that carried some pepper spray in her bag. Not to worry, I've worked on farms since I was a kid. I've got twice as much strength as a boy my age, if this bozo wants a fight, I'll damn sure give him one.

"Hey neighbor," a friendly voice calls from the cab of the truck. "Wanna ride to school?"

I stop and angle my head toward the truck to see…him. The boy from yesterday. His radiant smile seems to blind me almost as much as the scorching sun. I look from him to the beaten down old truck he's driving and expect him to look out of place, but strangely, he doesn't. The sleeves of his black Levi's shirt are rolled up to his elbows and his hair sits effortlessly at the nape of his neck. Not styled, but as if he has just run it through with his fingers. Bed head...but sexy bed head.

"How do you know where I'm going?"

"The books are a bit of a giveaway," he replies as he nods in the direction of my arms, filled with books the size of breezeblocks. "It looks like you could do with some help." He leans across the cab of the truck and flings open the passenger side door. I hesitate for a moment. I don't really know this guy and him being super-hot isn't really an excuse to just jump in his truck with him. I then look down at the weight beginning to pull my arms from their sockets. Coupled with the fact I can really do with not being late again today, I decide it's worth the risk. Plus, if he was a psycho murderer, he could have easily killed me when we were alone in the woods, right? Not really a scientific way of thinking, but deep down, I know I want to get in the truck and I'm looking for any excuse to convince myself. I walk around and launch my books onto the bench seat and climb in, making sure my books and bag create kind of a barrier between us. No harm in still being a little cautious.

As the truck moves off my attention is drawn to the inside. I expect it to be a mirror image of the outside, dirty with ripped seats and a footwell filled with candy bar wrappers and cans of soda–or beers. What I find though is the complete opposite. The seats are immaculate. So immaculate in fact that the inside looks brand new while the outside looks fifty years old. I could run my finger across the interior of the truck and wouldn't find a speck of dust

'He must clean this thing a dozen times a day.' I think to myself.

I look down at the floor and notice that apart from where my filthy sneakers currently rest, there isn't a spec of dirt, mud or gravel.

What I believe to be my covert scanning of his showroom quality interior isn't as covert as I thought.

"Find what you're looking for?" he asks with a smile in his voice.

I snap my head up. "Sorry. I just can't believe how clean it is in here." I look back down at the mess I've dragged in. "Or was."

"It's fine. I'll give it a once over with the dust buster when I get home later. I like to keep things clean."

"I can see that."

He focuses his eyes on the road in front of him with occasional glances in his mirrors. Quite the responsible driver. I find I can't take my eyes off him. His gorgeous hair, his perfect skin, which doesn't seem to have a mark on it–I find this makes me angry and then self-conscious about how my one or two zits must look like volcanoes about to erupt compared to his smooth porcelain surface. I see his eyes shift slyly in my direction and I look down at my hands, nervous he caught me studying him.

"What were you so interested in back there?"

"What do you mean?" I ask far too quickly, wondering if he was referring to me staring at him.

"As I was coming down the road you were rooted to the spot, staring into the woods."

"Oh, nothing much," I say, unconvincingly.

"You seemed pretty engrossed for 'nothing much'," he presses.

"There's an old burnt-out church there."

"Has it just happened?"

"No–been like that since I've been here. From what I heard it happened years ago."

"Why so interesting now then?"

I think whether I should bother to answer him or just brush it off and change the subject. The fact of the matter is I don't have an answer. Yes, there are the piles of dead animals that initially drew my attention, but there's something else. Something I don't really want to explain, or more accurately, can't explain. After a while I think, what the hell. I don't know him, who cares if he thinks I'm crazy. There's a sharp pain in my abdomen at this thought because of course, I care what he thinks of me. I try to ignore the thought and push it aside.

"I don't know–I can't explain it," I begin. "There's a pile of dead animals that seem to have come out of nowhere. Hundreds of birds, a dead deer."

"Maybe it was a truck or something."

"That killed a deer and then simultaneously managed to murder a hundred birds?" I ask, not remotely convinced. He shrugs as if he knows it's highly unlikely. "Well, that's what initially caught my attention, and then the closer I looked I noticed a huge blacked out section of grass. Like it had been burned. Trees around it lay on the floor, scorched. It was really weird." I look over at him to see if he's laughing, but there's no sign of humor on his face. Quite the opposite actually. He has his teeth clenched and his jaw bulges as he grinds what I'm sure are perfect teeth. *'In for a nickel in for a dollar,'* I think to myself and decide to press on. "The burnt patch...no, not patch, it's too big to be described as patch. The burnt section of grass is new, it wasn't there last week and on top of that it's a perfect circle. How is that even possible?"

"Aliens?" he asks with a little smile this time. Right, okay. He's now making fun of me.

"Haha," I muster up sarcastically. "It's weird–I can't really describe it–I just felt...drawn to it, like I couldn't take my eyes away." I can feel him looking at me as I look down at my lap, my hands automatically going to my necklace.

The silence drags. I can hear my heart beating.

"It's probably just kids messing around," he offers. I think about challenging him on how a bunch of kids would go about slaughtering hundreds of birds, but stop myself. If I'm honest, I would rather the change in subject.

We reach a stop sign at the end of the back road and he checks his mirrors, slows to a stop and clicks on his blinker. After checking left and right (several times) he slowly eases out onto the main road that leads into town. I was right before, he is quite the responsible driver, even on that deserted road I don't think he exceeded the speed limit once.

"Can you tell me something?" I ask, trying to end what seemed to be another mammoth silence. Well, that and because I was curious of course. His only response is a shrug and a slight nod that I interpret as go ahead. "Yesterday, down by the lake you knew my name even though I didn't tell you. How?"

He takes a moment to answer. I look at him, again unable to take my eyes away from his seeming perfection. His jaw pulses as he contemplates his answer. "It's a small town, when we moved here several people told me that I'd be living up the road from Tom and Abigail Lewis."

"How did you know that I was Abigail when you saw me in the woods?"

"I was told that Abigail was beautiful–you fit that description, so I took shot," he answers with a shrug.

I don't know what to do other than look down. I can feel the blood rush to my face. Part of me thinks he's lying even though I don't want to admit that. No one in this town, as far as I am aware, would ever call me beautiful. Especially if they attend the high school.

"I don't know your name," I manage to whisper while still looking down, too scared to lift my face toward him so he doesn't see my impression of a very ripe tomato.

"How rude of me, I can't believe I never introduced myself. I'm Mike." For the first time since being in the car he takes one of his hands away from the steering wheel and holds it out for me to shake. Hesitantly, I raise my hand and slip it into his. His hand seems huge in comparison to mine, completely engulfing it. I expect it to feel calloused and rough considering the manual work he must do on the farm, but no. It's just as smooth as his face looks. It feels as if an electric charge has jolted its way through my body. Waking me. I find it hard to catch my breath or get my words out. I snatch my hand away as if it has been burned. He looks at me oddly, but doesn't comment.

"Nice to meet you...Mike," I manage to say, or gasp.

What the hell is wrong with me?

I compose myself as we drive through the town. I look out of the window at everyone getting on with their lives. The towns folk who have known each other since they were kids. Gone to school together, worked together, go drinking together on a Friday night. The thought scares me. If Uncle Tom had his way that would be me–stuck here forever.

"I'm glad I ran into you actually." Mike's voice draws me away from the dismal look at my future.

"You are?" I ask, happier than is necessary.

"Yeah, being my first day and all. You can show me around, introduce me to a few people. Be nice to have a local show me the ropes."

In spite of myself I let out a harsh laugh. Mike catches that it isn't a happy one and looks at me, eyebrow raised. "I'm not the right person for that."

"How'd you mean?"

"You'll see soon enough." Is all I can muster as a response. I can't help but wonder if as soon as he sees how I'm treated at school, how uncool I am, if he will no longer speak to me.

I mean look at this guy, he's bound to walk straight into that school and immediately be a part of the 'cool clique.'

We continue in silence. We've left the main town square and are driving along Skipton Road which leads right into the school's main gates. The closer we get to the school the more my heart starts to race. I wonder what pleasures it holds for me today. From the corner of my eye, I keep catching Mike glancing in my direction. If I were a more confident person maybe I would think he was checking me out, but seeing as my confidence couldn't be any lower if it were buried six feet underground, I don't really entertain that thought.

"Find what you're looking for?" I ask, hoping he might laugh at the obvious reference to his question earlier. Unfortunately, he doesn't. He looks serious. He slowly reaches across the truck's front cab and lightly strokes my arm with the backs of his fingers. His touch is so light, but once again, that jolt of electricity courses throughout my body. Like I'm being shocked awake, Frankenstein's monster style.

"What happened?" Mike asks, his voice tight.

I look down at where he's touching and realize that it wasn't in anyway a romantic gesture. His fingers brush over the bruises on my arm, the five bluish black dots that are grouped pretty closely together. Immediately my defences come up and I snatch my arm away.

"What's it to do with you? What is it with everyone wanting to know my business…Heaver, Dr. Ainsley and now you? Why can't you all just worry about yourselves!?" I shout, my temper running away with me in a defensive outburst I am sure I will cringe about later.

"I'm sorry," Mike begins. "It just looks painful, and I thought…"

"You thought what?" I interrupt. "That by you asking these bruises will automatically disappear? I work on a farm. There's tools and machinery around, accidents happen, and people get hurt. Why can't anyone understand that!?"

"Tools that are the same shape as fingers?"

I don't answer. I know it's stupid of me to expect Mike, or anyone for that matter to believe that these bruises—that are so obviously the result of someone grabbing my arm—have been caused by farm equipment. I mean, you can see from a mile away that they're fingers marks.

One of the many times my uncle has grabbed hold of me in one of his drunken rages.

But I can't say that. I won't say that.

I turn my head and look out of the passenger side window. Mike doesn't press the matter any further and we just continue what's left of the journey in silence.

11

The school parking lot is heaving with people. Every space seems to be filled with a car, truck or bike of some description. Groups of students hang around waiting for the bell to chime.

It never ceases to amaze me just how big this school is for such a small town. Admittedly, if you were to drive on down to Austen or one of the other larger Texan cities, this would be the equivalent of a small elementary school. Maybe it just seems like there's a lot of people considering the building itself isn't huge–I mean, everyone knows who everyone else is so can't be deemed as that big. But seeing all these people just hanging around, it gives the impression of an enormous campus.

It's unusual for me to see this. On the rare occasions I catch the bus it drops us off a little further down the road and I never walk through the parking lot. On the days I miss it, I might come this way, but everyone else is usually in class.

Mike slowly navigates his way around groups of students idly standing. The navigating becomes less of a problem though seeing as the truck is so loud most people hear it coming long before we're near them. Initially, it's the noise and the battered bodywork that attracts most eyes in our direction, what keeps their eyes on us though seems to be Mike's face. I can practically see the girls in my class wide eyed and giggling to each other as they point at him. The boys seem to screw their faces up and wave their hand in some form of dismissal to the girl's reactions. Their admiration for Mike soon turns to shock though when they notice who's sitting next to him.

I feel I should duck, hide my face, but it is too late for that now, most people have seen me. I decide on a half and half technique. I rest my elbow on the inside of the door and put my hand to my forehead, semi shielding my face. Mike is oblivious to the reactions he has elicited from everyone, but seems keen enough to notice my half-hidden face. I catch him looking in my direction, but he says nothing. Maybe my outburst earlier has made him think better of offering his unsolicited opinions.

I hope so.

Mike circles the parking lot, unsuccessfully looking for a space. It seems to take forever and the agony of people staring at us gets worse and worse. Especially as I know exactly what they're thinking. *'What's this farm trash doing with this Greek God?'*

From my position of looking at the floor of the truck, I feel it start to turn.

Finally.

I look up and my relief is short lived.

I know on the face of it, all the spaces in the lot are exactly the same. Same size, same shape. But somehow, out of all the spaces Mike could have chosen, he has managed to pick the worst space here. Quite a miracle really.

I let out an audible groan. If there is a God, there's no doubt in my mind he is out to get me. To make my life an absolute misery. I look out of the driver's side window, past Mike and into the world outside. A huge black Dodge truck is in the space next to where we just pulled in. I would know the truck a mile off. It's Brad's. You'd be forgiven for thinking we were at a party instead of waiting for school to start. Brad and his gang, which includes Mia, crowd around with music playing, talking loudly and singing along. They crowd around the truck, sit in it or lounge about on the flat bed. Brad loves showing off how much money his family have, and this truck is his way of doing it. All they need is a few cans of beer and a bonfire and they'd have themselves a right little shindig.

You'd think that one of the teachers would come and tell him to turn it down, but they wouldn't want to antagonize the star of the football team, would they? Especially when his parents donate so much money to the school. Having a huge car dealership right on the outskirts of town has its benefits.

Mike doesn't even seem to notice the tail bed party going on to his left, or the fact that everyone is staring in our direction. Brad included. This isn't going to end well for Mike. It's one thing parking next to Brad's pride and joy, everyone knows that that's a no no. But having me in his old truck, the dirty farm girl. Well, that just adds insult to injury.

From my seat I can see Brad frowning in our direction, trying to recognize who this vehicle belongs to. Trying to see who would have the audacity to be anywhere near his truck.

"You couldn't have picked a worse place," I groan, deflated.

Mike looks at me for a long time, but doesn't say anything. I'm sure the corners of his mouth are twitching into what can only be described as a smirk, but I can't be sure. I'm not sure why he would be smirking, but I'm sure it will be short lived when Brad forces him to move his truck away. Mike is a tall guy, but so is Brad, and he's built like a barn door. If he wants Mike to move then I'm sure he'll make him.

This could get ugly.

It's an unwritten rule that no one parks next to the Dodge. A rule we just broke.

"Look, I think maybe we should move." I notice Brad and a few of his goons jump down from the truck.

"This space is perfect, right by the school entrance. I can't believe it was empty."

"There's a reason it was."

I take another quick look over my shoulder out of the trucks back window to see Brad pointing at the less than pristine condition of Mike's truck and laughing with his friends. I take a deep breath and open my door. No point in delaying the inevitable, we may as well get this over with. Mike doesn't make a move, he just sits there. Watching me.

I make my way around the back of the truck, books in hand and bag slung over my shoulder. Brad's annoyance over having someone park next to his truck seems to have turned to malicious happiness at the state of the offending vehicle. As I round the flat bed, he looks up and noticing who it is, his silent laughter turns to an audible chuckle. Like a pantomime villain.

"Well, well, well, what have we here?" Brad saunters around the truck and meets me at the back. "Dirty farm girl coming to school in a...dirty farm truck. It's just too perfect." He runs his finger over the body work, as if wiping dust away to emphasize the filthiness of it.

All his friends laugh, like a pack of hyenas. None more so then Mia who seems to have a real glint in her eye.

"Look, I'm sorry. He's new here...his first day actually and he didn't know not to..."

"I don't care how new he is. I don't want this heap anywhere near my baby." Brad scowls at the truck for added effect. "I'm worried it might catch a dent just by being close to it."

Again, the gang of Stooges laugh at a joke that wasn't remotely funny. I steal a quick look past him into the open door of the Dodge. It's the complete opposite of Mike's. While the outside is immaculate, the inside looks like the contents of a garbage can have been tipped into it. Candy bar wrappers, drinks, mud on the seats. I suppress the urge to smile, nice to look at on the outside and ugly on the inside.

I'm sure Brad can relate.

"So, who's the lucky farm boy about to get his ass whooped?" Brad kicks the wheel of Mike's truck as he angles his head to try to get a glimpse of the driver. It's no good. Brad squints his eyes as the sun glares blindingly off the driver side window.

I can't help but panic. I hardly know Mike, but that doesn't mean I want to see him get hurt. On his first day as well. What a welcome. I silently pray he just moves it without kicking up a stink.

"Hey, ass hat." Brad begins as he bangs the side of the truck with his brick sized fist, probably hoping to add another dent to the collection. "Move the rust bucket or you'll be leaving here in an ambulance instead."

Brad's friends start to exit the Dodge where they've been watching as if it was some prime-time sport. Which to them, it is.

Finally, Mike's door opens, and he swings out his brown cowboy boots. They make a crunching sound as they hit the gravel of the parking. He doesn't even look at Brad. He turns his back and shuts the driver's door. I look around and notice Mia stand up and take notice. She was paying attention before, happily watching as I was singled out in front of the school. This is different though, her attention has left me completely and is solely focused on Mike. She couldn't look more interested if she was standing next to him drooling.

"Hey, Mike maybe we should just find another space. No big deal." I try to defuse the situation, but knowing full well it isn't going to do any good. Brad looks over in my direction, eyebrows cocked, a Robert DeNiro style upturned mouth with arms raised to his side, palms in the air as if to say, *'well, what happens next is out of my hands.'*

Mike continues to ignore everything and everyone around him as if he's the only person there. He takes his key and locks his door. Manually—no remote locking on this old beast.

"Hey clown..." Brad calls to him.

Mike just turns and starts to walk toward me, again ignoring Brad, which only serves to anger him even more. Mike doesn't seem as if he's being rude or dismissive. It's genuinely as if they don't exist to him, like he doesn't have a care in the world. Actually, that is dismissive, but who cares? These jerks deserve it. The crowd of onlookers exchange confused glances. They've never seen anyone refuse to bow down to Brad. Mike's reaction is new to them.

"Shall we go, Abby? You can show me where the office is," Mike says casually, a cheeky smile playing on his lips. My panic for him starts to evaporate as his carefree attitude becomes infectious. It's short lived though. The panic comes right back when I see Brad advancing on him like a predatory animal. He reaches out with his huge paw of a hand, the very same hand he uses to launch the football down field in his role as QB. Also, the same hand he probably used to throw milk at me in the cafeteria. God I'd like to break that hand. He clamps it onto Mike's shoulder like a mechanical vice grip and uses his considerable strength to spin Mike around, so they're face to face for the first time since Mike had the 'insolence' to park near his pride and joy.

As the confrontation has finally got physical the pack of cackling hyenas get even closer. Knowing he has an audience seems to spur Brad on and he gives Mike a small push in the chest, like a bear batting a beehive. Mike doesn't move an inch. Doesn't even take a step back.

I want to do something. I want to help Mike, not just because I like him, but because I really hate these bullies. The trouble is, what can I do? It's futile to try and stop it and all that would result in is Mia and her lackies giving me a beat down as well. So, I just take a step back and hope Mike can handle this. Not very heroic I know, but I have come to realize in the last 6 months that when it comes to this lot, it's best to just stay out of it.

"I said…" Brad growls, but he stops almost as soon as he begins. They're almost nose to nose. Brad is slightly bigger, but not by much. Mike's face is calm. He looks completely untroubled…except…except for his eyes. They're hard. Unblinking. He stares directly into Brad's.

Brad's eyes widen. His face seems to be shaking ever so slightly. You'd have to really study him to notice as it's just a small movement–and study him I am. I'm in complete shock at what I'm seeing here. Brad's face is starting to go a dark shade of red. The veins in his forehead become more prominent as if they're a balloon that someone is blowing air in to.

My eyes shoot back to Mike who still has the same calm, smiling look on his face like he's in the middle of nothing more than a normal conversation. His eyes though, they seem to be glowing. They're super blue normally, but now they look as if he's wearing contacts powered by Christmas lights. No one else seems to notice, they're too busy giving Brad encouraging pats and punches on the shoulder while chanting and yelling things along the lines of "Kick his ass, Brad" or "C'mon superstar, you got this." But it's apparent to anyone with half a brain cell that no, he doesn't have this in the slightest.

Out of the corner of my eye, I can see Mia looking at me, studying me curiously as if this is some kind of trick.

Suddenly Mike looks away and for the first time he notices the crowd of what seems to be every single student in the school watching. His face changes. Gone is the stern, stoic expression he had while he was staring at Brad, and it's replaced by what seems to be shock and even horror. Brad on the other hand almost collapses. He's bent over, palms of his hands resting on his kneecaps as he lets out an almighty breath. Like a diver who breaks through the surface of the water after being down in its depths for a minute longer than their body would allow. Sweat prickles his brow as his cohorts' rush to be the one to help him regain some composure. Desperate to earn some brownie points and not devolve into the recesses of school anonymity.

I look from one to the other, trying my best to understand what in the hell just happened here. Not a single punch was thrown, but Brad looks as if he has just been ten rounds with an experienced boxer.

I fix on Mike, still staring at the crowd, worry etched on his perfect face. The creases in his brow threatening to crack his hard smooth complexion. His eyes finally fix on mine, and it becomes obvious he notices how confused I am. So far, in the short time I've known him, he has been nothing but cool, calm, and composed. Not anymore. He grabs his bag from the floor and slings it over his shoulder and starts to charge his way past the crowd. No words are spoken as he passes me and I in turn say nothing to him. I just watch as he pushes, head down and eyes fixed on the floor, through the audience. I follow him with my eyes until he is lost to me. Swallowed by the hordes of teenagers.

I turn back to Brad, who is now upright, pushing his 'friends' away as if he's in no need of their help when in reality he looks as if he could do with a doctor. It's definitely more than his pride that's been hurt here in this parking lot showdown. Unconsciously, I take a step in his direction. The veins in his neck and forehead look as if they're about to explode. Then I notice his ear–a small trickle of blood starts to roll down the side of his face. My eyes widen as I wonder–*did Mike do that?*

I look around to see if anyone else has noticed when I see Mia still staring at me intently. Her eyes are narrowed like she's a gumshoe in a noir thriller trying to crack a case. Her arms are folded across her chest, her foot tapping under her accusatory gaze. I can't help it. I fold like a sheet of paper and head through the crowd toward the main entrance, still feeling her eyes burning a hole in my back. Luckily, like Mike, I'm lost in the crowd almost instantly.

12

The day seems to drag on for an eternity. Lasting, it seems, twice as long as any normal school day. You can probably guess the reason for that. There was only one conversational topic on everyone's lips for the day–Brad and Mike. No matter where I went, that's what people were talking about. Not to me, of course, but I caught snippets of it all around the school and as usual, every version of the story I seemed to catch was different from the last. Initially the versions I was overhearing were pretty much true with maybe just one or two small details slightly fabricated or exaggerated, as you'd expect from teenagers eager to be the first to divulge the information. They wanted their story to be interesting so every now and again they'd embellish certain elements.

'Brad and some new kid squared off in the parking lot.' I overheard one boy telling another. True.

By the time lunch rolled around, 'Brad put some new kid in the hospital after he crashed into The Truck before school this morning.' False.

I didn't really expect anything different. I've been to enough schools to realize how these rumours circulate. Even though most of the school was watching, the story seemed to shift with each retelling of it. The trouble was even Brad was getting in on it.

"He just jumped outta his beaten up hunka junk and got up in my grill. He's lucky I was hungover or I'da schooled him big style." I overheard Brad telling Mitchell, one of his many followers. The worst part was Mitchell was there. He was one of the goons hanging out in the flatbed and yet here he was, mouth agape, salivating at every untruth. Brad caught me frowning at the horseshit he was spouting and for the first time, he sheepishly turned the other way, ignoring my existence.

At least one good thing came out of all of this. I was spared a moment of having to deal with Brad.

I notice Sam sitting at our usual table, the one furthest away and tucked in a corner. I make my way over and basically have to wave my hands in front of her eyes, as once again her face is buried in a book.

"Be with you in a second," she says to me without taking her eyes from the book.

I nudge the book closer to her face and bend my head to see the title. "Stephen King...again?"

She shrugs a response which causes me to smile. Finishing the chapter, she closes the book and lays it neatly on the table. She fiddles with it for a few seconds, turning it this way and that, making sure it aligns perfectly with the edge of the table. Again, my lips turn into a slight smile–she has complained about her OCD before, and I know sometimes it gets her frustrated, but I think it's cute. A little quirk that goes with her quirky personality.

I look down at my lunch tray and study the wonders that the cooks have rustled up for us today. Meatloaf, apparently. It looks more like something you'd feed a dog and even then, I'd think twice about it. I push that aside in favor of my fruit–a bruised apple and an over ripe banana. I'm looking at them both in disgust knowing full well that I'd rather eat those than the dog food meatloaf, when Sam nudges my arm. I look over at her and her face is etched with worry as her eyes look off into the distance.

"Do you think we should move? Go outside, maybe?"

I follow her gaze to see her looking at Brad's table. He is looking in our direction, but turns away as soon as my eyes reach his. I can see Mia laughing, holding court as her cheerleaders admire her and the boys leer lovingly at her. Like lovesick puppies.

"I think we'll be fine. Brad's had enough excitement for one day."

"Hmm...I heard about that. An ambulance had to take away some new kid." Sam sadly shakes her head.

"Mike."

"Huh?"

"The new kid, his name's Mike."

She looks at me with a cheeky grin on her face, raising and lowering her eyebrows. "I did overhear someone say that 'farm girl' came to school with the new kid. Care to explain?"

I feel my cheeks grow warm and look down at the floor.

"Nothing to explain. I ran into him yesterday and then this morning he was driving past me on my walk to school," I shrug, as if it's no big deal.

"Miss the bus again?"

I nod. "He was exploring the area, not that there's much to see in this town. He said he'd just moved into the old Anderson farm up the road, the one that's been abandoned for a while. We're basically neighbors."

"Just neighbors? Or is their potential love in the air?" She gives a wink.

I give her a 'as if' look. "Even if he did like me, which I can't imagine why, I mean, who'd want the stinking farm girl? five minutes at this school and he'd soon change his mind once he found out how popular I'm."

"He's not worth your time if that's the type of guy he is." Her head slightly tilted as if she were talking to someone who was ill. I appreciate it though. I may not have a lot of friends, but I'd rather have one Sam than ten Mia's.

"Thanks. It doesn't matter anyway–he only gave me a lift once and we've only spoken twice. I'm not even sure that constitutes a friendship, let alone anything more."

"I don't think it matters much now, him being in the hospital and all that. Unless you wanna nurse him back to health," Sam snorts.

"That doesn't sound too bad," I say through a smile. "But...he isn't in the hospital, or as far as I'm aware he isn't. I haven't seen him all day though." I scan the room, hoping to at least catch a glimpse of him. Partly so I can find out exactly what was happening this morning, but mostly because I just want to see him again. My heart races at the possibility. It beats so loud that I start to worry that Sam might hear it. But, as with the rest of the day, he's nowhere to be seen. I surprise myself at how horrible and crushing the disappointment is. The feeling of despair as my heart seems to drop.

I mentally tell myself to get a grip.

"Those stories that have been going around," I continue, after scanning the cafeteria like some kind of terminator, "aren't true. Nothing I've heard is, even the story Brad is telling. Which is funny considering that it looked as if the whole school was there."

"I saw the huddle of people, but took it as an opportunity to get to my locker without running the gauntlet of bullies." She indicates with her chin towards our favorite table.

I give her a sympathetic smile, but deep down, my heart breaks for her. To feel as if you should use that as an opportunity to get to class without being bullied is horrible. No kid should have to go through their school years like that. They're supposed to be the best years of your life. For most, maybe. Not for us.

"Well trust me, I was there–right in the thick of it. None of the stories you've heard are true."

She just sits there staring at me, eyes wide and arms held out. I let out a huge sigh, knowing she wants me to elaborate.

"We pulled into the parking lot and the only space we could find was next to Brad's...so we parked there..."

"The nerve."

"I know, how dare he use a perfectly good space. Well, obviously, Brad wasn't pleased with this which in turn meant that his gang of ghouls were also unhappy, because, you know, they have to mirror his every move."

"I know it well."

"We got out of Mike's truck and when they saw me that seemed to bring an extra bit of joy to whatever he had planned for Mike. Mia was at the back of the crowd, standing up in the flat bed of Brad's truck hoping to see me get another dose of public ridicule..." Sam nods sympathetically, but offers nothing else, what else is there? "Anyway, Mike jumps out and seems oblivious to the crowd gathering to potentially see him get his ass kicked, but when they came face to face...well...it's hard to explain. They just...stared at each other."

"They stared?"

"Literally. I'm not under playing it, they just stared into each other's eyes. No punches were thrown, not insults. They stared. Silently. But and I know it sounds crazy, it was really intense. Like Brad couldn't look away."

"Probably didn't want to look weak in front of his crew." Sam threw up some kind of strange hand gesture that was meant to look gang related, but actually made it look as if she had cramp.

"No, I don't mean he didn't *want* to look away, he definitely wanted to. I mean he *couldn't* physically do it."

Sam's face was more serious now, taking in exactly what I was saying. "You tryin' to tell me that you think this...this Mike guy was controlling him? Forcing him to look into his eyes?"

"Kinda," I shrug. "Brad's face was going blood red, and it was like the veins in his forehead were gonna explode."

"How was he doing it?" Sam asks.

"No idea. It wasn't just that. When Mike finally looked away, then so did Brad, like he had been...released." I look at Sam who is just frowning at me, never taking her eyes away. "Mike looked shocked to see the crowd that had gathered, like he was so zoned in he didn't see everyone. He just grabbed his things and marched off and kind of, disappeared. I haven't seen him since. Not in any classes or here at lunch." I scan the cafeteria once more as I say this.

"That sounds really weird, Abby..."

"Oh, and another thing that's even more strange. When Mike finally went, I looked at Brad and he had, like, blood trickling from his ear. I don't think anyone else noticed and he wiped it away almost immediately, but it was definitely there."

Sam looks off in the distance. "You think the blood was caused by his stare down with Mike?"

"What else!? He looked like his head was gonna explode. It was so weird." I look over at Brad's table again and he has his back to me, but seems to be rubbing the very ear I was talking about. The table are animatedly talking–mock fighting. Probably another farfetched story acting out what happened this morning. "I just need to speak to Mike. Find out exactly what happened. What he did."

Sam puts her hand on mine. A comforting gesture, but one she has never done before.

"Be careful," she says to me. "This all sounds really weird and if you're right and this new kid is responsible for making Brad's ear bleed and forcing him, basically against his will, to stare into his eyes–not that I care what happens to Brad, that guy is an absolute troll–then this Mike...he isn't normal. He could be dangerous. A witch...or a demon!" Her voice rising at the end as if she has just discovered something.

"A demon?" I frown. A smirk playing on my lips, disbelief dripping from my words like ice cream from a cone.

"If there's one thing I've learned from The Master of Horror himself," she pats her Stephen King book as she talks, her eyebrow cocked. "It's that people are not always what they make out to be."

13

I'm relieved when the final bell echoes throughout the school halls. Almost as soon as the first chime shrieks its way into my classroom, like a Banshee opening her lungs, I grab my tattered, almost falling apart book bag and shove my books and papers into it with no care at all. I'm sure I heard the work I'd just spent the last hour doing rip as I dumped everything in, but I don't care. I've more important things on my mind. Like, how did Mike do what he did? If he did anything at all that is, and where has he disappeared to all day? This is the real 'work' I need to spend my time on.

I'm up and out of my chair before anyone else has even moved. I nod to my English Lit teacher, Mr. Clarke on my way to the door. He's about fifty, but dresses as if he's half that. Jeans that are much too tight and leave little to the imagination. A white t-shirt, that once again looks too tight, but it's hard to tell under his little bum freezer leather jacket. He winks in response and does that cringy, finger shooting thing. He even does the clicky sound with his tongue. No dude, just...no. His mum needs to have a word with him about that as he must still live in her basement. No wife, girlfriend or boyfriend would let him get away with acting or dressing like that. On top of all of this, he likes the students to call him Justin, which is obviously his first name. As if we're all friends and he isn't a figure of authority. I don't of course. I barely talk to anyone in class unless I've been called on to answer a question. Even then I just answer the question, usually get it right and then return to my stoic position of silence.

Mr. Clarke doesn't take any notice of my haste. No one does. It's not uncommon. I'm always the first out of the room.

I'm out in the hall before anyone else and head towards the school exit. My feet moving so fast you'd think I was training to be a power walker. I round the corner and see the door at the end of the hall. I pass the bank of gray lockers on my right-hand side and immediately notice mine. The word 'TRASH' still visible even though Mrs. Cramer, our school janitor, has given it the good news with her trolley of cleaning supplies. It's still there and probably will be every day until the end of the semester. A ghostly reminder of my place at this school, and no doubt, in life. I slow to look at it, but the sound of my classmates spilling from the other classrooms and attacking their lockers causes me to pick up the pace again.

As I approach the door, my eyes travel upwards to the banner that stretches above it. A dark red background emblazoned with bright yellow lettering–the school colors.

Home of the Harton Hawks.

Huge black wings stretch the length of the banner and sit regally behind the lettering. It catches my eye, but I don't stand and stare. I see it every day. I walk directly beneath it and push the door open with more force than intended. It swings open and hits the wall, bouncing back as if on a spring. I see it coming directly for my face and with my left arm full of books and my right hand currently holding my bag strap, all I can do is close my eyes and wait for the impact. But nothing comes. Slowly, I begin to open my eyes and all I see is the door, taking up my whole field of vision. Inches, no, millimeters from my nose. It would have broken it had it connected.

My eyes shift to the left slightly, to the edge of the door where I can see fingers. Just floating fingers, perfectly manicured with the nails trimmed to absolute perfection. These fingers, no doubt attached to a hand which is again attached to a body positioned outside the door. I swallow hard, praying for it to be him. But what are the chances? He hasn't been around all day. In almost slow motion the door starts to pull back and there he is. His hair shining like gold, his eyes, iridescent in the Texas sun. My heart starts to beat at a pace I'm not sure my body can handle. A pace I've started to become accustomed to since meeting Mike. I find it hard to catch my breath and have to once again mentally remind myself to get a grip. I don't even know this guy and I shouldn't let his outward beauty (which there's a lot of) be my sole thought of him. How I judge him. I don't want to start acting like one of those crazy, helpless women in romance novels who fall for some dude just because he's hot even though he is so obviously a freak. I'm no damsel in distress. Bella Swan I am not.

"Do you and the door have some kind of disagreement?" Mike asks. His velvety voice like caramel for the ears. Smooth and sweet.

I look up at him, seemingly unable to create a coherent thought.

"Huh?"

That's it. That's all I manage to come up with—not even something polite like 'excuse me?', just a 'Huh'. I really am tragic.

"The door," he carries on, unaware of how much of a mess I am. Or at least too nice to bring it up. "You pushed it open with some force there. Has it done something to get on your bad side?"

"No...I was...I was just in a rush. Guess I don't know my own strength." I pull myself together enough to at least engage in conversation, or complete a sentence. Let's hope I can keep it up.

"That is most definitely true, Abby," he replies, a smirk playing on his lips as if he is privy to some information I'm not. I don't focus on it too long though as I fear the sound of my name on his lips is enough to cause me to hyperventilate.

Luckily, the stampede that is building behind me jolts me awake and I realize I'm about to be trampled Mufasa style as I stand blocking the door. I duck under Mike's arm that is still outstretched holding the door open and make my way down the side of the parking lot toward the concrete steps that lead to the front of the school building. Mike lets the door swing closed and jogs to catch up, my usual power walk proving a little too much for him.

"Slow up, Usain Bolt," he chuckles.

"As much as I appreciate the save back there, I'm sure a broken nose wouldn't be the best look, but I ain't got time to talk. I'm already late so my uncle is going to be majorly pissed without me standing around talking."

"Late? How can you be late? School literally just got out."

"If he had his way, I'd skip last period and go home to start my chores. He isn't the biggest fan of me even coming to school, but he knows he doesn't have any choice but to let me," I say, matter of factly.

"He sounds like a charming guy."

"You've no idea."

As we reach the bottom of the stairs, he places his hand on my shoulder and gently spins me around to face him. My breath catches and it feels as if every nerve ending in my body is tingling all at once. The feeling causes me to jump backwards and drop my books. He raises his hands in a 'I mean no harm' gesture which makes me feel a little guilty. I don't want him thinking I don't like him touching me. Quite the opposite actually.

"I'm sorry, I didn't mean to scare you or…"

"No, no it's fine. It's just…I just didn't expect it." I stutter, not wanting to tell him it wasn't fear, but excitement that caused me to jump.

He gives a sympathetic nod. "Why don't you let me give you a ride home? That way you can make it back in time and I can apologize for bailing on you this morning." Before I can answer him, he's bending down to pick up my books. When he stands back up, he's holding them all effortlessly under one arm.

I look up at him, raising my head, straining my neck and squinting my eyes from the blinding sun. He really is tall. His hair lightly blows from his shoulders. The natural waves in it framing his perfectly chiseled face, cheek bones so pronounced they look as if they could cut glass. He could have walked directly out of some shampoo commercial where the results they're promising are so obviously unobtainable…and yet, Mike has managed it. I then look down at myself. My dirty sneakers, ruined by outdoor work and more often than not, my trek to school. My faded jeans and t-shirt, and my hair, greasy and scrunched up into a half assed ponytail. A normal, natural look is how I would describe it. Like most people. Not this gorgeous, otherworldly creature in front of me. He could literally be talking to any boy or girl he wants. Instead, he decides to spend his time talking to me when he could easily get the attention of the Mia's of the world.

I don't kid myself into assuming that there's anything romantic in it. That's just too outlandish. He probably just feels sorry for me. What the hell I have got that would interest him?

The more I look at him–his broad shoulders, his angelic face, the fact that I have never, ever seen someone that looks like this in real life–the more my mind races back to my conversation with Sam earlier. Crazy as it sounded then, as crazy as it sounds now. As completely outlandish as the thought may be, and I would never utter the words out loud–maybe he is a creature that has crawled out of a horror novel. Maybe he is some kind of demon. You must have to do a deal with the devil to look like that.

"Weeeeelllll...?" Mike drags the word out as he looks at me through his long eyelashes.

I nod. "A lift would be great. If you're sure it's not too much trouble?"

"No trouble at all. I'm going that way."

I start to walk back up the stairs toward the parking lot when he calls after me.

"This way," he indicates to the opposite side of the street. "I moved it."

"You're learning," I look across the street and notice his truck parked on a grass verge. It looks as if it's squashed up against a tree to make sure it isn't blocking the road. Opposite the school is nothing but dense woodland. It goes on for miles. I have no idea how deep it actually is. In the six months I've been here the urge to explore it has been strong, but so as the fear of getting lost in it.

I go to take the books out of his hand, but he spins his body around, angling them away from me. I raise my eyebrows, throwing him what I hope is a disbelieving look. "I appreciate the attempt at chivalry, but I'm more than capable of carrying my own books. I usually do it the whole journey home, I'm sure I can handle the walk across the street."

"I'm not saying you can't handle it. I've got them now, I may as well hold on to them."

He turns to look down the street to make sure it's safe to cross. I mirror his actions and can see a car hurtling its way toward us. I plan to wait until it has past us, but then...

"After this car we should be okay..." Mike begins, but it is too late. You can commandeer my books all you like, but you aren't the boss of me. I run across the road just as the car zooms past me. I can feel the wind its speed creates blow across my back. The echo of the driver's horn rings in my ears.

I reach Mike's truck and look across the road to see him still standing in the same spot. Rooted in shock and horror would be a more apt description. I cross my arms in a pose I hope comes across as defiant, but more than likely looks cocky. Was it worth risking my life to try and prove a point? I think so.

Now there's no cars coming, Mike slowly walks across the street toward me. Really slowly. No doubt trying to prove a point of his own. He reaches his truck and unlocks the driver's door without saying a word. I continue to lean on the back, almost sitting on the rusted wheel arch, wondering if he is angry with me, but trying to pretend I'm not bothered either way. He opens the driver's door and gently places my books on the bench seat. Finally, he turns towards me, and I can see he is smiling.

"Point taken." Mike gives a slight nod. "Now, would you like to climb in through this side and slide across? Save you getting your shoes covered in mud. If you'd prefer, I can close the door and let you open it yourself?" He's having fun now.

I look across to the other side of the truck and see that he's right. The mud is so deep the soles of my sneakers would disappear, and while they're already a mess, I don't want to drag fresh mud into his truck.

"No need to close it," I say as I'm walking toward the door.

Once I'm there he holds his hand out to help my hop in. "May I?" he's still smiling. I look down at his hand and as much as I want to take it, the fear of another lightning bolt coursing through my body makes me take pause. A second passes and the desire to hold his hand outweighs the fear and nerves. I look up and return his smile.

"Thank you." I place my hand in his and the same energy courses through me again. This time I manage to handle it better as the expectation was there. I swallow hard and with my right hand grab the framework of the truck and heave myself in. I slide across the bench seats and instead of using my books as a barrier between us as I did this morning, I place them on the floor in front of my feet. Now there's nothing separating us.

Sam's words still ring in my head. I don't know this guy. Who is he? Where does he come from? There's a sense of mystery about him, but more than that, a sense of danger. Part of me is saying to keep my distance, but the other part wants to know more. The other part is excited by it.

He climbs into the driver's seat and looks across at me smiling. He turns the key in the ignition and the truck roars to life.

"Let's get you home."

14

The truck doesn't once deviate from the center of our lane. If I didn't know better, I'd say it was travelling on tracks that keep it from moving even a millimeter to the left or the right.

I sneak looks at him out of the corner of my eye and notice he doesn't once creep over the speed limit. The needle on the speedometer hovers perfectly over the fifty-five, never once faltering. It's refreshingly nice. I get to look out of the window and actually appreciate some of the beauty Harton Town has to offer. I can look at the woodland, or the houses and the shops. Usually, I'm either in Tom's truck with him travelling at warp speed, which turns everything outside of the window into a blur, or walking the backroads as they're quicker than going through the town. As much as I'm appreciating the scenery though, there's only one thing I really want to look at, so I turn my face back towards Mike. His eyes move effortlessly between the windshield, the rear-view mirror and his side mirrors, making sure he is completely aware of his surroundings. If he wasn't of school age, I'd say he'd been driving for a hundred years and even then, I'd still be impressed.

I look at him, half in awe and half in curiosity, in what I believe to be a sneaky manner. Side eyeing him while his attention is completely on the road. I assume I'm getting away with it.

"Do I have food on my face?"

My eyes shoot forward in a futile attempt to act as if I haven't been looking at him. *Well done, Abby. Fine spy you'd make. Double oh so useless.*

"Excuse me?" I theatrically turn my whole head in his direction, hoping to make it look as if I couldn't possibly look at him without doing this. I widen my eyes in a look which I hope screams innocence, but in reality, paints me with 'guilty as charged'.

For what I believe is the first time, Mike takes his eyes away from the road and looks at me. Amazingly, the truck still doesn't shift even half inch from the lanes center. He's wearing a heart thumpingly beautiful smile. Relief floods over me as I realize, he isn't angry. I mean, it is rude to stare, after all.

"If you want to ask me something, feel free," Mike adds.

I wonder what the best course of action is for getting to the bottom of what I want to find out and internally decide that asking if he is some kind of demon is not the way to go. I decide that trying to be tactful makes the most sense.

"How was your first day at school?" I ask, taking the scenic route to the answers I need.

His brow furrows as he lets out a deep breath. The perfect angle of his jaw line pulsates as he grinds his teeth. He doesn't answer right away. He takes his time. I swivel on the bench seat to angle myself toward him. I tuck my left foot underneath my right leg as I make myself comfortable. The shoulder strap of the seat belt cuts into my neck slightly so I release my arm from it, so it rests on my rib cage. Probably not as safe, but definitely less painful.

Mike still seems to be weighing up his response. His eyes continue to scan his mirrors as I wonder if he is going to answer me at all. I'm just about to speak up to end what feels like an eternity of awkward silence when Mike seems to have collected his thoughts enough to formulate an answer.

"I checked in at reception, but decided I needed another day to prepare, so went back home," he shrugs.

A slightly anti-climactic response. "Mr. Heaver was okay with that?"

"He agreed it was a good idea," he answers.

I see him smile, but he continues to keep his eyes fixed forward.

"I did assume you'd gone home. I didn't see you all day."

"You been looking for me?" one corner of his mouth upturns in a cocky smirk.

I start to blush and immediately jump on the defensive, when in fact, I *have* been looking for him...all day. "No. I just wanted to make sure you were settling in okay," I say pathetically, as if I spend my days making sure all newbies acclimate to Harton High. Abigail Lewis–Welcoming committee. That's me. "Plus, almost everyone was talking about you after what happened this morning with Brad," I add. Hoping to not only move the subject on to what I actually want to know, but to get it away from the idea of me looking for him.

He doesn't answer. I've started now, may as well carry on.

"What was all that anyway?"

"Things like that happen at school, right? Especially with idiots like...Brad, was it?"

"I get that. Brad's an ass. Stuff like that would happen every day if it wasn't for the fact that everyone is scared of him. I meant, like, what *happened?* How did you ...you know...do what you did?" I ask.

Mike definitely isn't smiling now. His Adams apple rises and lowers as he swallows. He doesn't look angry. He looks...nervous.

"Do? I didn't *do* anything. We just had a little bit of a stare out. Pathetic really."

"But Brad was in pain. You didn't even touch him, and he looked as if his head was gonna explode."

I hear a slight squeak and notice Mike has gripped the leather steering wheel so tight it looks as if he might break it. He rolls his fist over it as if he is revving the handlebars of a motorcycle.

A few seconds later he releases his grip and softens his expression into a relaxed smile once again. "I think you're seeing things, Abby. We just both didn't want to back down. Trying to prove our masculinity. Like I said, pathetic."

Maybe I would have believed him, questioned my own memory, but he gave himself away with his odd reaction. He's hiding something. There's no point in backing down now, I may not get another chance.

"No way, buddy. I wasn't seeing things. I saw what I saw. Veins were on show, his head was bright red, going almost purple, and when you left, it was finally like he had some control back. He looked really shaken up, and...and his ear was bleeding," I add, almost sheepishly, as if I'm accusing Mike of some enormous crime.

Mike removes his hand from the steering wheel and rubs his eyes, squeezing the bridge of his nose with his thumb and forefinger. As if nursing a headache after a long, hard day. My eyes shoot directly to the road in front, but deep down I know, even without him looking, the truck will travel completely straight. I'm right. "Abby, there are things, strange things. Things that I can't tell you." I listen to him intently and try to ignore the spike in my heartrate as he says my name. "Has anything like that ever happened to you? Have you ever felt like you've had control over someone like that?" he asks me.

I find the question odd. I seem to have no control...over anything. Let alone other people. I shake my head.

Mike nods. "Just know, I would never hurt anyone...especially you. I'm one of the good guys."

Mike looks directly at me, an intensity, no, sincerity, burning in his eyes. And I believe him. There's an energy I feel when I'm with him and deep down, I know that there's something different about Mike. But even with that feeling, that knowledge, somehow, I know he won't hurt me.

The truck goes silent again. I haven't really got the answers I was looking for. If anything, I have more questions.

"Are you a hypnotist?" I say, only half joking.

Mike replies with a smile.

"Or a demon?" I add. "That's what my friend Sam thinks."

His laugh shocks me. Not just a chuckle, but a booming, belly laugh. "A demon, really? You think that's possible?"

"Not really, but Sam reads a lot of horror novels, so her imagination can sometimes run away with itself."

"Who's Sam?" Mike asks through his laughter.

"My best friend. Well, my only friend."

"I'd like to meet her."

"Demon's not so bad, I mean Buffy dated two. Although I was never a fan of Spike, I'm an Angel gal."

"You watch Buffy? Wasn't that a bit before your time?"

"It's on Disney Plus, Sam gave me her log in. And anyway, I never thought demon, I thought you were a Jedi." I smirk, enjoying the fact that the conversation seems to have taken a more playful turn, and feeling more comfortable by the second in Mike's company.

"That's more possible than a demon."

"Well, apparently it's a real religion now."

"Yes. I have heard that," he replies, once again grinding his teeth.

"Oooh, you don't like that. Church goer, are we?" I tease. I can tell now from Mike's relaxed reactions to my questions the intensity of two minutes ago has gone.

"Something like that. Are you not? I thought everyone from this neck of the woods was."

"Most are, not me," I shrug.

"Can I ask why?"

I pause for a moment, wondering how honest I should be with Mike. I decide that telling him exactly how I feel will be of no harm. Just because he's religious, doesn't mean I have to be. Plus, it may have only been a few minutes in the truck talking, but I feel no reason to lie to him.

"If there is a God, and that's a big damn if, then what good has he ever done for me? Killed my mum, placed me with a drunk, abusive uncle. Any person that does that ain't getting no worship off me."

Mike stays silent and I wonder if my honesty was too honest.

"I'm sorry," is all he says.

"No big deal, some people have it a lot worse right?" I reply.

"Well," he reaches over and takes my hand. "I'm here now, and if there's anything you ever need. Just ask. In addition to Sam, you now have me as a friend."

"I told you on the way to school this morning, you don't wanna be friends with me. I'll do nothing to help with your street cred."

"I did already have a wild west style standoff with the most popular boy in school. Think it's safe to say I'm on the outside anyway."

He's right, of course. He's either going to be a total outsider now or he'll become the most popular kid in school for being brave enough, or stupid enough, to pick a fight with Brad. More than likely the former.

We carry on the rest of the journey talking about our favorite films. Mine–Indiana Jones. Mike's–The Matrix. I may have laughed more on this journey than I have in years. That laughter is short lived though. As we turn on to the gravel road that leads to the front of the farmhouse. I look out of the windshield. The happy smile that is plastered on my goofy face suddenly falls in horror.

"Oh, crap."

15

Tom hasn't always treated me the way he does lately. Sure, he was never the doting, loving guardian you'd expect. I mean, your sister dies in a fatal car collision and your niece is the only survivor of the traumatic event, maybe you treat her a little lovingly. Possibly even spoil her to overcompensate. No. He has always been ambivalent toward me. Made it clear he'd rather I wasn't there. But he was never out and out nasty. He never used to drink to the extent he does now, maybe a beer or two with his dinner, nothing to write to AA about. He never used to force me to do chores, or complain that I had to go to school, or that he had to feed me. I always got clothes when I needed them, sure they were second hand, but I got them. Most importantly, he never hit me. All that stuff is a recent thing. Things were changing. Year on year. Slowly, day by day, he was getting nastier. Then in the last 12 months, his verbal abuse turned physical. I suppose it's partly my fault. If he didn't have to take me in, then maybe he would have been able to live the life he wanted, whatever that was. But I didn't ask to be left alone. I didn't ask for him to take me in.

I damn well didn't ask for my mother to die.

At the thought of my mother my hand immediately goes to my broken necklace. I rub the sharp edge where one of the wings is broken, as if by touching it, it'll bring me some kind of comfort. It doesn't. But it's the one thing she gave me that I still own. In a sense, I suppose I still have a part of her with me. But she can't help me now.

As we continue our slow crawl to the farmhouse via the long-graveled track, I can see him standing on the porch. He's far away, but the face of fury he's sporting is unmistakable. I've seen it many times.

Tom stands on the porch that leads to the front door of the farmhouse. I very rarely, if ever, use this door. I always use the side door that leads directly into the kitchen. Probably because I'm usually in there cooking or cleaning. If you enter through the old wooden door with the two single glazed windows, you walk into a hallway that separates the kitchen and the living room and leads directly to the stairs. It's all open plan as there's no internal doors to separate either room. Just that hallway.

He's leaning on one of the wooden beams that travel from a small roof covering the porch, down onto the paint chipped wooden bannisters that are either side of the wooden steps. Everything here is wood. If a small fire broke out somewhere in the far reaches of the farm, the chances are it'll travel all the way around the property and take everything with it. Another one of the reasons I hate Tom's smoking. Something he's doing right this second.

He blows a puff of smoke from his lips which hides his face for all of a second. He looks like something from a horror film. Hiding behind mist and smoke, then it clears as he starts to make his way towards us.

He slides his hand along the white, or what used to be white, banister. His calloused hands surely too rough to succumb to any splinters. It's like they have a Kevlar layer over them, snapping the rogue needles of wood and paint as he walks. His hand slides over the wood as if in slow motion, loose chips of paint spring off as if his hand is made of sandpaper. It glides over the deep grooves which look like they've been left by some kind of wild animal's claws.

He's going slow on purpose. He knows I'm watching from the truck, and he wants to drag it out. Make me even more scared. Make me suffer. He flicks his cigarette into the air and I watch as it falls into the pile of other butts at the bottom of the porch steps. Even from this distance I can hear the creak as if they're about to give way under his weight. He stamps on the pile of cigarettes. No doubt to make sure the one he was just smoking has been well and truly extinguished, and also, to add a little bit of extra drama to the delay tactics he's already playing. He stands still for about three seconds, three of the longest seconds of my life. Three alternate dimension style seconds. Then he's off. Marching toward the truck like a man on a mission. His red and black checkered outdoor coat blowing behind him and I can't help but think how much he must be sweating in this heat.

I unclip my seat belt and open the truck door, hoping I can head Tom off before he reaches me...and Mike.

"Stay here," I order.

"Your uncle, I take it?"

I don't answer him. I grab my bag and throw it to the floor. I haven't got time to fiddle around trying to get it on my back. I grab my books and kick the truck door shut. I drop my books next to my bag and start to half walk, half jog toward Tom, who is only a few strides away from me.

"I got a ride from a friend so I wasn't late," I say, knowing that this response isn't going to calm the situation, but I have to say something.

"That the kind of girl I raised ya to be, huh? Jumping in the back seat with strange boys," Tom shouts.

"We were in the front seat."

"Don't get smart with me, girl." He jabs his finger into my face. "Goin' a school gives ya a smart mouth, does it? makes ya think ya can talk to me like trash, huh?"

"No, I was just…" I start, but I can't finish. He grabs me by the top of my arm, with such a vice like grip it causes an involuntary whimper to escape my lips. He almost lifts me off the floor.

"Now you get your ass inside that house and get to work, then we'll have a chat about you runnin' around town like some kind of harlot. It's actin' like that got your mother killed."

"My mother?" is all I can manage to get out as the pain in my arm intensifies, along with his grip. He's half carrying me and half dragging me now. What the hell's my mother got to do with me acting like a harlot? Even though I wasn't. My mother was killed in a car accident. Nothing to do with running around with boys.

"Get your hands off of her," Mike shouts. It caused Tom to stop and slightly loosen his grip on my arm.

"Mike, just go!" I shout to him over my shoulder. Partly because I'm embarrassed, but mostly because I don't want my uncle to hurt him as well. Mike just looks at me, sporting his own face of fury. Then turns his attention back to my uncle.

"Get back in the truck, boy."

"Not gonna happen, old man. And don't call me boy."

Oh, crap!

Tom lets go of my arm and I almost drop to the floor as my legs are back supporting my weight. He slowly starts to walk toward Mike, who doesn't retreat. Instead, he starts to walk toward Tom. I look on in horror as Mike's face begins to intensify. A face I've seen before, from this morning. But instead of seeing it side on, I am looking directly at it. His eyes are changing. Gone is the deep blue. Now they're glowing. A hot, bright white seems to fill his whole eye. Tom stops in his tracks and his hand shoots to his head. Just like Brad this morning he seems to have no control over his own movements. He's paralyzed.

I run in between them and push Mike hard in the chest. It was like hitting a block of cold concrete, but he stumbles back slightly all the same. I don't know why I'm stopping him, whatever he's doing, whatever it is he can do, I should let him. But I don't.

Mike's eyes return to normal and he looks at me half in disbelief and half apologetic. Its obvious Mike has a temper and also obvious that he can regret it the instant it rises to the surface. But what he said to me in the truck still rings in my ears *'I'd never hurt you'*.

"Abby, I'm..." he begins. But I haven't got time for his apologies right now.

"I know, just go...please," I urge.

"But..." He angles his head toward Tom.

I steal a brief glance over my shoulder to find Tom looking at the floor. His hands are rested on his knees and he's hunched over, taking deep breaths as sweat drips from his wrinkled brow.

"It's fine," I say, knowing he doesn't believe me. "Nothing I can't handle or haven't already been handling. I don't need you to save me."

Mike looks up to the heavens and bites his bottom lip, but begrudgingly he starts to retreat to his truck. "Call me if you need me."

"I'll be fine," I say, getting fed up. "Anyway, I don't have your number."

"You don't need it," Mike climbs in the front cab. "I'll hear you."

He takes one last look at Tom, clenches his jaw and slams the truck door. The truck is still running, I hadn't noticed in all the commotion. Mike slips it into reverse and drives away at a speed I hadn't seen him drive at before. Kicking up a cloud of dust and gravel, causing me to shield my face with my forearm. What the hell did he mean by '*I'll hear you?*' What is he, Superman?

Slowly, I turn back around to face Tom. He's now standing, and his face is void of the anger that was previously there. Replaced by worry and confusion. I take a few cautious steps toward him. I knew I was going to feel the back of his hand anyway after the way he approached the truck. But after the run in with Mike, it's going to be a lot worse.

I stand in front of him, my hands clasped in front of my body, like a little girl about to be scolded for doing something she knows she should never have done. I look up and find that Tom isn't even looking at me. His eyes haven't left the spot where Mike's truck was moments ago. Like he's hoping something will be revealed the more he stares into the dust that's slowly settling.

"Who was that?" Tom asks without looking at me.

"Mike," I whisper. "He's new. Moved into the Anderson farm a few days back."

"There ain't no-one in the old Anderson place. Been empty 3 months. Drove past it myself only yesterday." Tom's biting his lip, something he does whenever he's thinking. He's frowning so much his bushy eyebrows are threatening to cover his whole eye like he's wearing an eye mask made of caterpillars. "I don't wantcha seein' or talkin' to him again. Understand me, girl?" He's looking at me now, his gaze burning a hole right through me.

I nod slowly and close my eyes. I know what's coming next and I set my feet and brace myself for the blow that's about to connect with my cheek bone. Then I hear his footsteps, fading away. I open one eye to see him making his way back toward the house.

"Get ya things and start dinner. I been working all day. Gotta eat," he calls over his shoulder.

For a second, I don't move. Rooted to the spot through shock. I can't really feel too happy. I can't formulate much of a thought past surprise. Tom disappears under the porch and through the front door. The sound of it slamming pulls me out of my confusion enough to realize I better get a move on. I've had a reprieve, and I don't want to push my luck any farther.

I grab my bag and books and start walking. My thoughts filled with everything that just happened. The Anderson place is empty, so has Mike been lying to me? And what he did to Tom, the same thing he did to Brad this morning.

And his eyes.

These thoughts are going to fill my head all night, I know it.

16

I wake from a restless sleep, roll over and check the time–6 am. I sit on the edge of the bed and wearily rub my eyes. It's early, but I may as well get up. Sleep has eluded me enough through the night. The last thing I need is to fall into a deep sleep now and wake up late. I trudge to the bathroom and turn the shower on, letting the water heat up. I brush my teeth and study my face in the mirror. The sleeplessness evident on my face. Bags under my eyes complete with what appear to be dark purple rings.

I climb into the shower and let the water cascade over my skin. It's hot. Too hot. But I don't care. My mind runs over the nightmares that kept me from peacefulness only hours ago. It's funny, less than an hour ago I was lying in bed, tossing and turning. The Sandman and his sack of sweet dream were nowhere to be seen, and yet, the thoughts seem an eternity ago.

My usual nightmare was front and center. Ever present, as always. But this time it was different. This time things changed.

I was running through the school, the dawn sky its usual blood red, visible through the broken roof. But this time there wasn't just one person chasing me, there was two. The monster who is always in pursuit, but this time, he had a partner. Tom. I re-member running away, fearfully looking over my shoulder to see him marching on me. But it was different. He was different. His eyes were a glowing yellow, shining bright. He stumbled in my direction. Not in his usual angry, purposeful march, but like a creature from some zombie horror movie.

Tom looked possessed, as if he was some kind of monstrous ventriloquist dummy. I tripped at my usual spot and scrambled on the floor to create as much distance from myself and my two predators. Then, as has been the case lately when I fall into this nightmarish world, a hand reached out to rescue me. My eyes travelled from the hand, up the muscular arm and perfectly formed shoulder to the most angelic face I have ever seen. To Mike. He lifted me to my feet, and I immediately relaxed, knowing that in his arms I'm safe, and will always be safe. But then something changed, something became different as his grip on my arms began to tighten. They turned from the embrace of someone there to help, to the capture of someone there to harm.

I looked into his eyes, the eyes of someone who I thought was there to rescue me, but it becomes immediately apparent that is not the case. Like Tom's, his eyes began to glow, but not a bright yellow.

A demonic red.

I glanced over my shoulder and Tom and the faceless figure were getting closer and closer. Like a pack of wild animals advancing on a freshly killed carcass. When I turned my terrified face back to Mike, he was laughing. A maniacal cackle that seemed to echo across the nightmare version of the school. Then his face changed. His teeth turning into sharp, needle like pins. Horns began to protrude from the corners of his forehead as huge leathery bat like wings started to unfold from his back. He beat them and we rose slowly into the blood red sky. More demons fly around above our heads. They had gathered together in a horde and there was so many of them they turn the sky black. Monster Mike raises a hand to my cheek and where fingers used to be, there were now what appear to be hoofs with claws growing from the ends. He ran his fingers down my cheek, slicing the skin open and laughing as he went.

"Give her to me, Michael," the faceless man shouted from the ground. His voice sticking in my mind due to the well-spoken English accent.

Mike smiled at me and then let go.

I was falling. Falling into the arms of the man who has haunted my subconscious for as long as I can remember. Helped, not just by my uncle, but by the boy I thought was here to save me.

As I was about to hit the floor. I woke.

I switch the shower off as it becomes obvious that no amount of water crashing into my skull is enough to knock away these thoughts. I have another look at myself in the mirror. Slightly better, but it doesn't seem as if these dark rings around my eyes are going anywhere. I check the time again–6:30. I may as well get dressed and make my way to school. Be early for a change.

In the kitchen I make Tom's breakfast–pancakes and bacon. I've already laid the table with his cutlery and put his coffee and syrup next to his plate. If there's any benefit to being up early after a disturbed sleep, it's that I'm ahead of the game when it comes to my morning chores.

Tom walks into the kitchen, already dressed and been out on the farm for at least an hour. He sits down and I steal a look in his direction. Try and gauge what kind of mood he's in. It looks as if I'm not the only person to have been up all night. He's sporting the same dark rings I am.

I turn back to the sink and start to wash the pan I had used for the breakfast.

"Thanks." Tom looks at his pancakes.

I stop in my tracks. I put the pan on the draining board next to the sink and slowly turn to face Tom. He doesn't look at me. He focuses solely on his breakfast as he loads up his fork with food and places a large chunk in his mouth. I've no idea how to respond. I feel as if my heart has stopped beating. He hasn't said thank you to me, or been anything but aggressive and abusive, in well over a year. Not since he changed.

"You're...you're welcome," I stutter, breathlessly.

He doesn't look up. He just continues to shovel food into his mouth as if he hasn't eaten in days. I feel as if I'm on tentative ground. I don't want to do anything that makes him return to his usual angry self. I approach with caution.

"I'm going to leave for school now," I whisper. "I've got plenty of time so I can be early for a change." This is part of the reason, but by no means the only reason I want to get going as soon as possible. I need the walk to school to think. Turn my dream over in my head. What does it mean? *Nothing.* I think to myself, answering my own silly question. It's just a dream.

Tom stops eating. His fork, loaded with food hoovers a fraction from his mouth. I notice him clench his jaw, then he looks up at me for what I think is the first time since he came into the kitchen. My heart seems to fall into the pit of my stomach.

Idiot! I think to myself. Why did I have to push my luck? I lean against the sink as I brace myself for the attack I presume is coming. Hopefully, just a verbal one.

"On your own?" he says quietly.

"Yeah, I just feel like I could do with the walk. Didn't sleep so well."

Tom puts the food that had been teasing his lips into his mouth and chews slowly. Finally, he swallows.

My heart beats harder and faster.

"Stay away from that boy," he orders.

The only response I give is a nod. While I don't particularly want to talk to Mike at this moment in time, I have a feeling as soon as I see his face that could change.

Tom drops his knife and fork to his plate and it clatters loudly. He downs his coffee in one long gulp. He pushes his chair back as he stands and it squeaks across the old wood effect laminate flooring causing me to jump. I grip the sink once more. He grinds his teeth as he himself fights against some animalistic urge. Like two sides of him are having a battle.

"Be careful...and...don't be late," he barks and walks out of the kitchen. I'm left dumbstruck. Shock has me frozen like a statue. I grab my bag and leave through the kitchen door with plenty of time to make it to school and more importantly, plenty of time to gather my thoughts.

17

I load my books into my locker and slam the door. For the briefest of seconds, I look over the faded spray paint on it. Day by day fading further into non-existence. Then I turn to leave. As I spin around, I walk into something hard, or to be more specific, someone. Strong hands clasp me by the shoulders and prevent me from toppling over. The strong grip and now familiar tingle that course through my whole body, as if turning on a switch to every nerve ending, mean I don't even have to look up to know who it is.

My eyes focus directly in front of me on the white tee Mike is wearing. Not too tight, but still stretched against the hard, lean muscles of his chest. For the briefest moment, it once again makes me become completely self-conscious about the old, faded clothing I wear every day, but I push the thought to the recesses of my mind. I have more important things going on than worrying about my lack of fashion options.

I look up. Mike is looking down at me. One side of his perfect, wavy hair is tucked behind is ear while the other dangles down in his face, reaching almost his chin. One side of his mouth is upturned into a friendly welcoming smile and I feel my heart begin to race. Damn him for having this effect on me. I smile back, like the love-sick teenager I am. I gaze into the bright eyes that seem to change color every time he slightly moves his head. Looking like he does should be illegal. And then, out of nowhere his face changes. Morphs into the monster he became in my nightmarish, slumberland musings. I find myself in almost the exact same situation I was then. Held by Mike the monster, with his demonic features. If we were flying in the air, it would be a perfect re-enactment. I clench my eyes tightly shut and shake myself from his grip. Which isn't too hard considering he isn't holding me that tight. I take a couple steps back and find myself pressed up against my locker. With my eyes closed the roar of the corridor sounds twice as loud. Footsteps and conversations all blending to form an incomprehensible, almost deafening hum.

"Woah. Everything okay?" Mike asks. His smooth voice cutting through all the noise.

I don't answer. I take a deep breath and open my eyes. He's still a couple of steps away from me, sensing my unease he stays where he is instead of taking the two steps towards me. I make a mental note of this and appreciate it. His words from yesterday, when we were in his truck, echo in my mind, *'I wouldn't hurt anyone, especially you'*.

I look up toward his face. His brow is creased and concern is etched into his features. But no horns. No sharp, beastly fangs. Just pure beauty.

He begins to take a step in my directly and I hold my hand out as an indication I want him to stay where he is, for now at least. He reads the gesture perfectly and plants his foot back where it was.

"Abby, are you okay?" he reiterates.

"I'm fine," I reply. "I didn't sleep well and I'm just feeling a little jumpy this morning."

"Your uncle," he begins and then pauses, lowering his voice as he continues. "Did he...did he hurt you?"

"No," I answer. "Not yesterday at least," I add, with a bitter laugh.

"I just wanted to say sorry for yesterday, in case I made things worse for you."

"Quite the opposite, he didn't even shout at me, let alone hit me. He even thanked me for breakfast. He hasn't done that in a while," I shrug.

"Look, Abby," Mike begins as he finally takes his step toward me. This time I don't stop him. "You don't have to live your life like this. There're people that can help. I can help."

I look into his eyes and for the first time since meeting him his beauty doesn't even register. Instead, it makes way for anger and annoyance.

"Is that right? I never realized I had so many people in my life that cared. Everyone wants to help me all of a sudden. My knight in shining cowboy boots. Are you some kind of counsellor now and just forgot to mention it?" My words are dripping in sarcasm.

Mike looks shocked, maybe even a little hurt.

"I didn't mean to upset you. I just wanted you to know that I'm here. If you ever want to talk."

"Noted. And I just want you to know, and please listen carefully. I. Don't. Need. Saving. I've basically been on my own since my mum died and even more so since Tom woke up one day and decided he'd have more fun yelling and hitting me than ignoring me. I've managed this long, I'm sure I can manage a few more years. I know that it might make you feel good about yourself to help the farm girl 'trash', but trust me, it does me no good whatsoever." I jab my finger in the direction of my locker as I say trash, just to add emphasis to the word. I see Mike glance in that direction, but his eyes are back to me almost as soon as they've left. My voice is rising now and some of the students surrounding us begin to stop what they're doing and look in our direction, but I don't care. I barely even notice. I'm fired up and no one is going to extinguish it. This has been raging inside me, building up for a while and now it's reached boiling point. While it isn't all Mike's fault, he is getting the brunt of my anger.

I turn away from him and start to march off down the corridor, swinging my arms as I try to use them to propel me forward. I only get a few steps away when Mike grabs my hand, spins me around and pulls me close to him. Our bodies are touching as he holds my right hand with his left and places his right hand on the small of my back. To anyone else it would look as if we were dancing to music created by an orchestra of students walking and talking. My anger of just seconds ago is replaced by a light headedness as I struggle to take a meaningful breath. We stare into each other's eyes and once again the color of his are different. Gone is the bright blue of yesterday to be replaced by an emerald green that makes me weak at the knees.

It's a good job he has his arm around me, otherwise I'd fall to the floor.

Everything around me has melted into nothingness. Gone is the noise, gone are all the rest of the students. There's nothing around me but emptiness, sucked into a void I no longer care about. We are the only two people left in the world.

"You're not trash," Mike whispers, the cool warmth of his breath feeling like a summer breeze on my skin.

"Everyone else seems to think so," I croak out, my throat dry. "And if enough people start thinking of you a certain way, you start to see yourself that way, too."

"I don't see you that way." Mike starts to lean his head toward mine. "And I never will."

The tip of his nose brushes mine as his lips draw ever closer. I close my eyes as my heart beats so hard I'm worried it will spring from my chest and push him away from me. I swing my free hand around his waist and grip his shirt in my fist, holding him in place. I feel his bottom lip lightly skim mine. A ghostly graze. His smell, sweet and rich is intoxicating. A small moan escapes my mouth as the pressure of his lips on mine becomes firmer for a fraction of a second, and then...he's gone.

"That's quite enough of that."

Mr. Heaver's voice causes me to snap my eyes open in horror. He has pulled Mike away from me and has his hand on his shoulder. I look around and see the rest of the student body pointing and laughing and I want the floor to open and swallow me whole. Over Mike's shoulder I can see Mia. Leaning on the bank of lockers, her arms folded and her face screwed up. We make eye contact and then she flicks her hair behind her and marches off. Stacey and Lydia skittering after her like cockroaches.

"This space here." Mr. Heaver waves his hand in between us, "is the safe space. Any closer than this is what's known as the danger zone. Let's keep safe minimum distance, shall we? That goes for everyone," he shouts down the corridor. He pats Mike on the shoulder, takes a step toward me and whispers. "Nice to see you in on time...and making new friends." Then he walks away.

My face grows hot. I immediately look at the floor in an attempt to hide it. The rest of the school start to get back to their own business and thankfully, ignore ours.

"I'm sorry about that. I didn't mean to...I mean, I wasn't planning..." Mike stammers. This might be the first time I've seen him look nervous, or embarrassed, or without his cool exterior at least. In any other circumstance I might take this opportunity for some good-natured mocking, but seeing as I'm probably twice as embarrassed as he is, there's no point. Up until now I had never, ever kissed anyone before. I suppose, technically, I still haven't.

"It's fine. I know. I er, I didn't mind," I say, sheepishly. Trying to let him know that I won't mind if he tries again. All thoughts of my nightmare have been pushed out of my mind. I know there's something different about Mike. I know he can do things. Strange things. But how I feel when I'm near him, I just know deep down, there's nothing evil about him. Regardless of what my subconscious is trying to tell me.

He smiles. "Good."

"I better get to class, unless there was something else? Other than wanting to apologize for yesterday."

"Actually, there was something. I've been invited to a party tonight at the beach. I was wondering if you'd like to go with me?"

"Critton beach?" I ask.

"I believe so."

"I'm not sure I'm welcome."

"Why?"

"This is one of Mia's parties. I don't get invited to those. We're not exactly BFF's."

"Well, she's invited me..."

"Of course she has," I roll my eyes to the heavens.

"...and I would like to take you. As my date."

"Your date?" I almost scream.

Mike nods. "There's plenty of space down there and if you'd prefer, we'll stay out of her way."

"That might not be easy," I say. "She's invited you because she likes you...you know, as more than a friend."

"Well, I like someone else." Mike takes a step closer to me, "as more than a friend."

"Danger zone, remember," I say breathlessly. He smiles.

"Your uncle will be cool with it?" he asks, his face screwed up into a grimace.

"It's Friday. He usually leaves me alone so he can get drunk in the armchair. Or he will be out playing poker. Either way it'll be fine," I reply.

"Pick you up at eight," he backs away.

"Park at the end of the farm track, by the old oak tree. That way you can't be seen from the house. Just in case."

In seconds, he's swallowed up by the crowd of teenagers still lingering in the corridor. I'm left alone, bewildered at the mornings turn of events. I left home not wanting to see Mike, to shouting at him and storming off, to almost kissing him and then ending up with a date. My first official date.

The bell signaling first period rings, startling me.

I need to tell Sam.

18

I see Sam in first period, but don't have a chance to talk to her. I arrive a couple of minutes late, the mornings events slowing me up. Just my luck, arrive at school with plenty of time to spare and still end up late to class. Luckily, the rest of the class were still getting themselves seated and prepared, so Mrs. Spiff didn't seem to notice. By the time I sat down in front of Sam though, the class had begun, so talking to her wasn't an option. Even if talking to her was an option, I wouldn't have got much conversation out of her anyway. This was American History. Sam's second favorite class. Behind English Lit of course. Sam is a very studious student. Passing notes, whispered conversations, ignoring the teacher, all big no-nos in Sam's book.

We sit in single desk seats all in a row. Six rows across and five rows deep. Our seating is assigned by Mrs. Spiff and luckily for Sam and me, we're next to each other. Even if we don't spend our time talking, it's still a comfort.

First period is also the only class I have with Sam today. Our schedules are almost completely different. American History, Phys Ed and Geography are the only 3 classes we have together throughout the week.

"I need to talk to you."

"Y'all stop your talk. We don't have long and I'd like to get started," Mrs. Spiff shouts.

"At lunch, at our table," I whisper as I take my seat.
Sam just nods, eager not to get reprimanded.

The sea of confused chatter hits me again as I walk through the blue double doors. It's like someone turning the volume up on a television or a deaf person hearing for the first time by the flick of a switch. It washes over me like a tidal wave. Engulfing me as if I'm in the eye of a storm. Which from my perspective, I am.

I expect nothing different than any other day. Which is for most people to ignore me. Apart from the occasional bout of name calling from my usual tormentors, of course. Something I'm more than happy with. The ignoring, not the name calling. I'm less enthused about that. Today is different though. I grab my tray and make my way to the back of the queue of teenagers waiting for their less than appetizing school meal. The queue is small. Most kids here brown bag it. I don't have time for that in the mornings and it's much easier for Tom to give me a few dollars to buy the absolute minimum amount of food I can. Sometimes I will bring some fruit–that's about it.

The cafeteria lady splatters some brown, watery mass on to my tray. The liquid residue sprays all over my arm as she dumps it. Luckily, I'm wearing short sleeves, or my top would have got targeted as well. I walk down the line a few steps, grab my juice box and a juicy red apple and leave for my usual table. I weave my way through the large round tables of kids just milling around chatting, like I'm taking part in some crazy obstacle course that's part of some equally crazy reality show. Today the other kids don't ignore me as they do every other day. Instead, they seem to focus in on me. A chorus of *'Oooooooohhhhhhhhs'* and *'Aaaaaawwwwwws'* echo around the acoustic friendly hall. I look up, half in shock and half in horror to see all eyes on me. Boys pointing and making kissing sounds with their puckered lips. I start to speed up my walk, missing the days where I am all but invisible.

As I pass Mia's table, I prepare myself for onslaught of verbal abuse. No change there. Par for the course. But instead, I get nothing. It almost stops me dead to pass this group of a-holes and receive not even a cursory 'trash' or 'stinky farm girl.' It makes me feel as if something worse is coming. I timidly raise my eyes in their direction to see some of them joining in with the oohing and awing. Mia though is different, she isn't joining in. She isn't looking at me with the usual contempt she has in her eyes. She isn't pointing or laughing at me. She's not trying to trip me up or preparing to throw something at me. Instead, she stares at me, her eyes hard. Pure anger in them. For some reason this makes me feel as if someone has thrown a bucked of ice-cold water over me. I shiver involuntarily.

Since I moved to this school Mia has been the bully and I have been the target she has locked in on every day. As if she were a fighter pilot and I was the bogey she's hunting down. It's like she has a tracking device on me and can find me wherever I am. If she's bored, I always make for good sport. But she has never had this look in her eyes before. Never anger. She's looked at me with disgust. Pleasure when she's tormenting me. Indifference, if the mood takes her. But never anger.

Mike. He's the reason. She saw us this morning, that much was obvious when she stormed off. Inviting him to her party was so she could get him alone in some cozy corner of the beach while she's wearing one of the non-existent dresses she likes. Then, like a viper, she can strike.

I lower my eyes back to the floor and scuttle my way to the cafeteria's far reaches where I can see Sam. She isn't joining in the soundtrack the other kids had provided me with. Luckily, that's starting to die out now I'm out of the way. Oddly though, she isn't reading either. Her book sits on the table in front of her. Laid down at the perfect angle, completely parallel with her empty brown lunch bag, which has been flattened and folded. No doubt so it can be reused tomorrow. Her arms are rested on the table with her hands clasped together. She never takes her eyes off me, following me around the table, all the way to the seat I take. The one directly next to her. Her penetrating stare makes me nervous. I normally find her with her face buried in a book and have to coax a conversation out of her. Today she's ready. Today she's poised.

"Er...hi," I say through a confused expression.

"Does what you wanna talk about have to do with you making out with the new kid in full view of everyone earlier today?" she asks.

If I didn't know better, I'd say she was mocking me. But that isn't her style. This is genuine curiosity.

"You saw?"

"No, but may as well have. I've heard so many people talking about it that I got a pretty vulgar visual." Her nose wrinkles in what looks to be disgust.

"There was no making out. There wasn't even a kiss. There was an almost kiss. They're making something out of nothing...as usual." I start to poke my lunch with a plastic fork. The smell is disgusting, like sweaty feet. And it looks like roadkill. I push the tray towards the middle of the table, the thought of it going near my mouth makes me nauseous. I pick up the apple and decide a light lunch is the way forward.

"So, you spoke to him then?"

"Who?" I ask taking a tentative bite.

"The new kid."

"His name's Mike."

"Mike. You spoke to him? About the mumbo jumbo he pulled on Brad and about...you know..." she taps her Stephen King book "...being a demon."

Anyone listening in would think she was crazy. But her face is deadly serious.

"We spoke about it, kind of. He said he isn't a demon...or a monster," I shrug.

"Of course he's going to say that!" Sam shouts, her hands up in the air causing the table next to us to look over. She doesn't notice though. Unusual for Sam. She's usually so tuned in on what the people around her are doing, mostly out of fear.

"There's definitely something different about him, but I don't think it's bad. I just have a feeling...I trust him," I avoid making eye contact. I stare at my apple, turning it over in my hands.

"People trusted Ted Bundy too."

I purse my lips and look at her in a way that I hope conveys how ridiculous I think that is.

"Look, I just don't want you to get hurt. You don't know this guy, nobody does, and if what you told me is true...what he might be able to do...he isn't normal." She fiddles with her book, embarrassed to make eye contact and I think to myself how lucky I am to have her as a friend.

My mind immediately shoots back to Mike's confrontation with Brad. How Brad looked in immense pain and unable to do anything about it. Then to how he did almost the exact same thing to Tom yesterday. Then I think back to our journey home from school–his words echo in my mind.

'Abby there's things, strange things. Things I can't tell you.'

I don't want to lie to Sam, but I decide not to share this information. Because it doesn't look good. I know that's not a good enough excuse, but there you go. I'm only human. "He's a really nice guy, Sam. Honestly, if you just give him a chance, you'll see that. I'm sure of it...and it looks like now is the perfect chance."

I look up and see him striding toward us. I see people watching him as he walks. It's hard not to. I look over toward Mia who waves to Mike as he passes. He waves back, but doesn't stop as he makes his way to our table. Her face drops. I know it's petty, but this gives me much more satisfaction than I would openly admit. I chalk it up as a small win.

"You mind if I sit?"

I look over at Sam. She nods, takes out her asthma inhaler and takes a long puff.

Mike drops down in the seat next to mine. Considering the table is so small, we're now cramped in. I notice he has no lunch, but think nothing of it. It's not like the food here is particularly appetizing. We sit in awkward silence, Mike smiling happily while Sam looks down, studying the cover of her book.

"Abby told me she only has one friend, so, by my amazing powers of deduction I'm assuming you must be Sam," Mike asks with a friendly smile.

Sam doesn't even look up. Just nods.

"Well, I'm Mike." Mike holds out his hand to introduce himself. I don't know why, but I find this funny. His hand lingers in the middle of the table, waiting for Sam to take it in hers. As quick as a cat she stands, bundling up her belongings, shoving her neatly folded brown lunch bag into her book as if it is some kind of bookmark.

"I gotta go. See you later, Abby," Sam whispers as she continues to look down at her hands.

"Sam, wait..." I stand and call as she disappears amongst the crowd. I slump back into my seat, disappointment washing over me. I really wanted Sam and Mike to get along.

"I did shower this morning. I swear."

"She's just nervous. Shy around new people."

"It can't help that she thinks I'm some kind of monster. A demon, right?"

I laugh nervously. A nagging thought still lingers at the back of my own mind. One I don't want to let claw its way back to the forefront. "Sam reads a lot. A lot of horror. Sometimes her imagination gets the better of her."

"Or maybe she's more tuned in than she knows." He looks serious. His eyes clouding over with an expression I can't read. I'm about to ask him what he means when the bell indicating the end of lunch echoes around the cafeteria. The sound comes out of nowhere causing me to jump unexpectedly. Mike on the other hand doesn't flinch. His eyes still focused off in the distance.

"Mike."

He doesn't answer. I reach out and place my hand on top of his, which finally gets him to turn back to me.

"Sorry...daydreaming."

"I better get going." I stand, grabbing my book bag and uneaten lunch.

"See you tonight?"

"Yep...remember..."

"Park by the oak tree,"

I nod and smile. We stare at each other, lingering in each other's eyes. I give my head a shake and start to walk away, fearful a repeat of this morning's event may occur. I don't think I can handle anymore audience participation. I make my way to the exit door and stop to look over my shoulder. I see Mike stand and head for the fire exit door that leads to the parking lot. My brows knit together as I wonder where he's going. Ditching? He's heading in the complete opposite direction to all the classrooms.

He stops and looks over his shoulder as if someone had called his name. It becomes immediately apparent that someone has. Mia runs over to him, or more accurately, skips over to him. The hustle and bustle of the mass exodus from the cafeteria makes it impossible to hear even a fraction of their conversation from across the other side of the room. I clench my teeth and my cheeks grow hot with anger. I know it's stupid. I have no right to be angry, Mike isn't my property. He isn't even my boyfriend, but seeing him with someone as openly nasty as Mia makes my blood begin to boil.

Why does she have to keep putting her hands on his chest? You talk with your mouth, not your hands, Mia. Every so often she lets out, from where I'm standing, a silent giggle, and twizzles her hair between her fingers. I can't be sure what they're talking about, but it can't be as funny as her belly laugh seems to indicate. Mike isn't even grinning. Which gives me a small amount of satisfaction.

Suddenly Mike turns and exits through the door at the back of the cafeteria. The sun reflects off the doors silver frame blinding me momentarily. Like a laser beam frying my retina. I hold my hand up to shield my eyes. When I remove it, I have to blink several times to rid my vision of the floating ink blotches that I see in front of me. Like an internal Rorschach test. When my vision clears, Mia is staring at me from across the room. A huge smile plastered across her perfect face. She slowly raises her hand and blows me a mocking kiss. Whatever anger she had before has now evaporated. She flicks her hair over her shoulder and resting her small handbag on the inside of her arm, dances her way out of the cafeteria.

I spin on my heels and stomp down the corridor towards algebra. Grinding my teeth as I go. Somehow, even when she isn't even talking to me, Mia has a way of getting my back up. For the first time my dread of tonight's party disappears, and

I find myself wanting to go. Wanting Mia to see me out with Mike.

What could go wrong?

19

I stand in my bedroom. Unmoving. Rooted to the spot. Just staring. My arms hang loosely by my sides like two strings of spaghetti. My head, hangs to the right, almost resting on my shoulder as my eyes squint and my nose wrinkles. Like an explorer trying to decipher some strange new discovery, trying to interpret some long-lost hidden text. Instead, I'm looking at myself, or my reflection at least, in my battered full-length mirror.

Getting ready for a party is hard, especially when you've never been to one. Even more so when it's outside, and even more so still, when you're going with a guy. A guy who makes every single nerve ending in your body come alive at once with nothing but a touch.

A date.

I don't particularly want to go to Mia's party, but the idea of turning down a night with Mike was unthinkable. Got to take the rough with the smooth.

I study my denim skirt, check shirt and sandals and think '*that'll have to do.*' All day my excitement (and slight fear) for the night ahead had me imagining that my room would look like a scene from a cliched rom-com, clothes strewn across the floor, haphazardly creating a mounting. But it doesn't. First of all, I'm not that messy. I mean, why would you even do that?

Especially seeing as I'm the one who will have to clean it all up. Secondly, I don't own that many clothes. It would be more like a growing anthill in my room as opposed to a mountain.

I check the time. 7:51. I slowly and quietly head downstairs. Mike won't be late. I don't know how I know, I just do. Once I reach the middle of the wooden staircase I expertly step over the creaky step and stop. I stoop down low and peer around the corner directly into the living room. From this vantage point I have a perfect view of Tom as he lay slumped in his battered armchair. His back is to me. I can only see the top of his balding head and his right arm as it hangs over the side of the chair. A beer can is held only by the tips of his fingers and dangles at a precarious angle. It won't be long before his grip loosens and the beer splatters onto the floor, adding another stain to the already filthy rug.

I don't need to see his face to know he's asleep. The angle of his body, the beer can, the news blaring from the television and his deep breathing are enough. That's without mentioning the empty cans at his feet. I can already count five and that's without seeing the other side of the chair. Lone Star, what else.

I check the time again. 7:55. I better get out, the last thing I need is to be late and Mike knock on the door to be confronted by a very drunk and always mean Uncle Tom. I make it down the rest of the stairs and head for the door in the kitchen.

As my hand tightens around the door handle, something stops me in my tracks.

"The murder at Bethel Bible Village children's home occurred in the early hours of this morning..."

My heart starts to beat at double the pace and at first, I don't know why. Then it hits me. I know that children's home. I was there. I spin around and take a few silent steps toward the living room. Tom lets out an almighty snore that lets me know that a brass band could be rehearsing in the living room and he wouldn't wake up. My silence is unnecessary, but habitual. I turn my attention to the news report and continue to listen as a picture flashes on the screen.

"The home's warden was found when the day workers arrived ready for their morning shift. His murder, so shocking, and frankly, disturbing, that we're unable to broadcast any details at this time. Police say..."

I know him. I may have only been there for a few days, but I remember him. He is less spotty now and he fills out his uniform more, but his uneven hair is a dead giveaway. It's definitely the same guy. I don't know why, but my heart starts to beat uncontrollably. My breaths come in short bursts as if I'm about to have a panic attack. I rest my hands on my knees and try to control myself. *Get a grip,* I tell myself. You were only there for a few days and you didn't even know the guy. But something about the warden's murder seems to affect me for reasons I can't explain.

As I'm bent over, I notice the time in the corner of the television. 10:00. My heart starts to beat for another reason. I turn and almost run to the door. Being silent doesn't seem to enter my head at the moment. I just want to get out. I need air.

I hear the backdoor slam behind me as my feet crunch on the gravel just outside the kitchen. I know the slam won't wake Tom. He's dead to the world. The alcohol he has consumed has rendered him unconscious. A drunkard's coma.

The sound of the gravel echoes in my head as if it's an empty cavern. I pick up my pace, but my vision seems blurred. I stumble from left to right and have to hold the wall for support. One last deep breath with my eyes closed seems to do the trick and I carry on my journey. I try to avoid looking into the dense cornfield as I pass. The unease that washes over me every time I pass it is like water cascading all over me. I feel as if I am sitting at the bottom of the ocean, the weight pressing against my chest.

Ready to crush me. Considering I'm already having some kind of panic attack which I can't explain, the last thing I need is to add to that with my irrational fear of corn. But try as I may, I can't help it.

The wind picks up. A wind that wasn't there seconds ago. It whistles through the open barn as if a steam train is passing through. Clouds pass over the full moon. The lone spotlight sitting above the barn door flickers and then extinguishes, eliminating what little light there was. A chill passes over me as gooseflesh trickles up my arm. I hug myself, rubbing them as a shudder runs up my spine, feeling as if ice cold water has been trickled down my back.

Against better judgement, I stop and survey the corn that is moving more violently as the wind gets stronger. I don't want to stop. I don't want to look at it, but I can't help it. It's as if some unknown force is compelling me and no matter how hard I resist, I can't not look. I stare deep into the corn. Feeling as if someone, or something is staring right back at me. I can't see it, but I can *feel* it.

"Hel...hello." The words catch in my throat and only manage to come out as a croaked whisper. No reply comes. The only sound echoing through the farm is that of the unusual wind.

My heart thuds in my chest. The blood pounding in my ears.

The corn starts to part. Bending left and right as if someone is walking through, parting it to make a walkway. I want to run. I want to scream. I want to turn and make my way to Mike, if he's there, but I can't. My feet are rooted to the spot. My voice catches in my throat, like someone has gripped my vocal cords in their fist and is squeezing them until their knuckles turn white. A feeling starts to overpower the fear that is coursing through me. The urge to run is still there, but something else is stopping my flight mentality. If anything, this feeling is forcing me forward. Convincing me to walk into the corn. No, not convincing me. Summoning me.

The breaks in the corn get closer to the edge, closer to me. My eyes widen as I watch the corn moving like waves in the sea. Like that really old film about the giant murderous shark, causing ripples in the sea until his fin finally breaks the surface and his victims can see him coming.

I somehow, and with considerable force, manage to take a step backwards. I can feel my shirt sticking to my damp back. The force of will it takes to drag my foot back causing me to sweat.

Any second now, whatever it is that lurks inside the corn. Whatever monster it is that watches me, will break free and get me. The corn continues to part, reaching the farm track and then...stops. Nothing. I realize I've been holding my breath and exhale. A long shallow breath. I start to compose myself. Just as I'm feeling about halfway normal, something catches my eye. Slithering out of the corn is a snake. The largest snake I have ever seen. It's tongue flicks in and out as it heads toward me. Pursuing me. For a moment I'm rooted in shock and fear and then I finally get my mind back. I retreat, speeding up as the snake increases its own pace. My heel hits a rock and I stumble backwards, hitting my head on the floor as I fall. Finally, my voice returns and I let out a scream as the snake advances on me. It looks big enough to eat me whole. I shuffle backwards on my hands as it reaches my feet, and then...stops. It raises its head in the air, tongue flicking furiously. It looks around as if it's heard something or smelled something.

It turns around and as quick as it appeared, it's gone. Slithering away back into the depths of the cornfield.

"Abby!" I hear Mike's panicked voice behind me as he runs up the farm track. "What happened?"

I jump to my feet, trying to act as if nothing out of the ordinary was going on. Despite the fact that I'm lying on the floor, covered in dust and sweating much more than the short walk from the kitchen deserved.

"Yeah, I, er... I'm fine," I answer, trying to steady my shaking voice.

"Are you hurt?" he takes my hands in his. I feel the familiar bolt of electricity zap through me, causing me to shudder. But I get it under control. I look into his face as he looks at my hands, concern etched across his furrowed brow. "Well...are you?"

I realize I haven't answered his question. I was too busy just looking at him. I look down at my shoes, embarrassed. "I'm fine," I lie.

"You sure?" he answers, holding my hands up in front of me so I can see my palms. The heels of my hands are both grazed and bloody. All of a sudden, I can feel them throb. I must not have registered the pain. Too busy concentrating on the fear that was engulfing my whole being. I wince as his thumb lightly strokes the injured area. "What happened, Abby?"

I try to ignore the feeling I get every time my name leaves his lips. The race of my heart. The tingle in my skin.

"It's nothing, really. I get a funny feeling lately when I'm around the cornfield...like I'm being watched..." I pause, expecting him to laugh, but he doesn't. He looks serious. Concerned. So, I carry on "...when I came out tonight, I got that very same feeling, but something else as well, a feeling like I wanted to go into the corn, like it was summoning me. *Tempting me*. Part of me wanted to run, but this other part, a stronger part, wanted me to go into the corn and no matter how much I wanted to run, I couldn't. Then just when I think it's gone, when that feeling disappears, a huge snake comes charging out of the corn...Mike, what is it?"

Mike's face changes from concern to what can only be described as fear. He removes his hands from mine and takes me by the shoulders. He doesn't hurt me, but I can feel how strong he is as he holds my shoulders in a vice grip.

"A snake? You're sure?"

"Not something I'm going to get confused. Not every day you see the largest snake in existence slither out from your cornfield."

Mike moves in front of me. Standing between me and the cornfield, his arm across me, shielding me. He stares into the cornfield and I can see his jaw pulsing as he grinds his teeth. His eyes dart from side to side, scanning the edges of the cornfield.

"Mike, it's fine...it's gone. I'll tell Tom about it in the morning. It probably wasn't even that big, I'm sure I was just shaken up by what I saw on TV, even though I have no idea wh..."

"What did you see on TV?" Mike spins around, cutting me off midsentence. I'm caught off guard by his urgency.

"Just the news..."

"What was it?" Mike says, once again cutting me off.

"If you give me a chance maybe I can tell you."

Mike takes a deep breath and folds his arms across his chest. He looks me in the eyes and his expression softens. He gives me a small smile and nods his head slightly. My temper flaring seems to humor him.

"I'm sorry."

"Thank you."

"Tell me about the news report."

"A man was murdered. A warden at a children's home in Bethal Bible village."

"What man?" Mike asks, his voice clouded with confusion.

"I don't know," I say. "I...I don't really know who he is. I just remember his face."

Mike stares at me for what seems to be forever. I shift uncomfortably from one foot to another, feeling oddly venerable under his penetrative stare. "You were at the home."

It isn't a question, but I nod an answer anyway. "I can't remember the warden very well, but I recognized his face. He was there the night Tom came and collected me."

"Have they caught the person responsible?"

"I don't know, I kinda had a panic attack after that...the rest of the report is just a blur." I look at Mike and his expression is unreadable, and it makes me feel even more self-conscious. "It's silly, I know. This kind of thing is on the news every day, and I barely knew...no...didn't know him at all, but I couldn't help it," I shrug. Feeling more and more stupid at having such a reaction to someone who was a complete stranger. I've seen loads of news reports about horrible things and have always felt bad or sorry for the people involved, but never like this. Never to such an extent.

I watch Mike as he turns away from me and once again studies the corn.

"Are you sure there was a snake?"

"You think I'm seeing things?"

"No, it's just. You seemed pretty worked up already and maybe..." he begins, but this time, I don't let him finish.

"Trust me, Mike, it was a snake. A great huge snake. The Godzilla of snakes," I answer back, a bite in my words.

He holds his hands in front of him, palms facing me.

"Okay, ma'am." He laughs and then he drops his hands and takes on a more serious tone. "Look, if you'd rather stay home tonight..."

"No!" I shout out. "I mean, no. I don't want to stay in...I don't want to be alone," I say to him honestly, my voice nothing more than a whisper, but he hears it loud and clear. At first, he seems troubled by my response, disappointed or even upset. He looks at the floor and rubs his forehead with his hand. A low, deep breath escapes his lips. I think I've said something to upset him. I bite my lip, nervous he's going to go home and leave me. I'm just about to say something to break the awkward silence when all of a sudden, he looks up. His eyes lock with mine and he smiles, the most beautiful smile I have ever seen. The most beautiful *anything* I have ever seen.

"Then I suggest we better get moving, little lady. All the good spots on the beach will be gone."

He takes my hand and I realize I'm becoming better at controlling that current that runs through me every time his skin touches mine. He leads me to the passenger door of the truck, opens it and helps me in. He softly closes the door and smiles at me through the window. I find I can't take my eyes off him as he almost glides around the front of the truck to the driver's side. For the first time I notice what he's wearing and chuckle to myself. We are wearing almost exactly the same. Matching, except of course he is wearing the 'boy version'. His red chequered shirt has the sleeves rolled up, just like mine. My denim skirt is replaced on him with denim shorts and he's wearing flip flops to match my sandals. His hair, as usual sits atop his broad shoulders and looks equally like he has spent no time at all on it while simultaneously spending hours at some big city salon.

He reaches his door and places his hand on the handle. Then he stops. Once again, he looks behind him at the corn, his eyes moving at what seems to be an impossible speed from side to side. Then they stop dead. Slowly, his eyes travel upwards, then his head follows as he raises his chin. I watch him, confused. He studies the darkening sky, now an inky blue as the sun is almost set. His jaw pulses. It seems to be a habit for him whenever he is thinking, or more appropriately, brooding.

While still looking at the sky he yanks his door open causing me to jump slightly. He slides into the driver's seat effortlessly and ignites the engines. It roars to life. My eyes instinctively shoot to the farmhouse in the distance, studying for any movement. It would take an earthquake to wake Tom, but the truck is so loud that I look anyway. I feel that familiar bolt of electricity as something lightly grazes my hand. I look down and see Mike's hand on top on mine.

"You ready?"

"As I'll ever be."

20

The drive to the beach takes about twenty minutes. Twenty minutes of mostly silence. I keep stealing quick glances at Mike out of the corner of my eye. He seems nervous. Uncomfortable even. This immediately puts my insecurities on high alert. Was he regretting asking me to come with him? If anyone should be nervous it's me. First date at a party thrown by Mia is bad enough. Huge snake lurking in my cornfield, that's enough to make even the toughest person shudder.

As with the last two times I'd been in his truck, he drives slowly. Sensibly. Once again, he never deviates a millimeter from the center of the lane. This time though his eyes did shift. He was checking his mirrors, as any responsible driver would, but oddly, he also kept looking out of the window, and even more curiously, up into the night sky.

I turn my own attention back to the immaculately clean windshield. Not a spec on it. I see the ocean approaching in the distance. Still and lifeless. From where we are, it looks as if it could be a painting, like those used as backdrops in old films. It looks so peaceful and serene.

Long before we reach the parking lot and see anyone, I hear the music blaring. My heart seems to start thumping along with the beat. It must have been loud because Mike looks over at me immediately. His lips upturned slightly at the corners causing small creases to form on his perfect porcelain skin. His face, so chiseled it looks as if at any movement it may crack.

"It's gonna be okay. I won't leave your side," Mike says, never taking his eyes away from mine.

I swallow hard, my throat seeming to close up on me. I just nod. I can't seem to form any words. My first real party and I decide to make it one of Mia's. What the hell was I thinking? Although, I know that I'm not interested in the party one little bit. I just want to spend as much time as possible with Mike, and a night on the beach is pretty romantic.

I nod and try to offer a small smile that I'm sure must come across as a grimace.

We pull up to the car park. A height restriction barrier stretches over the entrance. The faded green paint on the underside of the rusted metal bar is all chipped away. Evidence of all the over height vehicles that have attempted to squeeze through. I wince as Mike drives under it, sure he is going to be one of the many that hit it. My eyes squint shut and I crouch down in the seat as if by doing so the truck will squash down with me. Like Mike is driving some kind of Harry Potter style night bus. I ready myself for the inevitable *whack* of metal on metal. But it doesn't come. Suddenly, my body rocks forward as the truck comes to an abrupt stop. I slowly open my eyes to see we've parked. I look out of the window and see we're neatly, and safely, in a space. Mike sits in his seat looking at me.

"Everything okay?"

"Yeah, why wouldn't it be?" I answer.

"You had your eyes clamped shut like you were watching a horror film."

"Well...I kinda thought you were gonna hit that barrier back there."

"Come on now, there was plenty of room. Could have driven a Greyhound through there." He undoes his door and swings his legs out.

"Tell that to the paint chips," I whisper as his door slams. Before I have time to remove my seatbelt, the passenger door opens and Mike stands there with his hand outstretched, ready to help me down. I place my hand in his and I can't help but think how perfectly it fits. I hop down off the seat and stand in front of Mike, our hands still intertwined. We stand looking at each other until Mike gives his head a little shake and slams the door shut. I look down at the floor, embarrassed.

"Giddy up," he holds his arm out in front of him in the direction of the concrete steps that lead down to the beach. I follow the direction of his arm and he starts to walk beside me. The car park is full of people. Some standing around talking while others sit in their vehicles, mostly trucks, playing load music and drinking. Several different songs seem to be blaring out of different speakers creating nothing but an unintelligible noise. Nobody seems to care too much though, as they laugh and shout at each other from one side of the car park to the other.

"Shoot," Mike says all of a sudden. "I forgot something, be right back."

He turns to jog away, then stops and comes back. "I also forgot to say, you look real pretty tonight." Then he turns and heads back to the truck.

I can feel my face burning as I blush at his words. I turn away from the truck and decide to take a slow walk while Mike grabs whatever he needs back at the truck. I look over the small concrete wall to my right that separates the carpark from the beach below. If I thought there were a lot of people partying in the carpark, it's nothing compared to how many people are on the actual beach. Twice as many...no, three times as many, at least. It looks as if the whole school is here. My heart rate starts to speed up again. Crowds are not my thing. *Probably should have thought of that before coming to the party, Abigail!*

"What the hell are you doing here?!" A shrill high-pitched voice cuts through the music and draws my attention away from the beach activities. Considering the volume of the cacophony of rap mixed with punk mixed with an assortment of country music, that's quite some feat. I needn't have turned around to find out who it is though. I've heard that *nails on a chalk board* voice dozens of times before. Screaming out in indignation at something meaningless, as if something not going her way was some kind of discrimination.

I turn to face Mia, hands on her hips as she stands tapping her foot, wearing a dress that leaves little to the imagination. Either side of her, as usual, is Stacey and Lydia, doing their best to look menacing. Which isn't difficult.

"I was invited," I answer, trying to sound confident and not the least bit nervous. I fail miserably.

"Who the hell would wanna invite your farm trash ass to a party," Mia demands as her henchwomen chuckle by her side.

"Me," Mike says as he returns, and not a moment too soon. He holds a cooler box in his left hand as I stand on his right.

Mia looks shocked as she looks at Mike standing by my side and coming to my defense, but regains her composure almost immediately. Her face changes in an instance as if it never happened, as if she has always been in control. A skill I am guessing she has been using her whole life. I look around me nervously, but luckily everyone else is either having such a good time or aren't interested, which I find hard to believe. Either way they're ignoring us.

"This is my party." Her voice is weaker than before, but her head still held high, nose pointing to the sky as she shakes her hair away from her face like she's auditioning for a shampoo commercial.

"Yes ma'am, I remember because you invited me," Mike answers calmly.

"That doesn't give you the right to invite other people to *my* party."

"Yeah," Stacey and Lydia echo at the same time, proving what loyal lapdogs, they are. "I understand that it's your party, Mia," Mike begins. Just hearing him utter her name sends a lightning bolt of jealousy through my body. "But respectfully, this isn't *your* beach. Now, if you'll excuse us, Abigail and I are going to find somewhere quiet to sit."

The look on Mia's face causes me to have to avert my own gaze to the floor, as if I'm studying the asphalt with microscopic scrutiny. Her mouth hangs open as her brow knits together. Stacey and Lydia look at each other, not knowing what to do, desperately looking to each other for instructions, but all that comes is silence.

Mike takes me once again by the hand and walks past Mia. Her eyes lock on Mike's hand holding mine and she finally closes her mouth. I can see her grinding her teeth as her wide eyes blaze with absolute fury.

Several steps after we've passed, something hard hits Mike on the shoulder causing him to drop the cooler box he was holding and stumble a step backwards. I look up from the floor, where I hadn't felt comfortable enough yet to raise my gaze, to see Brad standing in front of Mike. Brad does his best to try to look intimidating, but his eyes betray his tough guy exterior. He's scared, but trying to put up a front for his friends. Beads of sweat prickle his forehead. It could be the heat, most likely it's the memory of the school parking lot flashing through his mind. Creating a battle of dominance between nerves and fear.

I look at Mike. He moves to take a step toward Brad. Brad notices and involuntarily stumbles backwards a step, but regains his composure almost immediately. I tug on Mike's hand. A small gesture, but it stops Mike from taking another step. He turns and looks at me, shuts his eyes briefly and lets out a deep breath, composing himself. He turns back around and slowly and purposefully, bends down to pick the cooler back up. When he stands up straight, he looks Brad directly in the eyes. Brad swallows hard, his eyes as wide as a deer caught in the headlights of a Chevy truck. Then, Mike smiles. A warm and friendly smile. He raises his hand and Brad flinches slightly, but all Mike does is pat Brad gently on the shoulder.

"Enjoy the party, Brad."

We walk off toward the steps leading down to the beach. I steal a quick glance over my shoulder to see Brad and Mia standing together. Mia angry. Brad scared. I smile at them and raise my hand, the one that isn't holding Mike's, and give a little wave in their direction. Not surprisingly, Mia doesn't return it.

I know I am going to incur Mia's wrath come Monday morning at school, but right now, I don't care. Right now, I plan to enjoy my first real party and more importantly, as I look up at Mike, my first real date.

21

We walk to the side of the parking lot. Bushes run along the edge separating the lot from a grassed bank that leads down to the beach. At intervals, there's several flights of concrete steps that lead down to the sand below.

As we start to descend one of these flights, I get a better look at what awaits us. My observation from earlier seems to be correct. It looks like the whole class made it to the party. Bar Sam of course. The thought of Sam hits me with a twinge of guilt. Maybe I should have asked her to come as well, even though I know for certain she'd have said no. I'm pretty sure Mike wouldn't have minded. Although the thought of being alone with him fills me with excitement. Nervous excitement, but excitement, nonetheless.

From my bird's eye view, I allow my eyes to scan the beach. It's dark now and the bonfires scattered around the beach in the fire pits provided, immediately catch my eye. They light up the whole surrounding and look beautiful against the velvet backdrop of the night sky. I look up. Not a cloud to be seen. It looks like someone has got a sheet of black card and scattered silver glitter across it. I don't think I've ever seen so many stars. It takes me by surprise and I let out a small, involuntary gasp.

"Beautiful, isn't it?"

I nod. "Makes you seem so small. Insignificant."

"You're anything but insignificant, Abby."

Once again, the sound of my name on his lips causes my heart to race.

We reach the bottom of the steps and I feel the warm sand engulf my feet. I bend down and take off my sandals and carry them in my hand. My free hand. The one that isn't holding Mike's. I scoop my fingers through the straps and let them dangle by my side as we walk.

"Not a bad idea," Mike drops the cooler and starts to take off his own. I notice he never let's go of my hand, of which I am extremely happy about. He drops them on top of the cooler and picks it back up.

"I've been known to have a few."

The music from the parking lot fades into the distance the further down the beach we walk. The sound of the waves crashing against the shore is beautiful. It causes a shiver to run up my spin despite the warmth. A small breeze blows, but it's warm air that kisses my skin. The feel of the sand being pushed between my toe's tickles with every step. We pass several groups of people that don't even throw the smallest of glances in our direction, which is nice. Most are gathered around the fires, even though it's anything but cold. Others are playing silly games, chasing each other and laughing. I notice couples walking hand in hand, like Mike and me. Their feet being washed with the sea water every time a new wave comes in. I notice a couple kissing and for reasons I can't explain I feel my face grow hot and I have to look down, averting my gaze. I feel Mike's hand squeeze mine a little tighter. So subtle that I question whether it actually happened. Then all of a sudden, he pulls me into his arms. I'm pressed up against his chest and he has dropped the cooler box and has both arms around me. I feel like I can't catch my breath, but I don't have time to consider what's happening as a football whistles past my head. So close, my hair blows around my face.

A millisecond later some half-drunk jock comes diving by trying to catch it. Within seconds the ball, and the jock, are both gone.

I raise my head and look at Mike, whose chin is tucked into his chest as he looks down at me. I can feel his heart beating and I'm more than sure he can feel mine. He clears his throat and takes a step back, letting go of me for the first time since the parking lot.

"I'm er...I'm sorry about that. I saw him hurtling toward you and thought I better get you out the way," Mike says, rather embarrassed.

"It's fine. I mean, thank you."

We stand in silence for a second and then Mike bends down, places his shoes back on top of the cooler and takes a couple of steps forward. "I think I see a free fire down here, if that's okay with you?" Mike asks.

I nod.

We start to head further down the beach. I strain my neck to see the fire he's talking about, but I see nothing. Just darkness. "You've got good reflexes, he was coming fast."

Mike smiles. "I grew up on a farm too you know. That isn't the first time I've had to dodge out of the way of something last minute. Machinery...some demonic animal." He lets out a little chuckle and I understand exactly what he means.

"Speaking of living on a farm," I start, remembering what Tom said the other day about the old Anderson place. "Where are you living at the minute?"

"What do you mean?" Mike asks. "I told you, we just moved in up the road from you."

"Tom said he went past there a couple days ago and the place is still empty."

Mike opens his mouth to answer, but he closes it again before any words come out. He shifts uncomfortably. "Well, we haven't officially moved in yet. All our stuff hasn't arrived. Basically, just sleeping on the floor. Here we are."

Mike changes the subject abruptly. Another day I may have challenged it, but I'm taken a little by surprise. I look in front and see the fire. Exactly where I looked earlier and saw nothing. I stop in my tracks and Mike, a couple steps in front of me also stops and turns to look at me, confused.

"Where did that come from?"

"What do you mean?"

"I looked literally seconds ago and there was nothing there."

"Abby, of course, it was there. Why'd you think I was walking this way?" Mike asks, his eyes screwed up.

I give my head a shake and continue walking. Mike laughs and does the same.

Thick logs circle the fire pit creating makeshift benches. I drop down onto one, slightly harder than I intended and almost fall backwards. Embarrassed, I look at Mike who doesn't seem to have noticed, or if he does, he kindly doesn't let on. I compose myself, regaining my balance and hold my hands in front of the fire. An odd thing to do considering how warm it is out, but instinct takes over. It seems like the right thing to do.

Mike sits on the log next to me, much more gracefully than I did. He sits close. His arm rubs against mine as he shifts on the log. He drags the cooler across and asks what I'd like to drink.

"What you got?"

"You tell me what you want and it's yours," Mike answers, a mischievous smile playing on his lips. I tilt my head to the side and squint my eyes at him.

"You're a magician now?" I ask, sarcastically.

"Something like that," he answers with a small shrug.

"Okay," I say. "Coke."

Mike places the palm of his hand on the lid to the cooler, rather theatrically. He shuts his eyes. I watch him curiously, wondering where he's going with this. I continue to stare as he opens one of his eyes and peaks out to see if I'm watching him. I laugh and he smiles. Then, he lifts the lid off and reaches into the cooler pulling out two glass bottles of Coca-Cola. He effortlessly flicks the cap off one and hands it to me, then he flicks the cap off of his and holds it out in front of him. I hold mine out and clink it against the neck of his before we both take a long gulp.

"Impressive." He just shrugs as if to say, 'no big deal'. "How about some sweet tea instead?" I ask, playfully challenging him.

"I'm afraid I only perform one miracle a night. It's an unwritten rule I have."

I take another gulp of my Coke and curse myself for not picking a less common drink. Of course, he would have Coke in there. Everybody drinks Coke. What an idiot.

We sit in silence for a while. I watch the waves crashing against the shore as the moon reflects off its surface. It really is beautiful. With the sound of the water and the fire roaring in front of us I feel like I'm sitting back at my little camp and it's a welcome feeling.

The silence seems to hang heavy in the air. Having never been on a date I worry that if it stretches on for much longer, Mike might regret asking me, so I attempt to fill the void with the first thing that pops into my head.

"I told you when we first met that hanging out with me wasn't the best idea."

"Excuse me?" Mike asks, confused.

I gesture over my head toward the parking lot. "Mia and Brad. You could have been best buds with the popular kids and yet you decided to talk to me. Social suicide."

"Yeah, you're right. I'll go back up there and see if they'll accept me into their cult." I almost drop the bottle from my lips, causing some of the liquid to run down my chin. I wipe it away with the back of my hand and look toward Mike, terrified he might be serious. I can see by the goofy grin that he isn't and feel a shower of relief wash over me. Then his grin disappears.

"I know it's not easy, but you should just ignore those guys. They're not worthy of your time."

"It's easier said than done."

He nods. "Guys like Brad, they're nasty because they're unhappy with their own life."

"I'm not happy with mine either, but I don't go around taking it out on other people."

"That's because you're a better person than they are," Mike answers, never taking his eyes away from mine. "Just think, in twenty years' time they'll still be in this town, having never left and still talking about the glory years."

"The way my life is going, I'll be right there with them. Except, I'll have no glory years to talk about."

Mike goes silent for a while. He looks deep in thought, as if contemplating what to say. I start to worry that I've put him off with my self-pity, and then luckily, he breaks the silence. "You have an important future ahead of you, Abigail. You're meant for great things. I know it may not seem like that now, but trust me."

Mike looks in front of him, out to the ocean. What he said, and how he said it leaves me confused. The conversation seems to have taken a more serious turn than what I expected, and I regret my earlier comment about him talking to me when he arrived at school. Too late now.

"You know something I don't?"

Mike looks back toward me and the consternation on his face is replaced by a wide, playful smile. "Maybe."

I'm relieved that he's smiling again, but his mood changes leave me worried about what to say.

I look to my left down the beach. Everyone is still having fun, but the party seems a million miles away. They're only yards from us, but the breeze must be carrying their noise in the opposite direction because I can barely hear them at all. I drain the last of my drink and Mike takes the empty bottle from my hands and places it back in the cooler.

"So, what about you?" I ask, as I bury my feet in the sand up to my ankles. I shimmy them from left to right, like a crap concealing himself from a predator.

"What about me?"

"What's your story? You appear out of nowhere and I don't know anything about you. I shouldn't have come here really. You could be an axe murderer." I pause for effect. "You're not an axe murderer, are you?"

Mike lets out a laugh and I feel a tingle in my belly at being the person to have caused it. "No, not an axe murderer." I playfully wipe my brow as if I'm relieved. "Axes are too messy. I've seen American Psycho."

"Haha," I reply, deadpan.

"There isn't much to tell."

"There must be something. Anything. You didn't just fall from the sky!" I wave my hand about and raising my voice higher than I intended. This time Mike doesn't just let out a chuckle, it's full-on belly laughter. So much so that he falls off the log and finds himself lying on his back in the sand. I look at him strangely, never having seen him look so relaxed—or less cool than he does in this moment. He scrambles, not very gracefully, back to his sitting position on the log.

"What's so funny?" I ask.

"Nothing. Kind of an inside joke," Mike replies.

"An inside joke...between yourself and...yourself?" I ask, confused.

He opens his mouth to answer, but stops almost immediately. All traces of carefree humor fall from his face in an instant. Like a dog who has picked up some high-pitched frequency that no human could possibly hear. It's like watching a video play in slow motion. The creases around his eyes iron out as his cheeks fall. His teeth, immaculately white, retreat behind his lips as his mouth closes to form a thin, worried line. I know it's impossible, but his eyes, a bright blue at the best of times, seem to glow. A chill suddenly runs up my spine as a strong wind attacks us from out of nowhere. Mike's hair, sitting on his shoulders seconds ago now starts to blow around his perfectly chiseled jawline. The once warm sand turns harsh and cold as it blows across our face, feeling like grit sprayed on a frosty morning. The calm sea turns aggressive as waves begin to crash against the rocks surrounding us. The flames from our comforting fire rise to a height almost twice as large as they were seconds ago, and the heat reaches incinerator level temperatures.

I back away from it. Stepping over the log we were sitting on. Mike, without looking, takes a step in my direction, effortlessly stepping backwards over the log while his eyes still look in the opposite direction, scanning the distance. His arm reaches out in front of me, protecting me from God knows what as his head darts every which way.

Mike's reaction causes a fear to rise in me which I can't explain. My breath comes in short hitches. I look over his shoulder at the rest of the party goers who were moments ago running, dancing and playing without a care in the world. Now, they're gathering their belongings and trying to block their faces from the unusual sandstorm. Oddly, instead of being extinguished by it, the fires seem to thrive as sand is blown on them. The beach is illuminated a ghostly blue as lightning flashes overhead, looking like veins in the pitch-dark night sky.

My mind immediately goes to an old Frankenstein film I saw on television late one night when I couldn't sleep. Dr, Victor Frankenstein stands in front of the Monster laying prostrate on his medical bed. The doctor flips a huge lever causing sparks to fly from his crazy, over the top medical apparatus. Electricity begins to shock the monster to life as a storm, much like this one, appears from nowhere.

The thunderous clap that follows seems to make the whole ground shake. I hear screams from down the beach as the heavens open and a torrential downpour starts to soak the fleeing revelers. The rain comes so fast and heavy that the drops cause a wall of water to obscure my vision. The drops turn into hail. They strike my skin, stinging like iced bullets.

The beach, now empty as the last of the students scatter up the stairs towards their vehicles, seems almost eerie. I place my arm over my eyes in a futile attempt to stop the sand and rain that blows across my face. Mike, who moments ago was scanning the beach, now stands in front of me unmoving. Rigid. Statuesque. Apart from his hair which whips around his face. If it bothers him, he doesn't let it show.

I follow the direction of his unblinking eyes. They're steely. The pupils dilated as the surrounding blue glows as bright as the lightning. At first, I can't see anything except the roaring fire, flames rising high from the pit where moments ago my classmates were roasting marshmallows. I go to look back at Mike, confused by his behavior when something catches my eye.

"Mike, what's wrong? What're you looking ..." I stop myself as I see a figure behind the flames in the distance. If the fire, rain and high winds didn't make it hard enough to make out who it is, he is also wearing all black, blending into the canvas the night has created. Suddenly, a flash of lightning illuminates the figure. It's so bright it's as if God himself has flicked on a light switch. The man, maybe in his 20s, is wearing a long coat that reaches just past his knees. Black jeans, boots and a black sweater sit underneath the overcoat. The wind causes it to billow behind him as if he is wearing some kind of cloak. His hair, like Mike's, rests on his shoulders, but like his clothing, is jet black. The flames flicker in front of him distorting his face, but from Mike's reaction, he knows who he is. He disappears into the blackness once again as the night sky goes dead. The world having a momentary power cut.

"Mike," I say, my voice getting lost in the wind. "Mike!" I scream louder. It snaps him out of whatever daze he was in. He looks directly at me for the first time since this strange storm appeared. The fear on his face is unmistakable. Another flash of lightning puts the whole beach in the spotlight once more. Both Mike and I look back towards the fire, where the strange man in black was standing just moments ago. Now, there's nothing. No one.

Mike grabs my hand, spins around and starts to drag me in the opposite direction to which we came. His grip on my wrist is like a vice. I let out a whimper and he loosens his fingers, but he doesn't let go, and he doesn't stop. He's on a mission. A mission which seems to be fueled by fear.

"What the hell is going on!" I scream.

"We need to get out of here. Now," Mike replies through clenched teeth.

22

For the first time in the short span I've known Mike, he drives erratically. Usually, so calm behind the wheel, never once creeping over the speed limit. Now, he rockets down the street at breakneck speed. Several times he hits a deep patch of water and I fear we're going to crash into the woodland on the side of the road, or career into one of the oncoming vehicles. But Mike expertly takes back control of the beaten-up truck and centers it in the middle of the lane. As soon as we're straight again, he floors the gas, and I watch the speedometer rise at a speed I never thought possible of a truck of this size.

"Mike," I say, but my voice catches and it comes out as nothing but a raspy whisper, swallowed up by the roar of the truck and the howling winds. "Mike," I try again, this time much more forceful. Almost a shout. I know he hears me, his eyes slide to the corner of their sockets, side eyeing me without having to turn his head. But he doesn't answer me. He returns this gaze back to the windshield. Scanning the flooded road as his wipers go crazy. They move so fast they're nothing but a blur. Every now and again Mike's eyes leave the road and he scans the trees to our side and the sky above, looking for God knows what.

Before I know it, and much faster than the drive to the beach, we pull into the farm track that leads to the house. The back wheels skid as Mike takes the corner much faster than is necessary, or safe. As the wheels straighten up, speckles of mud splatter the back windows. I look out of the side mirror and see the large wheel arches are also caked in the thick brown substance. The storm turning the dusty track into something resembling artists' clay.

"My uncle...you should drop me here."

"Your uncle is the last thing you need to worry about right now," Mike says through clenched teeth.

I don't argue. One, because I can see that no resistance I put up will change Mike's mind. He's far too focused for that, even though I have no idea what he's focused on. And two, before I know it, we are at the side of the house by the kitchen door. Even if I wanted to protest, it's too late.

I sit motionless for a while, fully expecting the kitchen door to burst open and Tom to come rushing out in a drunken rage and drag me from the car. But nothing happens. Maybe the sound of the rain beating against the roof of the old farmhouse has drowned out the roar of the truck's engine. Or maybe Tom is still passed out. I can only hope.

"Go straight inside. Don't stop, don't hang around."

Mike's harsh tone causes me to jump. I snap my head away from the kitchen door toward him. He isn't looking at me, he just stares directly ahead.

"Mike, what the hell is going on? What freaked you out so much at the beach, you scared of a little thunder and lightning?" I ask, trying to be playful.

"Abby, I don't have time to explain."

"That's not good enough Mike. I ain't leaving until..."

"Abby!" Mike shouts. It stops me mid-sentence. He looks at me and seeing the shock on my face, closes his eyes and takes a breath. Composing himself. "I'm sorry, it's just...I don't have time to explain—I wish I did. Please, just do as I ask." Mike lays his hand on top of mine. I ignore the now familiar shock I get as his skin touches mine. I can see the earnestness in his eyes. Whatever is going on really has him spooked.

"Okay." I nod, still confused.

I open the truck door and just begin to swing my legs out when Mike grabs my arm, holding me in place.

"If you need me...call." Mike's voice is grave.

"We've been through this. I don't even have your number, remember."

Mike's mouth forms a small smile, although it's etched with concern. "That doesn't matter, just call me. I'll know."

"Mike, that..." I begin.

"You better go," he cuts me off, letting go of my arm.

My mind is a wired ball of confusion, not having the faintest idea what he means. I want to stay and question him. Get to the bottom of not only what happened tonight, but what exactly he's on about right now. *Just call him?* Has he got super-hearing? I've seen him immobilize someone with nothing more than a look so maybe he is a superhero. Or supervillain. I shake that thought from my mind as I hop from the trucks front cab out into the rain. The look on his face tells me that there's no point in questioning him further tonight. I'll get no answers. He doesn't seem to be in a talking mood.

Tomorrow is another day.

I half walk half jog to the kitchen door. Once I'm finally under the small roof that hangs over the door and safely out of the rain, I turn and look back towards Mike. The trucks headlights blind me and for a moment I can see nothing but white dots dancing in my vision. I hold my arm up in an attempt to block the light, but all I really needed was a moment to adjust. As my eyes become accustomed to the light, I can just make out Mike's silhouette behind the wheel. He's leaning forwards, his fingers clasped together as he hangs his forearms on the steering wheel. He isn't moving. I wait, staring at him. Then, he raises his hand and gestures toward the farmhouse with his thumb. His not-so-subtle way of telling me to get inside.

Hoping he can see, I roll my eyes and open the kitchen door quietly. It isn't locked–it never is. As I place my foot over the threshold, Mike guns the truck back to life. I lean back out of the doorframe and watch him disappear down the farm track and off into the darkness. I go to turn back into the kitchen when something catches my attention, or to be more specific, a lack of something. Quietly, I grab the umbrella that always sits just inside the kitchen door and slowly step back outside and shut the door until I barely here it click, open the umbrella and run toward the stables. Usually, even in weather like this the horses would be hanging their heads out of the stable door to see who had just arrived, and with a truck as loud as Mike's they'd have been extra curious, but tonight, nothing.

I run toward the darkened barn, the umbrella keeping my upper body dry, or to be more specific, from getting wetter than it already is. My lower half is soaked through, especially my feet. I hop over puddles as I go. Like a participant in some weird Crossfit competition. I reach the barn and peer inside. Not only were the horses not looking out of the barn at the world passing them by, but I can't even see them. I squint, looking into the far reaches of the barn, back into the pitch darkness waiting for my eyes to adjust. Then I see them. All four of them huddled in the far-right corner. All squashed together. All with their back to me, staring into the corner of the barn. Staring at nothing. Unmoving. Like statues.

"Samson," I call. "Daisy."

None of the horses move. I cluck and coo to them and scratch on the barn door. Nothing. I click my tongue, usually enough to make them run over for their apples or carrots. This time their ears don't even prick up or angle in my direction. The only sound that can be heard is the bomb sized raindrops that clatter against the roof. The uneasiness I feel seems to double as I slowly turn around and survey the rest of the farm. No sight nor sound of the pigs. The chickens-AWOL. I look over toward the corn, not just swaying, but aggressively blowing in the gusts of wind. I'm sure that if this rain and wind subsided there would be absolute silence here. My skin prickles and a weight seems to be pushing me down, resting on my chest.

All of a sudden, the wind gets worse and my umbrella is blown inside out. I wrestle with it, trying with all my strength to turn it back the right way. Then it is blown from my grasp completely and skitters across the gravel and disappears into the cornfield.

I take off toward the kitchen door, my hands in front of my face in a futile attempt to stop myself getting hit with the rain. It's useless, but instinct all the same. I sink ankle deep into every puddle I try–and fail–to dodge.

Finally, I reach the kitchen door, soaked through as if I had decided to go for a swim fully clothed. Much louder than before, I push the door open. As I jump in, I slip on the linoleum floor with my wet sandals. I let go of the door handle and grab the worktop for support and manage to stay vertical. I breathe a sigh of relief which is extremely short lived. The wind blows the door closed and it doesn't just close with a bang, the door hits the frame creating a *slamming* sound that echoes throughout the house. It's so loud that for a moment it eclipses the wind and rain. It feels like the whole foundations of the house shake. I freeze. If Tom wasn't awake before, he most definitely will be now. I don't move for at least ten seconds, but it seems much longer. Waiting for him to come around the corner, woken from his drunken stupor.

But he doesn't come.

I straighten up. For the first time I notice how dark it is in the kitchen. I flip the light switch by the door, but nothing happens.

I do it another two or three times hoping that by the third go it might work. But nothing. Just darkness. The storm must have knocked all the power out.

Slowly, I start to walk to the wooded archway that leads from the kitchen to the hallway and then the living room. My hands outstretch in front of me, feeling my way in the darkness even though I mentally know where everything is and could complete a tour of the house blindfolded. All of a sudden, like someone turning off a tap, everything stops. The wind, the rain, the thunder and lightning. They all stop immediately. I feel as if I've gone deaf.

I can feel the blood pumping in my ears. *Thump. Thump. Thump.*

Lights from the TV flicker in the lounge–so all the power can't have gone out. But there's no sound coming from it. But there is *a* sound. I stop and listen. With the storm having miraculously disappeared I could hear a pin drop. The sound...it's a buzzing.

The faint buzzing of flies.

I step into the hallway and see the swarm of flies scattered around the living room. At first, I don't see the horror that has attracted them here, but one more step which causes me to exit the hallway and enter the living room, and it becomes grotesquely obvious why we have these flying guests.

I hear a scream. I don't know where it comes from, but as I'm the only person here, it must be me. Strangely, no sound has escaped my lips. The scream is in my head. I'm too shocked, scared and horrified to even engage my vocal cords.

In the center of the room, hanging from one of the wooden beams that cross the width of the room, hangs Uncle Tom. I've always loved the wooden beams. The dark wood always made me feel warm and the thickness gave me faith in how strong they must be. I look now and think how I was right...they can support all of Tom's lifeless weight. I'll never be able to look at them the same again. He hangs upside down, like a side of beef at a butcher's market. His legs, tied together at his ankles as his arms dangle above his head. I realize how tall he is as his fingers lightly scrape small thin lines in the blood pooled directly below him as his body lightly sways. It looks like ketchup. Like when you've had a plate of fries and decide to slide one across a dollop of sauce and it smears across your plate. As soon as that thought enters my head, I know I'll never eat fries again.

As I look closer, I notice where all the gallons of blood have come from. His chest has been split open and his organs hang from the cavity in his torso.

I still can't force a scream from my mouth, but I can feel something rising in my chest, and then my throat. I turn away from the horror show directly before my eyes and lean on the frame that surrounds the huge open plan walkway. I bend over and vomit all over the floor. Oddly, I notice that it looks mostly like the Coke I had just drunk. Considering I was too nervous to eat anything all day, this isn't too surprising.

'*Christ*', I think to myself *'the beach seems like it was hours ago instead of minutes.'*

I start to feel my legs turn to jelly and I fall to my knees. Darkness closes in as my head becomes foggy. Just before I pass out completely, I manage one word.

"Mike."

It escapes my lips as nothing more than a breath. An inaudible whisper. Then my head hits the hardwood floor.

23

The warm breeze kisses my skin as I look out at the calm, peaceful ocean. I slowly raise my right hand and scoop my hair behind my ear to keep it out of my face. I don't want anything to obscure my view, not just of the ocean, but of my beach partner as well. I look to my left and my heart skips a beat, once again I can't believe that of all the people he could have chosen to come here with, he chose me. I study his face. His expression giving away absolutely no hint of what he's thinking or feeling. I'm like an open book. He's like ancient hieroglyphs.

It's so peaceful here right now, just the sound of the sea and our breathing, like meditating. Even with the rest of my class playing music and having a generally good time just feet away from us, it seems quiet. This might be the happiest I have ever been in my life. Definitely since my mom died. The thing is, I can't remember much from that time so I can't really compare, but it would have had to have been really happy to top this.

I notice Mike looking at me and lower my head to my feet embarrassed. Lost in my train of thought I have no idea how long he had been looking in my direction. I dig my feet into the warm sand, busying myself.

"Abby."

I snap my head around as I hear my name–nothing but a whisper, as if the breeze itself had uttered it.

"*Everything okay?*" *Mike asks.*

"*Fine,*" *I say.* "*I just thought I heard…*" *I trail off as I turn back in his direction. Just past him, where the rest of the class were just moments ago, now there's nothing. Now there's no one. The whole beach is empty, and an eerie silence stretches for what seems to be miles. Even the waves crashing on the shore create no sound. It's like I'm watching a silent movie.* "*Where is everyone?*" *I gesture to the empty beach.*

"*What do you mean?*" *Mike answers.*

"*Mia. Brad…everyone. Where did they go?*" *I ask again.*

"*Abigail, they're there,*" *he answers, talking much slower than usual.*

"*Mike, look. There's no one there. They're all gone.*"

"*I don't need to look, Abigail.*"

I look back toward the silent sea. Waves crash against the huge rocks and still produce no sound whatsoever. "*Something really weird is going on. Mike. I'm scared.*"

"*Don't be scared, you know I'll always protect you.*" *Mike holds my hand as he says this, but it's different. His hands feel like sandpaper and the electric pulse that courses through my body at every touch, isn't there.*

"*Abby.*"

I hear the whispered voice say my name once again. I turn in the direction it seems to come from. Just behind me. Once again, there's no one there.

"*What the hell is happening here?*"

I turn around and what greets me causes my stomach to lurch. It's Mike, but it isn't. His angelic face has contorted into some kind of demonic beast. What was once perfectly smooth porcelain skin has become coarse and deformed. Boils have risen on his cheeks and forehead and his mouth is twisted into some grotesque grimace. His smile, now widened by cuts at the corner of his mouth. His eyes, nothing but black holes in his face with blood slowly trick-

ling from them. His golden hair no longer there. Wispy strands spout from his scabbed head. There are so few that if I wasn't in such a state of fear, panic and confusion, I could have counted them all.

He smiles that wide smile displaying sharp, pointed black teeth. I fall off the log as I try and scramble backwards and begin to cry. My hand instinctively grabs for my angel necklace, but I clutch nothing but skin. My fingers search for it, but it's nowhere to be found.

"Abby!"

The voice in the air calls my name once more, only this time louder.

"Help me!" I scream. "Whoever's there, help me!"

"No one can help you now," demon Mike begins, his voice croaked, but high pitched all the same. He dribbles some type of thick black tar down his deformed, battered face. It hangs off his chin in long dangles of spit. "You're mine forever."

"Abigail!!"

My eyes snap open and I take a deep breath, sucking in all the air around me as if I've just been resuscitated. My breathing comes in short, sharp bursts. Something tickles my cheek, and I wipe the palm of my hand across to discover I have been crying. Not just crying, but considering how wet the palm of my hand now is, sobbing. I feel a sharp pain in my right hand, and I hold it in front of my eyes to inspect it. Blood trickles down it onto my wrist and then my forearm. I'd been clutching at my broken necklace and the pointed edge where the angel wing once was, has dug into the palm of my hand cutting me.

"Abigail, can you hear me?" Mike asks, panic rising in his voice. I lock eyes with him for the first time since waking up and notice the worry in them. They're wide. Like saucers.

"You were...some kind of monster...a demon..." I trail off, feeling disoriented. "Why am I on the floor?"

A small creaking sound draws my attention to something moving just over Mike's left shoulder. I focus my eyes in that direction and the reason I'm on the floor comes rushing back to me in an instant. The memories hitting me like a freight train. I see my uncle slowly rock into view and then disappear again behind Mike's back. The he sways back into my field of vision before going again. I feel as if I am going to be sick. Again. Using my hands and feet I try to back up, scramble away in a panic as my breath catches in my throat and I find it hard to breathe, but the wall I am resting against stops me from going any further.

Mike grips both of my shoulders in his hands to steady and hold me in place. He slightly alters his body, only a fraction to the left, but this small movement obscures Tom from my view.

"Abby, what happened here?" Mike asks, his voice calm.

"You..."

"Me?" Mike says, still calm, but confused.

"We were on the beach...your face...you were a monster...everyone...disappeared..." I stammer. My words coming in broken, short, stop starts. Nothing but incomprehensible yammering.

"Abigail," his voice firm. His eyes focused intently on mine. His grip on my shoulders tightens. I flinch slightly, but he doesn't let go. I look into his eyes. His bright blue eyes. Not the demonic black holes I saw while I was unconscious. "Focus. Tell me what happened when you came through the door. Did you find the room like this?"

That question seems to snap me out of my baffled state. "Of course I found him like that. You think I did this?" My voice rising.

"That's not what I meant. Have you touched or moved anything?"

"Yeah, I came right in and started playing around in his guts," I say sarcastically. I climb off the floor. Mike tries to help, but I shrug him off and slowly walk into the kitchen using the wall for support. My legs still don't feel confident enough to make the journey themselves. I grab a glass from the draining board, one I'd washed earlier before I went out, but Tom had been too lazy to put away. I pause at the thought. Maybe he wasn't too lazy. Maybe he couldn't. Maybe he was too busy being sliced open and hung upside down.

I turn on the cold tap and let the water run for a while. I wave my hand under it to make sure it's cold enough and then hold my glass underneath it. Adrenaline coursing through my body makes it hard for me to keep still. My hand shakes uncontrollably. The clattering of the glass on the running faucet seems to echo in the deadly quiet of the house. I never realized before how hollow it was in here. I lower the glass to stop the clattering, but the shaking persists. Water sloshes over my hand. Mike's hand envelopes mine, softly, but firm enough to hold it in place. My glass fills up and I turn off the tap. I look over my shoulder at him, he's close enough that our noses almost touch. He takes my right hand and still looking at me he wraps something around the palm. I look down and see he has wrapped a paper towel around my cut. A small pink dot appears on the white paper. I look at it, borderline mesmerized as the dot gets larger, and darker. Mike goes to add another layer of paper towel over this one, but I snatch my hand away.

"Thanks," I say curtly, and push passed him, slamming my glass on the table causing half its contents to spill out. Brilliant. All that effort to fill it up and I throw half of it away because I'm angry with Mike. Angry with him for reasons I can't really explain. Mike leans across me with a washcloth and wipes the table. "I don't need to clean up after me like I'm a child." Mike throws the washcloth into the sink and holds his hands up in surrender. I sigh and take an unsteady mouthful of water.

Mike sits down on the chair at the other end of the table. "Talk to me," Mike says. "What happened when you got in?"

"Nothing happened." I don't look up from my water. "I walked in and everything was quiet. I heard buzzing. It was the flies. I walked in and found Tom like that." A tear rolls down my cheek and I angrily wipe it away. Despite myself, more follow. I feel far angrier than upset. I have no real love loss for Tom, he never showed me any love, but I still wouldn't have wished this on him. But I don't want to shed any tears for him and the fact that they're coming in spite of that causes me to get angrier.

"Was there anyone else here?" Mike asks, ignoring my tears.

"No," I begin. "Well, I don't think so." I look past Mike to the stairs leading to a dark upstairs landing.

"What is it?" he asks looking over his shoulder, following my gaze.

"I never looked. What if there was someone, what if there still is?" I say, scared.

"There isn't," Mike says flatly.

"Did you look when you got here?"

"No."

"Then how do you know?"

"I just do."

"How!?" I ask, getting more frustrated by his unhelpful answers.

He just looks at me.

"Mike, tell me what's going on. Tell me what you know."

Again, he just sits. Staring.

"Since the day I've met you, you've been a closed book. I know nothing about you, where you came from. Why you came here. I've seen you do things–things to Brad–without actually, physically, doing anything. Now I know you know something. Tell me," I say, my voice getting higher as the sentence wears on.

He still doesn't answer.

"Tell me!!" I scream. No, not scream. Beg.

Mike opens his mouth and I lean forward, eager to hear whatever he has to say. Then, he sighs and looks down at his hands clasped on the table. I slouch back in my chair. Feeling defeated and all of a sudden, very tired. I force myself out of the chair and walk to the counter opposite and pick up the telephone receiver. We seem to be one of the only houses left with a landline. Tom was old school.

"What're you doing?" Mike asks, in almost a whisper. His head resting in the palm of his hand.

"What d'ya think I'm doing? Calling the cops," I answer.

"Stop," he answers sharply, snatching his head around.

"Huh?"

"That's a mistake. Don't call the cops," Mike says as he stands up from the table.

"Yeah, why would I do that." I put the receiver back. "I'll just pretend to everybody that Tom has taken a nice long holiday. Somewhere hot. Palm trees and umbrella drinks. I'll just ignore the body hanging in the room next door and the pile of guts on the floor. Hopefully the flies and I can become fast friends and the smell won't be too unbearable," I answer. "If you're not going to say anything useful, best not say anything at all."

I turn my back on him and pick the receiver back up and start to dial 911. As I hit the final 1, the line goes dead. I look down and see Mike's hand on the cradle, rendering the phone dead. I look at him and his face is serious. His steely eyes stare unblinkingly into mine. They're a lighter blue than usual. Much paler. My face conveying *what the hell* much better than my voice ever could.

"Just leave it. Let me handle everything," Mike says quietly.

"Aaarrgghh. For Christ sake, just tell me what's going on. It's obvious you know something, so just tell me."

"I know calling the cops would be a mistake."

"And what do you suggest I do, in all of your infinite wisdom?" I ask.

"Let's just say you call the cops. What do you think is going to happen? If they believe your story, then you're going to end up back in some children's home. Or Foster care. You're still a minor."

Concern flashes across my face, but I replace it with a look of determination. I can't remember much about the home Tom collected me from, but one thing I do know is that I don't want to be going back anytime soon. Or ever.

"What do you mean, if they believe my story? Why wouldn't they?"

"Come on. Nobody else here, there isn't a house around for miles so nobody would have seen an intruder. The bruises on your arms. They'll put two and two together and come up with five," Mike explains.

At the mention of my bruises, I self-consciously, and automatically cross my arms.

"You...you think that they'll believe I did this?" Mike just looks at me, eyebrows raised as if to say *of course. Don't you?* "How could I have done this? How could I have...cut him open like that...let alone have the strength to lift him off the floor?" By the time I've finished the short sentence I am out of breath. Panic rising in me as it's apt to do lately.

"They won't care about that. Something like this happening in this small town, they'll want to let everyone know they've closed the case and you'd be the easiest option. Plus, you'd have motive," Mike says confidently.

What he's saying seems unlikely, but still, it gives me pause. However unlikely, what if it's true? Mike takes a step toward me and goes to place his arms on my shoulders, but I flinch and take a step back. He holds his hands up. "Let me handle it."

"How?" I croak

"Go upstairs and take a shower, leave it to me."

I stare into Mike's eyes and he stares right back. All the evidence suggests that I shouldn't trust him. I barely even know him. The way he was able to basically incapacitate Brad with nothing but a look. His evasiveness when asked any type of question. Hell, even my dreams are warning me against him. And it's obvious he knows more than he's letting on, not necessarily about this, but, about something. And yet, even with all this evidence. Even with the frustration and anger I feel toward him in this moment, I trust him. For reasons I can't even explain to myself, I feel safe around him. Comfortable. I raise my hand instinctively to my broken necklace. I wince as the cut on my hand grazes the sharp edge, but I don't move it away. This necklace is my comfort blanket and the feeling I get when I am holding it, is the same feeling I get when I am with Mike. Or the closest I can get to explaining that feeling.

I feel tired. No, exhausted. The feeling washes over me like I'm caught under a wave at the beach. I push the thought from my mind, not wanting to be anywhere near the beach. Physically or mentally. I grip the kitchen worktop to keep steady, If I don't, I fear I'll fall over.

"Please, let me try and take care of this."

"But, how?" I ask, wearily.

"I don't know yet. Take a shower and I promise by the time you're out, everything will be under control."

Not knowing what to do, or where to turn I decide to go with my gut feeling, and my gut feeling tells me that Mike can help. If I let him. I turn and head for the stairs, I place my foot on the first one and turn back to Mike.

"When I'm out the shower, you're gonna need to give me some answers Mike, I don't care whether you want to or not. You need to," I say with more confidence than I feel at this moment in time. Mike looks to the floor. Then raises his head. His jaw clenched, he nods.

"I'll tell you everything. Everything about me...and you."

24

I stand underneath the shower head with the palms of my hands pressed against the white tiled wall. I notice the reddish-brown rust around the plug hole, it looks like it hasn't been cleaned in ages and yet, I clean it every weekend.

The piping hot water slaps my neck and shoulders as I lean my head forward. I stand like this partly because the water on my neck feels nice. Partly because I need the wall for support. I'm not sure my legs are up to the challenge of keeping me vertical.

I can't believe I'm in the shower at a time like this, when a body is in my living room. I must be crazy.

The water on my neck is soothing. Like a massage. Or what I would assume a massage to feel like. I've never had one before. I have this memory of when I was a little girl and I'd lay on the couch next to my mom with my feet on her lap and she would rub them while we watched television. I say memory. Maybe it's something I made up. The time before my mother died is all a blur, and that's being generous. In fact, I can barely remember a thing. Not even from the night of the accident that killed her. I only know it was a car accident because Tom has a habit of bringing it up in conversation whenever he's had a drink—which is often. He only does it to hurt me, and it works.

I've tried countless times to remember anything about my mom and our time together, but no matter how hard I try, it's impossible. I *want* to remember, but my mind won't *let* me. Like there's a wall in my brain that's blocking everything pre accident. Like it's separating my time with my mom from everything after and no matter how much I hit the wall with my fictitious sledgehammer, it won't collapse. And trust me, late at night when I'm alone in bed, or when I'm camped out in the woods by my lake, I really go to town on that wall. Sometimes I feel as if it is going to start to crumble, and then, nothing.

I take my palms away from the wall and see the circle of blood where the cut on my hand was resting. Immediately I place my fingers to my necklace. I hold my palm under the water and watch as it dilutes the red blood to a weak pink. It drops to the floor of the bathtub and dilutes further as it becomes streaks of pink that circle the drain in wispy strands and disappears down it.

Seeing the blood brings my mind back from the past, reminding me I have enough problems in the present to be dealing with. Big problems.

I look around and realize I can't see much. The water's so hot it's has caused the room to be nothing but steam, even the shower curtain is almost obscured and that's right in front of me. This is what it must feel like to live in a cloud. I raise my hand and swipe it through the steam as if by doing so I could grab a handful, but of course, it returns with nothing.

I know I should turn the shower off and get out. God knows how long I've been in here. Half hour? More? The sound of the running water in my ears and the drops hitting the hollow porcelain tub renders any noise from outside of the room mute. I have no idea what Mike is getting up to downstairs and a part of me is happy about that, but I can't put it off forever. Whatever his plan is, I've come to realize that calling the police must be a part of it. There's no way around that. I also know that staying in this shower for the rest of my life, however appealing that seems to me, isn't an option. Plus, my hands are starting to look like they belong to a ninety-year-old woman.

I grab the soap and shampoo and quickly wash. This may be the longest shower I've had, but consisting of the quickest wash.

I climb from the bath and wrap a towel under my arms and let the water drip onto the linoleum floor. I forgot to lay the bathmat down to soak up the water, but I'm not too bothered. It's not like Tom is going to express his anger at me anymore.

I stand in front of the sink and look at the mirror above it. I wipe my hand across it erasing the steam and look at the blurred image before me. I take a deep breath and just stare. I seem to have aged ten years in the last hour and to be honest, I'm not surprised. The events of today are not everyday occurrences. I think about what Mike said earlier, about not calling the police because they will blame me. I didn't believe it at the time, and I still find it hard to believe now, but I find myself looking at the scattered bruises on my arms. The very same bruises Mike used as an example of why they'd make me a suspect. Then, I open the towel hiding my body and inspect the other bruises. The ones on my ribs. My chest. My thighs. The bruises caused by Tom's punches. By his vice like grips and even the occasional kick to the leg. These bruises remain unseen, hidden by clothes. Strategically placed. But if the police were involved you can bet your life they wouldn't remain hidden for long. After seeing some of the bruises they'll want to see the rest.

Maybe Mike was right after all.

I wrap myself back up in the towel and turn around, lower the toilet seat and sit down. I rest my head against the wall next to the toilet and sob.

I wake. My head resting against the wall next to the toilet. For a minute I feel dazed. Confused. I have no real idea of where I am. I look down at the towel around my body and remember I had just climbed out of the shower. I then remember what happened before I climbed in. I straighten my neck with considerable effort. I feel like the Tin Man in *The Wizard of Oz*. I need some oil to get my joints working properly. Again, time seems alien to me and I've no idea how long I've been sitting here asleep. Long enough for my neck to set in place. I reach up and finger the hair that sits across my shoulder. Damp. Not wet. Long enough for my hair to have almost dried.

I lean across and grab the magnifying mirror that sits on the edge of the sink. The mirror Tom uses—or used—to (rarely) shave his nose and ear hairs. My eyes are bloodshot and my cheeks blotchy where I'd worked myself into such a state. It's rare for me to cry, let alone bawl like I did. My body, and eyes, probably didn't know how to react to this odd sensation. I study my face some more and notice the big red mark on my forehead. It's large and bright, so bright I don't know how it wasn't the first thing I noticed. Almost perfectly circular and in the exact spot where I'd rested my head against the wall.

I sigh. You're supposed to look good after a shower. I look worse and feel groggy and irritable. Drained of energy. Then again, the odd goings on tonight can surely make you feel a little out of sorts. Maybe I can find a support group in town that I can ask. 'Relatives of gutted family members' or something just as ridiculous. That thought makes me consider how crazy this situation is. My uncle was murdered, in this very house. Maybe by a drinking companion or someone he owed a gambling debt to, and here I am, showering and sitting alone in the same house. All because a guy I barely know said he will *handle* everything, and I trust him.

Maybe I'm the crazy one.

I hear a door downstairs close. The kitchen door that leads outside. The one I used to come in earlier. My body gives an involuntary jump and I drop the mirror smashing the side that magnifies. Brilliant. All I need is more bad luck, I don't have enough of it. My body tenses and I freeze, fearing the murderer has come back to finish me off.

"It's just me. Are you okay?" Mike's voice calls from downstairs.

My muscles relax. It's just Mike. Or, maybe it is the murderer, I think. I shake the thought away. Mike has secrets and he knows things, but deep down I know he isn't capable of this. Plus, he was with me all night.

"Be down in a second," I reply.

I walk down the stairs about ten minutes later, fully dressed. I had dragged a comb through my hair and threw on some old jeans (old is all I own) and a creased t-shirt I grabbed out of my bedside draw. Not caring at all how good or bad I look. I am well past caring. As I get to the bottom of the stairs, Mike exits the kitchen and is standing just below them.

A sympathetic smile on his lips.

"Did you call the police?" I ask.

"No."

The muscles bunch up in my jaw as I imitate what has become known to me as Mike's trademark. Mike can sense my frustration and quickly continues. "There was no need," he adds.

"Mike, I understand what you were saying earlier," I begin as I reach the bottom of the stairs, "about the police and my...well my bruises, but..." I stop mid-sentence. What I see in what will always be known to me as the 'body room'–which is in fact the lounge–renders me almost speechless. What I see is...nothing. No body. No flies. Not even stains left by the pool of blood that was trickling its way into the hall. That was seeping into the cracks of the hardwood floor. Even the putrid smell of rotting flesh seems to have disappeared completely. It actually smells nice. Like fresh linen from the dryer. Has Mike done laundry? Or just sprayed some freshener around the room.

I look at Mike, my face scrunched up as if I am trying to solve some impossible sum. I think I see a look of nervousness cross Mike's face. Or panic. But it's gone in an instant.

"Where is he?" I ask.

"He's at the hospital. Turns out it wasn't as bad as it looked. I told them it was a farming accident. He's going to be fine," Mike answers rather nonchalantly. As if I've just asked him what he wants for dinner and he replied he wasn't hungry. Waving his hand in front of him to dismiss my question much the same way a child would swipe past a video they don't want to watch on their tablet or iPad.

"Wasn't as bad as it looks." I almost scream. "His insides were on the outside."

"You were shocked. In a panic. You must've been seeing things," Mike replies.

"Seeing things?! Are you for real? I saw exactly what was in front of me, blood and guts and flies. His lifeless eyes were wide open. It was quite obvious what I was seeing. And farming accident? A tractor came in here and hung him upside down as well, did it?"

"Obviously it wasn't a farming accident. I just told the doctors that. He had probably just passed out. You were panicked. Scared. Come sit down and have some water, you'll feel better."

Mike turns his back on me and heads toward the kitchen. I stand rooted to the spot, looking from Mike filling a glass with water from the kitchen faucet to the now immaculately clean body room. The floor looks so shiny that I swear I could see my face in it if I went close enough. I've no desire to see that though. I turn back and Mike is in front of me handing me the glass. I take it. Look at it for a second, then launch it across the room. It clatters against the wall and lands in broken shards exactly where Tom was swinging moments ago. Swinging. Dead. I know he was dead. No matter what Mike says, he was as dead as dead could be.

"Tell me what the hell is going on." He doesn't answer. Doesn't even move. With all the strength I can muster I push him hard in the chest. He doesn't budge an inch. He stays rooted to the spot as I stumble backwards. Angry (and slightly embarrassed) I slap him across his left cheek. I regret it as soon as my hand connects with his face, but I don't let him see that. My anger overpowers my regret. Mike Looks back at me, his eyebrows raised in shock. Then his face changes and he has the decency to look ashamed at least.

"I want to tell you everything, Abby. I really do, but I don't see that it'll do any good."

"So, you're keeping secrets? Did you've anything to do with what happened to Tom?"

"What? No of course not. How could you even think that?" he replies, hurt in his voice.

"Because you're so secretive. You show up days ago out of nowhere and for some reason you've taken an interest in me when no one else ever has. Was this all some plan put together by you, Brad and Mia, to mess with me? Murdering my uncle seems a little excessive though, even for Mia." I pause. "Wait, the warden at the home, earlier on the news. He was murdered, quite gruesomely according to the report. So gruesome they wouldn't even mention the details. Are they connected? Am I connected?"

"Abby, just..."

"It is, isn't it? I am. This is about me," I walk past Mike in some kind of daze. The realization seemingly making things make some sense. The only thing is it isn't clear what sense it's making. I still need Mike to tell me what it is he knows.

I sit at the kitchen table and place my head in my hands. My body feels exhausted. Like I could sleep for an eternity.

"Please," I say to Mike. "I feel like I'm losing my mind."

"Your uncle is going to be fine. Why can't you just leave it at that?" Mike asks and for the first time, seems tired himself.

"Because it doesn't make any sense and if I don't get answer, I'll drive myself mad wondering."

"It'll seem crazy. It'll be hard to hear and even harder to believe," Mike says, seriously.

"I don't care."

"It'll change your whole life. Everything you know or thought you knew. Are you ready for that?"

I nod.

Mike runs his hand through his hair, pulls out the dining room chair at the other end of the table and looks directly at me. I notice his eyes are exceptionally bright. Brighter than I've ever seen them and that's saying something.

"I guess I better start at the beginning then. The reason I'm here, is because of you."

"Because I called you, like you said. Which is weird enough on its own. I barely whispered your name. How did you hear that?"

"No questions until I've finished, and I didn't mean that. I meant the reason I'm here, in this town, is because of you. To...to protect you," he says, with no trace of humor in his voice whatsoever.

"Okay, I'll play along. Protect me from who? Tom?"

"Something much bigger than that. Much worse. Although, trust me, I wanted to sort him out as well," Mike says angrily. "But I didn't," he adds quickly, his hands in front of him defensively.

"But you know who did," I say. It wasn't a question.

Mike nods.

"And that's who you're here to protect me from?"

Mike just nods again.

"Who is it? Or, what is it?" I ask nervously. It takes a while for Mike to answer, like he's struggling with the words. Choking on them almost. He looks down at the table, his hands in front of him, clasped together as if he's ringing an invisible neck. Finally, after what seems like forever, he lifts his head and looks back at me.

He looks scared.

"Mike, just tell me. No more secrets. Who are you here to protect me from?"

"My brother."

I look at Mike. Shocked and confused. He looks back at me. We just sit staring at each other, the silence seems to pound in my ears. I don't know what to say or how to break it. In the end I don't have to, and neither does Mike.

"Hello, Abigail. It's a pleasure to finally meet you." A strangely familiar voice echoes through the empty farmhouse.

25

He came out of nowhere.

I heard no door open or close. No footsteps on the hard-wooden floor despite the fact that he was wearing black boots that definitely would have made a sound. Has he been here the whole time? No. He can't have been.

Could he?

I scoot my chair back a foot as if the extra distance was the difference between danger and safety. The wooden chair legs create a nails on a chalkboard style screech, but nobody pays any attention. Mike immediately stands up and positions himself in front of me in a defensive stance. He isn't close to me, he's on the other side of the dining table, but he angles his body so that I'm all but blocked from this stranger's view. I say stranger, but I have an unusual feeling in the pit of my stomach that we're not strangers.

My mind flashes to the blood red sky complete with monsters of some kind flying high above. Wings flapping in a blur like a swarm of human-sized locusts. A figure dressed all in black pursuing me through the school halls. Having never seen his face before, somehow, I know that this is the person from my nightmare.

I follow Mike's cue and stand up, taking a step behind the chair for extra protection. From my standing position I get a better look at the man leaning against the doorframe leading to the kitchen. He looks to only be in his late teens, very early twenties at the oldest. His hair, like Mike's sits effortlessly on his shoulders. But unlike Mike's whose hair is a messed-up surfer blond, this guy's hair is coal black. His clothes are also all black, topped off with an over coat that hangs just past his knees. My immediate thought was that he must be extremely hot in that coat, but he doesn't look it. He looks relaxed. Calm. The grin on his face indicates that he's enjoying himself very much. As with Mike, his skin is as smooth as porcelain. Just as I know that this is the person from my dreams, I also instinctively know that this is who was on the beach when the storm hit out of nowhere. This is who Mike saw. This is who he was talking about just seconds ago. For all their differences, they essentially look the same.

This is Mike's brother.

"I'm surprised, Michael. I expected you to make up some elaborate story about what was going on. I don't know, you're an undercover policeman and this was a drug deal gone wrong, but no. You told her your brother was responsible, and I have a feeling you were actually going to tell her who you are. Or what you are to be more specific," the man in black says. I barely register what he's saying because I'm too taken aback by his English accent.

As he talks, he slowly and deliberately walks into the kitchen, stroking his fingertips gently over whatever he passes. Slowly caressing it. Barely even looking in our direction as he does so. He moves in such a fluid motion it's as if he is floating. With every movement he makes, Mike readjusts his position so he's always in front of me. His body is tensed and his fists clenched as if he's ready to strike at any moment. The two of them remind me of wild cats circling each other waiting for the opportune moment to attack.

"Luc. Don't do this," his voice sounds gravelly. Dry. As if he hasn't spoken words for days and needed a glass of sweet tea.

Luc barks out laughter.

"Oh, sweet Michael, you know that isn't an option. If it were as simple as you asking me, then we wouldn't even be here, would we?" Luc turns to face us for the first time since entering the kitchen. His attention seeming to be on everything he had walked past instead of us. "Why so tense? Relax, we're family," Luc adds. Mike doesn't relax. Far from it.

Our maneuvering around the kitchen as led to Luc standing in the heart of it, by the back door and Mike just in front of me by the archway that leads out to the hall.

Luc places his hands on the kitchen worktop next to the sink and hauls himself up so he's sitting on it. He crosses his ankles and places his hands on his thighs. Still smiling at us. Toying with us much the same way a cat would a mouse before eating it. "So, Michael, how have you been? It's been, what, a few thousand years since we spoke last? And the lovely Abigail, what an absolute pleasure it is to finally meet you. It sounds as if you're rather nervous," Luc gently taps his ear with his finger, "I can hear your heart beating ten to the dozen. Calm yourself. I'm not here to hurt you."

"Is that what you told my uncle?" I ask. My voice much steadier than I thought it would be, and I'm proud of that fact, considering I feel as if all my insides have dropped to my knees. Mike angles his head towards me and gives it a slight shake.

Don't engage.

Did I hear Luc right? He hasn't spoken to Mike in a few thousand years? *Thousand?!* He couldn't have said that, I mean, who were these guys?

"No. Him I did mean to hurt. I thought I was doing you a favor."

"A favor? By murdering my uncle?"

"He hurts you, no? Regularly. I thought I would put a stop to it for you. It was obvious Michael wasn't going to. Someone as important as you shouldn't be treated like that. You're not just some common human like the rest of these hairless apes," Luc waves his hand in front of his face as if swatting away flies. "I didn't want you hurt anymore, Abigail."

"Ignore him," Mike says through gritted teeth.

Luc's smile widens, displaying a mouth full of immaculately white teeth. Not true what they say about the British and their dental care then. "Still, obviously I didn't do that good of a job though did I?" Luc begins as he leaps off the counter. "I'm sure I heard Michael say your uncle was going to be fine. Unlike me to not finish a job properly. I certainly didn't intend for him to make a recovery when I opened up his chest cavity and put his organs on display. I can always take a trip to the hospital and finish the job though."

"I'll call the cops. You won't get anywhere near him. Especially Now I know who you are. What you look like,"

Luc looks to Mike and bites his bottom lip. "She's cute, Michael."

"You didn't have to kill him or hurt him if what Mike is saying is true. Did you?" I ask, frustrated for answers.

"Yes."

"Why?"

"Because I wanted to. Because I can," Luc says happily.

"Luc. Please, let's talk about this. Me and you. Like we used to. This doesn't have to go down this way. We can…we can come to an arrangement of some kind. She's just a girl."

I feel slightly insulted by Mike's '*just* a girl' comment, but am smart enough to know that this isn't the time to bring it up.

"But she isn't just a girl, is she? You know that and so do I. Even if she doesn't. You know what's ironic. You led me to her. She was well cloaked but, as soon as you decided to come down here, I sensed you. Your presence here led me to her. If you hadn't have come, I probably would never have found her. So here I am, in the Hillbilly Hall of fame," Luc's arms are spread wide.

"I am begging you, Luc. Please..."

For the first time Luc's smile disappears and is replaced by another look. Anger? Disappointment? Disgust? I can't tell, but whatever it is it's aimed at Mike.

"Begging me. You know that that won't work either. Plus, did it help me when I begged father to forgive me, and he still cast me out?" Luc's smile returns as he takes a step closer to Mike. "I've never seen you like this Michael, ever. You're scared. You're never scared. What is it? I know you're not scared of me." Luc's eyes travel over Mike. His stance. The ways his hands are stretched out in front of me, shielding me from Luc. Then his evil grin grows into a huge smile, and he claps his hands. "It's her. You're scared for her. You've actually developed real feeling for young, Abigail. Tut, tut, tut–come now Michael. You know that's forbidden. It's how this mess all started in the first place."

I look from Luc to Mike and for the first time, Mike's eyes leave Luc, and he looks at me. He does look scared. In the short time I've known him, his face has never looked this tense. Almost immediately he returns his gaze to Luc. His stance still cat like, ready to pounce.

"Listen to me, brother," I look at Mike, slightly shocked. Even though I had thought they were siblings, hearing him say it out loud seems strange, especially considering what Luc has done and how agitated Mike seems. "It isn't too late for you, it doesn't have to be this way. Go to him, ask for forgiveness. He will listen to you. You always were his favorite." Mike straightens his stance and moves to Luc, his body more relaxed, but his fists still clenched.

"Forgiveness," Luc spits, like a cobra spitting venom. Mike stops in his track's and takes a step back. Luc relaxes after his momentary lapse and regains his confident smugness. "I don't want forgiveness, Michael. In my mind I have nothing to be forgiven for–well, in regard to the original 'transgression' that is–I've done a few things since as you well know that may require some overlooking," Luc says this with such glee. Like a child talking about drawing on the wall of their parent's house. Not murdering my uncle. Or whatever else he may have done. You gut someone, it's quite obvious you've done more. Worked your way up to disembowelment. That's advanced level stuff. "I mean, look around you," Luc continues, quite theatrically now. "I'm winning. You must see this?"

"Winning?! This isn't a game!" Mike shouts, showing some anger for the first time since Luc entered the room. So much so that it causes me to jump. I have no idea what game Luc thinks he's winning, but it's obvious in Mike's eyes there is no winning. Or definitely no game.

Luc continues as if there was no outburst from Mike at all. Walking around the kitchen, almost in a small circle, counting things off on his fingers. "Murders, rapes, wars...we're already living in hell. It's here, on earth. What a glorious time to be alive."

"You're wrong," Mike says, unconvincingly. His face troubled as if he believes what Luc is saying, but doesn't want to admit it.

"Really," Luc replies, eyebrows raised. "This world is a cesspit of evil and debauchery, whether you want to acknowledge that or not. I can see it in your eyes. You know it's true. These hairless apes are one step away from living in hell and I have barely had to do a thing. A nudge here, a whisper there. As I said eons ago, they will disappoint. But no one wanted to listen to me."

I have no idea what they're talking about, but it doesn't stop an added fear rising in my chest. I can't help but feel that whatever Luc is talking about, and however much Mike wants to disagree, Luc is right. The world is plagued with hate. Every day I hear about some unspeakable evil that is happening around the world. The biggest threat to people, is us.

"You're wrong. They're good. I know it," Mike whispers.

"Don't be so foolish, Michael. You know the prophecy. The only way any kind of order, any kind of peace will ever fall upon the earth is if she..." Luc points at me with a steady index finger, "Is allowed to live." He takes a step closer to me and Mike mirrors his movements. Luc's response is only to smile. "...and you know, I'm not going to let that happen."

"Abby," Mike's voice strong and firm. His eyes never leaving Luc. "Run."

I stand unmoving, having no idea what is going on, but knowing instinctively that it isn't good. My belly feels like a washing machine on spin cycle. I place a hand on Mike's shoulder. In stark contrast to Luc's, I can't stop mine from shaking. Mike doesn't look around, doesn't even flinch at my touch.

"Mike," I whisper.

"Go!" he bellows. I jump as his voice echoes around the wooden walled kitchen. I Grab the keys to Mike's truck which he had left on the kitchen worktop. I don't take my wide eyes away from Mike as I stumble backwards, my feet not feeling like their own. Then in a blur, no, not a blur, much faster than that. As if Mike was in some *Star Trek* episode and he was beamed or transported across the room. He appears out of nowhere in front of Luc and punches him in the face. Luc's body lifts off the floor and careers into the wall above the sink. I've never seen anything like it. The hardest and fastest punch I have ever seen. Not that I'm an expert in physical combat.

I'm sure that punch alone would have killed a human man, but it was becoming immediately obvious to me that Luc, and Mike for that matter, were not human. But that's crazy. If they weren't human, what were they? Vampires? As stupid as that sounds I can't think of another explanation for the way they're talking.

Luc scoops himself off the sink and I can see the huge crack in the wall where his body hit. Shockingly, he has no blood on his face. What he does have is the evil smile he has sported since he entered the room.

I stand rooted to the spot, partly through amazement, but above all, fear.

"*Get out of here*!" Mike takes his eyes away from Luc for the briefest of seconds to shout at me, and Luc is on him. Much like Mike when he shot across the room, Luc is the same. Almost disappearing and reappearing. He grabs Mike by the front of his shirt and with one hand he raises him off the floor. Instinct takes over and I grab the wooden dining room chair in front of me and smash it across Luc's back and shoulders. The chair shatters into splintered pieces, but Luc doesn't move. He slowly angles his head in my direction and his evil smile, which has up until this point been playful, intensifies. It becomes more of a snarl. His upper lip curling to reveal his perfect teeth. My eyes widen, realizing what a mistake that was. Mike notices the look Luc is giving me and tries to distract him with another Godlike punch. This time Luc barely moves. His head just snaps to the side and then right back to face Mike again. Luc lets go of Mikes shirt and grabs him by the throat, holding him off the ground one handed. A low, animalistic growl rumbles in his throat. Mike's eyes shift towards me. His head, unmoving. Clamped in place by Luc's hand. Mike's eyes tell me exactly what his mouth did moments ago. Run.

My brain finally starts to fire signals to my legs that they need to get a move on, and as much as I don't want to leave Mike, my legs start to carry me from the kitchen into the hall. I mouth the words 'sorry' to Mike as tears start to fill my eyes.

Finally, I turn and run to the front door. I sling it open, and it crashes into the wall. I run haphazardly down the porch steps.

"Don't go too far, love. I'll be needing a word with you after I'm done with Michael," Luc's posh English accent calls from the kitchen.

Running as fast as my jellified legs will carry me, I stumble my way across the graveled driveway and rip open the unlocked door of Mike's truck. I leap into the driver's seat and fumble to get the key in the ignition. After two tries, I keep missing the hole. A huge crash from behind me causes me to snap my head around and I drop the keys into the trucks footwell. The sound, like a volcano erupting directly over my head obviously came from the farmhouse. There's no movement. The house looks still, like a painting. The sound of the horses stamping their feet and snorting in the still night is the only noise outside of the truck, but it's barely audible to me. The sound of the blood pumping in my ears makes everything else sound as if I am underwater.

I sit staring at the house. So still, I'm not even blinking. Then I jump out of my skin as the same loud crash echoes through the night. So loud that even at this distance, it may cause my eardrums to explode. I don't have too much time to dwell on it though because milliseconds after the crash I see Mike's body break through the side of the farmhouse and skid across the graveled drive. I make an attempt to get out of the truck to help him to his feet, but he waves a hand at me and rolls his eyes. Upset I haven't yet left.

I look up at the farmhouse and there he is. Walking as if in slow motion. There's no wind, but Luc's long black coat billows behind him as he takes slow and deliberate steps toward the front of the porch. His lazy, almost evil grin has completely disappeared. He now looks animalistic. Demonic.

I reach down to my feet and feel around for the keys. It seems to take forever, but finally, my fingers grip the cold metal. I stab the key into the ignition with more force than needed and gun the monster to life. Slamming my foot onto the gas I speed off. Looking in the interior mirror, all I see behind me is a cloud of dust. My eyes switch every second from the dark path in front of me to the slow clearing dust behind. As my vision becomes clearer, I see Mike slowly get to his knees as Luc approaches him. Mike tries to get to his feet, but Luc hits him, keeping him down.

My vision starts to become blurred as tears fall freely down my cheeks. I turn from the farm track onto the main road and the last thing I see is Mike's unmoving body, laying prostrate on the floor as Luc stands over him.

26

If the pitch black of night didn't make it hard enough to see, the tears now freely streaming down my face make everything in front of me look wavy. My constant checking over my shoulder and around me causing the truck to sway over both lanes.

The trees to my left pass by in nothing but a blur, and that isn't just because of my uncontrollable sobbing. The speed at which I am driving is dangerously fast, but right now I deem the danger back at the farm, the danger that is possibly following me, much more terrifying. At least this danger is more or less in my control.

My mind goes back to Mike laying on the floor, helpless. Luc, his own brother, staring down at him. Ready to deliver what looked to be a final blow. And how did they do what they did? The speed. The strength. It was otherworldly. Like something you'd see in a Zack Snyder film.

My thoughts are interrupted, as out of nowhere, something drops from the sky. Something big. A black, indistinguishable mass. I scream and my foot comes off the gas and instinctively slams on the brake causing me to skid across the road.

I steady the truck and put my foot back on the gas gently. The whole hood of the truck is dented by the weight of this object. Then, it raises its head and looks directly at me. Luc. His pale, smooth, unblemished face is emotionless. I yank the wheel to the left, and then the right. An attempt to fling him away from the truck, but I know its futile. He holds on to the hood with a vice like grip and I know deep down that nothing, and nobody, would be able to pry him off if he wishes to stay attached. If he can withstand the punches I saw Mike throw his way, then a little bit of swaying, however forceful, isn't going to bother him too much.

Luc's face starts to sport the same demonic snarl I saw when he was beating down on Mike. Then he raises his right hand and smashes his fist through the windshield. The glass drags down his forearm, but it does about as much damage as a child running a plastic ruler down their own arm. No blood. No cuts. No marks whatsoever. The shards of sharp glass just snap off into little chips as if he has skin made of leather, or steel. I scream and lean back trying to place myself just out of his reach. My body is pressed up against the back of the truck's cab. I squeeze against it, squashing myself, but it's no good. Unless I can somehow learn to walk through walls, I can't get myself any farther away.

He just keeps coming.

Pushing his arm further and further into the truck until the hole he has made reaches his shoulder. His fingers stretch out. I look at his hands, his fingernails long like claws. His veins, bulging as his fingers spread out trying to get any kind of grasp on me. His sharp nails, which seem to be growing longer before my very eyes, pierce the sleeve of my shirt, ripping it. I scream and angle my body away, but it has the opposite effect. By snatching my right side away, I have put my left side within his reach, and he wastes no time in grabbing my shoulder. His grip, like that of a Terminator, is strong and painful. I feel like my shoulder is burning. He pulls me closer and then releases my shoulder and immediately grabs a chunk of my hair. Instinct takes over and I do the only thing that I feel I can do—push the gas pedal all the way to the floor.

The truck springs to life, roaring in protest. It sounds as if the engine is going to fall out, but I keep it pressed down all the same. The pain in my scalp intensifies. Either from Luc's firm grip or because his claws are piercing the skin on my skull. Either way, it's becoming unbearable. I hold out for as long as I can stand the pain, and then, when it becomes too much to bear. I slam my foot on the brake pedal. The truck skids and almost comes to a complete stop as a loud screech echoes through the trees surrounding us.

My plan works. The momentum flings Luc from the hood and causes him to go skittering across the road. What I didn't anticipate happening is him never letting go of me.

I come crashing through the windshield, shattering it. I can feel the glass scratch my skin to pieces. My face, my arms, my legs. From head to toe I can feel sharp pin pricks. Like being pecked to death by a thousand birds.

I hit the road with a thud that takes the wind out of me. I can barely breathe. I gasp for air. I'm sure every bone in my body is broken. As I lay on my front, my cheek bone pressed against the concrete, I try to lift myself off the floor, hoping I can make it to my feet before Luc does. I place my palms on the floor and push. A searing pain shoots through my arm and my collar bone and I think I'm going to pass out. I fall back to the floor and notice the small pool of blood where my face was resting.

I try one more time to get up. I owe Mike that much at least, considering how he fought to protect me.

Try as I may, I can't do it. The pain is too much. Finally, I manage to get from my front to my back. With considerable effort. As I roll on to my back, there he is. Looking down at me. The same, stupid smile on his face. If I didn't hate him before, I do now. With the intensity of a thousand suns. No. A million.

He doesn't have a mark on him. No cuts. No grazes or bruis-es. Even his hair looks immaculate. The only indication that he has been in any kind of distress, let alone a major car accident, is his coat. Rips through the arms and shoulders and dust and dirt all over the side where he had skid across the floor. *Good* I think to myself *I hope it's his favorite coat.* A little victory, but in situations like this you've got to take what you can get.

Luc bends down, his forearms resting on his knees as he looks at me. Surprise on his face.

"Well, Abigail, I must say. I didn't expect that of you. How brave...or stupid. I haven't yet decided."

"Go to hell," I choke out through a mouthful of blood. He smiles. He's enjoying this. It's sport to him. I can tell by his expression.

"I've already been," he stands back to his feet. "For now, though, I think it's time you and I spent some time alone." He stands over me. He's tall, but from this angle he looks like a giant. He places his black biker boot on my shoulder and presses down. The pain is the most intense I have ever felt. He presses harder. I scream, but that brings with it a whole new pain somewhere in my abdomen. Through blurred vision I can just make out Luc staring at me with a mixture of curiosity and satisfaction.

Finally, it becomes too much. Darkness completely sur-rounds me and I give in. Everything becomes black.

It's a cliché, but from this angle the stars really do shine like diamonds. They're literally covering the whole sky. The velvety canvas of the night sky is the perfect backdrop for how beautiful they really are. I can't see anything in my periphery. The sky fills my whole vision and if it wasn't for the fact I can feel I am laying on something hard, I'd really believe I was floating.

For a second, I think I've fallen asleep at my camp, like I so often do after an argument with Tom. Finding peace at my sanctuary by the lake. My fortress of solitude. All the events that happened only an hour or so ago could have easily been a dream. But then I am pulled right back to reality and the night sky retreats away, stealing the stars from my vision and causing my heart to drop to the pit of my stomach as I realize, none of it was a dream. It was all real.

"Good evening, love. So glad you've decided to join me. It's a beautiful night, hardly worth spending it napping now, is it?" I may have only known him for the briefest of time, but the English accent coming from my left-hand side, just out of my vision, causes beads of sweat to start prickling my forehead. I turn my head to look at him. He sits nonchalantly on a small wall that looks as if it surrounds us in a huge square. Like some kind of courtyard. His feet are crossed at the ankles and his palms are rested on the wall behind him as he leans back. He couldn't look more relaxed.

I gingerly go to get to my feet, anticipating a barrage of pain, but as I roll over to my side and then eventually to my hands and knees, I realize there isn't any pain. Not that there's a subdued amount or that it isn't as intense compared to after the crash. There just isn't any whatsoever. Shocked, I climb to my feet and start to study my hands and my arms, which were earlier covered in cuts and bruises. Now, almost nothing. A few pink scratches that look to belong to wounds that have long since begun to heal. Not injuries that were sustained a matter of hours ago. Even the bruises Tom had given me on one of the many times he had lost his temper, finger marks where he had grabbed me, old bruises from the odd kick, were gone. Or faded into almost non-existence.

I turn my hands over, my eyes wide in shock and amazement. I look all the way up my arms, raising the sleeve of my shirt and can't see anything past a faded bruise or a barely there pink line. I look over at Luc, forgetting for the briefest of moments what a monster he is, my mouth open, completely unable to comprehend what I'm seeing. Or feeling. I should be unable to move, in a hospital bed somewhere, or maybe even dead. But as it stands, I feel fitter than I did before. Luc returns my gaze with a smile. Not the same, sly, evil one I have become accustomed to in the last couple hours. An honest smile.

"How?" I ask.

"You really don't know anything do you?" Luc asks with a slight shake of his head. "About who you are, your lineage?"

My mind races back to the night my mother died. The fragments of memory I have of that night - and they're just fragments—coupled together with the stories I had heard from Tom or my brief stint in the home. The car accident that killed my mother. The one in which I sustained absolutely no injuries. I'd always thought I'd just got lucky, or mom was unlucky. But now I'm not so sure. How can the same unbelievable thing happen to the same person twice?

"I shouldn't be shocked," Luc continues as he gracefully stands up from the wall he had been lounging on. "Michael has always been the kind to keep things close to his chest. I thought he'd have been a little more forthcoming with you in regard to information. Oh, well, not as if it matters now is it."

I ignore his comment. He wants a reaction, but I'm not going to give him one—if I can help it. I walk to the edge of the courtyard surrounding us and look over the wall that travels all the way around us. We're up high. Really high. It must be the early hours of the morning because the whole town is eerily quiet. Silently sleeping. Not a care in the world, or their cares are pushed to the back of their mind at least while they're lost in the land of dreams. Not one car passes by. Not one person can be seen or heard walking through the town. It looks beautiful from up here. Maybe I never appreciated this town enough in the short time I've been here. The immaculately cut grass. The scattered benches in the town square where elderly friends can be seen of a morning on my way to school, sharing a coffee and stories of old. They've probably known each other their whole lives, having grown up here. Friendships that have stood the test of time. One of the things I used to hate about small towns, everyone knowing each other. Knowing their histories and even their futures to some extent seeing as people hardly ever leave. It becomes easy to know where they're going in life because it's been seen dozens of times before. Now I yearn for it. Standing here, knowing that this could be the last thing I see, I wish I'd have made more of an effort to appreciate its beauty.

I think about the time Sam and I shared a sweet tea and sat on those very benches. Maybe that could have been us in fifty years. Still sitting there. Still complaining about the same things. Watching Mia walk by with her grandchildren and laugh to ourselves at how her life never turned out the way she always dreamed it would. Nasty, I know. Petty even, but still. A nice thought.

I study the darkened shops surrounding the square. The little coffee shop. There were reports of one of those chains, Starbucks or the like opening here, but the town got together and put a stop to it. It would have run Mr. Gomez out of business, and no one was prepared to let that happen. He was as much a part of the town as it's foundations. Everyone was according to Mrs. Williams who ran the petition. I sigh to myself for not making more of an effort. Too little too late.

I feel completely alone. The only sign that I'm not alone in this world is that I can just about make out Earl, the town drunk, asleep on his bench.

I think of Mike, who I can only assume is dead. Or he'd be here, protecting me, like he said he would. We've known each other only days and yet here without him, I feel lost. Scared. For all his secrets, he made me feel safe.

"What are you thinking about?" Luc's voice cuts through my thoughts. He sounds genuinely interested.

"Nothing. Just...Looking."

"It is quite beautiful, isn't it?" he muses as he walks over to stand by my side, surveying the town, dead silent. Dead. Quite fitting really. "Apart from the vermin that inhabit it of course. Don't tell anyone I said it was beautiful though. I have a reputation to uphold."

Luc stands next to me, so close our shoulders are almost touching. I try and side eye him in secret, but he catches me, much the way Mike always does. I don't avert my eyes. What would be the point now? Instead, I turn and face him directly. I'm scared, of course I am, but if my fate is inevitable then what I say or do now makes no difference.

"If you're going to kill me, why not just get on with it?" I ask, sounding bored. I'm talking about my death as if I am asking him if he would like a drink. Even I'm slightly shocked by how unaffected by the whole situation I am. I can feel the fear in me, but it isn't rising to the surface.

"I'm not going to kill you," he begins, still looking out over the town from our perch on top of the clock tower roof. "Actually, I am, just not now."

"Why? Just get it over and done with, why waste time?" I ask him, not wanting to drag my death–no, my murder–out any longer than it needs to be.

"Because I don't want it over and done with and I don't see it as a waste of time. I like to play with my food before I eat it." He shrugs his shoulders.

"I'm food now, am I?" I turn and face him. Arms folded. Anger overriding what little fear I was feeling.

"You humans. So sensitive," he chuckles.

"*You humans.* So, what are you then if you're not *human?*" He smiles.

"I was thinking of explaining everything to you, but now I may take a leaf out of Michael's book and keep it a secret for just a tad longer."

"First you kill Mike and then you want to act like him. You really are messed up," I scoff at him. He laughs out loud at this and it seems to echo around the empty town. A flock of bird's scatter from a nearby tree. The only movement in the town other than ours.

"I can see why he likes you. You're quite the feisty one. Most other people would be terrified right about now. Maybe all you've had to endure, however awful it may have been, has made you tougher. A survivor," Luc says, the admiration evident in his voice. "And in any case, *Mike* as you so affectionately call him, isn't dead. He's much too tough for that. As much as it pains me to say. I know that more than anyone else."

"You're lying," I say, confused. "I saw. If he were alive, he'd be here...I know he would."

"Oh, trust me, he'll be here." Luc cocks his head to one side, slightly raising his face to the sky. His eyes squint for a fraction of a second before a smile spreads across his face. A smile that for the first time since I met him earlier, reaches his eyes. His face, like Mike's, is beautiful. But on the inside, he might be the ugliest person I've ever met. "Much sooner than I thought actually. Even I underestimated him. He really is strong. I thought that beating would at least incapacitate him for a few more hours yet. Give us a little quality time together, my sweet." He winks at me. "Well, best let the games begin."

Luc grabs me violently by the arm and drags me closer to the ledge at the edge of the platform we are standing on. He takes a step on to the small concrete wall and tries to drag me up with him. I attempt to resist, but it's useless. He's much too strong. He pulls me up next to him and I wobble slightly, fearing I'll fall, but Luc's grip steadies me. Instinctively, I grab on to Luc with both hands. The top of the ledge is rounded and it's impossible to stand without rocking, although I notice Luc manages it with ease.

He looks down at me, holding on to him literally for dear life and winks at me again.

"I knew you'd come around in the end. Be careful, Michael will be awfully jealous."

I want to push myself away, but know it's pointless. If he decides to let me go then I'll fall, certainly to my death, and if he doesn't want me to, he will just use his vice like grip to hold me in place.

"Ah, here we go," Luc says, slowly.

I follow the direction of his gaze. Following the road that leads out of town, but see nothing. It's deserted, like everywhere else in the town square. I squint my eyes toward the woodland in the distance, willing them to adjust to the pitch darkness. A mass of trees and no street lighting makes seeing anything virtually impossible. I try to listen instead. For something, anything. Footsteps, a car engine, but the beating of my heart blocks out any other sound. If there was any to block out. For the first time in my life, I understand what the saying 'the silence was deafening' actually means.

"Well, Abigail. It has been an absolute pleasure to host you this very early morning for our alfresco chit chat, I just wish we had longer." Luc takes a quick glance over my shoulder in the direction I was just looking. "But it really is time for you to go. Don't be too upset."

Using his free hand, he gives me a theatrical wave.

"Bon voyage."

And with that, he pushes me from the ledge. In spite of myself, I scream. The cold morning air rushes past me, blowing my hair in my face. I'm not sure if being unable to see anything makes this fall better or worse. Every now and again, through strands of wild blowing hair I see the concrete floor rising to meet me and I know in a matter of seconds, fractions of seconds, I will collide with it. I turn around mid-air, so my back is to the floor that's approaching, and I flail my arms and legs as if by doing so I can climb the air around me like a ladder and make my way back to the top of the clock tower.

People say your life flashes before your eyes, but not mine. All I can think about is how much this is going to hurt and how time seems to have slowed down. Maybe my mind is just working faster as death looms. Getting as much in as it can before it ceases to operate any longer.

Then, all of a sudden–*thud*–I hit something. It's hard, but not as hard as the floor. It takes the wind out of me momentarily. More from surprise than because of the impact. Then even weirder, I start to go back up again, in the opposite direction to the floor below me. Like I've just fallen down a lift shaft, landed on top of the lift as it was heading up to a higher floor. I start to wriggle. Trying to angle my body to see how I'm not a pool of sludge on the floor. But the voice that whispers in my ear stops me dead. Makes me freeze almost.

"Stay still, I don't want to drop you having just about stopped you from using the floor as a trampoline." Mike's voice causes me to immediately stop my thrashing around. I turn, slowly. There he is. A cut on his forehead that has already healed, like mine. A grave smile on his face. His beautiful face. I grab his head in my hands instinctively and kiss him. He doesn't pull away, instead he kisses me back. Suddenly, I remember the situation we're in, and how I seem to be traveling through the air, and I snap my head away. Mike breathes in deeply, my kiss having taken his breath away. I don't have time to take satisfaction in that as I look around and realize, unbelievably, that we're flying.

Then I notice why. Or more precisely, how. How I never noticed before is beyond me considering how huge they are. Two massive, bright white, feathered wings protrude from Mike's back. They're not flapping. They're still. Like a bird when gliding, and yet, we're flying. Higher and higher. Up past the clock tower I was just pushed from.

"Bravo, Michael. Just in time. I knew you wouldn't let me down." Luc's voice carries on the breeze Mike, and I are currently riding. Mike doesn't answer him. Instead, he turns in the other direction and heads out over the trees into the woodland opposite.

I feel as if I have a million questions and yet, I can't formulate a word let alone a sentence. Mike notices me looking at him, opened mouthed. Despite everything he allows himself a smile.

"So," he gives a slight shrug, or as best a shrug he can produce with me in his arms. "I'm an angel."

I swallow hard at the revelation. My hand instinctively goes to the necklace my mother gave me. What has been with me every day since she has been gone. My guardian angel. I rub it with my thumb, expecting to wince at the cut I made earlier, but then realize, it has probably healed with all of my other injuries. I remember now that I have many more questions that need answers, not just about Mike's wings.

Mike's wings. I can't believe I'm actually thinking that.

"Mike. It really is time to tell me everything. And I mean, everything," I manage to choke out through my amazement as I stare at his glorious wings.

Wings. Wow.

"You're right. It's time. For me to protect you, you need to know it all."

27

Mike slowly lowers us to the ground.

Apart from my initial questions, we haven't spoken since he caught me in the square. The whole experience was so weird I'm not sure I could have taken part in any kind of conversation, let alone taken in any information. I'm still not sure. What I am sure about is how safe I feel in his arms. How glad I am that he caught me. Not just because I'm not dead, that's obvious, but because he's also alive.

For the first time since seeing Mike with his wings on show, they flap slightly. Controlling us impeccably as we softly land on the ground. He moves them so effortlessly, like I would my arms or legs—which I suppose is exactly what it is like. They're a part pf him. Like limbs.

As we land I back away from him slightly, only two or three steps, and survey my surroundings. I was so caught up with the fact that the boy I'd been spending my time with over the last few days has wings—is an angel—that I didn't realize where he was taking me. Until now. I look over at the familiar, makeshift lean-to roof of my camp. The stillness of the lake. The charred fire pit. Instantly I feel at home.

Mike looks at me. The corner of his mouth half turns up in a kind of smile, come shrug, come unspoken apology. He turns away from me and walks to the edge of the lake, doing what

I have done dozens of times before, and just watches the still water.

I just watch him.

I can't take my eyes off his wings. Not just because there's a boy with wings, that's enough to make anyone stare. But because they're so beautiful. They glow. Luminescent.

I watch as he bends down and picks something from the floor. Unconsciously, I walk forward. My feet carrying me without much thought. I look at him as he stays in a crouched position, cradling something in his hands. His wings, so big the tips rub across the leaves and dirt behind him. The bottoms becoming dirty as he moves fractionally on the balls of his feet. I walk to his right-hand side and angle my head to see he is holding a dead bird. A robin, I believe. Not that I'm any kind of ornithologist. It's unmoving. Stiff as a board and looks as if it has been dead for some time.

Mike holds the bird in the palm of his hand and places his other hand over the top, covering the bird completely. I watch, mesmerized. Not just by what he's doing, but by how he looks. How the situation would look if anyone else were to walk through. Which never happens. A boy, crouching by a lake that's so still it could be made of glass. The full moon reflecting on the surface. An iridescent bluey, green sheen shining from the top of the lake when you move as little as one foot to the next. With wings so big they're more or less the length of his body. Maybe bigger when they're spread wide.

The scene looks like a painting.

He takes a deep breath and his eyes start to glow that bright blue I've seen a couple times before. Almost a hot white. I can't make up my mind whether it makes him look more beautiful (if that were at all possible) or terrifying.

Maybe a bit of both. Maybe that danger, that mystery, is part of what I like about him.

Slowly the glow of his eyes returns to normal, which is still a much brighter blue than anybody's I've ever seen before. He lowers his head, his eyes focused on his cupped hands. Slowly, he opens his hands, and the chirping of a very alive bird fills the silence. It flies out of his hand, full of life and lands on one of Mike's wings. He stands and smiles at the bird which chirps a thank you and flies away into the night. I laugh. I can't help it. This is all so ridiculous and unbelievable, but also so amazing that the choked cough of a laugh escapes my mouth involuntarily.

It was so beautiful to watch.

Mike's eyes leave the bird as it disappears amongst the trees. Going to find its family, I hope. He looks at me and smiles. Initially I return the smile, but then it falters. The gravity of the situation hits me, and my amazement and wonder are replaced by annoyance and borderline anger.

"I shouldn't do that you know, change the natural order of things."

I ignore him. "Time to start talking, Mike. If that's your real name," I say, rather childishly, but I don't care.

"That's my name. Or Michael actually," he replies, smiling. His teeth seem to sparkle like you'd see in some animated film from Prince Charming. I try not to let it affect me. It's not easy. I turn away from him and head over to the log that has fallen just outside my camp. My own private bench. I can feel Mike watch me as I walk away and while he can't see my face, I take the opportunity to try and steady myself. I close my eyes and take a deep breath. I turn and sit, my eyes back on Mike who is now facing me. He heads in my direction and as he does so, his wings start to shrink away from view. Getting smaller as they disappear behind his back until they're gone completely. As he turns to sit on the bench next to me, I steal a quick look at his back. No sign that there were any wings there, apart from the fact that his shirt has two rips in it. Two diagonal rips right by his shoulder blades, going out at an angle. Like somebody has tried to cut an A into his shirt, but forgot the middle line.

As he sits, I avert my gaze.

"Shoot," he says.

"Who are you?"

"Mike."

"What are you?" I ask, delicately.

"I told you. I'm an angel," he answers, sounding nervous.

"Like...an angel, angel. Or like, an X-Men kind of angel?"

"Are you calling me a mutant?"

"No, no...not at all. I just. It's a lot to take in," I add quickly, afraid I've offended him.

"I'm kidding. An actual angel–yes. Angel with a capital A. Full of grace and divinity," he laughs.

We're both silent for a while. I feel as if I have a tractor load of questions and yet, nothing is immediately coming to mind. I look out over my lake. A bird flies down and skims the surface, breaking the perfect stillness. I wonder if it's Mike's bird.

"Why didn't you tell me when we first met?"

"Really? 'Oh, hey I'm Mike. I'm an angel of the lord by the way.' You'd have run a mile. Plus, I was hoping I wouldn't have to tell you anything. That I could do what I was here to do, and you'd be none the wiser."

"And what is it you've come here to do?"

"Protect you."

"But why? I'm nobody. Farm trash, remember."

"You're as far from a nobody as you could possibly get."

"How?" I ask, my confusion rising instead of dissipating at every answer I'm given. "Wait!" I exclaim as I look down at the wounds that should have rendered me hospitalized, but have instead pretty much healed completely. "Am I like, you know, *The Chosen One*, like you know, *Buffy* or something.

With superpowers and a destiny to fight demons? Like Luc?"
My voice trails off, the excitement seeping away with every word
as I realize how ridiculous that sounds. Then again, the whole
thing is ridiculous.

Mike just stares at me, his eyebrows raised. "Sorry. That's
stupid. Vampires aren't real."

"Well, actually…"

"Vampires are real!?" I shout.

"Abby…"

"Sorry, go ahead."

Mike takes a deep breath. "You don't remember anything
from before your accident, do you?"

"I don't remember anything from directly after either. It's
like my memories start as soon as I left the home. I've only
fragments from being in there. Like when I saw that news report
and remembered that the warden who was murdered was there
when I was."

"The wardens murder. That was Luc." Mike looks down, like
he's embarrassed to be letting me in on this information. Even
though I'd pretty much guessed that after tonight.

"But why? I don't understand any of this, Mike."

"To get to you. The reason you can't remember anything.
The reason your mind is blank is because a block was put on
you. To stop you from remembering," he admits, hanging his
head in shame.

"By you?" I ask.

"Not me. Another angel. I was against it, but was outvoted.
Not that that should matter to you now. We still took away your
memories, essentially."

"Why would taking my memories away make me any safer?"

"They–the celestial order," Mike rolls his eyes, "thought if
you had access to your memories you could slip up, be found

easier. I disagreed and thought that if we watched you, we could keep you safe."

"Mike...this isn't making any sense. Your answers are confusing me more, giving me more questions. What memories? Safe from what?" I run my hands through my hair and tug in frustration, almost pulling a handful out.

Mike lets out a huge sigh. It causes me to wonder whether angels actually need to breath, but that's one of the really unimportant questions I can ask another day. If I live long enough. Mike raises his hand toward my face, but I flinch. He looks momentarily hurt and then smiles sympathetically. "Do you trust me?"

I think about his question. The things he has done for me. The way he has treated me and realize that I do.

I nod.

Close your eyes. I do as he asks and realize that in this vulnerable position, I don't feel the slightest bit scared. I really do trust him.

"This is going to be a lot to take in."

I feel the tips of his fingers lightly touch my forehead. The initial electricity jolts through me, but I've become accustomed to that now, so the reaction is not only manageable, but nice. What follows is a feeling I've never had before. A feeling that is almost impossible to explain. Like someone pouring images into my brain. Overloading it with visuals. Like that scene in Mike's favorite film–*The Matrix*–with John Wick in it, where he lives in a computer. They plug him in and download all manner of stuff into his brain. Kicky, punchy stuff. This is kind of how I imagined that would feel. Like someone had put a huge fan just behind my forehead and turned it on full power. I feel as if I am being blown backwards at 100mph and yet, I haven't moved. I'm still sat on the log and Mike's fingertips still gently caress the center of my forehead. Just above my brow and between my closed eyes.

Then, as quick as it started, it stops.

I'm sitting in the back of a car, and yet, I'm not. I'm still on the log with Mike yet my mind is elsewhere. I look around the car. It's not familiar, but deep in my bones, I know I've been here before. I look out of the backseat window. It's pitch dark out and while it isn't raining, it's obvious it has been. Lots. There's nothing out there. We're on a long road surrounded by nothing but open space.

"June, just pull the car over and let me out," a man's voice says, sympathetically, but firmly. I've no idea who he is. He looks to be in his thirties, but really reminds me of Mike, and even Luc. His skin, like theirs, is perfect. Not a mark on it. His hair, unlike theirs is short. He angles his head to look at the woman driving and I notice how bright his eyes are. A green-blue, but once again, like Mike and Luc's, they're unnaturally bright. Almost glowing.

"No. I'm not going to leave you," June replies.

"They'll find us wherever we go. You know this. It's safer for you–for both of you–if you just drop me here," the man turns to look in the back seat at me. He gives me a smile. A beautiful, heart-warming smile that brings a lump to my throat.

"We're in this together. We're a family," June takes his hand in hers. My heart wants to explode in my chest. June is my mum. Her face is burned into my memory and this man, I don't know how I know it, but he's my dad. "Isn't that right, kiddo," my mum finishes.

"Right," I manage to croak out as my throat closes with emotion.

As I scan my parents in the front seat, I get a glimpse of my reflection in the interior mirror. It's me, but it's not me. It's kid me. In the back of a car and I come to the realization that this is the night of the accident that kills my mum, and my dad is here. Does he die too? Does he run and leave us? I have never known who he was or what happened to him, but these must be the memories that were blocked from my mind.

Now, it looks as if I may find out.

"June." My father's face is grave. Pained. His face may be perfectly smooth, but somehow, I can see the conflict etched there. "You know how much I love you, love both of you, but we can't escape this. Listen to me. The only way to keep you both safe is for me to get as far from you as possible." I watch in stunned silence. The love he feels for my mother, and for me, is obvious in every strained word that escapes his lips.

"How? How is you leaving, what's best for us?" My mother shouts through sobs. Not out of anger. Out of love. Exasperation. "Surely, the best way for us to stay safe, is if you..."

"*Look out!*" my father shouts, causing me to jump out of my skin. I can feel my fingers tighten around Mike's arms even though he isn't here with me in the car. Even though *I'm* not here in the car.

It's a weird sensation.

Out of the windshield I momentarily glimpse a shadow standing in the road. Just a shadow silhouetted by the full moon behind him. What catches my eye the most in the split second I get to adjust my vision, is a sight I have only seen very recently. The huge wings that are spread wide behind him. Like Mike's, but slightly smaller.

In a panic, instinct taking over, my mother yanks the wheel hard to the right and slams her foot on the break. The car skids, jack-knifes, and topples over. The momentum causes the car to continue its trajectory until it rolls to a stop on its roof. I hang upside down, my seat belt stopping me from falling headfirst into the roof of the car. I look over at my mum, blood stains her forehead and she sits motionless, eyes closed.

"Mum!" I scream, hoping to get some recognition, but knowing full well that I won't.

The winged figure rips the passenger door off and drags my father from his seat, he's badly injured, but his groaning lets me know that he is alive at least. He's flung to the side of the road like a piece of garbage. I unclip my seat belt and brace myself for the impact as I fall. I land, a crumpled ball on the roof. I touch my head and study my bloodied hand. My shoulder also has a cut. For a second, I freeze. I was always under the impression I had no injuries from the accident. It's short lived though as I notice the winged man, the angel, rip my mum's door from its hinges and start to drag her body out.

"Get your hands off of her," I cough. Unsurprisingly, he ignores me. I watch as he drags her body across the road by her arms. She starts to stir, but her eyes remain closed. Her feet are dragging behind her as if she were nothing but roadkill. Anger rises in me, and I feel a surge. A feeling I have never felt before. Or can't ever remember feeling before. Like fire burning through my veins. I scramble to my knees and try to open the door. It won't budge. Using all the strength I could muster—which I didn't expect to be much considering I'm in my body as a six-year-old—I forcibly push the back door, and it swings open with such power that it almost comes back and hits me. Pushing my shock to one side, I get out of the car and stand up.

In my mind I'm like a bystander. I'm in the body, but not controlling it. I'm just watching as if on autopilot as the events from my childhood unfold before me and my memories once more come back to me. Like a tidal wave of thought. Even if I wanted to change these events, I couldn't. I'm powerless.

I start to walk towards my parents with purpose. I feel no fear as I watch this angel begin to lift both my parents, one in each arm. Then he stops as he notices me making my way in his direction. He drops their limp bodies to the ground. My mother, still barely moving. My father, groaning whatever life he has left out of him as he tries, and fails, to crawl his way to the woman he loves.

"No need to panic, little one. You'll be coming with us as well. I won't leave you behind. Abominations like you can't be left to roam the earth," the angel utters and even with his perfectly chiseled face manages to project a grotesque smile. I say nothing. Instead, my arms slowly rise out to my sides. His smile falters, but only for a split second. My eyes light up, glow so bright it's as if I am going to burn him alive with them.

"Calm down now, lassy," he says, a hint of fear in his voice as he holds his palms out to me in surrender. But I ignore him. "Just relax. Look, I promise I won't hurt you," he continues as he edges closer to me.

The surge of energy in my body reaches breaking point. I can feel it. Like I'm about to explode. When he's but a couple of steps away from me, I snap my palms open. He stops still. Frozen in place. His hands grip the sides of his head as his face goes the color of a lovely ripe tomato. I continue to walk toward him, my hands gripping nothing but thin air, and yet it's as if they're squeezing his brain. Turning him into knots of pain.

He screams. An earth-shattering noise that sounds inhuman, which I suppose, it is.

I get closer. Within touching distance, and yet, I don't have to touch. Just when I think he's about to implode, when the pain and pressure is all too much for him, he lets out an almighty scream and throws his hands in front of him. At me, but not touching me. I shoot back off my feet. Soaring through the air. The fire in my veins dissipates. My eyes return to their normal green. I hit the road, skidding backwards adding more grazes and cuts to the ones earned in the car accident moments ago. Dazed, but surprisingly fit for a child who had just been supernaturally thrown into the air, I get to my knees. He has my father over one shoulder and is trying to pick my mother up with his one free hand. Whatever I did to him has had some kind of effect. He's unsteadied on his feet and struggling to get a hold of her limp body. I notice my father's shirt, ripped and bloodied. On his back are two huge scars near his shoulder blades. Their shape is exactly the same as the rips in Mike's shirt made by his wings. seventeen-year-old me is confused. six-year-old me continues her pursuit.

I start to make my way in his direction, my walk turning into a jog. He hears me coming and panic crosses his face.

No, not just panic.

Fear.

He drops my mother, bends his knees and leaps into the sky, disappearing into the blackness.

Silence. It fills everything. Like a beating drum inside my head.

I kneel by my mother's side and try to shake her awake. I pick up her arm and let go. It just drops by her side. She starts to groan, a gurgled choke coming from deep in her throat, as if she's choking on water. She coughs and splatters blood over her face and mine. Tears begin to fall down my cheeks. With considerable effort she forces her eyes open slowly. She tries to smile at me, but the look is frightening. Her face pale and her teeth covered with her own blood. Her hand limply raises to her chest where she grips her necklace. The necklace my father gave her on her birthday. Using the last of her strength, she tugs, snapping the chain and holding the angel wing pendant in her hand. The tears fall more freely, teaming down my face as if my eyes were faucets. She hands me the necklace. I clamp my fist around it as my mother's arm drops to her side. Her chest stops moving and her wide eyes stare lifelessly at the sky.

She's gone.

I lay my head on her chest, hearing nothing.

I don't know how long I stay like that, shivering in the cool night air before someone arrives. It could be hours. It could be minutes. The sound of footsteps behind me causes me to snap my head around. As I do, my eyes glow brightly. The person behind, a woman, holds her hands up in a 'I come in peace' stance. The brightness in my eye's dims. The unusual perfectness of her face is something I have become accustomed to as seventeen-year-old Abigail. No blemishes, no lines of worry or laughter. Smooth as a china plate. Her eyes, a pale blue, almost all white from a distance, with a tiny black dot in the middle. She's dressed casually, but smart. Jeans and dress boots with a beige raincoat that stretches to her knees.

"It's okay, Abigail. I'm here to help," the lady says. I don't think to ask how she knows my name. Relief just floods through my body that I'm not alone. Help is here.

"My mum...she's. She's not breathing." I lay my head back down on her chest.

"I know, poor thing." She crouches next to me, stroking my hair in a maternal way. I don't shrug her off. I just lay. Unmoving. Except for tears. They still trickle down my cheeks, rolling to the corners of my mouth. Instead of wiping them, I catch them with my tongue. Tasting the saltiness.

"We need to call an ambulance," I utter, barely a whisper. "And the police. Someone took my daddy. A man with wings."

She bites her lip. "I know. I can help. Look at me."

I lift my head off my mum. Eager for the help.

"Look into my eyes," she says. I do as I'm asked, unquestioningly. I want to scream at myself. Tell myself not to trust her, but I have no control. I'm a bystander in my own body. She places her hands on either side of my head and holds them there. Not tight, but firm.

Her eyes begin to glow. The sight panics me and I try to struggle. It's no use, her grip is too tight. Her palms grow hot on my head and my eyes begin to roll back, showing only the whites. I look possessed. The lady's eyes intensify. A red glow emits from her hands. My body starts to shake and then...nothing. Everything goes black.

I open my eyes and I'm back in the clearing with Mike.

Slowly, he lowers his hand from my head. His face apologetic.

I feel something on my cheek and raise my fingers to it. I notice they're shaking. I wipe them across my face and feel wet. I study my fingertips and clearly see the tears on them. From the corner of my eyes, I can see Mike watching me. Unsure of how I am going to react. I take a deep breath and try and steady myself.

"Why did it stop there?"

"That's the point at which your memories were blocked. After that...you were unconscious and the angel that was there, Agatha, she called the police. Waited until they arrived and then left. The rest you know."

I pause. Unsure of what to say. Trying to keep my anger and disbelief in check. But I can't.

"You're monsters," I whisper.

Mike has the decency to hang his head.

"You're angels...you're...you're supposed to help people. Look after people—not ruin their lives." My voice gets louder as I stand and turn away from him.

"I didn't agree with taking your memories. I know that counts for nothing, but I was against it. The others, well, they thought they were doing the right thing at the time," he says, quietly, as if he knows that's not really going to hold any water with me.

"And the one who tried to kill me. Who actually did kill my mum? Was he doing the right thing?" I say venomously, swinging around to face him with such speed that my hair whips my face.

"Ariel was acting alone. I can assure you he was not acting under orders, and he was dealt with appropriately," Mike answers forcefully.

"He was killed?" I asked, shocked.

"You're upset about that?" This time it's his turn to be shocked.

"No," and I wasn't. I was glad he was dead and I hoped it was long and painful. What I was shocked about was that these were supposed to be angels and here they were, thinking nothing of killing other angels, and humans alike.

"Angels are not these fluffy winged creatures in robes that sit on clouds playing the harp," Mike sighs as he gets up from the log and walks toward me. "We're soldiers of light fighting battles against darkness on a daily basis. It isn't our job to be forgiving and good natured. It's our job to be formidable and fearless."

What he said kind of made sense. As much as any of this did at least.

"Why did he–Ariel–why did he call me an abomination?" I ask, not quite sure I *wanted* to know the answer, but knowing I *needed* to.

Mike briefly closes his eyes and lets out a low deep breath. I get the impression we are finally getting somewhere, and wherever it is, he doesn't really want to go there.

"It's because of who you are. Or more specifically, what you are."

"And what am I?"

"A Nephilim," he answers, seriously.

"A what?"

"A Nephilim. A child of the sons of God," he waves his hands to the sky, "and the daughters of men," he sweeps his hand low, indicating to the ground. "Or more commonly...half angel." He looks me in the eye, never taking them away. I try to process what he's saying. *Half angel. Madness.* Yet, I saw what I did. Similar to what I've seen Mike do, and if I've learned anything over the last couple hours, it's to believe the unbelievable.

"My father..."

"Was an angel."

"The scars...on his back..."

"Where his wings...used to be. Your father was one of the fallen. To fall, you have to remove your wings. An extremely painful process. Not unlike severing a limb." Mike winces at the thought.

"But why would he do that, if it's so painful? Why would any angel?" I ask, baffled by the choice.

"Simple," Mike begins. "For love."

I study Mike. My heart beating.

"Love," I whisper. Not a question. Just a statement.

"Your father fell, because he loved your mother. So much so that he was willing to go against one rule that even other fallen angels won't break. To be with humans. It's forbidden. Most fallen angels. Almost all of them to be exact, fell at the time of the rebellion. When Lucifer defied our father's wishes and refused to serve man...and woman," he adds with a small smile. "They severed their wings and fell from grace. Except Lucifer of course. He didn't fall as much as was...pushed."

"I know the story," I interrupt. "He was cast out by the archangel Mic..." I stop. Realization finally dawning on me. I look at Mike. Take in all of his glory. His beauty. The image of him with his wings on full show. "By you. You're the Archangel Michael." He doesn't answer. His face gives away no reading whatsoever. "Which means," fear washes over me like water cascading over my whole body, "Luc. Luc is Lucifer." Again, it wasn't a question, and Mike doesn't confirm or deny it. He doesn't need to. "Oh, shit."

I turn around and start pacing. If things weren't bad enough this revelation is causing me to have a well justified panic attack.

"Abigail." Mike grabs me by the arms. "Calm down."

"Calm down! Literally, the devil wants to kill me and your answer to that is, calm down," I say, exasperatedly.

"I won't let anything or anyone hurt you."

"You think that will stop him?"

"No. But I won't stop either."

"Why Mike? Why is killing me so important to him? Because I'm a neph...whatever it is. Because I have angel blood?"

"You're not supposed to exist, Abigail. A human with the blood of an angel. You've no idea the power you possess. That scares Luc. That scares a lot of angels."

"Is that how I healed my injuries, in my memory and after Luc stopped my truck?" I ask.

"Your angel blood, yes," he nods.

"Then why, all these years when I've been hurt on the farm or when Tom had hurt me, why didn't those heal?" I question him.

"You must've suppressed your grace. Your angel blood. Being around me, it must've awakened it somehow."

I think about this for a while and it makes sense, kind of. Since being with Mike I have felt different, and every time we have touched, it was like something was being shocked awake inside me.

"There's something else. Another reason why Luc wants to harm you," he says, this time sheepishly, looking at the floor.

I don't say anything. I look at him, wide eyed, lips pursed. An expression that says *well, go on.*

"There's a prophecy." He turns away and heads toward the lake.

"Of course there is."

"It says a Nephilim will, at some undisclosed time in the future…" I can feel him rolling his eyes even with his back to me, "…will give birth to a child who will bring peace, or destruction to the earth."

"And that Nephilim is me?"

"It doesn't say you by name, but as it stands, you're the only Nephilim on this earth and I don't see that changing any time soon. Anyway, Luc *thinks* it's you, so at the moment that's all that matters."

"And I thought I had it bad before I knew about all of this. Hang on, wait a minute…" I say, something just dawning on me "Are you trying to tell me the whole purpose of me being here is to give birth to some kind of Jesus savior?! Like, I don't matter at all. I'm just some kind of Sarah Connor?"

"You like The Terminator?" Mike asks with a smile.

I don't answer. I just give him a look that makes him well aware that now isn't the time for jokes.

"Okay. Bad time. No. That's what this prophecy says, but your future is in your hands. If you don't want children–then don't have any. You alone are important enough. Don't let any-one tell you what you need to do," he answers passionately.

It calms me down a bit. With the red mist gone I can think a little better.

"Who's supposed to be the father of this baby?" I ask, gen-uinely interested in who the powers that be have me doing the dirty dance with.

Mike turns his back on me again.

"Mike. Answer me."

"It doesn't say," he turns back to me. "It just…it just says the father will be…an…an angel," he stutters and for the first time since I have met him his complexion changes slightly. He's blushing.

My heart starts to pound. Running through my mind the implications of what that could mean should this prophecy come true. If I want it to come true. The uncomfortable silence lingers between us and I hunt for words to fill it.

"So, it's such a bad thing for an angel and a human to be together. So bad in fact that my father had to sever his own wings–which is still crazy, my father had wings." I shake my head to juggle the thought around enough that it might start to make sense to me. It doesn't work. "But it'll be okay for me to have...well...be with, an angel?"

"You're not a human, or not wholly at least. Surely that memory I released into your mind showed you the power you possess?"

I think about what he said and push all the other thoughts aside. The thoughts of Lucifer wanting to kill me. My destiny as a vessel for some savior child. My father being an angel. All the things I can't quite wrap my head around just yet. Instead, I think about what I saw myself do. The power I harnessed. How not just that night, but tonight, I managed to heal all the wounds I had. It really was amazing.

Suddenly, tiredness hits me like a wrecking ball. I turn and walk into my camp and almost fall onto the blanket I've stashed away in there. Out of nowhere, it becomes a mammoth task just to keep my eyes lids from closing. Tonight, has been a night of revelations. I thought I wanted them all, but it's made my head hurt.

Fear, information overload, emotional overload. It's not every day you realize you're half angel. That your father was an actual angel, and your mum died trying to keep your family together.

"They must've really loved each other," I say to myself. To Mike. To no one in particular. Just thinking out loud.

"They did. They risked everything for that love. It's admirable."

I yawn. Big enough and wide enough that I feel as if I could swallow the whole clearing.

"You need to get some sleep." Mike pulls the blanket up over my knees.

"You'll stay?"

"I'll be right here," he answers, patting the blanket next to me.

I lay my head down, wondering, even after how exhausted I feel, if my mind will let me sleep.

I close my eyes and take a deep breath and within seconds.

Darkness.

28

The burned out, dilapidated church looks the same as it did the last time I saw it. The roof, charred to ash. Gaping holes making it look as if it's about to cave in at any second. The stained-glass windows, smashed to smithereens. The animal graveyard still littering the grounds. Some of the animal bodies, half eaten by other wild creatures. Others, half buried by the fallen leaves from the surrounding forest.

It's dark out. The middle of the night. The moon and stars hidden behind a heavy cloud covering. A strange mist settles just above the ground surrounding the whole church and rendering my feet invisible.

I feel as if I am walking through the set of a Tim Burton movie.

There's an eerie silence. The only sound is my feet crunching the leaves and twigs that sit hidden beneath the mist. Not to mention the stiff bodies of birds I must be trampling on. Strange sounds can be heard echoing through the night. They must be animals, but they sound wrong. A shriek more than a chirp or growl. No animal I can put my finger on.

I look down at the long white dress I am wearing. Confused as to why I'm wearing it or what I'm even doing here. I look around. I feel like there's eyes watching me from deep in the shadows. Instead of turning and running away, which deep down I know I should do, I head toward the huge wooden church door. I have *no idea why, but it feels as if something is calling to me. Mentally forcing me to enter. I stand and watch as the mist rolls through the broken and splintered door as it hangs precariously from its hinges and continues down the aisle. Like a wave rolling to the shore.*

I reluctantly step over the threshold, angling my body to navigate past the awkwardly hanging door. The pews are filled with people. But they're not themselves. Not the way people should be. I notice Sam sitting on the end of one of the rows, her skin, a pale sweaty gray color. Sores cover her face as she dribbles a black tar like substance from her mouth. A low grumbling issues from deep in her chest, like an animal unable to form words. She looks in my direction, but not at me, straight past me, as if she can't focus on anything. Tears fill my eyes and I want to run to her, but my body won't let me. I'm rooted to the spot. I look around and see Mia and Brad along with their gang of bullies. They're all in the same condition as Sam. I don't like them, but seeing them like this fills me with sadness. They're not people anymore. They're Zombies.

I start to move down the aisle, not walking, floating. As if on a conveyor belt that is moving me along against my will. I try to turn my eyes away from my zombified classmates and towns people, but they're everywhere. I decide to look off into the distance, but what greets me there is just as bad.

No. Worse.

In the corner of the church, off to my left, is Tom. Hanging upside down, his insides on the outside. A perfect recreation of when I found him at home, but this time, he's awake. Smiling even. He raises his hand and sticks his thumb up to me. I have to swallow down in an attempt to keep anything unwanted from coming back up.

I keep moving forward. No matter how hard I try to turn and run, I can't. My body is held in place as I am forced toward the front of the church. As I get nearer, something stands up and approaches the alter in front of me. A monster. Sharp canine teeth protruding over its bottom lip. Massive horns sprout from its forehead. In its hand there's a book. A copy of the bible. Smoke emits from the monster's hand as if the bible is burning it, but it gives no reaction. Around its neck, it mockingly wears an ill-fitting priest's collar.

It suddenly dawns on me what's going on as I look down and finally realize that the dress I'm wearing, is a wedding dress. Adrenaline hits. I try with every fiber of my being to turn. To about face and head toward the door. I scream. I groan and grunt as I use all my strength. It's no use. The monster behind the alter lets out a booming, demonic laugh that echoes around the room. My zombie friends get riled up at the sound and begin to bang on their pews and make weird, animalistic noises.

The demon priest extends his arm as I get closer to the front of the church. He holds out his hand, points his finger at me and then slowly, turns his hand so the palm is facing up, then curls his finger in a creepy, come here motion. His bony finger is twice as long as a humans and his nails are more like talons. He sidesteps the alter and I see the robe he wears is ripped where he has forced it over his unusual frame. It hangs in shards of fabric. My vocal cords begin to work again as a scream erupts from my mouth when I notice his feet, which are not feet at all, but hooves.

Whatever is dragging me forward stops as I reach the front of the church. Someone sitting in the front row stands up and turns to face me. I'm expecting to see another zombie so when a perfect, blemish free complexion greets me, I'm shocked. My shock is then replaced with anger and revulsion as Luc gives me his smarmy smile.

"Don't be scared of Asmodeus," Luc indicates to the demon priest. "He's a pussy cat really. Or maybe a goat. I'm not too sure," he continues, looking at his hooves. Asmodeus laughs hysterically, his booming voice shaking the precarious walls. "Wait until you

meet, Samael. There's time for that - shall we?" he says as he raises his hand and strokes my face. I try to pull back, yank my head away, but it's no use, I'm frozen to the spot.

"Oh, I almost forgot. Your wedding gift, how rude of me." He flourishes his hand to a huge black curtain hanging above the alter. High above our heads. My rigid body is released enough that I am able to lift my head in that direction. Luc waves his hand as if he's a magician performing a trick and the curtain falls to the floor. Whatever I had seen before is nothing compared to what I see now. A range of emotions fight for dominance. Anger, fear, revulsion, panic, horror, sadness and every other human emotion it's possible to feel.

Mike's shirtless body hangs above the alter. Blood running down his muscular torso. His arms are stretched to the side, as if he has been crucified. His wings, detached from his body, hang behind him, outstretched. They're in the same position they would be if they were still a part of his body, just hung further away. I can see the joint where they would have been attached to his back. Roughly severed, dripping in his blood. His head rests on his chest. His eyes, lifeless.

I try and scream, but my mouth won't cooperate. It's stuck shut and won't budge. A series of muffled, humming vibrates from my lips, but no real sound comes out.

Luc erupts into malicious laughter, which sets Asmodeus off on more of his booming, floor shaking, howling. The rest of the church comes to life and my zombie friends, including Sam, break out into hysterics. It's like Luc's laughter is a homing beacon for them and they advance on me, like a pack of hyenas. Their faces fill my vision. Face after face. They start to crowd me. They're almost on top of me. I fall to the floor, and they follow. Tripping over each other as they land on me. I can't breathe. All the air has left my lungs and I try to take deep breaths, but my mouth is still clamped shut. I try to gasp, but it's no good. The pressure on my chest is too much to bear. I'm suffocating. My hands reach for the sky as if that will help, but then I disappear beneath a mass of bodies. Everything goes dark. I manage to tear my lips apart. Like ripping a wound open that has just been sewn shut. I ignore the pain and scream with whatever strength I have left. It isn't much. The sound doesn't break through the mass of bodies that now squash me to the floor. Even I can't hear it. The only sounds that penetrate my ears are Luc's laughter and the snapping of zombie teeth.

I can feel the tears wetting my cheeks. Ooze drips from their mouths and lands on my face. It burns.

A break in the bodies as they shuffle around gives me one last slither of a look at Mike, his body hanging, blood dripping. Then he's gone. Darkness engulfs me once more and I let go. Give up the futile attempt at escape as the weight of corpses continue to crush me.

I wake with a start.

My scream echoes around the dark, empty woodland. A few birds scatter from their trees.

I immediately grab for my mouth. Running my fingers over my lips. They're fine. My hand then grips my chest. The feeling of suffocation coming back to me. I gulp in air, just because I can.

It takes a minute or two, but I manage to calm down and control my breathing.

I scan the clearing for Mike. Not seeing him, I get up and head to the lake in front, peering through the trees ahead. Nothing. Remembering what happened back at the farmhouse when I discovered Tom—which seemed like days ago now instead of hours—I decide to try something.

I close my eyes and whisper, ever so gently, "Mike."

Slowly I open one eye, while keeping the other pinched shut, feeling like an absolute moron. Nothing. I open the other eye and have another look around. Still utter silence. I'm alone.

"Idiot," I say to myself.

As I turn back around to head toward my little lean to, I notice Mike's truck parked on the track between some trees, it wasn't there last night so he must have brought it here. The huge dent where Luc landed is still on the hood, but it must run well enough for Mike to have got it here. The windshield is completely missing.

Wondering why he would have left me, after everything that has happened, starts to give me palpitations. If it wasn't important then he wouldn't have gone, and if he didn't think I was safe, he wouldn't have left me. Still, the panic starts to rise in me like water in a bathtub. I know part of it's the dream I just had, but another part is everything that has happened to me over the course of the last few hours.

I need to find Mike.

And just like that it dawns on me. I know exactly where Mike is. I don't know how I know. I just do.

I jump into the truck's cab and find the keys already in the ignition. I sit and wonder if the angel blood I now know is coursing through my veins gives me access to some invisible wings. I don't have time to try and make them sprout. I gun the truck and listen to what has now become the familiar, comforting roar. I look out of the window knowing that day will break at any moment, maybe before I even get where I'm going. I can smell the sunrise, as silly as that sounds. I know it's coming, and it can't come a moment too soon. Something about the sun burning the darkness away, illuminating it, gives me a calming feeling.

I shift the stick into reverse and look over my shoulder as I launch the truck backwards and disappear amongst the trees.

29

I park the truck a five-minute walk away from the church. I know Mike would probably still hear it, but I thought it best to be cautious. He came here while I was asleep because he either didn't want me coming, or he didn't want me to know where he was. But I'm certain he's here.

I walk along the edge of the trees toward the front of the church. As always on this road, barely any vehicles go by. It's even quieter than usual considering the early hour. The sun is just rising, but it's a gray morning. The sky is full of clouds all looking to dispense of the rain they're carrying.

As I reach the gap in the trees I slow down. Conscious not to make too much noise as I head toward the entrance. I stop almost immediately. The animal graveyard taking me by surprise, even though I'd already seen it.

I look up from the animals to the door of the church, hanging from its hinges. Exactly as it was in my dream. I've walked past this church dozens of times, maybe more. I had never realized I had studied it enough to know little details about where windows were smashed. Where exactly the cracks were. How the door hung. But evidently my subconscious did. It's exactly the same, right down to where the animals are situated.

My head snaps to the entrance as echoed voices float out on the breeze.

I make my way around to the side of the church not wanting to go in. Worried about what I may find. I stand on a fallen log underneath a broken window and peer in. I grit my teeth and swallow hard with what greets me. There's only two people in there, not the hordes from my nightmare.

Mike and Luc.

Luc stands at the altar, almost the same place he was in my nightmare, his hands in the pockets of his long black overcoat. Mike stands a couple steps inside the church door. At opposite ends of the aisle. Broken pews surround them on either side.

I stand still, frightened to breathe in case it alerts them to my presence. Plus, I want to hear what they're talking about, knowing full well that I will be at least part of the topic of conversation, if not all of it.

My heart stops when I hear Mike's voice echo around the large hall.

"You could have at least cleaned up the massacre outside."

Luc barks a laugh. "Massacre. I've been involved in a few in my time, I wouldn't exactly call it that."

"What would you call it?" Mike asks.

Luc thinks for a bit. "An accident. You know how much I like animals, a damn site more than I do humans, that's for sure."

Mike doesn't answer. Luc turns to face him.

"It's not my fault, brother. You know I expel a lot of energy when I come here. It can't be helped. Plus, I think it looks rather fetching out there, matches the décor in here. Death and destruction—right up my street," Luc says, gleefully.

Mike, to my shock, allows himself a small smile.

"You don't change, do you?"

Luc replies with a smile of his own and a slight shake of the head. For all their differences, I can see that they're brothers.

"So, where's Abigail?" Luc starts to look around theatrically, behind curtains and under pews. "I know you won't have left her too far, protective guard dog that you are."

"She's safe," Mike says, not rising to the 'guard dog' bait.

"So, diligent. You're basically a guardian angel now. Have you been demoted?"

Mike doesn't answer.

"So serious," Luc says in a deep, mockingly official voice.

Mike puts his hands in the pocket of his jeans and his shoulders slump slightly. He looks tired. Disappointed. "I came to talk."

"Trust me, Michael, if I wanted to fight, you'd already be unconscious–again," Luc says the word *'again'* slowly, with added emphasis.

"You've gotten stronger, no doubt about that." Mike's eyebrows are raised and he nods.

"You'd do well to remember it." Luc doesn't mask the threat in his words.

I stay frozen at the window, as still as a statue. Worried any movement could not only cause them to see me, but make me miss something one of them may say. I'm not prepared to let that happen. I'd rather die from lack of breath than miss a sentence.

There are a few seconds of silence as the two just look at each other. Mike doesn't seem to want to get drawn into Luc's angelic bravado contest.

"Leave Abby alone," Mike says. Not threateningly. Not angrily. Just a simple honest request. My muscles tense tighter than they already are.

"Urgh," Luc groans. He throws his head back and closes his eyes as if bored by the turn the conversation has taken. "Haven't we already had this chat?"

"Please...brother."

Luc stops his amateur theatrics and looks at Mike, his face serious. I swallow hard and for a second it sounds so loud in the silence.

"It's been a long time since you've called me that." Luc looks serious for a moment, his mask slipping. He looks touched. Emotional even. Then seconds later the mask is back, and his grin reappears. "Aren't you taking this whole love thy neighbor thing a little too far? Then again, you've always been a bit of a daddy's boy. Not as much as Gabrielle of course. How is he anyway, still father's messenger boy?"

"I'm not here to talk about Gabe."

"No, you're not. You're here to beg for my leniency. Why don't you bow or get down on one knee and ask me?" Luc says with a flourish and his trademark smarm. Like he is on stage in some play.

"Can't you take anything seriously?" Mike growls.

"You want me to take things seriously. Fine..." Luc begins as he takes a few steps toward Mike, his coat billowing behind. A chill runs up my spine as I see him strut his way forward. I see Mike tense up. His body goes rigid, his fists clench together. Preparing himself for what's to come. Only, nothing does. Luc stops about halfway. His face has changed. Gone is the smarmy, cocky smile and it has been replaced by a venomous anger. His teeth are bared and, I swear, just for a moment, his eyes flash a hot red. "I'm going to haunt her every day, for as long as I find it amusing. I'm going to stalk her every minute until her fear drives her insane. When she's just about ready to end it all..." as Luc is talking, he is taking slow steps toward Mike, now, he is just one step away from him. They're right in each other's face. "...I'm going to drive this hand through her chest and snap her spine. All while you stand by and watch. Unable to stop me. Serious enough for you?"

I become paralyzed by fear. Deep down I already knew it, but hearing it from Luc's very own mouth makes the realization fly to the surface. He's going to kill me and there's no way Mike will be able to stop him. I swallow hard and wait for Mike's reaction which I assume–and slightly hope–will be a physical one. But once again, he shocks me.

"What happened to you?" Mike's voice is clouded with disappointment and confusion. "After all these years I still can't understand it. You were the favorite. He loved you more than all of us..." Mike slowly reaches his hand up and touches Luc's cheek gently. Lovingly, even. "The Star of the Morning. My brother. Then, you threw it all away."

At first, I think Luc is feeling some shame. He looks down to his feet, averting Mike's gaze. But when he looks up, his face is filled with anger. Almost snarling.

"What happened to me? How dare you. My whole family turned their back on me–cast me out to live in Hell, literally. You say I was his favorite, rubbish. He expected me to bow down to his pathetic creation. His pets. He has given them everything and us nothing!" Luc's voice booms around the dilapidated hall. He pokes Mike hard in the chest causing him to take half a step back.

"Nothing? He has given us everything–life, paradise, a purpose."

"Don't be so naïve, Michael," Luc spits. "This pathetic creation has been a disappointment at every turn, just as I said they would. He has given them everything and yet half of them don't even believe he exists!"

"Yes, they're flawed..."

"Flawed," Luc shouts. "They murder, rape, go to war–mostly in his name–and what does he do? Nothing! He forgives them. What did I do? Have a difference of opinion. That's it.

I disagreed with him on something and that warrants me being cast out of heaven. His favorite, you say."

"It had nothing to do with you having an opinion and you know it. It was your pride! We all saw it coming. You weren't content with your position, you wanted more. Craved more power," Mike replies, his voice steadily getting higher. "Ask for forgiveness, beg him to take you home and he will. This madness, the eons of fighting will all be over."

Luc is silent. His eyes never leaving Mike. "Never," he answers after a brief silence. "I will not bow down to anyone, least of all that Tyrant. I'd rather rule in hell than serve in heaven. And when I finish ripping the heart from your girlfriend's chest, I'll be completely unstoppable."

Mike pushes Luc hard in the chest with both hands. Luc almost falls, but manages to regain his footing. His response is only to emit a high-pitched laugh as he stumbles.

"I'll be with her every step of the way. You won't get near her," Mike says through gritted teeth.

"It's her coming to me you want to worry about. I'm quite persuasive. Kind of what I'm known for."

They stand staring at each other. Luc smiling. Mike, his face stern.

Mike shakes his head and turns around, heading back toward the door. It's obviously become clear to Mike, as much as it has me watching from the wings that there's no getting through to Luc. I could have told Mike that before he came.

As Mike reaches the church door, Luc speaks up. "No one knows who this child's father will be, Mike. It just says the father will be of angelic blood. She's had a very tough life has young Abigail. Most of her problems have come at the hands of angels. Maybe I can convince her that coming with me, fighting against you, is what's best for her." Mike stops. He doesn't turn around, but he doesn't take another step either. "If I father that child, you know what will happen. What it will become," Luc continues, quietly.

My brows furrow, confusion once again hitting me like a brick.

"I'll do whatever it takes to protect her," Mike says, without even turning around. "Remember that...brother."

Mike walks out of the church, leaving Luc alone.

30

"Let's go, Abby," Mike says wearily. His voice causes me to stumble from the unstable log I'm standing on. I let out a small yelp and instinctively look back through the window to where Luc was moments ago, but apart from a few rats that look big enough to mount a saddle on, it's empty.

I steady myself and jump down from the log. I look over my shoulder to make sure no one is behind me.

"He's gone." I worry he may be angry with me being here, but he's wearing a smile. A tired smile, but a smile all the same.

"How did you know I was here?" I ask.

"I always know where you are."

"Did he know?"

"He knew you were close, but not this close. I've kept you pretty well hidden. Like an invisibility cloak, if you like," Mike says with a small shrug.

"You like Harry Potter?"

"Who doesn't? Where's the truck?"

I point down the road. My head filled with images of angels wearing white diapers, siting on clouds having movie night. Luc would have definitely been in Slytherin, I think to myself as we start to walk up the road to the truck.

"What you smiling at?" Mike asks me.

"Nothing important."

I open the door to the farmhouse kitchen, but I needn't bother. It's hanging on by nothing but a splintered shard of wood. When I push it, it falls off completely. I let out a pathetic yelp, but Mike catches the door and lays in down on the hardwood floor. I look around and am speechless. If I were a cartoon character my chin would be on the floor. The place looks as if a tornado has passed through, liked it, turned around and went back again.

I'm sure the floor is damaged, smashed to pieces maybe, but it's almost impossible to tell considering it is covered in debris. The walls have huge cracks down them. Some are almost completely knocked down. Windows are smashed and the sink is spraying fine spouts of water. A huge puddle sits on the floor underneath it.

I look around in wide eyed amazement wondering how two people could do this much damage, and then I remember. They're not normal people. Or people at all. They're other-worldly.

"Sorry about this," Mike says sheepishly. "Couldn't be helped."

I look up at the roof. A huge crack in the wall travels all the way. "Are we safe to be in here?" I ask.

Mike looks around, raises an eyebrow and shrugs. "I think so."

"Reassuring," I say as I step over the broken dining table, sidestep the kitchen worktop that's now on the floor and head to the hall which is showing signs of the same tornado like destruction.

"I'll sort it out, go and have a sleep or something. Whatever you like. I'll have it as good as new in no time," Mike says, rather cheerily.

"You run a construction company I don't know about?" I ask.

"Trust me," Mike says through a smile that lights up the room and causes me to feel faint. He's been through a hellish beating, a night in the woods and not to mention flying through the night sky, which I still can't wrap my head around and yet, he looks gorgeous. Barely a hair out of place.

"Maybe a shower is a better idea. A cold one," I say, only half joking.

Mike looks away, embarrassed. Blood rushes to his cheeks and I can't believe I've made him blush. I smile to myself, happy at the thought.

I turn and head up the stairs, Inspecting the cracks in the wall as I go. Praying I don't fall through the stairs or that the wall doesn't collapse on me. Instinctively, I know it isn't going to happen. Mike wouldn't allow it. The thought makes me warm inside. As I reach the top of the stairs, instead of turning left for the shower, I head right to my bedroom and fire up my old laptop, keeping my fingers crossed the whole time that the clash of the titan's downstairs hasn't caused the Wi-Fi to stop working. It hasn't. I can hear Mike banging something downstairs so I put my headphones on, click on some random Spotify playlist (Country Music–I can get on board with that) and type Michael and Lucifer into the search bar and hit enter. My breath coming in short sharp bursts as I do.

Within seconds, a list appears on my screen. I scroll through and click on one at random.

'Lucifer had wisdom, ability, beauty, perfection and yet he wanted more... he wanted to be worshiped like God... He was removed from the presence of God... Cast out like a bolt of lightning.'

I close the tab and move on to the next one.

'...prior to his downfall, Lucifer was a magnificent being... Unfortunately, pride overtook his heart and sin cost him everything.'

I lean back in my chair, the soundtrack I'm listening to meaning nothing. Just background noise as I try to take in everything I'm seeing. Everything I'm reading.

"This is crazy," I whisper to myself as I rub the bridge of my nose. Or hope I whisper, the music in my ears making it hard to tell. I could have shouted it. I look towards my door. Still closed. I turn back toward my screen and then something catches my eye. The next website down.

The War In Heaven.

I read on. Eyes wide. Heart pounding.

'And there was a war in heaven, Michael and his angels fought against the dragon, and the dragon and his angels fought back. But he was not strong enough, and they lost their place in heaven. The great dragon was hurled down - that ancient serpent called the Devil, or Satan, who leads the whole world astray. He was hurled to earth and his angels with him.'

And underneath there was a picture. The Picture. The one everyone knows or has seen at some point. Michael standing victoriously over Lucifer. His sword in hand, his blond hair blowing behind him as he floats, his foot on top of a fallen Luc. Neither of the images on the painting looked much like the real thing (the real thing, how crazy this still seems to me), but it was still a powerful painting, nonetheless.

I stare for what feels like forever. Just looking. I pull my headphones off and throw Garth Brook's off into the distance, aiming for my bed, but finding the floor instead. Sorry Garth. I can't seem to take my eyes off the painting on the screen, trying, and failing to wrap my head around it all. Not just what has happened to me over the last day, or really my whole life from the day my mum was taken from me, but this picture. Millions of years of history that weren't just Sunday school stories.

It was real. All of it.

"Abby, you coming down? I'm done." Mike's voice snaps me out of my mythical daydream, and I slam the laptop shut, not wanting him to know I was researching him. It seems a bit stalkerish, even though I'm sure it's perfectly natural of me considering recent events. I mean, it's one thing being religious and believing angels are real. It's another thing finding out they *are* real, and that the boy you have a thing for, is one. Your dad is one and you're half of one. It's enough to send you into a state of mental paralysis.

I leave my bedroom and quietly close the door and head for the stairs. At the top I pause. The same nervous feeling in my stomach as when I walked up, scared the stairs may collapse on me the moment I put any kind of weight on them. As I stop at the top of the stairs, the wall catches my eye. The cracks are all gone. The walls are perfectly smooth. The railings on the stairs are fixed in place. I place my hand on the ball on the railing at the top of the stairs and give it a little shake. Solid. I shake it more forcefully and it won't budge. My brow furrows as I study the rest of the wall and the stairs. How could Mike have done this in that short amount of time? I couldn't have been gone for longer than thirty minutes.

I make my way down the stairs and realize that the creak on the third step from the bottom is also gone. That had been there since we had moved in. Once I reach the bottom my shock is replaced by utter amazement. The wall that was basically knocked down, is up again, as good as new. Better even. I peer into the kitchen which is also immaculate. Nothing on the floor, which looks as if it has been waxed and polished. The small flood. Gone. The sink. Fixed. I about-face and head into the lounge. Again, it's spotless. Half an hour ago it looked as if a construction company would need to come in here and rebuild from scratch. Now, it looks like a new build. The only indication of Tom's demise now being the mental images I have which I'll never be able to shake from my mind's eye. As my eyes scan the room, I find Mike sitting in the corner on the arm rest of the couch.

"How did you…?" I start, but don't finish.

"Angel, remember," Mike answers, rather cockily.

"Right. You'd make someone a great housekeeper one day."

"Is that right?" he asks, standing up and walking towards me. "Mikey Poppins. Has a nice ring to it."

"You like Mary Poppins?"

"Abby, I do like to watch films," Mike answers, his arms folded.

"It's just…it seems odd. Angel's chilling out with a bucket of popcorn watching Mary Poppins."

Mike doesn't answer, he just rolls his eyes.

I look away smiling, enjoying the ease of banter between us. Even with everything that is going on, Mike seems much more relaxed around me now that he has told me everything. Now I know what, and who, he is. I like it.

I notice a holdall by where he was sitting.

"Is that clothes?" I ask, pointing at the bag.

"Yes."

"We're leaving? Good–I'll grab some stuff and be back in a minute." I turn around and go to make for the stairs. Mike grabs me by the wrist gently, pulling me back toward him.

"No, we're not leaving. I grabbed some of my stuff quickly. I thought I'd stay here, if that's okay with you of course?"

"You. stay here. In my house. You're going to sleep here, with me?" I ask, my words coming out in a jumble. The thought of Mike staying the night is making me tongue tied.

"On the couch, of course," he says quietly.

"Erm…yeah, of course. On the couch…but…" I trail off, partly embarrassed, partly in thought.

"Look, I can go—or sleep in the truck if you're more comfortable…"

"No, it's not that," I cut him off. "I'm comfortable. More than comfortable, but shouldn't we be leaving? I mean, isn't that the sensible thing to do?"

"Look, I understand you're scared. That's normal, I'd be a little bit concerned if you weren't, but it would be pointless to run. Luc wouldn't stop, he would continue to hunt you and regardless of how well I managed to keep you hidden, he will eventually get to us." He moves closer to me, placing his hands on the tops of my arms, looking deep into my eyes. "I can protect you. I promise."

Looking at him, I one hundred percent believe he will do all he can to protect me, and to be honest, there're worse ways to go than being with him.

"What about the army?" I blurt out, suddenly, shocking even myself.

"You want to call the army?" Mike asks, his face screwed up, producing almost no line on the smooth surface of his face.

"No, your army. You beat him before with an army of angels. Let's go, call in the troops, Mike!"

"Wow. Someone's been doing their research."

Damn.

"Just a teeny bit," I say, indicating with my finger and thumb the tiniest gap.

"There is no army. Not this time," Mike sighs, avoiding eye contact the whole time.

"What? Why?"

"I'm all there is, and even that was contentious. The others, my father–getting involved is forbidden. To them, if the prophecy doesn't come to pass then it wasn't meant to happen. Things have to run their course."

"But you came," I whisper.

"I wasn't going to leave you to fight this alone." He takes my hand in his. We stand silent, just looking at each other. It feels as if something is going to happen or should happen. My heart starts to pound out of my chest, so I try and break the awkward silence. It's either that, or I'm going to grab him and kiss him, but I'm scared as to how he will react.

"But...you can beat him right. I mean, angels can be killed. You can finish this."

Mike drops my hand and turns away from me. Immediately I regret saying anything. Should have just gone all out for the kiss.

"He can't be killed?" I ask hesitantly.

"He can be killed, but only by another angel." His back is still to me, his head angled to the floor.

"Well, that's good news...right?"

"Abby, I can't kill him." His voice is low. Strained.

"But you said..."

"I said he *can* be killed," he answers, turning to face me again. "I can't do it. He's, my brother."

"Are you kidding me?!" I shout, taking a step toward him. "He's a fricking monster...he's...he's the devil for crying out loud."

Mike flinches, as if I've just slapped him. It could be because of my reaction, but I believe it has more to do with me using the word devil.

"Abby, you need to understand."

"He's a monster!"

"There's still good in him, I know there is. I just need to...reach it," Mike says, desperately trying to convince me.

"Mike, he murdered my uncle. Ripped him open–is that him expressing the good in him?" I ask, the sarcasm dripping from my words.

Thirty seconds ago, I thought we might kiss. Now, we're arguing. Maybe we are a real couple.

"Your uncles not dead, I told you that. He's going to be fine, the hospital think it was a farming accident."

"Only because you fixed him up using your angel mojo! Nothing to do with Luc's kind nature!" I shout.

Mike rubs his hand over his face, tired, frustrated. A completely human emotion that takes me by surprise considering the otherworldly acts I've seen from him this past day. I feel a twinge of guilt. After all he has done to keep me safe, here I am questioning him. But he's wrong, there's no doubt about it. There are only so many second chances you can give someone, and it sounds to me like Luc has had his fair share. Since the beginning of time. I fold my arms and refuse to give into my inclination to apologize. I'm doubling down on my annoyance.

"You need to understand..." Mike begins, his voice low, but I don't let him get any further.

"No, you need to understand. He killed my uncle. I don't care how or why you brought him back, he was dead. He wants to kill me. He's made that clear–or convince me to give birth to some demon spawn to use whichever way he chooses–either way, he's evil and needs to die." Mike doesn't take his eyes off of me during my whole tirade, he just watches, "What are your plans if you can't talk him round then? Offer him a jolly old cup of tea and hope for the best? And what's the deal with that anyway, why does he have an English accent and you don't?" I shout, all my thoughts tumbling out at the same time, my anger finding it hard to keep the important topics at the forefront.

To my shock, Mike's expression changes to one of amusement. "Don't laugh at me," I say, kind of sulkily. "I'm being serious."

He changes his expression. He can't fully hide his desire to chuckle though.

"The only thing you need to know is that I will protect you and I'm willing to do anything–absolutely anything–to make that happen. I just don't want it to have to come to that if I can help it," Mike stresses. I nod, in semi-approval. I'd rather him say he was going to lay waste to Luc, but this will have to do. "As for the differences in our accents, all of us have different accents or dialects. All the different accents in the world are represented in heaven through the angelic order. It's where they all started," his grin returns.

I think about it for a second or two and shrug. "Makes sense."

As I finish my sentence, my belly lets out a low, loud grumble. I never realized how hungry I was until now. I haven't eaten in hours. I put my hand over my belly and the other over my eyes, wanting to disappear from embarrassment. Through my fingers I can see Mike laughing.

"Hungry?"

"A bit," I say, still hiding.

"Sorry, I don't need to eat so it slips my mind."

My hands come flying down. "You don't eat?" I almost scream.

"I can eat, I just don't need food to survive," Mike shrugs, as if it's no big deal.

I shake my head in wonder. Not eating or having the satisfaction food brings when you're hungry is unthinkable to me.

"I suggest we get you something to eat, before that monster in your gut decides to eat both of us..."

I close my eyes. I don't know why I'm embarrassed, it's a perfectly natural response when hungry. But I am all the same.

"...then we get ourselves washed up and ready for school tomorrow," Mike finishes.

"School? Seriously?" I ask, amazed at the thought of going to school after everything that has happened.

"Tomorrow is Monday."

"Yeah, I know, but do you really think it's a good idea? Shouldn't we hunker down for a while? Try and stay as low key as possible."

"Luc is going to come after you, Abby, but chances are if you're at school he may be less likely to with all those people around."

"Really? Luc doesn't strike me as the shy type. He probably prefers an audience," I say sarcastically.

Mike shrugs. "Maybe you're right. Either way, once all of this is over, you're going to need a good education. College, career. No point in cutting class for no reason."

"No reason?" I ask him, eyes wide in disbelief.

"Well, no point cutting class when there's a strong chance nothing is going to happen. Just live your life as normal and I'll be there."

I look at him. I don't answer, I just study him. Thinking over what he said and decide that he's right. It was bad enough having Tom try and keep me away from school to be his personal maid. No way I want Luc now making those decisions for me. Or having me make those decisions based on what he may or may not do.

I nod.

"Cool. Now let me do us something to eat. Fried chicken?"

I nod again. This time, much more enthusiastically.

31

"So, I heard your uncle is in the hospital."

I turn away from my locker to find, Sam. Her latest read–The Outsider–another Stephen King book, is clutched tight to her chest, like she's nursing a baby. I look at her–me, her only friend–her, my only friend. Her love for all things weird and wonderful. Her quiet demeanor and the way she shuffles her feet when she walks, and I think to myself that, even though I have no idea what the book is about, the title is apt. To me, she's one of the nicest people I have ever met, but to others, she probably does seem an outsider. Especially in this town. We both are, in all honesty. When being on the inside means you've to act like Mia and her cohorts of small-town misery, then I'm happy being on the periphery.

"Wow, news really does travel fast in small towns."

"Unfortunately. Is he going to be okay?" Sam asks, actually concerned as opposed to asking because it's the right thing to do or because she's being nosey. Just another reason why I'm glad she's my friend. I may not have any love loss for my uncle, but at least she cares enough about me to ask.

"I'm sure he'll be fine. I haven't been to visit him because, well, because I had to look after the farm and haven't had time. It was a small accident though. He'll be back to his charming drunken self in no time at all," I answer. "What exciting things did you get up to this weekend?" I ask. She doesn't respond with words, but makes it perfectly clear what her weekend consisted of by holding up her tome of a book and waving it inches from my face. "Was it good?" I ask, through laughter.

"It's amazing," she enthuses. Coming alive in front of my eyes as she so often does when talking about a book. Going from this meek, demure, little thing to bouncing around from foot to foot. Her face lighting up and her words coming in fast sentences with barely a breath in between. "It's about this guy, right and maybe he isn't all he makes out to be and..." She stops dead. Mike has just arrived. Immediately Sam averts her eyes and adopts her shy stance of angling her gaze toward her feet and clasping her arms close to her body. Mike looks at me apologetically.

"Sorry, did I interrupt?"

"No, Sam was just telling me about her book," I say, indicating to the book she's holding. "What happens to this guy then?" I try and prompt Sam to continue knowing that with Mike here, it's a futile attempt.

"It er, it...he...nothing," she mumbles nervously before turning around and shuffling off. "See you at lunch," she says quietly over her shoulder as she disappears amongst a throng of students.

"Yeah, see ya," I call after her, sadly.

"She hates me."

"She's just shy," I say. "It isn't easy, ya know, being different. Being new. With years of bullying, you can't help but become wary of people." I look to Mike, and he gives me an understanding smile. He may never have experienced it himself, but at least he's trying to empathize.

"She'll be fine. She has a bright future ahead of her if she continues down the path she's on."

"Is that right," I say, intrigued. I look at him, eyebrows raised, and my lips pursed together. He reads me as easy as Sam does her books.

"Oh, no," he's shaking his head. "It's no one's business to know parts of the future. Anyway, she only has to make a few different decisions and that future all changes anyway. She has to stay on her current path for what I see to actually happen."

I ignore most of what he's saying and give him my best puppy dog expression. I push my bottom lip out like a sulking child and knit my eyebrows together. He looks at me and just shakes his head. We start to walk down the corridor, and I playfully keep up my sullen expression, enjoying the easiness between us. Gone are my nerves at being around him. It's easy. Natural.

He looks at me and laughs. My lip coming out further, my eyebrows almost covering my eyes.

We continue to walk down the corridor slowly.

"Let's just say, in a few years' time there might be some young girl, and she *might* be standing by her locker, and she *might* be holding a huge novel written by your friend. Possibly," he adds with a wink and a smile.

My heart fills as if it has swelled to three times its size. I'd want nothing more than for Sam to be happy and I know that being a writer would be the thing that makes her happiest, and she deserves a huge dose of that. I feel as if I'm floating down the corridor as opposed to walking. I'm not sure any other news could have made me as happy as that has. *Except maybe Luc taking the first bus back to Hellsville.* Sam was the first person to talk to me at this school when I came here. One of the only people really. That's a kindness I've never forgotten and never will forget. Two outcasts drawn to each other, now best friends. Hopefully for many years to come. As the thought of us as old ladies, sitting down for a coffee, laughing at the teenagers that walk past us in town and complaining about the way they dress and how it wasn't like that in our day enters my mind, it immediately starts to become hazy. Blurry. Like dipping a paint brush into a jar of water to clean it. The water becomes contaminated with the paint. Discolored. It becomes something else. As do my thoughts.

Like heat waves emanating from the pavement in the Texas sun, my thoughts become hard to see and blur into something completely different, and I know what's coming. Old lady Sam disappears and is replaced by Sam lying on the floor. Her eyes, wide, but lifeless. Blood trickling from her mouth and nose.

I squeeze my eyes shut, even though I know the thoughts in my head and not in my field of vision. I shake my head trying to dislodge them. I feel a hand on my shoulder and snap my eyes open. I realize I've stopped in the middle of the corridor. I look to my right to see a concerned Mike looking back at me.

"Headache," I say, and realize it's true. A sharp pain throbs just behind my eye.

Mike raises his hand and touches my temple lightly, and as quick as the pain came, it's gone again. I look at him in amazement. I'm about to ask how he did it, but catch myself just in time. For all the amazing things he can do, being around him feels normal. Natural. Then I forget what he is.

"So," he begins, snapping me from my thoughts of angelic beings. "What time am I picking you up?"

"Excuse me?"

"Did you want to get something to eat first? See, I remembered you need food. Or did you just want me to pick you up around 8:30?" Mike carries on as if I have the slightest idea what he is on about.

"I'm lost."

"I know I'm staying at your place, but I'll make a show of going back out and coming to the front door. Do things properly."

Mike's mouth is upturned, his shoulders slightly shrugged as if he is weighing up his options.

"Mike!" I shout, causing a few surrounding students to look in our direction. A few were looking anyway, as they do when someone like me is standing with someone like Mike. But my raised voice causes a few more turned heads. "What the hell you rambling on about?" I finish, at a lower decibel than before, almost a self-conscious whisper.

Mike cocks his head upwards slightly and raises his eyebrows. I follow his gaze, slowly and as if it is a huge effort for me to do so. Showing openly that I'm bored of this game already. There's a banner hanging above us. I take a step back so I can make out what's written on it. When I finally do see it, I wish I'd have stayed where I was.

Homecoming Dance–This Friday–7:30 p.m.

I start to laugh. Mike returns my laugh with a confused smile of his own.

"You...you can't be serious?"

"I'm deadly serious," he answers.

"Mike, we can't."

"Why can't we?"

I stare at him, exasperated. Then I take a step closer toward him, closing the distance so I can talk at a volume only he will hear. "Oh, I don't know, maybe something to do with the fallen angel looking to finish me off."

"That's not a good enough reason," he replies, brushing it off as if my excuse was an ingrowing toenail.

"Not a good enough reason. Death by the hands of a Supernatural being isn't a good enough excuse. Being pursued by the devil himself isn't a good excuse. I've heard it all now. Plus, It's not an excuse. It's a fact."

"Luc is going to come, at some point, whether you go to the dance or not. Not experiencing all the things you're supposed to as you grow up is something you'll regret. If you don't go, Luc wins."

I think about what he says. Yes, he's right. Not going to the dance because of Luc would give him some kind of mental upper hand. But what if that's not the only reason.

"Fine. On that account you're right," I say, as he starts to look smug with himself. "But in addition to having a crazed killer on my tail, I also don't want to go. I barely like being forced to spend time with some of these kids when I'm at school, why would I then choose to spend my free time with them?"

"What about Sam?" he asks.

"She won't go," I scoff.

"She might if you do. Please. Do it for me," he replies with a smile.

"You? How does me going to the dance help you?"

"I've never been to a dance. We don't have them back home. We're soldiers remember, we don't organize dances that often and I'd really like to experience it. I've seen a lot of John Hughes films. Dances always look so much fun."

"Are you trying to guilt me into going?"

"I mean, I have saved your life once or twice. Least you could do," he answers with a mischievous smile.

"Blackmail, how very male of you," I answer, returning his smile. He's playing around and I have to admit, I like it. "I don't have a dress," I continue as I cross my arms and turn down the corridor heading to class. I lighten up, starting to like the idea of going to a dance with Mike. Like a date. The thought gives me butterflies. He's already won me over. Our last date at the beach didn't go too well–finding a corpse when you get home is enough to put a dampener on even the best of nights.

I mean, I don't have to talk to anyone else, bar Sam of course. She can come with us.

"You'd look beautiful in whatever you decide to wear," he brushes a strand of hair from my face.

"It's homecoming." My face grows warm from his touch. "I need a dress."

"We'll find one," he answers as we stop once more. Face to face.

My eyes catch some of my class walking past looking at us and I take a step back. As much as I want to kiss Mike, and I believe he wants to kiss me, I don't want it happening in front of a corridor full of people. The last thing I need is a similar reaction to last time in the cafeteria. I'd rather just fly under the radar.

Easier said than done.

"Wait," I say, something just dawning on me. "We need tickets. It might be too late now." I'm shocked by the disappointment I feel saying this. Thirty seconds ago, I had no desire to go.

Mike smiles his brilliant smile at me. His perfect teeth glowing as he reaches into his back pocket and produces three tickets. "I got one for Sam as well. Just in case."

"You really are an angel," I say through laughter.

"Get a room," some random student shouts as he walks past us.

"He's right, I better get a room. A classroom." I check my watch. "See you at lunch."

I head down the corridor to my math class. It's all the way to the end, past the water fountain and turn right. Probably the furthest class from the school entrance. Luckily, I have a little bit of time. I could get used to these rides to school. Mike walks with me. I say nothing assuming his first class must be this direction as well. When he turns right at the end of the corridor, the same way I'm headed, I turn and stop him. There's only one room down here–not counting the library–and it's the room I'm going to. I know he's not in my math class.

"As much as I enjoy your company, I don't need a personal escort all the way to the door," I say to him with my arm across his chest, stopping him in his tracks.

"If you don't move your arm, I'm going to be late for class."

I look toward the class door. "You're not in my class."

"I am now. I paid reception a visit and had a little talk with the lovely lady, Brenda I think her name is, who handles the schedules. She was kind enough to change mine to match yours."

"They do that?" I ask, a little shocked. I didn't think they'd change a student's schedule unless under extreme circumstances, and while being hunted by a fallen angel is certainly extreme, I doubt that's what Mike said to her.

"I can be very persuasive," he grins. Then he leans forward and gently kisses the tip of my nose. "Hurry, we don't want Mr. Tully giving us detention now do we?"

He walks off and into the class. I'm stuck rooted to the spot. My stomach doing somersaults of excitement. My face burning hot.

Persuasive indeed.

32

The cafeteria doors swing open as someone exits and the familiar roar of the packed hall hits me like a ton of bricks. The sound bounces off the hollow walls and attacks me. It's funny–after all I've been through the last couple of day's you'd think that this would seem like nothing. A walk in the park. But it doesn't. it's everything.

The devil is one thing. A gaggle of nasty, bitchy teenage girls. Well, that's another thing altogether.

A flock of seagulls have taken up residents in my abdomen and are flapping their wings in a manic effort to break free. I stop and take a deep breath anticipating what's to come. Mia and Brad will be sitting at their usual table, no one else dare sit there. As soon as they see me their usual greeting of mockery and insults will commence. Once again, I marvel internally at my ability to withstand the physical barrage of an abusive uncle and the murderous rampage of Luc, but wince at the thought of bullying from teenagers.

Mike puts his hand on the small of my back and gives me a half smile. Slowly he begins to walk forward and gently eases me with him.

As we enter, I immediately look around. A survival technique. Know your surroundings. I can see Brad in the distance, not because of how tall he is, but because he sits on the table as opposed to the chair. Like a king sitting on his thrown with his loyal subjects gathered around his feet. Eager to hear his words of unfiltered wisdom, usually about last night's football match. They sit on the chairs around his feet looking up at him worshipfully. Mia will be next to him, although I can't see her tiny frame behind the hulk of his quarterback physique. I know she's there because her followers, her cult, are also scattered around the table looking up longingly. No doubt taking in every word of whatever it is she's complaining about today. The list of subjects could be as long as your arm.

"What would you like?"

"Huh?" I snap my head away from the table of jocks and cheerleaders and look at Mike.

"For lunch," he inclines his head toward the long queue of students waiting to pick up a hot meal.

"You're really taking this 'making sure I eat' thing to a whole new level, aren't you?"

"If I keep asking then it'll become habit and I won't forget," he says with a smile, obviously pleased with himself.

"I'll just have some fruit, please."

"That's it?" Mike asks with a screwed-up face.

"Yeah, that'll be enough. Not too hungry," I answer with a shrug.

"Fair enough. You go and sit down, I'll bring it over. No point in both of us queuing here."

I look at the queue again and he's right. Dozens of kids waiting haphazardly with their plastic trays. Jumping around, play fighting. Acting out the latest action films. There's a good ten-minute wait there. I nod to Mike and head to the back of the cafeteria. I make sure to take a different route than usual. I don't want to pass Mia's table if I can help it. Avoid at all costs. She's probably heard that Tom is in the hospital and will have some kind of snarky comment to make about it and I'm really not in the mood.

I make my way to the table in the far-right hand corner where I can see Sam sitting. Well, I say I can see her, that isn't exactly true. What I can see is tiny fingers wrapped around a huge breeze block of a book which is hiding her small face. I plop myself down in the seat next to her and drop my bag on the floor by my seat, letting out a sigh as I do so. Sam slowly lowers the book from her face and has a look around her, as if she's looking for someone. Her face is colored with mock confusion.

"Everything okay?" I ask, slowly.

"It's just unusual to see you lately without the new guy," she answers, turning her attention back to her book.

I notice the sharpness in her words, as if her tongue is a razor blade. At first, I contemplate answering her back in the same manner. It's bad enough I try to avoid Mia because of stuff like this without having to worry about getting it from my friend as well. Then I reconsider. For six months it has just been the two of us. Us against the world. So, I can understand her annoyance at seeing me with Mike, even though it doesn't deserve her catty remarks.

"He only lives up the road and he's given me a lift a couple times," I shrug, trying to act as if it isn't a big deal. "Plus, he found Tom. Got him to the hospital," I finish, hoping this good deed can make her see how nice of a guy he is.

"Nice of him," she dismisses, never taking her eyes away from her book.

I can feel annoyance rising in me at her response to me having another friend. I keep it in check, trying to understand how I would feel if it were her. Still, it makes me angry, but I don't want to argue with Sam, especially over a boy. "Give him a chance, Sam. You'll like him. Trust me. I'm a good judge of people, that's why I'm friends with you," I say, buttering her up a little.

She side eyes me, but I can see the corner of her mouth twitch. "I'm sorry. I'm glad you've another friend. I really am." She looks directly at me as she lays her book on the table. I can see the honesty in her eyes.

"Thank you. But he's your friend, too."

She turns back to her book, not acknowledging what I said.

I turn my attention back toward the lunch queue. More time must have passed than I thought because Mike was now making his way over, a tray full of fruit in his hands. Sam doesn't see him coming, her attention firmly in the thrilling world Stephen King had created. She usually does this, gets so caught up in what she's reading the real world around her just fades into non-existence. Most likely the main reason she reads so much—to escape the real world and all its problems. As Mike drops the plastic tray on the round plastic table top, the clattering sound causes Sam to jump. A small yelp escapes her lips involuntarily. Her book slips from her fingers and lands on the tabletop with more of a thud than the tray. Such is her life at school that any unexpected sound is greeted with fear rather than harmless curiosity. It may look humorous from the outside, but knowing exactly how she feels, my heart breaks for her.

"Fruit," Mike proclaims, oblivious as he takes a seat opposite me and Sam.

Sam looks at him nervously and then shifts in her seat, edging closer to me. She lifts her book covering her face once more. A very robotic movement that stems from nervousness and a desire to hide from the outside world. I swear, if she could disappear into one of her books, even the horror ones she loves to read so often, I'm pretty sure she'd do it.

I turn away from watching her, not wanting to add to her nervousness. "You got enough?" I study the tray filled with an apple, an orange, a banana, pineapple chunks and a pear.

I only wanted one piece.

"Five a day, right?" Mike asks, his face etched with concern as if he's made some great mistake.

"Yeah–a day. Not all in one sitting," I answer, with the purpose of being playful. Instead, his face drops as if I've just slapped him.

"Sorry, I was–just trying to remember you need to eat so wanted to bring enough."

I look immediately to Sam to see if she had heard what Mike had said, or how he had said it to be more specific. Slowly she lowers her book, so just her eyes can be seen above the top.

"You *remembered* she needed to eat? Of course, she does, why wouldn't she?" Obviously, she wasn't as lost in her book as I'd assumed. As soon as the words leave her mouth though, her eyes widen as she realizes she has spoken the words out loud. She tries to hide behind her book again, but I reach across and lower it back down with my hand. Her cheeks are red with embarrassment

"He just means because he isn't hungry, he had to remember that other people still are," I answer in a poor attempt at making an excuse.

"Well, if you're not going to finish them all," Mike begins as he inches the tray toward Sam. "Maybe Sam can help you?" he asks, flashing his brilliant Tom Cruise smile. If he's hoping that will put her at ease, then he is sorely mistaken. If anything, it will give her a panic attack.

Sam's hand immediately goes to her pocket and she pulls out her asthma pump, places it to her lips and pumps herself with a lungful of air. She takes a deep breath and swallows.

"I'm er...not hungry," she whispers, trying to hide behind her book again, but unable to lift it with my hand still on top.

"Put a piece in your bag for later."

"I better go," Sam replies, her voice low and meek.

"Please don't go, Sam."

"I have to...I er...have some work to finish in the library."

My face drops. I want her to get to know Mike, I know they'd get on. I try not to take it too personally and consider telling Mike to leave so I can talk with Sam, but it isn't out of the ordinary for her to do this. Sometimes she does go off to the library at lunch preferring the solitude to even my company. I tell myself that's what it is, and not because Mike is sitting here.

She packs her things away in her backpack and mutters a barely audible goodbye as she starts to head for the fire exit door at the back of the cafeteria, keen to avoid passing the other tables.

"Sam," Mike says as she starts to head off. She stops and turns toward Mike, angling her body in his direction while her head is aimed to the floor. I look across to Mike, waiting for what he's going to say. For some reason, feeling nervous. "Abby and I are going to go to the dance on Friday evening..." Sam shoots me a confused look, but says nothing. "We would love it if you'd come with us. All of us go together...as friends."

I look at Mike and smile. Then turn to Sam. "Please Sam. We never do anything like this. It'll be fun."

"There's a reason we don't do anything like that," Sam adds as she adjusts her gaze to look across at Mia and Brad. I turn and look too. They're throwing bits of their food at the table in front of them.

"I know, and it's about time we stopped letting them stop us from having fun."

Sam looks from me to Mike. Then back again. "I'll think about it," she turns around and shuffles off, not giving us a chance to answer.

We watch her exit the cafeteria. Mike exhales, picks up the apple from the tray, leans back in his chair and rolls it from his hand, down his arm, flicks it up, catches it and takes a bite. "She really doesn't like me, does she?" he says through a mouthful of apple.

"Don't take any notice, she's like that with everyone. Give her time," I say. He runs his free hand through his hair as he takes another bite of the apple. "What happened to not eating?" I ask, laughing. "That apple's almost gone, and you've only had two bites."

He looks down at the apple and shrugs.

❦ 33 ❧

The rest of the week seemed to pass by as if in slow motion. My anticipation for the dance on Friday seeming to make every day drag. A nervous fear was battling it out with my excitement every time I thought about it, which was often. My first ever dance. After our very short lunch together Monday morning, the week was better in terms of how comfortable Sam became around Mike. On Tuesday we all sat together again at lunch, although Sam never uttered a single word. Still, she didn't leave so I took that as a win. By Wednesday lunch, she was responding to questions with one-word answers. She was still hidden behind her book, but the answers were audible. Come Thursday she was in full flowing excitement mode when Mike asked her about the book she was reading. She spent the next forty-five minutes barely taking a breath as she waxed lyrical about the greatness of Stephen King. She even forgot about her inhaler, which she never used once the whole time. Then earlier today, she spent the whole of lunch never picking her book up once. She wasn't overly involved in the conversation, jumping in here and there, but to keep her away from her book for that length of time, this was real progress. So much so that she even said she will come to the dance with us, but she wasn't dancing. Which was fine by me.

On top of all of this, we never saw, nor heard from Luc. Maybe he'd decided to give up? Doubtful, but one can hope.

Of course, the whole week the panic of what to wear was ever present, especially considering I still didn't own a dress. Not one. Mike had told me not to panic. He would handle it, and if you can't trust an angel, who can you trust?

Now with the night finally here, I stand in front of the mirror barely recognizing myself, and marveling at how much has changed, especially in the past week. I'm not even talking about the fact that the existence of angels isn't just a leap of faith, I have one sleeping downstairs on the sofa. I'm talking about the fact that I'm actually sitting with more than one friend at school. That I'm standing here, in a beautiful dress ready to go to a school dance. Something I would never have thought would be a reality a couple of weeks ago. I have no idea where Mike got the dress, or how he knew what size to get. Just another of his *angel powers* I assumed. I lightly rub my hand down the front of the soft blue fabric. It's beautiful. I look beautiful–not that I'd utter those words out loud.

"Abby, you coming?" Mike's voice echoes up the stairs. Immediately my heart starts pounding in my chest. I push the thought of this being a date from my mind. Sam is coming with us, which I'm more than happy about, but obviously, not a date. Plus, Mike is an angel. It isn't like there's much future there. It's forbidden, as my mum and dad found out. That being said, Mike did say the prophecy stated that the father of my child, (at some point in the *very* distant future) would be an angel. I shake my head to bully the thoughts out. Trying to rationalize the fact that there could be a future between the two of us when I know full well it's an impossibility, is frankly, idiotic.

"Coming," I holler back.

I take one last look at myself in the mirror. The stranger in the dress looks back, her face etched with nerves. I close my eyes and steady myself. Unsure of what tonight will bring, but knowing, with Mike and Sam with me, everything will be fine. I will not let the thoughts of Luc, or even Mia and Brad, ruin my night.

I walk out of my room and slow my steps as the unfamiliar sound of my high heeled dress shoes clip clop on the wooden floor. A far cry from the sound the rubber soles my sneakers make. It feels alien. Yet, nice to be able to dress up in a way I've never done before. I wish my mum could see me. I rub my necklace at the thought of her. She's always with me. I try to creep in an attempt to silence the sound. It doesn't work, it just increases the length of time between each echoed clip. Each echoed clop. I slowly descend the stairs. My shaking hand firmly on the handrail to make sure I don't trip. As I reach about halfway down, I see Mike standing at the bottom, his back to me as he faces the front door. Slowly, he turns around and he takes my breath away. His suit is jet black, as are his boots. His white shirt is open at the neck as his golden hair rests effortlessly on his collar. On anyone else it may look scruffy, but on Mike, he looked as handsome a man could possibly look.

I reach the bottom step and stop. We stand still, just looking at each other. It's as if the world has frozen in time. After a moment, Mike takes a step toward me so he's standing just in front of the bottom step. Even though I am standing on the step, he is still about an inch taller than me, and I'm in heels. He is directly underneath the hallway light, the glow lingering above his head like a halo.

"You look amazing."

"It's the dress," I answer, embarrassed.

He places his finger under my chin and gently raises my head so I'm facing him again "It's not the dress. It's you," he whispers.

I start to feel uncomfortable. I'm not used to being paid complements.

"You look...handsome," I say, feeling stupid. This whole boy/girl thing is new to me. Mike senses it and takes a step back. Part of me is glad, the other part wants to grab him by his lapels, pull him toward me and plant my lips firmly on his.

Mike pokes his elbow out so I can wrap my arm around his, like some old-fashioned gentleman.

"Shall we?" he asks, a goofy smile plastered across his face.

I smile and slip my arm through the gap in his and we head toward the front door. The only sounds that can be heard is my heart beating and my heels hitting the floor. I'm not sure what's louder, but I'm positive that Mike can hear both.

"What time are we picking Sam up?"

"She said she wanted to make her own way there," I shrug. "I offered, but she was adamant. I don't think she wants her dad seeing a boy picking her up. He gets kinda protective."

Mike nods as we head out onto the front porch. It's warm out, but I still shiver as a warm breeze caresses my bare shoulders. Mike doesn't seem to notice. The sun is just setting creating a scorching ochre glow across the horizon. The barn, the paddock, the now orange land that stretches behind the house as far as the eye can see. It's beautiful. I study my surroundings, somehow expecting something to burst from the cornfield and attack us, like that huge snake. To ruin the night before its begun, but nothing comes as we head toward Mike's still battered and dented truck.

"All the things you can do, but you can't fix your truck."

"I could, but I like it. Its imperfections add to its beauty," he replies. "I was going to get a limo, but I thought that was a little extravagant."

"Just a little. We could fly," I say, jokingly.

"My wings would rip my shirt and jacket."

"You could take them off."

Mike looks at me wide eyed, surprise coloring his face. The corners of his mouth run up in a smile and I have to look away. "I could, but I think it would be frowned upon," he answers as he pulls the passenger door open for me. I climb in, still averting my gaze.

"Well, Cinderella. Let's get you to the ball." He slams my door closed.

We arrive at the school and the parking lot is packed. Queues of mostly trucks are backing out onto the street. Kids are scattered everywhere. It seems like there's a greater number of people here than actually go to the school. Mike sits patiently, waiting for the line to clear so he can finally get into the parking lot and find a space. He finds one almost immediately and I wonder if he used some kind of angel mojo to materialize one out of nowhere. I erase the thought from my mind. It's highly possible, but I'm not sure he'd have done it out in the open like that, especially with this number of people around.

The drive here was mostly silent. The butterflies in my stomach seemed to grow to the size of crows with each passing minute. Mike tried talking to me, but soon stopped when my one-word answers made it clear that I was too nervous to form coherent sentences. My mind was working overtime about potential situations that could arise tonight. My first school dance, with a bunch of people who don't particularly like me and a rogue angel that wants to polish me off because of something I'm supposed to do years down the line.

I think nerves are a valid response in the very least.

Mike kills the engine and turns to face me. "Ready to enter the lion's den?" he asks, playfully. I give him a look that expresses that now isn't the time for jokes. His smile is sympathetic. "Come on. We're in this together. Plus, Sam might already be in there and she'll need our support. Strength in numbers."

I nod.

Mike comes around to open my door. He takes my hand and helps me slide off the bench seat and onto the ground. My heel turns over as I try and balance myself, the shoes feeling very new to me. I steady myself, look Mike directly in the eyes and firmly nod.

"No turning back," I utter.

Mike slips his fingers into mine, our hands tangled in a knot. We head toward the school entrance, our arms touching. Our hands clasped together and while the nerves are still there, I know no matter what the night throws my way, with Mike and Sam with me, I'll be able to handle it.

We make our way down the corridor toward the hall which is hosting the dance. The only time I have seen it in use is when Mr. Heaver has decided he wants to talk to the whole school, which is usually the start of the school year. Or when they have had some kind of performance in there. A play or concert of some kind. None of which I have been to in my time at the school. Even if I wanted to, Tom wouldn't have let me.

For the first time in what seems like a long time I wonder how he is doing. A twinge of guilt pangs in my chest at having not thought about him sooner or been to visit him. It seems like a lifetime ago. Plus, if Mike managed to bring him back and make it look like a farming accident, then I'm sure he's fine.

He doesn't deserve any visitors anyway.

I can hear the music floating its way down the corridor as Mike and I approach. A few kids are scattered about, leaning against the lockers, loitering. A group of boys to our right, all holding red plastic cups filled with some kind of fruit punch, are huddled together to hide the fact that they're adding what I can only assume is alcohol. Completely unaware that their attempts to go unnoticed are doing nothing but drawing more attention to themselves.

Further down, just tucked out of the way under a small alcove that houses the water fountain, a couple are wrapped in a passionate embrace. I can't make out who they are as their faces are squashed together. I tentatively look up at Mike, who angles his eyes down at me. I look away sharply, my face growing hot. I slowly look back toward him and can see that he's smiling back at me. We both laugh, more from embarrassment than anything else.

We reach the double doors that lead to the hall. Mike pulls one side open and moves aside allowing me to enter first. As I walk in the wall of sound hits me. Much the same as entering the cafeteria at lunch, except the roar of talking is replaced by the echo of music. It's hard to make out what the song is, it sounds like Tim McGraw, but the acoustics in here are so bad it could be anything. I angle my ear to try and focus on the distinctly southern voice and I'm sure I can hear Tim growling to anyone that will listen.

Definitely Tim. My uncle has him on all the time when he's out tinkering with his truck.

I take some time as we stand just inside the door to admire the decoration. I must say, even I think it looks beautiful. Luckily, Carrie, our class president decided not to go for some cheesy theme like 'The Under the Sea' dance or something equally as vomit inducing. Instead, it's just a formal dance. Carrie has done wonders with turning this bland hall into a feast for the eyes. Lights flicker from the DJ's equipment catching the streamers that hang from the ceiling just right. Sparking an iridescent light show from the shiny tinsel type décor plastered on the walls.

I scan the dance floor which is full. Kids contorting their body in all sorts of shapes that seem to not go in any way, shape or form to the song that is playing. If anything, they look possessed. My eyes continue around the edges of the hall, looking at the people that are too cool to dance. I immediately see Mia, Brad and their horde of cretinous bullies. I have to admit, she looks beautiful, a little too much skin on show for me, but on her, it looks amazing. I study her for a moment longer, laughing and fawning over Brad. They're not a couple, but they may as well be. They spend all their time together and are basically king and queen of the school. Her shiny pink dress throws off shades of green and yellow and blue every time the lights catch her just right. She may as well have her own spotlight above her she's glowing so much. Their friends, as usual, float around them awaiting any orders they may be given.

I can't help but feel a sense of Deja Vu as I scan around the hall. In most cases this could probably be put down to the fact that if you've attended one dance, you've attended them all, but considering this is the only dance I have ever been to, this isn't the case.

"Everything okay?" Mike asks, obviously noticing the concentration on my face as I try to figure out why it feels like I've been here before.

"Yeah, I think so—it's just..."

"Hi!" Sam's voice is barely a whisper even though she's shouting over the music.

My words trail off as I say hello to Sam. The feeling of having been here before disappears and is replaced by sheer happiness. There was a part of me that thought Sam may pull out last minute and not come to the dance. I couldn't be happier that she's here.

"You look lovely, Sam." He's right, she does. She's wearing a trouser suit with Converse sneakers and a white tee with a picture of Pennywise the Clown on it. She looks more herself than I have ever seen her. Relaxed even.

"Thank you," she replies, shyly, looking away.

"You really do, Sam," I add as I give her a hug. "I'm glad you came"

"You look great too," she says into my ear as we hug, "really pretty, and I'm glad too. It actually looks quite fun."

"It will be. We'll have a great time," I tell her, enthusiastically. Unsure whether I believe it or am trying to convince myself.

"Shall we head over that way and try and grab a seat?"

We make our way through the obstacle course of possessed human beings, weaving in and out, trying our best to avoid arms that appear from nowhere. Sam and I giggle as we have to bob and weave like a boxer more than once to avoid a stray elbow to the face. Mike leads the way, effortlessly moving in and out of the gaggle of dancers as if he knows exactly what's coming. I hold Sam's hand now instead of Mike's making sure neither of us get lost in the crowd.

Finally, we are out of the 'line of fire' and have made it to the bleachers at the side of the hall overlooking the dance floor. A few people are scattered about on them, talking and observing the dancers. A few pointing and laughing good naturedly at their friends acting ridiculous with their breakdancing attempts. Sam and I follow the direction they're pointing and giggle to ourselves. This is all very new to us.

"So, who's first?" Mike asks as he stands in front of both of us, his left hand in his pocket, his right hand held out to me and Sam as if he expects one of us to take it.

"First for what?" I ask, my eyebrows creased.

"To dance. Or all three of us can go up together?" Mike says, a friendly smile spread across his face. Sam leans as far back as the bleachers will let her. Her back pressed against the wooden footrest behind her. Her hands waving furiously across the front of her body emphasizing the no that she's saying, but none of us can hear.

"Dance?" I shout.

"I believe it is customary at these types of events. I mean, it is literally called a school *dance*."

"Not me thanks, I'll watch from a safe distance. Abby will," Sam says as the music dies down and another song starts. She pushes me in the small of the back lifting me off the seat.

"Thanks," I say, through laughter.

I take Mike's still outstretched hand, and we head toward the dance floor. Somehow Mike seems to find a route to the center without bumping into anyone. I keep a tight grip on his hand and follow behind him. The base in the noise that blares from the huge speakers on the stage (I say noise because it definitely isn't real music) causes the floor to rumble.

"How are we supposed to dance to this?"

"Huh?" Mike leans into me.

"How are we supposed to dance to this!" I shout directly into Mike's ear.

He angles his head up as if hearing the music for the first time. Raises his hand and clicks his fingers. All of a sudden, the music stops. A slow ballad starts to play. Classical music of some kind. It sounds like a harp.

The hall, sigh en masse. I look over at the DJ who is frantically fiddling with his equipment. Pressing buttons and turning knobs, but no matter what he does, the song continues to play. I can't help but laugh as I watch the poor guy scratching his head in confusion and disbelief.

Mike takes my hand and pulls me close to him.

He holds my right hand in his left and rests it to his chest. His other hand he places on the small of my back and pulls me closer, our bodies touching. He smells nice. I can't quite place my finger on what it is. Candyfloss? Whatever it is, its sweet. I breathe it all in. It makes me feel lightheaded.

I look into his eyes, shining a brilliant blue. Like the clearest sky on a summer's day. The rest of the hall disappears. All of my classmates fade into nothingness, and it feels as if we are the only two people in the world. My heart swells just looking at him and I realize, regardless of if it is allowed, regardless of if there's a future there–I love him. With every part of my being, with every fiber of my soul. I love him completely.

It feels as if we are barely moving. If I wasn't fully aware that there's a room full of people, I'd have thought we were floating in mid-air. We slowly turn in a circle, becoming one with the beautiful, haunting music. Over Mike's shoulder I can see Sam watching us. Smiling. I lift my hand from Mike's shoulder and wave. She waves back and then gives me a thumbs up. I smile to myself and place my hand back. Then, I lay my head on Mike's chest. For once, not caring who's around. Not caring who's watching us. I feel Mike press his face into my hair, breathing me in. I raise my head to look at him, our faces millimeters apart. Our noses almost touching. We look at each other, getting lost in each other's eyes and then Mike leans down and presses his lips against mine. The electricity I feel when we touch is nothing compared to this. My whole body comes alive as if a current is passing through it. The music fades away. The rest of the people on the dancefloor, in the hall, disappear. We are the only two people here.

I wrap my arms tighter around his neck and pull him closer to me, never wanting this to end. He grips me tighter around my waist, both hands circling my body. My hands travel up and into his soft, golden hair and then–

"Okay, okay, that's enough. This isn't some seedy drive-in movie." Mr. Heaver's voice, perfectly ruining the moment–again–snaps me back to reality. I step back from Mike. My breathing coming in short sharp bursts. I look around to see other students watching us, some looking shocked. Other's looking entertained. Mike on the other hand hangs his head, looking embarrassed, and slightly ashamed with himself. I try and tell myself that this is because he isn't allowed to get involved, not because he doesn't want to. It doesn't help. The look on his face still makes me feel upset. The music stops abruptly. The hall now filled with a cacophony of mixed conversations and movement. "You two again," Mr. Heaver continues, mock annoyance in his voice when he can finally see our faces. "Didn't you pay any attention to what I said in the corridor only a matter of days ago?"

"Yes, sir. Sorry," I mutter, awkwardly.

"Won't happen again." Mike looks over at me, embarrassment still coloring his cheeks. Mike holds out his hand for me to take. I do, and we start to head back to Sam at the bleachers.

We get back and everyone, including Sam, is quiet. No one utters a word. Sam's lips are pressed together, obviously suppressing a smile. None of us talk. I look over my shoulder at the DJ, still frantically messing about with his laptop.

"Nice dance?" Sam asks, no longer hiding her smile.

I tilt my head and look at her, exasperation on my face. A mini eye roll thrown in for added effect. "You know, I think I preferred it at the beginning of the week when you were too embarrassed to talk around Mike," I say, good naturedly.

She responds by throwing an obscene hand gesture my way. Mike and I both laugh at Sam's out of character outburst.

"Well, I think I need a drink of some kind. Anyone else?" Mike asks.

"Me please."

"Be careful, I heard two guys talking about how they spiked both punch bowls," Sam chips in.

"I'll find some soft drinks."

"There's only two bowls and if they're both spiked, you won't have much luck," Sam answers with a shrug.

"I'll think of something," Mike says with a knowing grin in my direction.

"I doubt it, unless you're some kind of magician. If so, I'll have a cup of something."

Mike the magician. I suppose she isn't too far off. He does do some pretty unexplainable things.

"Hey, farm girl!"

I audibly sigh. I don't need to turn around to know who it is. The high pitched, shrieking is a dead giveaway. I don't even turn around to face her as I answer. "What do you want, Mia?"

"I wanted to introduce you to my date. You may feel the need to show off on the dance floor, sucking face..."

"I wasn't showing off," I interrupt, bored. Mia carries on as if I haven't even spoken, as usual, no one else exists in the world she has created for herself except for her.

"...but you no longer have bragging rights for having the hottest date at the school..."

"I never brag."

"...my date is now the hottest guy here," she finally finishes.

I've no interest in turning around, getting into it with her or seeing her date. It isn't until Mike responds that I become interested and intrigued.

"What the hell do you think you're doing here?" Mike's voice is low, almost an animalistic growl. I can barely hear it even though I'm just a few steps away from him. Some of that may have to do with the fact that the rest of the kids at the dance are now starting to turn on the DJ for his lack of music. I turn my head ever so slightly in Mike's direction and the look on his face is that of pure fury. Slowly, I turn around, anticipating exactly what is about to greet me. At first, I see a smug, Mia–arms folded across her chest, her foot tapping as her lips are pouted in some kind of imitation of a fish. A look that says '*I've won*'–won a battle I didn't even know we were having. My eyes slowly travel up, knowing what I'm going to see, but like looking at a car crash, I can't draw my eyes away. Standing just to Mia's left, a step behind her, is Luc. Dressed in what I have come to realize is his customary black clothing. His black suit sits over a black collarless shirt. His biker boots have been replaced with smart, dress, ankle boots. Like Mike, his hair is hanging effortlessly on his shoulders, but looks as if he has been for a four hour blow dry.

"Abigail, so lovely to see you again," Luc says in his smarmy way.

"I said, what the hell are you doing here?" Mike repeats his question, louder this time due to not only his anger, but the fact that the DJ has managed to get his noise playing again.

"The same as you, Michael." Luc acts shocked. "I'm here to have a good time with the beautiful, Mia." Mia, stares directly at me, satisfaction oozing out of every pore.

"Get out of here now, Luc," Mike takes a step forward. The threat obvious in his tone. Sam gets up and takes a step toward us, intrigued by what's going on.

"I should have known the hanger on would be here. No date of your own?" Mia says to Sam.

"No date. Just friends," Sam answers back. I feel pride swelling inside me at witnessing Sam answer Mia for once.

"Who is this lovely little thing?" Luc takes a step closer. Mia's face at Luc calling Sam lovely was marginally fun to watch, but I don't have time to revel in the feeling. I step in front of Sam, blocking her from Luc.

"Don't you dare go anywhere near her," I say, my voice strong and unwavering.

"So brave."

Mia looks from Luc, to me, to Mike and back to Luc again. Understandably confused by this exchange. "Do you guys already know each other?" I ignore her, not wanting to take my eyes off Luc and definitely not wanting to be the one to clarify anything for Mia.

"Abigail and I have only just met, haven't we love? But Michael and I, well, we're practically family," Luc answers, obviously enjoying every minute of discomfort he is bringing on me.

"There's a lot of people here, Luc. Don't do anything stupid," Mike warns.

"I'm just here to have a good time," Luc's arms are out in front of him, palms up in a childish attempt to show us he has nothing planned.

"That's what I'm concerned about."

"Unless you think my dancing is stupid of course," Luc Laughs. It isn't funny and Mia has no idea what's going on, but she laughs with him. Starting a second or two after and being out of time, but she still laughs.

I take a step toward her. Mike initially holds out his hand to stop me, but I shrug him off. I look at Mia earnestly and honestly for maybe the first time ever. Dead in her eyes. Pleading with her to put her feelings about me aside for one second and just listen.

"Mia, please. He isn't a good guy. Stay away from him. Trust me," I urge.

"Trust you? You're just jealous that my date is hotter than yours." She brushes off what I'm saying much the same way as she brushes her hair off her shoulder at the same time.

"Mia!" I shout, grabbing her. Her eyes widen. Maybe in fear. Maybe in shock. Most likely a bit of both. This time Mike does come forward and try to lead me away. I don't let him stop me though. "Listen to me. He is dangerous. Very dangerous. Don't go anywhere alone with him–stay with friends. Hell, stay with us if you have to."

Luc takes a step forward and much more forcibly than Mike is pulling me, he yanks Mia away. She stumbles back, but he holds her up. His face still has a hint of a grin, but there is a fire in his eyes. "Come, Mia. Let's go enjoy ourselves," he finishes before they walk away, his voice oozing with implication.

Mia looks over her shoulder at us. Gone is her usual superiority glance. It's replaced by a curious, almost fearful expression I have never seen before.

"We have to help her," I say out loud, but am mostly talking to myself. Wracking my brain as to how I can get her away from him when I know she has no intention of listening to me.

"How?" Mike answers. "Short of my flying over there and tackling him out of the room I'm not sure what can be done."

"Flying?" Sam asks, confused, not just by the interaction between Mia and me, but also by the conversation going on now.

"Figure of speech," Mike turns to face Sam. His face etched with worry. His smile, a troubled one.

"Abby, who is that guy? What's going on here?" Sam asks.

"He's...well... it's..." I start, but can't seem to finish. My brain not working fast enough to think up some excuse. Also, I don't want to think up an excuse, I want to tell her the truth. The whole truth, but how can I?

"He's my brother," Mike says, firmly. Not taking his eyes away from Luc and Mia who are now dancing goofily together. Neither looking over here. Luc mocking us in his own little way. I whip my head toward Mike, surprised he made this revelation. His face is set. Determined.

"Wait, what? Your brother? I mean, I can kind of see the likeness, but also, not. He's British, right?" Sam asks, a confused jumble of thoughts and questions spilling from her mouth.

"He was sent to boarding school over there," Mike answers quickly, not missing a beat. He carries on before Sam can enquire any more about his family history. "Abby, you were right. This was a bad idea–I gave him too much credit. I never thought he'd come here, but he's just toying with us now. We should go." He holds out his hand for me to take. I look at Sam, her eyes cloud over with intrigue. She's a writer at heart, she knows there's a story here. I scan the rest of the hall. My class, having fun without a care in the world. The decorations, beautiful. Streamers hanging from the ceiling. Lights flashing not just from the DJ's table, but from the walls where spotlights usually focus in on performers taking part in yearly theater productions. The table at the back of the hall filled with trays of food and bowls of now spiked drink.

"Abby," Mike calls, but I barely hear him as I look down at the beautiful dress I'm wearing. The shoes that I initially struggled to walk in. I realize that now I'm here, I don't want to leave. It's my first school dance and I'm spending it with my best friend and...whatever Mike and I are. I'm not going to let it be ruined by a murderous demon.

"Abby," Mike says again, lightly taking me by the elbow to snap me out of my own thoughts.

"No," I say, turning back to him and pulling my elbow away. Not in anger or with any force. Just to let him know I'm not going anywhere. "You were right all along, Mike. These are the experiences I should be having and I'm not going to let anyone, especially Luc, ruin that for me. I came here to enjoy myself and that's exactly what I'm going to do."

I look from Mike to Sam. Mike looks worried. Sam like she hasn't a clue what is going on, which, she hasn't.

"Are you sure?"

"Surer than I've ever been about anything in the world. We stay. We have a good time. That's it. That's what's gonna happen," I say with a small stamp of my foot and nod of my head.

Mike looks across the hall, no doubt eyeing up Luc and weighing his options. Risk assessing. I follow his gaze. Luc and Mia are off the dance floor now. They lean against the wall at the back end of the hall. Luc, stroking her face and her hair while she looks up at him adoringly. If she were a cartoon, love hearts would be springing from her eyes right about now. From a distance most people would say it looks sweet, maybe even sexual. For me, knowing who Luc really is, knowing what Luc really is, it's just creepy. Mike sighs and closes his eyes. He shoulders slump slightly in defeat. He can sense the resilience in my voice. He knows my mind is made up. I walk toward him and place my hand on his cheek. From the corner of my eye, I can see Sam look away, embarrassed. He turns back and looks down at me. I smile at him. It's forced and my lips are set tight, but the meaning behind it is real.

"If we go, he wins anyway. If I live the life of a prisoner, locked away for fear of what may happen then I may as well just let him have me," I whisper to Mike. His jaw sets and I know he's heard me over the music. He has one last glance back toward Luc before he turns to me, a sadness in his eyes I don't want to dwell on or question. He nods. I rise up on my tiptoes and lightly kiss his cheek before turning back to Sam who is still looking away. I take her hand and go to sit on the bleachers again. She still looks confused, but sensing something serious is going on, she grips my hand tight and puts her other one on top of mine. A real friend. I love her for that small gesture more than words can say.

"So, about those drinks," I say to Mike who is watching me intently.

"Abby, I don't think I should leave you..." he begins as he takes a step closer to me. I hold up my hand and stop him.

"We're here to have a good time remember, and you promised us both a drink, didn't he Sam?"

Sam looks from me to Mike, not wanting to get caught in the middle, but loyalty winning out. "Yeah, you did, and I am pretty thirsty," she answers quietly.

"I'll be fine Mike. It's five minutes and we're in a room full of people. Plus, Sam is here," I say, holding up our still clasped hands as if I was a referee in a boxing match announcing the winner.

Mike runs his hands through his hair, his blond looking more and more golden as the lights pass over him. Struggling with the thought of leaving, but knowing he can't be with me every second. "I'll be as quick as I can."

"We'll be fine," I say, firmly. Not sure who I'm trying to convince.

Mike lingers for a second or two, sets his jaw in his characteristic way and spins on his heel disappearing into the crowd. I take a deep breath once again and feel my bravado fade away as fast as it came. My shoulders slump slightly. Whatever energy was in me creating this will to not be scared was also holding me upright. Now it's gone, I feel as if I may crumble to the floor. I wasn't lying before, I do want to stay. I don't want Luc dictating my movements any more than I want Mia doing it. The chest puffing on the other hand was all show. Just knowing Luc is in the same room as me, taunting me, feels me with dread. Knowing what he is capable of also makes me scared for Mia. I may not like her, but I don't want her to get hurt.

"What's going on?" Sam asks delicately. "Is everything okay?"

I look at her. My best friend. Wanting to spill my guts and tell her everything, but scared doing so could put her in danger. "Everything is as far from okay as it possibly can be. I want to tell you, Sam, I really do. I just can't. Not right now. I promise you I will try to explain when all of this is over–if it's ever going to be over. For now, though, just stay away from Luc, if he comes near you, just come to me, or Mike, but don't go anywhere near him. Understand?" My voice rises at the end. My eyes wide as I try and drive home the point. I may not be able to tell her much, but I'm damn sure going to get home to her that Luc is bad news. I know Sam would never willingly go to Luc, but I'd never rest if something happened to her, and it was because I never warned her.

Sam nods, emphatically. Her face serious.

"Just keep thinking to yourself that it's like one of your books come to life. Monsters are real," I add as I turn my gaze back to the dance floor, scanning for Mia and Luc. I spot Mia, arms folded, face sour as she looks around the room. Luc on the other hand is nowhere to be seen. My heart starts to race as I look around the room in a panic. I spot Mike, his back to us as he queues at the punch table.

"I'm here for you, when you're ready to talk."

"Thank you."

"What about Mike though?" Sam asks, tentatively.

"What do you mean?"

"If he's Luc's brother–is he okay? I mean, are you sure you can trust him?"

"If there's anyone in the world you can trust wholeheartedly, it's Mike. If you trust me at all, then believe that. He's one of the good ones, unlike Luc."

"That isn't a very nice thing to say, love."

I snap my head around and there he is, standing in front of us. Two plastic cups in his hand. Smiling his smarmy smile. Immediately my eyes dart past him to the punch table, searching for Mike. He isn't there. My eyes travel over the whole hall. I can't see him anywhere amongst the mass of people. A jumble of bodies all in huddles around the room. You could hide a herd of dinosaurs in here and not find them. I have no chance with Mike.

"Get away from us."

"Now, now, play nice. I brought you both a drink." Luc holds up the cups.

"We don't want your drink. Mike's getting us a drink, and he'll be back any second. I suggest you get lost."

"Mike is, well, Mike is going to be a while," Luc says, cryptically. My heart rises to my throat as panic causes sweat to prickle my brow. What does he mean? What has he done with Mike? "Hello again Samantha." Luc turns his attention to Sam. Creepiness dripping with every word he utters.

I jump to my feet and position myself in front of the two of them, just in time to see Sam retreat within herself. Shuffling backwards as her eyes shift to the floor.

"Don't you dare talk to her, don't even look at her," I say through gritted teeth.

Luc sighs. He raises one of the cups and downs the drink throwing the empty on the floor. "Come with me, Abigail," Luc says. It isn't a request.

"No chance," I laugh.

His eyes momentarily shoot past me to where Sam is. He gives a slight flick of his hand in front of his face, in between us, and I hear a little thud behind me. I spin around to find Sam lying unconscious on the bleachers she was moments ago sitting on. I run to her and kneel. She's still breathing. I shake her, but she doesn't react.

"It's no use. She won't wake unless I want her to."

I jump back to my feet, almost run toward him and hit him hard in the chest with both fists. He doesn't move, doesn't even budge. What he does do is laugh.

"You're spunky aren't you. I like it." He laughs.

I slap him across the face. His smile vanishes instantly and is replaced with a look of utter fury. My pleasure at hearing the satisfying 'clap' as my palm connects with his cheek is short lived as the look on his face fills me with dread. I hide it, or try to, at least. Setting my face, my chin pushed outwards, my jaw pulsing the way I've seen Mike's do so many times, readying myself for whatever is coming. My stomach seems to plummet to my feet at the thought of Mike and what may have happened to him, but once again, I don't let him see it. I'm done with giving other people satisfaction from seeing me struggle. From the day my mother and father died at the hand of one of his acolytes, I've been bullied and beaten. That ends right now. I refuse to bow down to the likes of Luc. Even if he is the devil himself.

"Come with me. Now," he says. Gone are the pleasantries. The words come out in a low growl through his gritted teeth.

"Are you high? I'm not going anywhere with you," I shout.

Luc rubs his forehead in a forced, theatrical movement. As if he is playing a part rather than acting on instinct. "I wanted to do this the easy way. The nice way. Give you a chance to come without causing a scene but you're forcing my hand, dearie." He takes a step closer to me, towering over me as he looks down his sharp nose directly into my eyes. "Come with me now...or I will murder everyone in this room before you've a chance to blink. I will massacre them all in ways so painful they'll be begging me to finish them off and I'll start with her." He nods his head toward the still unconscious Sam. "I'll ram my hand through her tiny chest and snap her spine and then drag you from here anyway. So, you see, either way you're coming with me, it's just up to you whether your friends, and enemies in the case of the colossally stupid Mia, die along the way. Your choice, love."

I hesitate. Not because I'm considering it, but because I am trying to process what he's saying. He'll do it. I know he will.

"Fair enough," he shrugs, heading in Sam's direction, taking my silence as an invitation to start the murder spree he seems intent on doing. His movements wake me up to the reality of the situation and I place my hand on his chest.

I nod.

"Let's go," I whisper. The smirk that raises one corner of his mouth tells me he heard me loud and clear. He grabs my elbow and unnecessarily starts to drag me along with him.

"What about, Sam?"

"She'll be fine. They'll just assume she's a little tipsy," Luc answers.

He half drags, half marches me toward the exit door. I have to work up a little jog to keep up with him. One of his steps being two of mine.

Luc pushes his way through the dance floor. Literally shoving people out of the way. Some fall over and a few scattered shouts of "Hey" and "Watch it dude" drift over the music into my ears, but he doesn't stop. Doesn't even look around. As we reach the exit, I have a quick scan over my shoulder, through an array of bodies obscuring my vision I just about glimpse Sam unmoving on the bleachers. My eyes dart to the other side of the hall where I see Mia, standing by herself obviously searching for Luc. One of the papier-mâché decorations comes unstuck from the ceiling and falls in front of her. It won't hurt her, but she jumps back, avoiding it. Seeing her panic causes my mind to flash elsewhere. To something I've seen play out before me many times before. In my own subconscious mind. Mia laying on the floor, in a beautiful dress. Rubble on top of her. Blood covering her beautiful face. Bodies. Everywhere. Some soaked in blood. Others trying to lift breezeblock sized chunks of wall off their weakened torsos. Some crawling for safety. Sam, a metal rod poking through her stomach as she lay motionless, eyes lifeless and wide open, seeing nothing.

I can see it all in front of me as if it's real. The nightmare that has haunted me for months. I finally know what it is. It's here. Now. This dance. It's what's going to happen to everyone here, because of me.

I look up at Luc. His eyes glowing a terrifying, demonic red. His lips curled back over his teeth in a terrifying smile come snarl.

I never should have come.

<h1 style="text-align:center">34</h1>

I'm pushed through the door with such force that it swings open and hits the wall with an almighty bang. It barely misses me on its way back as I tumble to the hardwood floor with a thud, my knees throbbing as my arms sprawl out in front of me. Luc, walking behind me with all the ease of a man out on a summer's day stroll, stops the door hitting his face with the palm of his hand, enters and gently closes it behind him. He smiles at me. A smile that makes my insides crawl. He turns back to face the door and places his fingers tips to the lock, there's a red glow and seconds later, a small click. He gives the door a tug. Satisfied, he turns back to face me.

"We wouldn't want to be disturbed, would we?" he asks. I don't answer, knowing a rhetorical question when I hear one. I let the silence hang between us like a dense fog.

I look around studying the gym. I knew where we were coming the moment he started heading this way, but I look around as if I've never seen it before, for no other reason than to give me something to do. I don't want to look at him. At the face that's going to make the nightmare that has haunted me for so long, a reality. Now I finally know where that nightmare will take place, when it will take place. I wonder if it's worth resisting. I saw Sam and Mia, and everyone else here, squashed under a pile of rubble. Dead. Wearing the same clothes as they have on tonight. It becomes clear to me that it was never a nightmare, but a premonition.

How could I have been so stupid?

Mike must be dead, or incapacitated in some way, otherwise he'd be here. I feel another pang of sadness at the thought, but it's accompanied by a throb of anger at his desire to still see the good in Luc and not entertain the thought of killing him. Then again, it's one of the reasons why I love him. He isn't evil like Luc. He sees redemption as a solution.

But it looks as if he has failed.

I look behind me at the basketball hoop, remembering the last time I was in here. Gym class. When Mia took me out and then had her goons flush my clothes down the toilet. It seems like forever ago now. That's the only time I've ever been in here, gym class. I never attend any of the games, never wanting to get involved. Never really being allowed to. I start to regret it now. Now I can see the end of the very dark tunnel which has been my life, I wish I'd have got involved more. Made an effort.

Too late now.

I look over my left shoulder at the banked seating. I allow my eyes to travel upwards to the small windows that line the back wall. All the way up, the top of the windows reaching the ceiling. Impossible to get a clear view out of unless you were sitting on the top row of seats. I can see a crack through one of the windows, no doubt the result of someone expressing their anger at their team losing. A full moon hangs high in the sky, the only light in this room coming from the slither cutting through the window and across the wooden flooring. A huge triangle of white light covers the space between us. Any other night it might look beautiful, romantic even. Tonight, it looks like a frame from a horror movie. Which I suppose is fitting, considering I'm seated on the floor in front of a monster.

"What are you thinking about?" Luc asks, pleasantly.

I look back to him. His hands clasped in front of him. Looking as if he hasn't got a care in the world.

"Mike," I answer. Staring him directly in his eyes, which have lost the blood red color they had on the way here.

"Of course," he answers, maybe a little annoyed. "You're scared. I can smell it." Luc wafts his hand under his nose as if he's a chef trying to tempt the smell from a nice meal to enter his nostrils. "It's pungent. Like mold or damp. Stand up."

I don't move.

"Get up." He waves his hand upwards in a get up motion. "I won't hurt you."

I slowly get to my feet, more so because I'm uncomfortable on the floor than because he told me to, but either way, I know that if I don't, he will just drag me up anyway.

"You won't hurt me, where have I heard that before? Oh, yeah, right before you dangled me off a building," I say.

"A misunderstanding. I knew Michael would come for you."

"And now? Will he come for me too?" I ask.

He smiles. "Unlikely."

I swallow hard. The implication of his words clear.

"You know, I'm not as bad as everyone thinks I am. As everyone *assumes,* I am." Luc starts to walk around the huge court absentmindedly.

"I find that hard to believe."

Luc snorts laughter. "So, Michael has told you everything now I assume. About your future. Your past?"

I don't answer.

"This...future child of yours," Luc begins, with a dismissive wave of his hand. "Could cause me all manner of problems." He takes slow, methodical steps toward me.

"Aww, and stop your murderous reign of evil. I'm distraught for you."

"I'm not evil. Or wasn't always at least."

"Oh, please, your own father kicked you out because you're so freaking evil. What does that say about you!?" I shout, my words echoing around the empty hall. I can still hear the *thump, thump, thump* of music from the dance, but it seems a world away. My thoughts are still with my nightmare though. If I can't find a way of stopping him, Luc will kill everyone in there.

"That's not strictly true." Luc holds his finger up as if he's an adult lecturing a child. Which I suppose in his eyes, is exactly what's happening. "I was banished because I loved my father *too* much. I didn't think it was right that someone as powerful, as glorious as he, should spend all of his time on you humans. Giving you infinite chances and you failing him at every turn. He gives you free will, to think and feel whatever you wish, and you repay him how? Destroying the beautiful world he created for you and to add insult to injury, half of you don't even believe he exists. I didn't believe that his greatest creation, Angel, should bow down to you ants. I showed you no ill will until he tried to force us to serve you, watch over you, bow down to you. I showed him unapparelled love and yet, he rejected it. Rejected me. His so-called favorite. You tell me how loving your father that much can ever be wrong. How that love can ever justify your own brother, the loyal servant, throwing you from the heavens. You can't can you?" Luc finishes, his eyes manic, getting more and more worked up as he goes on and on.

He takes steps closer to me and for each one he takes forward, I step back. Shifting uncomfortably under his gaze.

"There's no point in retreating. There's nowhere to go and even if there were, I'd find you."

"What do you want?" I ask.

"You."

"What?" I stop in my tracks, genuinely confused.

"I know Michael told you about your future. About the power you possess, not just what you could give birth to, but you yourself. A power so great even angels would fear you, but you seem unable to tap into it, which is good news for me I tell you. The role your child will play, how he or she, is to be born of angelic blood. Well, if that child is mine, born of my angelic blood..." Luc lets his words trail off, leaving them hanging in the air.

"You want my child to be the spawn of Satan?! Literally!" I scream the words, not believing what I'm hearing.

"Come with me." His hand outstretched. "I promise, you'll never be hurt, by anyone, I won't allow it. I'll give you a better life than you've ever been given here if you come with me. To my home."

I can't quite process what he's saying. Can't wrap my head around what it is he wants me to do. I look at him in disbelief, unable to form a sentence as I stand looking at his smirking face. I want nothing more than to run over and slap him again, but my feet won't move. Rooted to the spot as I try to make sense of what he is asking. The silence drags on until Luc, who likes the sound of his voice a whole lot, decides to fill it.

"It's not as horrible as people say, sure a few nasty souls get tortured, but they deserve it. You. You'll be treated like a goddess, my goddess. You'll have whatever you want, whenever you want. I promise. Just say yes."

Again, I can't answer. Can't form any words. I thought he was here to kill me, prevent this child from being born. Apparently not.

"I don't have to hurt anyone, Abigail. But I will. Everyone in that room." He points to the wall in the direction from where the music is coming, and I realize he's playing his trump card as I picture Sam lying motionless under rubble. Her dead eyes looking directly ahead at nothing. He knows, and so do I, that I will do anything to save her. To save all of them. Even the ones I don't like.

"Please, don't hurt them," I whisper.

"Then say yes. Say you'll come with me. If you don't, not only will I kill you, but I'll rip a hole in the fabric of this universe bringing forth an army of monsters that will rid this world of the plague of humanity...starting with your friends. Starting with Sam."

I weigh up my options. Say no... and he kills everyone, bringing hell to earth. I know he will do it. I've seen it. Say yes, and my life may be a misery, but I can save theirs. And with Mike gone, I see no other choice.

Slowly, I nod.

"Say. It. Say yes. I need to hear the words." Luc's eyes wide in a manic stare. His teeth on show, looking more demonic than ever. Saliva filling his mouth and dripping to his chin as excitement starts to get too much for him and his true colors, his true face, begins to show.

I open my mouth, ready to utter the words that will condemn me to hell, but save my best friend and every other person in that room. But before a word comes out, an almighty crash fills the room, drowning me out. Luc and I both snap our heads around toward the direction of the sound that is still echoing around the hollow room. Both doors to the gym hang from their hinges, splintered pieces of wood fly like arrows in all directions. One door broken clean in half and there, in the center of the door stands Mike. The light from the corridor behind him making him nothing but a silhouette, but his strong stance and flowing hair are unmistakable to me.

I steal a glance at Luc, his cocky, know it all demeanor is gone. Replaced with shock...and anger.

"Alright," Mike says, "dance is over."

35

My heart jumps to my throat at the sight of him. He's not dead. But he's definitely beat up. As he takes a step into the hall he stops in the sliver of moonlight. His face is bruised. Blood trickles from his bottom lip. I want to run to him, wrap my arms around him, but my brain tells me to stay put.

I snatch a quick look at Luc. His face twitching. Every nerve ending on fire with anger. His eyes returning to their demonic red as his teeth seem to have become vampirically sharp.

Mike's eyes dart between me and Luc.

"Get away from her. Now."

"Michael, impeccable timing as ever," Luc says through gritted, dagger-like teeth. Gone is his jovial demeanor. The carefree laughter he had when he dropped me from the roof in town, knowing Mike would save me, is gone. He knew Mike was coming then. This. This is unexpected.

"Abby, come over to me." Mike's hand is outstretched for me to take.

"Not so fast, love." Luc side shuffles in front of me. "We were just having a lovely chat, Michael. So rude of you to interrupt. Abigail was just about to say something, weren't you, dear?"

I swallow hard. Luc's changing appearance becoming more and more unsettling with every passing second. "He wants me to go with him." I blurt out.

Mike looks at Luc confused. His brow creasing. "To Hell...why...?" Then his face relaxes, and I can see his eyes widen in the moonlight as realization dawns on him. Luc obviously sees it too, as a raspy laughter starts to rumble deep in his chest.

"The prophecy," Mike whispers.

"It states the father will be an angel...well..." Luc opens his arms wide. "Angel. Right here." Luc holds his arms high, his index fingers pointing down at himself. I suppose he's right, he is an angel, although at the moment he looks anything but angelic. His hair is sticking to his skin with sweat. His skin looks almost gray as his eyes grow ever redder. Even his face looks as if it is mutating. His chin elongating. His forehead bulging. I take a step back, wanting to be near him even less than I did before his monstrous transformation. He's becoming angrier too and trying to hide it, but it isn't working. The snarls and growls rumbling in his chest are giving him away.

"Don't say anything, Abby. He needs your consent to take you there. No living soul can enter unless they give permission," Mike says to me, never taking his eyes off Luc.

Luc roars. An actual roar. He arches his back, sticking his chest out. His arms wide at his sides as he faces the ceiling. The whole room seems to rumble as this other worldly sound erupts from his now slobbery mouth. The anger he feels impossible to hide. I jump back, the sound terrifying me. Mike inches closer to me, but stops when Luc returns his blood red gaze toward him.

I stare at Luc in bafflement. Gone is the handsome man he was minutes ago. Replaced by a grotesque half monster. Like a werewolf from a horror movie mid-transformation. He's slightly hunched over, his legs bending at an unnatural angle. Stretching his black trousers as if they're about to rip. His hands, curling backwards as his once manicured looking nails protrude from the tips of his fingers creating demonic claws.

"Luc, for the last time, please let this go." Mike begs.

"Never," Luc growls. His voice, like his physical appearance has also changed. More gravel, more demonic. More inhuman.

"Look at you," Mike says, the emotion evident in his voice. "You've been gone too long. You need to get back. Your true form is showing. You can't keep this up much longer."

"My true form!? I am Lucifer–the most beautiful of all the archangels. This wasn't my true form until you threw me into that pit of despair. You caused this," Luc bellows, waving is hand over his body, highlighting his hideous appearance. He doesn't need to draw attention to it. It's impossible to miss, now. His feet have broken from his shoes, only, they're no longer feet, they're hooves. His legs are bending awkward at the ankles as if they're the legs of a goat.

"I'm sorry." Mike hangs his head, taking his eyes off Luc for the first time. I shift uncomfortably. A palpable tension hanging in the air.

"You're sorry?" Luc asks, disgusted. "You're a millennium too late, brother."

"Not for that. For this."

Mike launches across the space between himself and Luc. Almost as if he's flying without sprouting his wings. He clatters into Luc sending him careering into the banked seating behind him. Luc smashes through them and disappears beneath the broken piles of wood. The sounds of their bodies colliding echoes like two lumps of concrete being crashed into each other at supersonic speed. The force seems to create some kind of supersonic boom. Seconds after they touch, an invisible wave rolls into me and knocks me from my feet. The same wave hits the wall opposite causing it to crack. The high windows shatter and shards of glass fall over the now broken seating.

I struggle to a sitting position to see an obviously weakened Mike looking at me gravely.

"Run."

"Come with me, Mike," I say as I get to my feet. "Let's go. Hide."

"No. This has to end. Tonight. Go to the dance, get everyone out...and run."

A rustling comes from the destroyed seating.

"Now, Abby. Go!" Mike shouts.

I start to back off, walking slowly toward the broken doors as I keep my eyes on where Luc is. The broken seating on top of him starts to move and fall to the side. A shadow starts to emerge from the rubble. I don't hang around to find out what happens next. I run from the gym as fast as my legs will carry me. I notice a sharp pain shooting from my right ankle up my shin, but try to ignore it. I must have twisted it when I was knocked from my feet. Either that or the high heels are impossible to run in. My only concern now is getting Sam, and everyone else out of this school and as far away as possible.

I round the corner and slip. I hit the hard linoleum floor with my knees and palms, out of breath and my heart racing. I reach around and pull my shoes off, throwing them against the lockers opposite. I jump to my feet and sprint much faster down the corridor to the dance hall. As I approach the door two boys exit, concerned looks on their faces. I ignore them and push through the middle, eager to get to Sam as fast as I possibly can.

"Yo, what was that noise?" One of them asks.

"Yeah, felt like the whole school shook." the other adds.

I try to think of an excuse, something to explain away the noise and get these two, and everyone else, to leave.

"Gas leak." I blurt out, without really thinking. My mind nothing but a jumble.

"Gas leak?"

"Yeah, it's really bad...there's been an explosion in the basement. We have to evacuate." They both stand there staring at me. "Go!" I holler. They look at each other for the briefest of seconds and then turn and run toward the front of the school. "Two down, two hundred to go," I mutter to myself as I spin on my heel and push through the doors into the dance.

I'm not in there ten seconds before Mia is on me. Shouting over the music, one hand on her hip, the other pointing in my face.

"Where is he? Don't think I didn't notice you both went missing at the same time!"

"What? Who? What're you even on about?" I ask. My eyes scanning past her at Sam on the seating in the far corner. Sitting up, her head in her hands.

"My date. Y'all think you can steal him do you, well not on my watch," Mia shouts, clicking her fingers as she does.

"Mia, I haven't got time for this," I shout back, knocking her hand away from my face. "And neither have you. There's a gas leak, we all need to get out."

"Like I'm going to fall for that. You just want me gone so you can have both to your-" I grab her by the shoulders before she has a chance to finish her sentence.

"Shut up. I'm not kidding, get out of here." Her face drops. Fear? Concern? Anger? I can't make it out. "It's not safe to be here right now," I shout, then push my way past her and jog barefoot over to Sam. I kneel. She looks up at me through watery, bloodshot eyes.

"What happened?" she asks, dazed. "My head feels awful, and this music isn't helping."

"We need to go," I say, ignoring her question.

"Good, let me just get some water first," she answers, standing up and going to walk away. I grab her by the arm and stop her in her tracks. As I do, another loud crash erupts from outside the dance hall. Mike and Luc. A few kids turn in the direction of the noise, then turn back to whatever they were doing. Others don't even acknowledge it.

"We don't have time, Sam. We have to go, *now*." I start to pull her toward the door. She doesn't resist, which is good.

"Where are your shoes?" she asks from behind. I don't answer. If we make it out of here alive, maybe I'll tell her. As I reach the door an arm reaches out and grabs me. Panicked, I turn, expecting to see Luc, but instead seeing Mia. Gone is her fury, replaced by what looks to be concern.

"What's going on? Really going on, and not some bull about a gas leak," she asks.

"Mia, I don't have time to tell you, just for once on your life listen to me. We have to go. We all have to..." I stop midsentence and look around the hall. The couple hundred or so students without a care on the world, dancing. Enjoying themselves. My mind flashes back to my nightmare, where they're all laying in this very room, dead. My mind starts to race, trying–failing–to come up with a way to get them all out.

"What is it?" Sam asks.

"We have to get them all out. Every one of them."

"How?"

"I don't know, but we..." a high-pitched ringing stops me midsentence. I notice the dance floor slow down as people start to look around for the source of the noise. Over their heads I see Principal Heaver by the fire exit door. He's pushed them open and while I can't hear him over the ringing and the music, he is calling for people to exit.

I turn around and look over my shoulder to find Mia, standing by the entrance door, her hand on the fire alarm. She smiles at me and shrugs "You wanted everyone out."

I smile back, even in the current situation, I can't help it. "Thank you. Now follow me," I shout in Mia's direction, hoping she hears. I grab Sam again by the arm and notice she's still nursing her head. I pull her toward the dance floor, which is now easier to cross considering most people are heading for the fire escape at the back of the hall. More than half the students have left, and I start to breathe a sigh of relief. They'll make it out and if Mike fails, there will be no one here for Luc to murder.

By the time we reach the fire exit we're the last three people in the hall. Principal Heaver ushered out the group in front of us and then followed them, noticing we were right behind. Just as we are about to pass through the door into the open air beyond, the loudest crash of all erupts behind us. We all stop and turn. The whole back wall where the door to the dance hall is–or was–has collapsed. Mike lay, bloodied and bruised in the middle of the dance floor. The music now off, but the lights constantly flashing. His clothes are ripped, his face barely recognizable. I go to run to him, but he painfully holds up a hand to stop me.

"Mike!" I scream, my throat catching with emotion.

"What's happening?" Mia asks behind me. More to herself than anyone else considering her hushed tones.

"Abby...run..." Mike coughs. His voice strained. It's painful for him to speak. As he finishes, he coughs up thick lumps of blood that look almost black in the flashing disco lights. My eyes fill with tears as I stand rooted to the spot. Unable to turn and run, but unable to go to his side. I feel a hand on the top of my arm gently pulling me backwards. I don't turn but I know who it is from the gentle touch and then the followed-up whisper in my ear.

"I don't know what's going on, Abby, but we need to go, now," Sam whispers.

I can't even turn my head let alone move. Then a noise from out in the corridor breaks whatever it was that was keeping me still. It sounds like footsteps, but not. Not footsteps of a human at least. I watch Mike slowly stand and painfully turn towards the now huge hole in the wall. My eyes follow.

An echoed clip clop sounds travels to my ears. I can feel both Sam and Mia tense up at my sides, their bodies shifting toward the now absent wall. What enters the room causes gasps from behind me. I feel the same shock they do, but nothing leaves my lips. They remain tight shut as I find myself clenching my teeth. Half in anger and half in horror.

Luc is unrecognizable. He's grown about two feet in height, and he was already tall. Now he looks gigantic, but what's worse is his monstrous appearance. His legs have completely morphed into some kind of animals. Bending backwards by the ankle and leading to huge hooves. They've also grown thick and hairy by the top. His hands look to have completely transitioned into claws. His upper body, grown so thick and muscular that he has ripped almost completely out of his shirt, like the Hulk. What's most horrifying is his face, which has gone from the perfect, blemish free, porcelain skin, to a hideous, sweaty, pockmarked mess. His teeth, now fangs curling over his bottom lip. What's most nightmare inducing though is his forehead, where two huge horns have started to grow. The vision really is demonic. In every sense of the word Luc has become the very personification of evil.

"What the hell...?" Escapes Mia's lips.

"Wow." Sam breathes in fearful disbelief and awe. One of her horror novels come to life and she seems unsure whether to be scared or amazed. She will puff away on her inhaler at any sign of another student talking to her, but face to face with a monster, not a problem.

Luckily, I know exactly what to feel. Fear. We should be afraid. Very afraid.

"Mike," I call out, my voice cracking with emotion.

"Get her out of here!" Mike shouts, coughing more blood as he does so.

"Abby, let's go!" Sam shouts as she grabs my arm firmer and pulls me backwards. I stumble slightly, but make no move to retreat. Luc slowly advances toward Mike. It's hard to tell, but he looks to be smiling. His fangs on full show.

Sam continues to try and pull me back, I'm vaguely aware of it, but most of my attention is on Mike. The state he's in, and the fact that Luc is looking to finish him off. I try to take a step forward, but Sam's grip holds me in place. Another hand grabs my other arm, with much more force this time and drags me back. The force of the pull is that much stronger that I almost fall to the ground. I tear my gaze from Mike and look at Mia. Her eyebrows raised, fear in her eyes. She grips my arm like a vice and looks me dead in the eyes.

"We need to get out of here."

I look from Mia to Sam and realize that I need to get them away from Luc. I have one last glance over my shoulder at Mike and tell myself that as much as I would like to, I can't break down. Not now. I watch him as he struggles to his feet, waiting to meet Luc who is still slowly and purposefully making his way toward him. The clip clopping of his hooves sounding so loud I fear my ear drums may burst. The spinning lights from the DJ equipment highlighting him one minute and plunging him into darkness the next.

I turn back to Sam and Mia, shake my arms loose from their grip and start to walk toward the fire exit door. They follow without command. I step outside and my feet squash into the warm, damp grass and I remember I have no shoes on. It's pitch dark out and I can barely see one foot in front of me. Lucky enough, the car park where we are headed is lit by streetlamps, so I just make my way in that direction. The car park is full of bodies moving around. I can't make out anyone in particular because they're too far away, but it looks as if everyone from the dance is already up there. Hopefully, no one is left milling around the corridors of the school.

"What the hell was that thing?" Mia asks.

I don't answer. What can I say? The devil. I'm pretty sure she wouldn't believe me. Although, after witnessing what she just did...you never know.

"I'm pretty sure that gas leaks don't have that kind of effect on people," Mia continues after receiving no response. She doesn't get any explanation from me on this either. I just continue to power walk through the damp grass of the school grounds toward the parking lot. I look at the rest of my class as we get closer. Some looking annoyed, some having a laugh and a joke. Not a care in the world. I can't help but envy them.

I notice Principal Heaver pacing back and forth. A phone to one ear and his finger in the other to block out the noise. Probably calling the fire brigade.

"Mike looked in a bad way," Sam whispers. Her voice hesitant as if she wasn't sure she should say anything.

The mention of his name causes a tightening in my chest. I try to swallow, but my throats too dry. As usual, whenever I'm feeling like this my hand goes to my necklace. I rub my fingers and thumb over the sharp broken wing and my mind leaves Mike and goes to my mother. How she risked everything, her own life even, to be with my father. How she wouldn't leave him, even when he told her too, to save herself. They were stronger together, she had said that to him.

"What's the deal? Let's get out of here." Mia's voice rings through the quiet outdoors and I realize I've stopped. Mia and Sam are a few steps in front of me. They're looking at me, concern in their eyes. Even Mia. I hold my necklace in front of me and study the broken wing. I turn heel and start to head back to the dance hall, my feet squishing in the damp grass, my dress billowing in the small breeze. I feel something inside me, an energy coursing throughout my whole body.

"I have to go back. I have to help him."

Sam runs in front of me and puts her hands on my shoulders to stop me. "You can't, that…thing…"

"She's right. Don't be an idiot," Mia adds.

I look at them both and then focus on Sam. I drag her to me and hug her tight, holding her for a second longer that any normal hug, then push her aside and march back toward the fire exit doors.

"Abby!" Mia calls.

"Leave her," Sam whispers. A lump catches in my throat as I realize the probability is that I'll never see her again. I refuse to look over my shoulder at them. My mind is set on one thing. Helping Mike.

As I near the doors a huge bang erupts from the hall. The force is so strong I'm thrown from my feet. The walls look as if they shake right down to their foundations. Dust emits from them and fills the air around me. I hear screams come from the parking lot in the distance. No doubt they think the fire has caused some kind of explosion.

I rush to my feet, and sprint toward the door.

The whole back wall of the hall, behind where the DJ was standing, is caved in. Mike lays slumped on the floor underneath it, having obviously just been hurled through the air. He's trying to struggle to his feet, but has nothing left in him. He collapses back down.

Anger rises in me unlike anything I have ever felt. My whole body feels as if it's on fire. Flames course through my blood igniting every fiber of my being. It's so intense I feel as if I might spontaneously combust.

"Ah, Abigail, I knew you'd come back to me," Luc grunts. His voice seeming to have lost the English accent and become nothing more than a monstrous growl. As if his voice is coming from deep in his throat as opposed to from his mouth. He's more beast than man...or angel, now.

"I've not come back *to* you. I've come back *for* you," I say through gritted teeth, my eyes focused in on him, unblinking. Completely in the moment. Mike pushed to the back of my mind, it's like the whole world falls away as I focus all my energy, all my anger, on Luc. He starts to make his way towards me, doing what I can only describe as a smile as a thick black liquid oozes from his mouth. Instead of retreating, I start to make my way toward him, arms at my side.

I sense Mike shuffle to my right, but I don't look.

"Abby...what...are...you...doing..." Mike coughs and splutters his sentence out, but I ignore him. Like my mum would never leave my dad, I will never leave him. If I have to, I'll go out fighting. Not running. I'm done sitting back. I'm taking control. It's my time to save Mike now.

Luc smiles as I walk toward him. His fangs digging into his lips. He takes a step or two toward me, looking to meet me halfway. The energy coursing through me keeps me focused. I feel like I'm going to explode. Luc's beastly figure already causing a shadow to fall over me even though he is a few feet away. That's how huge he has become. I think back to the vision Mike showed me. How I managed, through no rhyme or reason, to incapacitate the angel attacking my parents with some unknown force. The same force I feel running through my veins this very moment.

Maybe I can do it now, because I've already seen myself do it then.

When we're nothing but a few feet apart, I slowly let my arms rise from my sides, and concentrate on nothing but Luc. I tense my hands, fingers, arms. My whole body. Letting the energy build and build and build until I can take it no longer. My arms still outstretched at my side, I spin my hands around and aim my palms in his direction, focusing all my pain, anger, frustration and now this unknown force, at Luc.

He stops dead in his tracks. His claws grab the side of his head as he squeezes his eyes shut. The pain, obvious on his face becomes even more evident when he lets out an almighty roar. So loud the walls begin to shake, but I don't stop. If anything, I focus my mind more to intensify whatever it is I'm managing to do to him. I notice movement in my peripheral vision. Mike getting to his feet, his eyes wide in wonder.

I continue to advance on Luc, increasing the intensity of my attack. I don't understand it and I can't explain it. Yet, the power flowing though me feels completely natural. His pain growing as I angle my hands more in his direction, aiming this invisible force directly at his chest. He smashes his fists into the hardwood floor creating a hole at least a foot deep with his strength.

I can see Mike moving closer, but refuse to let him distract me.

All the times Mike touched me–the tingles, the electricity I felt–was it this power awakening inside me? My angel grace?

Luc begins to writhe around on the floor. Throwing his body this way and that, having no idea what to do with himself as he is overcome with the kind of pain he has inflicted on so many others. I squeeze my fists tight shut as I try to use every ounce of energy flowing though me to cause as much hurt as I possibly can.

As he lay on the floor, Luc's back starts to bulge, mutate. The skin begins to rip away in flakes. Falling to the floor in a mass of dry skin. What looks to be bone starts to sprout from his back, similar to the look of the horns that now stand proud and pronounced on his forehead. I watch in amazement as the growth continues. Then I realize, it isn't bone, It's his wings.

Unlike Mike with the huge, almost blindingly white feathered wings, Luc's are a reddish brown, and leathery. They're as big as Mike's, maybe bigger, but they look like giant bat wings.

I'm caught off guard. My surprise causing me to falter slightly. Something tickles my top lip, and I raise my hand to touch it with the tips of my fingers. As I pull them away, I see blood there and realize my nose has been bleeding. I stumble on my feet, as if seeing the blood made my brain realize how much all of this has taken out of me. I wobble, feeling woozy. Dizziness blurring my vision. I tightly shut my eyes and rub my face as if trying to wake myself up. When I open them again, the short, sharp breaths I had been taking catch in my throat.

Luc is on his feet.

He's hunched over. Breathing–or growling–heavy. He looks tired. His wings making him look like a giant and his hooves making him a terrifying image to behold. He stamps his hooves on the floor like a bull ready to charge a red rag. His head is aimed slightly down as if he plans to spear me with his horns. I try to focus in on him as I did before, cause whatever unimaginable pain I was forcing his way moments ago, but no matter how hard I focus, no matter how tight I clench my fists. Nothing. I'm like a battery that has run out of juice. Luc raises his head to the heavens and lets out another roar. It's so loud I have to cover my ears with my hands to try and dampen the sound. It doesn't really work. The loudest clap of thunder I have ever heard erupts overhead. Instinctively, I turn and look out of the door. A flash of lightning illuminates the school grounds. The heavens open and rain starts to hammer down.

I turn back to Luc. He's moving nowhere near as fast as he did before, but it's enough to make me ready my stance. I take a couple of steps back, but my feet are firm on the floor, knowing that physically, I'm no match for him, but outrunning him isn't an option. I wish it were, I'd lead him away from the school, away from Mike, but I know that even in his weakened state he'd catch me with ease, and I don't want him having that satisfaction. My angel powers don't seem to stretch as far as speed or strength. My abilities seem to go just as far as causing some kind of aneurism. Which to be fair, has proven useful.

I ready myself for his attack. His onslaught. I don't blink as I look into the glowing red of his demonic eyes. I reach up once again, as I always do in times of panic, for my broken angel necklace. It steadies me. The fear is still there, but I also feel as if my mum and dad are with me too.

He moves fast. Not the lightning speed he was before, he isn't a blur, I can see every movement. I take a step back, planting my bare foot on the floor. I close my eyes and brace for the impact. It'll surely kill me, but maybe then, this will all be over. Not just for me, but for everyone. Mike. Sam. Maybe they'll all be safe without me around to have to protect.

There's a loud *crunch*. My eyes snap open to see chunks of the roof falling inches from my feet. But nothing else. No Luc. I take a step back to avoid being crushed–I look through the holes in the roof at the sky, which is now turning a blood red, with occasional flashes of brilliant blue light. The thunderclaps coming just as loud and aggressive as the first one. Panic rises in my throat like bile as I fear I may be crushed to death by the falling debris. Puddles start to form in the hall as the rain plummets through the gaps in the roof. I scan the room quickly and see Mike and Luc at the far-left hand side of the hall. Luc, imbedded into the almost demolished wall, his eyes closed, unconscious. Mike, out of breath and barely able to stand, holds him in place with one hand. Mike's full wings on show, seemingly giving him some much-needed extra strength.

As Luc was charging, Mike must have caught him halfway and with the last of his strength, smashed him into the wall. Saving me, as he swore to do, from almost certain death. We saved each other. Luc is left unconscious, but how long he will stay like that I don't know.

The thunder seems to be getting louder and coupled with the sound of the bomb sized raindrops hitting what's left of the roof, I can barely hear my own thoughts.

"Mike!" I scream over the apocalypse.

He looks back at me and offers a strained, apologetic smile.

I frown. Confused by his expression in this exact moment, considering everything that's going on. I tear my eyes away from him as huge cracks start to travel up the length of the walls. The whole building is about to crumble.

I take a hesitant step toward Mike, almost slipping on the now soaked hardwood floor. I stop as the wall breaks. A bouquet of papier-mâché flowers falls from the wall and land with a splash. Bulbs explode and smash on the floor, their loud noise eclipsed by the chaos surrounding us. Again, I step toward Mike whose hand is still pressing an unconscious Luc into the wall, holding him in place. Mike holds out his free hand toward me, palm facing me. He speaks no words, but I know he wants me to come no further. I scream as a huge chunk of wall falls over his head about to crush him, but his wings come up over him. The wall shatters into pieces as they connect with his wings.

"Go!" he screams at me. "The whole place is going to cave in."

"Come with me!"

He looks back toward Luc and then hangs his head. Luc begins to stir, but his eyes haven't opened.

"I can't," he whispers, but I hear him despite the noise. "I have to finish this."

The whole back side of the hall caves in. The wall collapsing in on itself as if a demolition company had just sent a wrecking ball through it. I jump back and raise my hands like they would protect me even if the wall were close enough to hit me. I take a few steps back, subconsciously heading toward the exit behind me.

The whole place is going to collapse in seconds and crush us all.

Mike looks up at what's left of the roof, swaying precariously.

'*Go,*' he mouths.

The tears falling from my eyes mix with the rainwater on my cheeks, the saltiness settling on my lips. I turn and run, slipping as I go. I fall and my head bangs off the hardwood floor. My vision goes blurry, but I don't have time to wallow in the pain. I stagger to my feet as the building falls around me. I touch my forehead peeling my damp hand away expecting to just see rainwater, but instead seeing bright red blood. I make it out of the door and collapse in the pouring rain onto the soaked, muddy grass. I roll over onto my back and stare, in blurred vision at the blood red sky and the demolition before me. The whole building, nothing but rubble. I try to rise to my feet, but a searing pain in my temple causes me to drop back to the ground. My blurred vision getting worse. Nausea overcoming my whole being. The world begins to spin as darkness engulfs my double vision.

Then, nothingness.

36

I stand in front of the mirror running my new tangle tease brush through my hair. I stare at myself. I feel like I look different. Older. Not *old*. Just, more...mature. Then again, the events of a few weeks back would be enough to age anyone.

I drop my brush onto my bed side table and pick up my new cell. Another gift from Tom to go with my new brush and the wardrobe full of new clothes he has bought me. It's amazing how something as simple as some clothes that fit can make you feel better about yourself. Can make you feel clean. They're nothing special. No designer labels or anything like that, but they're new. They fit. They're mine. My new jeans actually reach my ankles which is new for me. I smooth my hands over the design on my t-shirt. Stranger Things, a show I've become obsessed with in the last few weeks. I couldn't watch it before because Tom wouldn't pay for Netflix. Since coming home from hospital though, that's all changed. I've managed to binge watch it all. Twice. I smile as I look at the logo - *'Stranger Things.'*

Ain't that the truth.

My hair—always a thick, dark brown—now seems thicker, shinier. More luscious. Like I don't have to do much to it now to look pretty much perfect. Weird. And also, not so weird.

The blinding sun through my window sparkles off my necklace. I reach up and gently rub it. Like Aladdin rubbing the magic lamp. If only that was the case. If only touching it could make people appear or give three wishes. I shut my eyes and continue to gently stroke it. I open one of my eyes slowly, half expecting to see someone there, but it's just me. I laugh as I open both eyes fully, feeling every bit the idiot I am. I snatch my hand away quickly catching my thumb on the broken wing, you'd think after all this time I'd remember it's there, but I never do.

I check the time on my phone–7:14. I'm going to miss my bus and be late. Somethings change, I think looking at myself in the mirror. Somethings stay the same.

I swing my door open and head down the stairs, moving fast, but cautiously watching my feet to make sure my flip flops don't catch on the stairs. I still expect to hear the creaking as I descend, but since Mike gave the house a complete renovation after his titanic battle with Luc, the old farmhouse seems more solid than ever. I swallow hard at the thought of Mike. Trying to push down my heart that now feels as if it has become lodged in my throat. I want to push the thought of him from my mind, but as usual, I'm unsuccessful. The wall I have put up to protect me from the thought of him, from his three-week absence, is weak. Its foundation held together by a watery glue, with Mike on the other side punching it with all his angelic might. The pain I've felt at not seeing him, at not even hearing from him pounds at me like fists. I try to be angry at him, but I can't.

I just miss him.

"Off out?" Tom asks.

His voice causes me to jump as I reach the bottom step. I audibly gasp and take a step or two in the opposite direction, back toward the kitchen. Operating a minimum safe distance. Tom holds up his hands and takes a step away from me. He lowers his head, pain in his eyes and shame on his face. I can't help but have that reaction to his voice, especially when it catches me by surprise. His voice is usually followed by some kind of pain or discomfort. I start to feel bad, but quickly suppress that feeling knowing full well I have absolutely no reason to feel bad for him. He should feel pain. He should feel shame.

I steady myself, straighten my back and take a deep breath. "I'm meeting some friends at the beach." I check the time again. "But I'm going to be late."

Tom strides into the kitchen, a smile formed on his weathered face. It looks odd. Unnatural. "I'll take you," he grabs his keys from the kitchen worktop.

He heads to the back door and opens it. Standing aside, he waits for me to walk through. I stand rooted to the spot, not knowing what to do. He's never offered me a lift anywhere before, even when I've been late for school. His need to be nice is unsettling. He's trying too hard to atone for his past and it makes me more nervous than when he used to be on the rampage. That, I knew how to deal with, I knew what was coming next. This is all new to me. Maybe a near death (or in actual fact, real death) experience has made him question himself. His smile falters and his shoulders visibly slump as he can see I'm not as happy or enthused by the lift as he wants me to be.

"Abby, I...I know I've been...I'm trying..." he begins, but I cut him off. I don't want to hear it. One because it's awkward and two because I don't care. He doesn't have the right to feel bad or sorry for himself.

"Okay," I say as I march past him out in the warm night air.

The drive to the beach doesn't take us long–fifteen minutes at most, but it was the longest fifteen minutes of my life. It felt more like an hour. Tom trying to make small talk and me, sitting as far away from him as the trucks front cab would allow, almost molded into the passenger door, giving him one-word answers while looking out of the window at the setting sun. After five or six of these failed attempts to start conversation, Tom gets the picture and gives up. We make the rest of the journey in silence which does absolutely nothing to alleviate the tension and awkwardness that hangs in the air like a bad smell.

Tom slowly pulls into the parking lot just up from the beach. It's pretty full and as with the last time I was at one of these things, my classmates are milling about, listening to music and talking around their trucks. Tom leans forward, his eyes squinted as he studies the group before him.

"Lotta kids here," he says, not looking at me.

"It's a party," I say rudely, as if he's stupid.

"There gonna be drink here?"

"It's a party," I say again, even more rudely this time as I drop from the high cab on to the concrete floor.

"Well…" he begins hesitantly. Wanting to say something, but not really knowing what that something is. "Don't drink. And er…y'all stay away from any drugs."

I turn and look at him, shock and amazement on my face. *The nerve of this guy.*

"Don't drink. Really? Coming from you?" I say, spitefully. He flinches back as if my words have grown hands and slapped him across the face. I slam the door and march off toward the stairs. I feel good, I know I shouldn't, but I do. The satisfaction at hurting him, even with a few spiteful words, is childish and petty, but after the years of emotional hurt he has put me through, and the occasional physical pain, I can't help but feel he deserves it. To be fair to Tom, the past few weeks he hasn't touched a drop of drink. He's been clean shaven every day and he's wearing clean clothes. Still, there's enough hurt in my past to gleam a small amount of satisfaction out of talking back.

I march across the parking lot feeling self-conscious. Like all eyes are on me. Like I'm a fish swimming around a glass fronted aquarium. No one says anything, which I'm thankful for. The name calling and heckling has stopped since Mia and I have become 'friends.'

I hear the truck reverse and drive off. I resist the urge to turn around and watch. Trying to quash the guilt I'm feeling for being nasty to Tom when he was obviously trying to be nice to me. *For a change* I remind myself. I push the thought away and pick up the pace. I can see her standing at the edge of the parking lot alone, hugging her elbows and shiftily looking from the floor to her surroundings. Like prey looking out for a predator. She lifts her head up and sees me, her face changing immediately from the worrisome frown into an infectious smile. I can't help but return it. I pick up the pace turning my fast walk into a jog.

"I was wondering if you were going to come."

"I'd never stand you up," I say, linking my arm through hers and leading her to the stairs that lead to the beach front. "I was running late, missed the bus, but Tom offered to give me a lift."

Sam looks at me with wide eyes and raised eyebrows. Sam is the only person I have ever told what my life is like with Tom–or was like.

"Turn up for the books. How's he been since getting out of hospital?"

"Fine. Completely different. Scarily so. He must've had a visit from the ghost of Christmas past while he was unconscious," I reply.

As we reach the bottom of the stairs Sam stops so abruptly and with our arms still linked, it almost causes me to fall backwards. Catching me by surprise, I stumble.

"What's up?"

I follow Sam's gaze as she surveys the scene before her.

"You sure this is a good idea?" she whispers.

"Of course, we were invited."

"No, *you* were invited."

"Look," I say, taking my arm out of hers and standing in front of her, "let's give it twenty minutes, if it doesn't work out, we'll go. Deal?"

Sam is silent for ages, her eyes still scanning the beach before she finally looks at me and slowly nods. We descend the rest of the stairs and finally reach the sand. We bend down and take our flip flops off. The sand is warm, almost hot, which surprises me considering the sun is all but set.

"You came!" I hear Mia's voice before I see her. She comes barreling out of nowhere and wraps her arms around me and kisses me on the cheek. I'm caught by surprise and try to hug her back, but it's awkward and unnatural. "And you've brought a friend," she adds, decidedly less excited as she looks at Sam. Sam looks at me with a 'I told you so' look on her face.

"I'm going to go get a drink," Sam says flatly. She turns and trudges off toward a cooler someone has placed over by the stairs.

"I hope you don't mind," I say to Mia. "She's my best friend, and she could really use a chance to have some fun."

"No problem at all," Mia answers, shaking her head, and it looks as if she's being sincere. "After what the three of us saw—we're like—bonded now, or something." She gives me a little pat on the arm. I force a smile.

"Yeah, I suppose."

"So, we haven't spoken much about it, what with you being in the hospital, although, it doesn't look like you have a scratch on you now. You heal quick." Mia narrows her eyes. Self-consciously, I look down and let my hair fall over the side of my face.

Mia ignores my obvious awkwardness and carries on, taking the conversation down a road I really wish she wouldn't. "No one seems to have any clue what the frick happened–Heaver still telling people it was a gas leak, but he didn't see what us three did. That...thing..."

"Have you told anyone what you saw?" I ask, quickly.

"No way! People would think I'm crazy," she shouts.

Relief washes over me. The last thing I need is for more people to start asking questions I can't answer.

"What was that thing?" Mia asks, quieter this time.

"What thing?" I ask, playing stupid and not remotely pulling it off.

"Come on, you know what thing. The thing that was kicking Mike's ass. It was like something out of an episode of Supernatural. I kept expecting Jensen Ackles to come running through the door. Thinking about it, that wouldn't have been half bad," Mia says, looking off into the distance at an imaginary Jensen.

"It was just...a man..." I say. Seeing the skeptical look on her face I speed up pretty quickly. "A big man...a really. Big. Man?" I finish. More asking for her to believe me than saying it with any kind of conviction.

"Abby. It was a monster. A real monster. An out of this world horror movie style monster. A hide under your bed and in your closet style monster. A rip your heart out and..."

"Okay, I get it," I blurt out cutting her off. "But it wasn't," I carry on in an unsuccessful attempt to convince her. "The lighting, from the DJ. That made things distorted...and..." I continue, raising my finger as if I'm some kind of Sherlock Holmes that's cracked a case, "someone spiked the punch...with a hallucinogenic. What you think you saw wasn't real. It was just a fight."

I'm out of breath by the time I've finished. Talking much too fast to sound even remotely convincing.

Mia looks at me with her eyebrow cocked slightly. "I know the punch was spiked. I'm the one that spiked it."

"Someone spiked it after you?" I say again, making it sound more like a question than a statement of fact. I really suck at this lying gig.

Mia pauses. Just staring at me. I feel as if I am being interrogated even though she isn't saying anything. My forehead prickles with sweat and my palms become damp. What the hell is wrong with me? I faced down the Devil himself and yet I become nervous under Mia's gaze.

"Whatever," she finally blurts out. "Live in denial if you want. I know what I saw and what's out there. Maybe I'll become a demon hunter." She finishes and once again looks off into the distance. I can't help but think she would be really good at it. "What did Mike have to say about the whole thing, considering he was the one on the receiving end of the ass kicking?"

My heart speeds up at the mention of his name. I try to speak, but the words get stuck in my throat, refusing to come out. As if they've grown claws and are clinging to my insides for dear life. I'm hoping Mia will notice, but subtlety isn't her strongest characteristic, so she just stands and waits for me to start talking. Finally, some words come out, albeit weak and croaked, as if I have a sore throat.

"He moved away. Him and his family. They're...they're not coming back." I hang my head. This comes easier than everything else I've said to Mia because it's technically not a lie. He has gone away. He isn't coming back. I feel like the sadness in my voice is evident, but once again, Mia doesn't notice this. It's just her way I suppose.

"Good riddance, I say, to him and Luc. You know he just left me there that night. Up and left. Me. Who does he think he is? Probably got one sniff that there was going to be a fight breaking out and ran with his tail between his legs. Coward.

We're better off without them," Mia says passionately. I smile at her outburst even if I don't agree. "Come and sit over here with us," she angles her head behind her. I look over to see her friends sitting there. The ones who spent their whole time at school being nasty to me. Lydia sees me looking at waves emphatically in my direction. I half-heartedly wave back.

"Is that a coffee table by the fire?"

"Yeah, I brought it from my room so we can lay some food out."

"You have a coffee table in your room?"

"Of course. Where else am I going to put the water dispenser?" Mia says, completely serious.

I suppress my desire to chuckle. "Maybe we'll come over in a minute. I'll wait for Sam to get back."

"Well, make sure you do," Mia's pointing her finger at me, giving me an order, but smiling all the same.

She turns and heads back to her group of friends as I turn and head over into the corner where Sam is standing holding two cans of Coke.

"How's your bestie?" she asks sarcastically.

I smile. "You know you're my BFF," I say as I take the Coke. "She was asking about that night."

"Of course, she was. Why wouldn't she? If you saw what she did, and had no idea what was going on, then you'd have questions too. I know I did. What did you say?"

"Not the truth. Some bull about the disco light and drugs. Can't even remember."

"I just can't believe. Angels. The Devil...you, half angel," Sam shakes her head.

"Gonna write a book about it?"

"Maybe I will," she says, a huge smile lighting up her face.

We start to walk the beach aimlessly, heading away from the crowd as we always do. Even when we're on 'friendly' terms with the populars, we still inevitably revert to being loners. Loners, together.

We walk in silence. The sound of the party goers drifting into nothing but background noise as the sound of the waves crashing on the shore drowns it out. The light from the fires and the overhead car park gets duller as we get further away, like the blackness of the night sky swallows them whole. The darkness being kept at bay by nothing more than stars.

"Penny for the 'em."

"Huh."

"Your thoughts."

I shake my head. Walking through the darkness of the beach is my only savior from Sam seeing the tears in my eyes.

"Mike?"

I nod. "I barely know him. Haven't known him for hardly anytime at all and yet, the thought of never seeing him again..." my voice trails off.

"Did he say whether he was coming back? Ever?"

I shake my head. "He isn't coming back. I just know it."

We continue to walk in silence. The ocean becoming louder and yet, more soothing.

People loose people. Throughout time love is found and lost. People all over the world, and beyond, know the pain of having your heart broken and yet, I feel as if I'll never be able to move past this.

Sam stops beside me and I stop to look back at her. She's smiling. A real smile, one that reaches her eyes. I wipe a stray tear from my cheek and smile, a much less genuine one, back at her.

"What?"

She walks up to me and takes my drink from my hand. She looks past me, over my shoulder, off into the distance.

"Every now and then people surprise you."

I frown, confused. I turn and follow her gaze off into night. There he is.

Standing casually in the shadows. His black jeans and white shirt fitting him perfectly. His sleeves rolled up to his elbows as the small breeze causes his hair to tease his shoulders. No trace of the battle with Luc on his face at all. It's perfect.

I look back toward Sam in shocked disbelief. She nods toward Mike with her head, telling me without words to get a move on. I don't need telling twice. I drop my flip flops by my feet and turn, running far more awkwardly than I'd want because of the sand, toward Mike. As I reach him, he opens his arms and engulfs me in them. We kiss. Mike picks me up and holds me in his arms as my hands run through his hair, clenching it in my fists. We kiss for what feels like hours and it still isn't enough.

Much too soon Mike lowers me back to the ground and has to untangle my hands from his hair. He takes a step back and I gasp for breath. Every nerve ending in my body feels on fire and yet, I want more.

Mike looks down at me, his jawline pulsing as usual. I want to run my hand down it, but I fear if I move, I may pass out. He reaches out and holds my hands in his.

"Let's sit. Talk," he says, breathlessly.

There's a log behind us, but he doesn't go to it. Instead, he just glides down into the warm, soft sand. I drop down next to him much less gracefully and get as close as I can without sitting on him. My legs squashed up against his as if I'm trying to meld them into one. I scoop my arm through his and hold his hand. He breaths in a deep sigh of satisfaction as he closes his eyes and smiles. I smile too, happy that it isn't just me feeling like this. I make him happy too.

Neither of us utter a word. I lay my head on his shoulder and listen to the ocean. The foamy waves fold in on themselves as they crash on the sand. The sound of the party is hard to decipher. Like a television left on in the background. The sky is as clear as I have ever seen it. What appears to be millions of stars blinking at me from the cloudless sky. I wonder to myself if that's Mike's doing, freeing the sky above us of any blemishes to add to this perfect moment. The warm breeze caresses my cheek, and I close my eyes wanting this night to never end. Enjoying the silence. Quite possibly for the first time in my life, feeling content.

"I'm sorry. For leaving the way I did. Without saying good-bye. Without checking if you were okay," his voice is low.

"It's okay."

"Is it?"

"Not really," I laugh. "But I know why you had to."

"With Luc incapacitated like that. I couldn't give him a chance to get his strength back. I had to go."

For a second, I don't answer. An image of the horrific monster Luc had morphed into creeps back into my mind. I close my eyes and grit my teeth in true Mike fashion.

"Where is he now?" I ask, surprised at the fear I feel just talking about him.

"He won't be a problem anymore. He's...tied up. I think that's the best word for it," Mike answers, gravely. "He won't be causing problems anytime soon. You saved us, Abby. You saved everyone. You saved...me. Your power is remarkable."

I smile at him, not really knowing what to say.

"How are things with your uncle?"

"Fine. Weird. He's being nice...too nice. I don't know how to react to it after all these years. He's not getting my sympathy though. Or my forgiveness. He doesn't deserve it," I spit in anger. "If he thinks a few rides and a few days without any slaps in the face are enough to make me forget everything then that attack from Luc has really frazzled his brain."

"You should maybe ease up on him just a little." Mike turns to look at me, his eyes soft.

"Ease up on him? Are you serious?" I answer, pulling my head away from his shoulder, but never letting go of his hand.

He starts to move, and I worry he's going to get up, move away from me, leave, but he just angles his body toward me. We are now more or less facing each other, our hands still clasped. "When you were taken in by your uncle, we...angels I mean, put a kind of cloaking device on him. To shroud you both from being found. It was powerful, so powerful that Luc never knew where you were until I came to earth and he realized why I was here." Mike turns to face the ocean. A regretful look on his face. I reach up with my free hand and stroke his face.

"I'm glad you did," I whisper.

He looks back and me and smiles. Not a happy one, a sorrowful smile that breaks my heart.

"What we didn't realize," Mike continues, "Is that Luc was one step ahead of us. While our combined angelic powers were enough to keep you both hidden, what we didn't know was that Luc had already got to your uncle first. He put that hatred of you inside your uncle. He wanted him to hate you, to hurt you. For you to question what the whole point of your life was so that when he did finally get to you, it would be easier to tempt you away from...well from everything. Because you would hate this world. You'd hate God and everything he stood for. You'd hate me," Mike finishes.

I look away from him. Studying the grains of sand that cover my feet as I try to wrap my head around what he just said. "So, Tom..." I trail off.

"He never wanted to hurt you. That evilness. The nastiness. It was all Luc. How your uncle is acting now. That's the real him."

I let the words linger in my head for a while and as crazy as it sounds, it makes sense. "Why did you leave me with him?" I ask, not looking him in the eye.

"I didn't know. I haven't been watching you all these years. It was someone else's assignment. Until you moved here 6 months ago, and I decided to check in...and saw you for the first time. Then I decided to get involved."

"Thank you."

"If I'd never came to you, then Luc would never have found you."

"And I'd never have found you."

I lean forward and kiss him gently on the lips. When we part, I spin myself back to our original position and lay my head back on his shoulder. This is perfect. A literal depiction of perfection. The distorted reflection of the moon in the rippling ocean. Like everything in life, beautiful, but imperfect. The stars flickering brightly like glitter as the sand warms my bare feet.

We sit in silence. I grip his hand as if for dear life, never wanting him to leave my side and yet, knowing deep down, this can never be. *We* can never be. The minutes pass and Mike speaks, his voice cutting through the silence like a knife though a child's birthday cake.

"I have to go." He looks up sadly into the night sky.

"Already?" I answer, almost jumping up. My hand instinctively gripping his tighter. My body telling him I don't want him to go. Ever. My mind, knowing full well that he has to.

"I shouldn't even be here, Abby. I came back to apologize for leaving the way I did. To say goodbye."

"You can't stay, even until the end of the party?" I say, clutching at straws.

Mike looks to the heavens, once again. He closes his eyes, grits his teeth in frustration. His only answer is to look down at the floor and slowly shake his head. He stands up, gently pulling me to my feet. He looks down at me and I can feel my eyes welling up, but I refuse to let them spill over.

"I love you," I whisper. Knowing it's true. Knowing that I may never see him again and the pain is almost unbearable. Understanding why my mother risked everything to be with my father. Knowing how dangerous it was, she stayed with him, keeping us all together. A family. I know deep within my bones that I would do anything, risk anything, to be with Mike.

He takes my face in his smooth hands and places his lips on mine. Gently at first and then growing firmer until he pulls away, short of breath. Once he regains his composure he reaches out and takes my broken angel necklace in his fingers and smiles to himself. Then, he leans back down and kisses the tip of my nose.

"I love you too." He turns away, marching in the opposite direction. I want to chase after him, beg him to stay, but I don't. I just watch.

"Mike!" I call after him as he almost disappears into the shadows of the night. He turns to face me, his porcelain skin glowing in the dark. "The prophecy, about my..." I hesitate, not knowing how to phrase it.

"Destiny," Mike finishes for me.

"You said that the father of my baby will be an Angel. Do you know who?" The words are barely a whisper, but I know he heard me. One corner of his mouth curls up into an unmistakable half smile.

"Stay safe, Abby. Luc has a lot of crazy acolytes out there."

I smile back, knowing he isn't going to answer me.

His wings slowly unfold from his back with a *swish*, as beautiful and glorious as I remember. Without even flapping them he rises into the sky. His wings begin to move. Hardly noticeable at first and then one huge flap and in the blink of an eye, as quick as he came, he's gone. I look up and the beautiful scene that was laid out before me moments ago seems duller. Quieter. The stars all seem to have retreated behind a thick cloud covering that moments ago was nowhere to be seen.

EPILOGUE

T he heel of my right foot catches the bottom step as I rush down the stairs. I clatter to the hallway floor, my phone and keys skidding across the hardwood. My knees pounding the ground with such force I fear I might have broken a bone. Or the wood. Luckily, instinct kicks in and my hands stop my face from hitting the ground as well.

Uncle Tom rushes from the kitchen into the hall and helps me to my feet. He gathers my phone and keys and hands them to me. I look down as I put them into my pocket, my embarrassment completely outweighing any pain I feel.

"You okay?" Uncle Tom asks, genuinely concerned.

"Yeah, fine thanks. Just don't want to miss the bus," I answer, head still down. I lift my trouser leg to inspect my knees, the throbbing pain already non-existent. Tom jerks his head back in shock and confusion. Not even a red mark.

"Wow, you're a tough one."

Angel blood. I think to myself. Ever since being around Mike, the angel DNA in me seems to have awoken big time.

"Yeah, don't mess with us farm girls," I lift my arms and flex my biceps.

"Darn right," Uncle Tom gives me a high five.

After what Mike told me, about Luc putting some kind of mojo on Tom and the way he's acting now being the real him.

I've cut him a hell of a lot of slack. I can't forget it, every time I see his face, I remember, and sometimes if he walks into a room and I'm not expecting him, I still flinch. It's second nature, but I'm getting better. He's treated me with nothing but kindness since coming home from the hospital.

"Sorry, I can't give you a ride today, I've got so much to do around here."

"It's fine. When schools out, I'll come straight home and give you a hand."

"No, you won't. You go out and enjoy yourself. You're only young once," he smiles and for the first time I can see my mum. See that they're related. Since he had stopped drinking, smoking and started shaving every day, he looks ten years younger.

I notice the clock above his head and realize that even though I don't have a myriad of chores to do every morning or breakfast to cook, I'm still going to miss the bus.

"Shoot," I say as I grab my bag from the dining table, sling it over my shoulder and run to the kitchen door. I grab a slice of toast from a plate Tom has cooked on my way past.

"See you later!" I yell, spitting toast as I do.

"Be careful or you'll fall again!" he shouts as the door slams.

Concern, I think to myself. It's nice to finally have someone feel that toward me. A warm glow burns in my belly, and I don't think it's the toast.

I shove the last piece of toast in my mouth and speed up into a jog. It's a gorgeous day out, I'm barely halfway down the farm track and my forehead is already prickled with sweat. I look at the shiny, dark brown fence that separates the corn field from the track. It looks great. Uncle Tom replaced it all last week and I helped him varnish it. There's a real sense of pride looking on the success of hard work, especially when you enjoyed doing it. We've stashed the broken, sun kissed fence pieces of old out back and are going to have a bonfire when the weather starts to cool down. Maybe some S'mores.

My eyes travel from the new fence to the old corn field, the huge corn swaying in the almost non-existent breeze as it has done many times before. I smile to myself. The fear I used to feel at just looking at it has now gone, hopefully forever. Knowing now that the presence of the snake, was just Luc playing games with me. I pick up the pace, not wanting to miss the bus, especially now I have no excuse. The past couple of months I have been late exactly–zero times. An achievement I am extremely proud of and something that hasn't gone unnoticed by Mr. Heaver.

About halfway down the track a noise from behind me causes me to stop dead. The fear I thought had evaporated moments ago comes rushing back in an instant. In seconds my mind runs away with me. Images of a demonic Luc rush through my mind's eye. The huge snake that slithered its way through the corn slithers its way through my brain. I drop my book bag to the floor and clench my fists, ready to use my newfound angel powers against whatever is coming from behind me.

I turn and immediately open my palms and raise my arms to my side. Except, there's nothing there. I relax the frowning concentration on my face and lower my arms naturally by my side. I scan the farm in front of me and the cornfield on my left and see nothing but vast, empty space. I shake my head. Laughing to myself I turn back around ready to continue my journey. As my eyes refocus in front of me, I see it. The school bus, just pulling away from the end of the farm track.

"Well, shit."

I breath a huge sigh of frustration. I look up to the clear, cloudless, bright blue sky and close my eyes. I breathe in through my nose and back out through my mouth. Five times. Trying to steady myself and calm the frustration at missing the bus, mostly because I know it's all my own fault this time. No one to blame. Once I've composed myself, I bend down to pick up my bag, and there it is. For a moment, I just look, making no attempt to pick it up. Common sense tells me it should blow away in the breeze, but it barely even moves. It just sits there on the ground. After a few seconds I take it in my hand and the familiar tingle courses through my body. A smile forms on my lips as I hold the giant white feather in my hand. It feels like he's right here with me, standing next to me. Like that night on the beach three months ago, holding this feather feels like I'm holding his hand. I stand up and look around me, but see nothing but corn and open fields. I open my bag and place the feather inside one of my books never wanting to lose it. I smile to myself knowing this is Mike's way of telling me he's always here, always with me. Watching over me. I zip my bag and throw it over my shoulder.

Who cares about the bus anyway? It's a lovely day for a walk.

Tom Carter is an author of horror/thriller novels. Other works include "The Doctor Will See You Now," "The House of Whispers," the YA PNR/Teen Horror "SWISH," and he also has a short story in the horror anthology "Bloody Hell: An Anthology of UK Indie horror." He worships at the altar of the two Steves: King and Spielberg. He resides in England.